Call of the Dark

A Dream Walker Novel

MICHELLE MILES

Book Cover by Erin Dameron-Hill

First Edition May 27, 2020

ISBN: 9781393479758 (ebook)
ISBN: 9781734306828 (paperback)

For my husband, who never stopped believing in me or this book.

There has to be evil so that good can prove its purity above it.

Buddha

Don't let evil conquer you, but conquer evil by doing good.

Romans 12:24

CHAPTER 1

Dallas, Texas, June 2038 A.D.

D REAM WALKING A PATIENT in the hospital during the night shift wasn't the best idea I ever had. It ranked right up there with taking a stroll alone in the park after dark with a serial killer on the loose. But Emma Cox was catatonic patient number fifty to arrive in the ER that month and I had to do something.

Emma. I'd known her. We'd been in community college together. She was the first friend I made when I returned to the States ten years ago, alone and scared and trying to figure out what to do next. Hell, she'd been my only friend. Until we both met Ryan in physics class. Cute, dimple-faced Ryan. Then all bets were off. She went after him with low cut tank tops, skinny jeans, stilettos and hips a blazing. The fact he asked her out instead of me had nothing to do with us not speaking to each other again. Ever.

Now here she was, laying face up on a gurney, staring into space like some sort of wasted zombie. I was a night owl phlebotomy technician at All Saints Hospital working the graveyard shift. That night, I picked up my assignments like normal and headed off to do my rounds when I caught sight of the woman with colorful hair. Emma liked to experiment with unique hair color. When I saw the crown of platinum violet, my gut told me to check it out.

At first, I didn't recognize her. She looked like all the others who arrived lately staring out of sightless, pitiful eyes. Their faces were nothing more than vacant skulls with skin sagging off the bones like flaccid leather.

Her youthful, smooth skin that once held a healthy rosy pallor was pale and paper thin. The freckles she hated dotting her nose were more noticeable than ever. Her once bright blue eyes now held a dull sheen. Had I not once been her friend, I wouldn't guess she was twenty-eight, the same age as me.

Even though I wasn't supposed to, I read the charts on patients with this malady. It violated all kinds of ethics, but I had to know what was wrong. Plus, I was tech savvy enough to get into the system. Their initial symptoms arose from sleep disorders, then odd behaviors manifested, until finally the patient would go eerily still and merely stare into space. One guy stared straight ahead, unblinking, for four days, but when tested, he caught a tennis ball tossed at him with the reaction time of an all-star MLB outfielder.

The doctors couldn't explain it.

But maybe I could. If I could get inside Emma's head, inside her dreams.

I hadn't done this in a long time or for any other patient, but I knew her. We'd been friends once, even though she got the guy and I didn't. She helped me through a lonely period of my life before she introduced me to Ben. I owed it to her to find out what was going on behind those sad hollow eyes.

With a cocky confidence, I sat before the girl at death's door, ready to step into her mind.

I checked Emma's vitals. The steady *beep-beep-beep* of her heart monitor was the only sound in the room. Her eyes never focused as she continued to stare into the distance to someplace she saw.

"Hi, I'm Anna." My voice sounded high and tinny and I cleared it to untangle my nerves. I inhaled a deep breath, let it blow out and started again. "And I'll be your dream walker tonight."

I smiled, amused at my joke. She didn't respond. She didn't even blink.

"Remember me, Em? This won't hurt. Promise."

I grasped her hands, held them in mine. Her icy fingers cut through my warmth. Determination steered me, though I had no idea if this would work. In the past, when I dream walked, the subject was already asleep. She wasn't asleep, although technically she wasn't awake either. I took a deep breath and cleared my mind.

Then it happened. Her pupils expanded from pinpoints to large black pools. I had her. I was sucked into her mind, pulled along like a helium balloon on a string buffeted by the wind. I no longer stared into her face, but into her subconscious, a bystander in her dream. I was with her, watching and waiting.

We stood in a strange house with scarred wood floors, walls the color of mint julep, and red curtains adorning the windows. There was an overwhelming sense of urgency, panic and dread, though I couldn't decipher if those were her emotions or mine. Emma walked through the house with unhurried steps, placing one bare foot deliberately in front of the other as her fingers trailed lightly on the walls. She stepped through a swinging white panel door to the kitchen. On the floor lay a man with a pool of blood spreading in a dark red circle underneath him.

No, it wasn't a man. Alabaster wings splattered with blood grew from his back. One wing hung limp as if broken, perhaps even ripped from his back. The sharp tang of damp copper hung in

7

the air between us. Gooseflesh prickled my arms. Emma turned to me, her blue eyes meeting mine. Not a glimmer of recognition was there.

"I know who did it." Her voice sang out in an odd melody. Her words cut through me like a cold north wind.

"Who did what?" I asked, shaken.

"Who killed the angel, Anna."

Surprise flickered through me at the use of my name. She realized I was there and remembered me.

Was this why she was in her current state? Why she could no longer speak?

"Who?" The word slipped out of my mouth, a whisper of ice. She didn't answer.

"Who did this, Em?"

"I—" She paused, her lower lip quivering.

"I did it, of course. Hello, Anna."

He had appeared from nowhere, suddenly there in the blink of an eye. Standing in a wash of pale light, his black wings glistened as they ruffled, like something out of a nightmare. He had a sinful, savage look about him, his wide face punctuated with a wolfish grin. Obsidian eyes scrutinized me with an unsettling gaze that promised wickedness.

The thing that bothered me the most was the creeping sensation I had seen that feral face before.

"Who are you?"

His black eyes rounded giving him the visage of a wounded puppy. He clutched his chest in mock anguish. "You don't know? I'm heartbroken."

I searched my memory but came up with only dust bunnies. His face was unique enough I ought to remember it. But I couldn't place it. For sure I would remember those spectacular wings. I didn't. My past was sometimes a blur. My early life wasn't exactly full of leisure and extravagance. Not knowing him didn't mean anything. Seeing him in a shared dream did.

"No matter. I will not be offended." He waved away the insult. "I am Azriel." He paused, looking expectantly, as though the name might stimulate some memory.

I feigned indifference and tried to ignore the fear rattling through me. "Never heard of you."

"Now that is tragic. You wound me deeply, *chérie.*"

I had enough of his phony outrage. "Why did you kill the angel?"

"I had no choice. He was trying to protect the girl. He had to die."

Emma still stood behind me, clutching her elbows with wide white-rimmed eyes. She witnessed the brutal murder. But in real life or in her mind? Was that what sent her into the catatonic state? Witnessing the murder of an angel—in real life—didn't make sense. She must have seen it in her dream, or nightmare. And this Azriel guy...who was he to her?

"Was he her guardian angel or something?" I half meant it as sarcasm.

Azriel nodded, his reply deadpan. "Yes, he was."

A cold tendril crawled up my spine. Emma's guardian angel was now dead. What did that mean for her? What did Azriel want with her?

A hundred questions swirled through my head. I didn't know where to start or even if I should ask this black-winged bringer-of-death.

"What's the matter, Anna? You seem to be troubled." He took one step, then another, toward me, closing the gap between us.

I swallowed my panic and tried to break the dream connection but couldn't. Something or someone kept me there. In all the times I dream walked, that had never happened. I never had a coherent one-on-one conversation with someone else either.

The dead angel at my feet was troublesome. The only thing between Azriel and Emma was me. And Azriel—whoever he was—could speak to me and control my dream state.

"What do you want?"

"I've come for the girl. How fortunate for me I stumbled upon you." He stepped over the dead angel and circled me as a though I were his prey. "I've been wondering where to find you. I've been hunting for you. It's been a long time, *chérie*."

I didn't like this familiarity between us. He'd used the word *hunted* instead of *looking* like perhaps it was a new sport. I shifted from one foot to the other, watching him as he halted in front of me. His eyes flickered to Emma, who still stood behind me with wide eyes. She hadn't moved a muscle since Azriel showed up. Her bottom lip quivering was the only thing indicating she still breathed.

"I need you. You need me." His eyes glinted with a dark malevolence that told me I had no choice.

"I don't need anybody." I proved that when I uprooted myself and left England to return to the U.S. at eighteen. "And anyway, you're just a dream."

The corner of his mouth lifted in a half smile. "Am I?"

It was enough to make me question the thought. *Was* he a dream? "I don't know who the hell you are but I don't want anything to do with you."

Up close, Azriel had a god-like appearance. It almost hurt to look at him. Yet I found I couldn't look away.

"You will change your mind about that." His eyes lingered on my face then dipped down to my lips before flickering once more to Emma. "And now it's time for me to go."

He blew me a kiss then he flashed around me, moving so fast it was like a burst of light. He clamped one hand on Emma's shoulder and the other flattened over her heart. Her scream so loud and fierce, I thought my ears would bleed.

I watched, horrified. The color drained from her face. I couldn't move. I was frozen in place. Her appearance changed, as if she aged fifty years in mere seconds. Her hair turned stark white and lines and wrinkles adorned her once youthful face. Suddenly she went limp, falling to the floor as though all her bones had melted.

Azriel removed his hand, pulling away a pale pink light. His hand closed into a fist around it, the creases of his fingers glowing with the light. He flashed a grin and disappeared.

The second he was gone, I snapped out of her dream. I became dimly aware of the cacophony of alarms indicating she'd gone into cardiac arrest. I jumped up as more medical personnel burst into the room.

"What happened? Why didn't you call for help?"

"I-I...it happened so fast—"

"Get out of the way."

The nurse pushed me toward the exit. I stumbled and paced in the hallway, peering through the window of the room, trying to make sense of what happened. All I knew was Azriel touched her and she died in the dream.

Unable to be revived, Emma died that night in the hospital.

✦――――✦

After the doctor pronounced Emma's time of death and they carted her off to the morgue, I was done for the night. Tired and haunted by what I'd seen, I left the hospital.

As I exited, a guy leaned against one of the concrete pillars of the portico. The moment he saw me, he pierced me with his lethal gaze. His massive forearms were folded over his starched white button-down shirt. He wore faded jeans and scuffed cowboy boots. His devilish good-looks were criminal. It looked like he was trying too hard to be Texan. Dallas was home of the urban cowboy, pick-up trucks, Friday night lights, and fierce Texas pride. He might look the part, but I could spot a transplant anywhere.

A little warning bell screamed in my head. At first, I thought cop, but this guy didn't look like a cop and something was off. I couldn't put my finger on it.

As soon as I exited, he pushed off the pillar in a slow methodical way that turned my knees to water. He walked toward me with a brisk confident stride. Dawn stained the clear summer sky, fading from indigo to blue to indigo again. But it was still too early for the lights in the portico to turn off. His face was bathed in a garish yellow glow as he approached, giving him an authoritative look as his green-gold eyes pierced through me making me wish I was anywhere but there.

"You Anna Walker?" He spoke with the hint of a Texas drawl that sounded forced.

I gave a cautious nod. "I am."

"Kincade Harrison." He flashed a badge so quick I only got a glimpse of what looked like a gold star. "I want to ask you a few questions about the death of Emma Cox."

Great. Just what I needed. It hadn't been my finest hour and I wasn't sure how to explain what happened. I certainly couldn't tell him I dream walked her or he might lock me up in the mental ward. Straitjackets were so last season.

"What about her?" I tried to act casual without letting him know I was acting casual.

"You were the last one to see her alive."

It wasn't a question but I nodded as though it were.

"Witnesses found you sitting on her bed holding her hands. You're not a nurse so what are you?"

His odd phrasing of the question took me aback. I regarded him coolly. "I'm a phlebotomy tech."

"Phlebotomy tech, huh." His voice was tinged with disbelief. "Mind if you tell me what happened?"

Oh, I minded plenty. I shrugged. "I'm not sure. One minute she was fine. The next she'd coded."

"It was sudden?"

Well, now. I didn't have the answer to that. I assumed it was sudden but since I was in her dreams, I couldn't say.

"It was."

"Why were you holding her hands?"

He certainly had a lot of information about the incident for having just showed up.

I bit my lip, my mind racing for a quick explanation and then it hit me. "We were praying. Well, I was praying rather. It's something I do with patients." I hesitated. He lifted a brow in question, something Azriel had done. "I don't like the others knowing I do it."

He pressed his lips together but he understood and was smart enough to read between the lines. Sometimes folks were weird about that stuff. When he didn't ask another question, I continued, letting the words spill out of me in a frenzy.

"I pray with those patients because I like to think it gives them a sense of comfort here." I tapped my temple with my forefinger.

What a load of crap that was. I was totally making it up and he probably knew it. Well, it wasn't entirely a lie. I *was* a believer but I hadn't been to church in years. I *did* pray, but not with patients and not that often.

The guy's eyes narrowed, making my gut twist. "That so?"

I nodded.

He glanced up at the hospital's sliding doors, peering through the smoked glass at the neon sign above the receptionist's head that read *All Saints Hospital* in bright blue letters. I shifted from one foot to the other as he returned that sharp gaze to my face.

"What happened to her?"

"She coded."

"I *know* that." Frustration edged his voice. He stepped closer and I got a whiff of sandalwood and patchouli that was oh-so-masculine. "What happened, Miss Walker?"

"What happened was she went into cardiac arrest. She died while I held her hands and there wasn't a damn thing I could do to save her. I don't like watching patients die. I especially don't like seeing my friends die."

"You two were friends?"

"We were once, yes."

The closer he got, the bigger he looked. It was as if he sucked up all the air around me. I inhaled deeply and took a step back, his intimidation tactics working like a charm. He towered over my five-foot-six frame, forcing me to crane my neck to look up at him. I wasn't exactly petite, either. But standing so close to him gave new meaning to big and tall. We stared each other down. The whoosh of the sliding doors behind me indicated someone exited the building, followed by their footsteps on the concrete as they moved away.

"I don't imagine you enjoy seeing a friend die. I'm sorry for your loss." At last, he stepped back out of my personal space.

I stifled a yawn, pretending like none of it affected me. "Now if you don't mind, I'm exhausted and I'd like to go home."

He stepped aside and let me pass. As I walked by, I had the distinct feeling it wouldn't be the last I'd meet Kincade Harrison.

I drove home in a fog of grief and confusion, trying to puzzle out the things in Emma's dream starting with Azriel. He alluded to being real, not someone's dream image. While I believed divine influence worked at times, I didn't believe they walked among us.

It bothered me a lot he seemed to know me. And then there was the matter of what he did to Emma. Near as I could figure, he ripped her soul right out of her body and killed her. An icy ball of fright took up residence in the pit of my stomach and refused to go away. I arrived at the apartment I shared with my boyfriend. Ben recently landed his first legal job at a law firm in downtown Dallas specializing in commercial law. We lived in Uptown and had a small but classy apartment. We had the perfect life. But in my experience whenever things appeared perfect, shit was about to hit the fan. I opened the door to the delicious aroma of breakfast—bacon and sausage frying. My stomach immediately grumbled.

"There she is! My gorgeous girl."

Ben was a morning person. His sunny disposition rivaled the dawn. Not only that, he loved to cook which was great because I couldn't boil water without burning it and my disposition was far from sunny. He was tall, dark and certainly handsome with golden skin and a head of thick wavy black hair. His deep blue eyes were full of depth, life and unquenchable warmth that drew me in from the first moment we met.

He stood in the kitchen with a dish towel over his shoulder. His face practically beamed with his cheer. Here, with a spatula in his hand, he was in his element. I rounded the corner and spied crispy bacon on a platter. Sausage was cooking in a pan and pancakes were on the griddle.

"You're in a good mood." I snagged a piece of bacon and munched on it. He knew exactly how I liked it—burned and extra crispy. Yum.

He smacked me on the butt in greeting. I got a whiff of undertones of coffee, his aftershave and bacon. "I'm always in a good mood when you come home to me." He kissed my cheek.

That was Ben. Always saying the sweetest things to me. He was in touch with his emotions, unlike me. I tried not to feel too much about anything. Even Ben. We'd been dating for nearly a year and I still had trouble saying those three special words.

Lately, he kept dropped hints about getting married. I wasn't sure about having the white picket fence and two-point-three kids, either. And while I was happy with Ben and loved him and could imagine myself married to him, something about being married wasn't my destiny.

"How was work?" he asked.

I snagged another piece of bacon, not ready to talk about Emma. "Boring. Big day today?"

"I have an early meeting. Some big wig oil and gas tycoon is about to be sued." He scooped pancakes off the griddle and onto a plate. "I'll see you later?"

I nodded.

And then he was out the door. As he left, I didn't miss the disappointment on his face. We didn't have a lot of time with each other since I worked the night shift. So, I ate more bacon, the pancakes, had a cup of coffee and headed to bed with a giant yawn. Breakfast was my dinner.

I shimmied out of my scrubs and climbed into the soft bed, curling my arms around my pillow. As I drifted off, I couldn't help but think back on the dream walking I did with Emma.

I've been wondering where to find you.

I could still hear Azriel's voice in my head, as though I'd seen him in person. I wasn't sure what he meant by that, nor was I sure I wanted to find out. I shoved it out of my mind as I drifted to sleep.

But then something strange happened. The faint brush of a wing, feather soft, grazed my cheek. I stood in a forest. The wind blew, clacking dead tree branches together and swishing dried leaves. The huge moon hung low in the sky. The blue-white light glinted across his black wings and my breath caught in my throat. *Beautiful and dangerous.*

Black wings fully extended. Moonlight glistened off the feathers. The only other part of him I could see was his head, a black orb above the wings. When he turned, I glimpsed his face. Azriel snapped in his wings, folding them close to his body, and fully turned to face me.

His dark eyes glowed, mesmerizing me, tempting me. Taunting me. His face was all hard angles. He smiled a feral wicked smile. He swiped his tongue over his lips, leaving a damp sheen. A flicker of recognition hit me but it was faint and I couldn't grasp it.

"I'm coming for you."

I sat up and screamed.

CHAPTER 2

I CLUTCHED THE SHEET to my chest, my heart beating double-time. I could have sworn the dream was real. That I could feel Azriel's wing brushing my cheek. Calm sputtered through me as I came to the realization it was not real. Thank God. Glancing at the clock, only an hour had passed. I yawned again but I was wide-awake now thanks to the adrenaline rush.

I shoved the blankets off and stood. I needed a latte and the only place to get one was down the street. Ben and I lived in a trendy part of Uptown where shops were only a brief walk away. I pulled on a pair of jeans, a rumpled t-shirt, slipped on shoes and swept my black hair into a low ponytail.

A few minutes later, I exited the coffee shop with my favorite latte. As I headed back to the apartment, two big men with piercing dark eyes lumbered toward me. I glanced around to see if they were looking at someone else but nope, it was me.

I stayed where I was, waiting for this to play out. They halted in front of me and the biggest one looked me up and down. He had a switchblade in one hand, flicking it open and closed repeatedly.

Like that was supposed to impress me. Or intimidate me. I was neither. The second guy had a face like a bull with a smashed in nose and bushy eyebrows the color of ink. All that was missing was a ring though his nostrils.

"You Anna?"

"Could be. Depends who's asking."

He gave me a toothy grin that made me shiver as if spiders crawled down my spine.

He flicked the switchblade. Open. Close. "Someone wants a word with you." Open. Close.

I huffed out a sigh, trying to sound tough. "Someone like who?"

"Can't tell you."

"Then I can't help you." I started to step around them but the second one moved in front of me. When I turned around to go the other way, a third was behind me. I took a step backward but he put a hand in the middle of my back to stop me.

"Now, you can come with us real quiet like. Or we can make you come with us not so quiet like." Switchblade dude leaned down to speak in my ear, his rancid warm breath tickled the fine hairs on my neck.

"All I have to do is scream," I said.

He laughed. His voice still too close to my ear. "All you have to do is scream, huh? Boys, what do you think? Should we show her?"

They laughed as though it was the best joke ever. "Show her, Ox. Show her." This was from the second guy behind me, the one with the bull face. I decided to call him Bull.

His hot hand pressed between my shoulder blades, pinning me between him and the other guy who had forearms the size of a small tanker truck. The world around them moved into slow motion. It was as though an opaque veil dropped down to separate me and these creeps from everyone else. My stomach cramped and my hand tightened on the paper cup. Passersby walked around us as though we were invisible. I tried waving to grab the attention of several pedestrians but it was useless. It was like we stood inside some sort of bubble.

The reek of death and rot permeated the air around me, sticking in my nose and the back of my throat. I looked back at the three guys who had accosted me and realized they weren't guys at all. They were something else. Something I couldn't explain. Something terrifying.

They looked similar to their human appearances, but they were clearly not human. What were they?

"I don't understand." I tried to ignore the panic rising in my gut.

"You will. Boss wants a word with you. And I do what Boss says. Let's go." Switchblade's meaty hand clamped around my upper arm.

"Who's your boss?" I croaked.

"Time to find out, ain't it?" He grinned, showing two rows of sharp white teeth, a contrast against his tanned face.

He turned me around and wedged me between him and Bull. Tanker Arms with the huge forearms took up the rear. Meanwhile, as we walked toward a black sedan parked up the street, Switchblade started the open, close, open, close, thing again.

Tanker Arms took the wheel while Switchblade shoved me in the backseat and followed me in. I was sandwiched between him and Bull. I lost the taste for my latte. My stomach was in turmoil.

They took me through town and turned onto the road leading into Greenwood Cemetery. Not exactly my idea of a swell time. The gravel made for a bumpy ride and it jostled me between Switchblade and Bull. At a corner, the driver hung a left.

The car stopped at a large stone crypt with four columns dominating the front steps leading to a medieval-looking door with heavy iron hinges. Two leather-clad guys flanked the door. The name *Luciferus* was in large stone letters across the top. Somehow, I didn't think that bode well.

It seemed odd two guys stood guard at the entrance to the crypt in the middle of the day, but who was I to judge? Were they afraid something would be stolen? The peace of the dead would be disturbed? I wasn't sure.

Bull pushed open the car door and ushered me out. Switchblade gave me a shove to indicate he wouldn't tolerate any hesitation.

"What are we doing here?" I asked.

"Follow me," Switchblade said. Open, close, open, close.

Switchblade (a.k.a. Ox) led me toward the crypt. Tanker Arms led the way with Bull bringing up the rear. One of the leather-clad guys at the door descended the steps and flanked me, thereby pinning me between four overly muscled guys ensuring I didn't lose my nerve.

Good times.

Switchblade pulled open the door, his muscles straining. It must have been as heavy as it looked. I got a friendly shove to continue following him. Inside was what I expected. A stone tomb. It was so quiet and dark it gave new meaning to the phrase silent as the grave. A horror-chill rushed through me, turning the hairs on the back of my neck into ice.

Tank pushed something on the tomb and a trapdoor opened in the floor. Stairs led down into the ground. A damp earth smell wafted upward.

A flicker of warning invaded the shadows of my mind. Bull pushed me forward and I followed them down. My sneakers thumped off the concrete stairs as we descended. At the bottom, Switchblade opened the door. Bull shoved me inside and I stumbled forward.

Awful pushy, these guys.

"Easy," I snapped.

But he gave another push propelling me into the hallway. I could hear music thumping and vibrating the walls and realized I was headed to an underground club in the cemetery.

Guess it was the perfect place for it since there weren't any neighbors who'd complain about the noise.

Switchblade opened another door and led us inside a dark room with blaring music. Fluorescent paint was splattered on all the walls, floor, tables and chairs. My stomach cramped again. My mind began to grasp this was not a club for humans. I blinked, thinking maybe I was seeing things. Or maybe I was still dreaming. But no, this was all real.

Scantily clad waitresses swirled through the room with trays of drinks in colors I'd never seen before or thought possible. A vampire couple—vampires!—snuggled together in a booth. The man sliced open the woman's arm then leaned over to suck and lick her seeping blood. She closed her eyes in total ecstasy. Winged men and women crowded the dance floor enjoying each other's company. They all had a similar look to them. Wings colored from soft gray to black suggested they were far from angelic.

The stench of sulfur and death and decay nearly overpowered me, making me gag. I had no doubt the guys who accosted me on the street were demons, just as there were demons in this club.

Demons, vampires and fallen angels...oh, my. I had a bad feeling about this.

To say it took me by surprise would be an understatement. I had no idea this place existed, much less these supernatural beings. I gawked so hard it garnered the attention of one surly looking vampire who didn't particularly like it by showing his fangs. I shoved my eyes back in my head and snapped my head around. Sure, I heard the stories vampires and all the rest were real, but I ignored them like any other normal human.

But then, I wasn't exactly normal.

And the fact angels were real made me wonder about Emma and her dead guardian angel. Had that really happened?

The demon guys led me past all the grunge demon rockers, past the funky vampires, past the wicked angels. All from the wrong side of the underground tracks.

Switchblade halted at the back of the club outside a door with a sign reading Office in white block letters. He didn't knock before entering. As the door swung shut, silence enveloped us. My ears rang from the sudden change in decibels.

A plush red carpet covered the floor. A settee and several chairs were in front of a gas fireplace. On one side was an oak bar loaded with colorful bottles and shimmering glasses. A couple of doors led out of the room. The place looked more like an apartment than an office.

"Wait here," Switchblade ordered.

They scattered across the room. They poured drinks and lit cigarettes, making themselves quite at home. I, however, was left in the middle of the room trying to ignore the tightening in my chest, the prickling hairs on the back of my neck and my heart beating too fast for its own good. Not to mention the heated sweat on my palms.

Switchblade disappeared through one of the doors. I glimpsed another hallway before it closed. Uncomfortable silence. If I had been smart, I would have left. Turned and run through the club but I couldn't make my feet move. Fear rooted me in place despite the gut feeling telling me to get the hell out of Dodge.

I tried to decide where to look, still holding my paper coffee cup. They ignored me and I ignored them. Minutes passed until the door finally opened and Azriel swooped inside. He walked with a confident gait, his arms swinging by his side and his head held high. He exuded confidence.

Azriel. He was real. And he was the boss. The latte churned in my stomach. The dream with Emma was real.

We eyed each other for the first time. He sized me up as I did him. He was taller than I expected with a full head of wavy black hair slicked back from his handsome face with all the razor-sharp angles. He still had that same feral look. His black eyes glittered as though they had stardust in them.

He didn't bother to hide the expanse of his iridescent black wings and I wondered how exactly that worked. Did he have special wing holes cut out of his shirt? A shirt, by the way, that strained against the muscles of his chest, abs and biceps. His waist tapered down into dark blue jeans ending in a pair of black motorcycle boots complete with shiny silver buckles.

He smelled like cinnamon.

Not that I noticed.

"Leave." His gaze never left mine.

His abrupt order made the men scatter like scurrying mice, disappearing through the door the way they'd come. Azriel eyed me for a long moment before smiling that wolf smile. "Thank you for coming."

"What do you want?"

He chuckled. "Direct and to the point. I like that in a girl. I appreciate the opportunity to speak with you in person, Anna."

"Like I had a choice."

He advanced, closing the distance between us. His lusty feral gaze raked over me making me want to skinny dip in bleach.

"True I considered extending a personal invitation to you, however I didn't want to take a chance you'd refuse. I wanted to see you in person."

He reached a hand toward me and I flinched backward, out of his way. He didn't bother to hide his disappointment. "Lovely as ever. But why do you wear your hair like that? It should be down, not up."

I stepped away from him. "I'll ask again. What is it you want from me?"

He walked to the bar and poured a drink. "I have a proposition for you. Could I offer you a refreshment?"

"I'd rather drink a glass of tacks."

He laughed. But I was serious. He came around the bar, holding a highball swirling the amber liquid. We eyed each other and I wasn't sure where this was going. "Get to the point already."

He ignored me, took a sip and perched on the edge of one of the plush chairs. "Will you sit?" He propped his ankle on a knee and waved to the opposite chair but I shook my head. I wanted to be ready to run at a moment's notice. "Suit yourself. You and I have something in common."

"We have absolutely nothing in common." I shifted my weight from one foot to the other, still clutching the cup to keep my hands from fidgeting.

"We can both dream walk."

"We can."

That was true, yes, but he was lethal. I learned from my uncle certain lines should never be crossed. Sort of like the unwritten rules of dream walking etiquette. I doubted Azriel would follow those unwritten rules or even give a damn about them.

"You are, perhaps, wondering why I was in that girl's dream."

"Not really." I made sure I sounded as bored as possible. "But you're going to tell me anyway."

"There are a great many things you don't know, Anna. But I will teach you if you'll let me."

"I don't think so." No way in hell was I going to take lessons from this guy. I had enough lessons from my now-estranged uncle to understand what I could and couldn't do and I didn't need any pointers from this dark angel. "What about the girl?"

"She deserved to die. She was nothing." His gaze never left my face, a flicker of hatred in his eyes.

No, she wasn't. She was my friend. She wanted to be a high school English teacher, marry and have kids. She wanted to travel the world. She had hopes and dreams like I did. I never knew if she and Ryan got married or had kids and I wondered about that now.

Had I stepped into the Twilight Zone or something? None of this made sense. Demons and vampires and angels patronized the nightclub. What did that mean exactly? I decided to play it cool. Like it was all situation normal.

"She had her whole life ahead of her. You didn't have to kill her."

"As I said, she was weak but her soul will make an excellent addition for us."

"Us?"

"The Fallen."

"The Fallen?" I repeated.

He rolled his eyes and huffed, exasperated. "Have you forgotten everything? We are here to claim what is ours."

I had no idea what the hell he was talking about. I'd never heard of the Fallen. Again, I shifted from one foot to another, remaining silent and waited.

"I'm in need of your unique talents."

The heated lust in that look gave me a serious ick factor. I could feel the prickle of his mind pushing against mine. An image of us having sex burst into my mind. I imagined a thick stone wall and blocked him out. My free hand clenched, nails digging into my palm.

"Stop it."

He chuckled louder this time. "Did the image not please you?"

"What do you want?" I ground out.

"I do so love toying with you but I'll get to the point." He took a sip of his drink. "A war is coming. A war that will end all. All that anyone knows. I've been authorized to hire you to help us."

"Who's 'us'? Who authorized you?"

He clucked his tongue as if I were a failing student disappointing him. "You know who I work for."

"Who?" I ground the one-syllable word between my teeth. I had a solid guess but I had to hear him say it.

He sighed. "We are the Fallen." He sneered at me as if I was as stupid as the rest of the human race. "Lucifer. Who else?"

My blood turned to ice in my veins. Chilling me from head to toe. The Fallen. Angels who lost their place in the heavens. What the bloody hell did they want from me?

"I want nothing to do with you." As an afterthought, I said, "Any of you."

His feathers ruffled. "Come now. Don't be that way. We're not a bad lot."

Ha. Right. "Hilarious." No way was I going to work for Lucifer. So not going there.

"At least listen to the reason why we seek you?"

I didn't say anything. But I didn't run either even though I should have.

"You, my dear, are going to help us get what we want."

I didn't like the sound of that. "And what is that?"

"Redemption."

I nearly choked on my own spit. My mouth went bone dry and my stomach knotted. The only way they would achieve redemption was if they could return to the heavens. Pretty sure that wasn't going to happen. Maybe if Hell froze over.

Maybe Hell was going to freeze over. Oh, shit.

"And, uh, how do you propose to do that?"

"With your help. You are the only one that can find what we seek."

He dragged out the explanation on purpose to keep me there. It got on my nerves. He was trying to bait me. With this game of Twenty Questions, I'd never get out. I stood and waited.

"No questions?" he asked.

"Cut to the chase." I jiggled my cup. The remnants of my latte sloshed in the bottom. Not enough to drink and probably cold by now.

He laughed a dark bitter laugh. "You're going to help us find the Holy Relics. Starting with the Horn of Gabriel." He rose, placed his empty glass on the nearby bar, and then moved to me. A little too close for my comfort.

"The Horn of Gabriel, huh? Never heard of it or the Holy Relics. And why would I do that?"

"Because you do not wish to die."

Good reason. When I didn't come up with a snappy comeback, he narrowed his gaze and moved closer.

"Refusing us would be a grave error."

Grave error. Was he joking? "Okay, I'll play along. Say I agree to help you. Then what?"

"You will search for the Horn of Gabriel and deliver it to me."

"And how would I find this horn?"

"That is up to your discretion."

Like I was supposed to pull that out of my ass. "And how many of these artifacts are there?"

"Five. Once you bring them all to me, I will hand them over to my lord master."

"Five? Are you smoking crack, too? I have no idea where to find this Horn of Gabriel much less four other artifacts." I didn't know where to begin. I didn't even know what the other four artifacts were. "If I do, then what happens?"

"So inquisitive. I like that about you, Anna. Lucifer uses them to achieve his ultimate goal."

"Which is redemption?"

"Yes."

"And...that involves what exactly? Control of the world?"

"Something like that."

My eyebrows knitted. "How exactly does having five Holy Relics give you redemption?"

His wings rippled with annoyance. "Redemption comes in many different forms. When we have what we want, the Seven Seals will be broken. The Four Horsemen will arrive. Your god will fall. And Man will worship my leader instead."

Armageddon. That's what he was talking about. I refused to allow that to scare me as I tried valiantly to ignore the dizzy fear sweeping through me.

"Blah, blah, blah. Holy Relics. Blah, blah, blah. World domination." I waved my free hand around like I was over it when I was really trying to hide my shaking limbs. "Sounds like a lot of hard work to me. Not my idea of a good time. I'm afraid I'll have to decline your offer."

Pure straight-up bravado but I wasn't about to let him see how freaked out I was. I didn't want to be a part of Armageddon or whatever it was. And, uh, what were the Holy Relics?

"I find your lack of enthusiasm disheartening."

"Sorry, bucko, but you've way over estimated my abilities. Besides, I have no idea what these relics are or even where to find them so I doubt I'd be very much help."

"You have no clue as to your abilities, do you?"

"I can dream walk. So what?"

His eyes never left mine. Even though I wanted to look away, I couldn't. That hint of a wolfish grin was on his face.

"Oh, but you are more than a dream walker. So much more. You are the only one who can find the relics." He reached for my hair. His fingers trailed through my ponytail, the strands falling like silk. The tips of his fingers grazed my neck.

I slapped his hand away. "Maybe I wasn't clear. I'm not helping you." I tried to sound confident as I enunciated each word.

"You are making a mistake." Again, his lethal gaze went down my body. He licked his lips.

"Why don't you put your eyes back in your head?" I gave him a violent shove backward.

"Clearly, you need further persuasion. You will be given another opportunity to agree to help us." He ignored me and continued to look at me as though he'd ripped every article of clothing off my body. As though he was ready to lick every inch of my naked flesh with his hot damp tongue.

Stop it. Just stop it. Think of Ben. Only of Ben.

"Ah, yes. Your attractive boyfriend. Ben Turner, is it?"

Fury spilled through me and my hand tightened on the cup so hard I crushed it. Remnants of latte spewed out onto the garnet rug. I recognized the veiled threat. Azriel chuckled.

"And if I don't help you?"

"I will be forced to convince you in other ways."

Ben. He threatened Ben's life without saying it. "Stay away from me. And Ben."

I left my crumpled paper cup on a nearby table. I hurried from the room, my hands shaking and my gut twisting.

◆————————◆

I stumbled my way through the club pounding acid rock music to the stairs and out the crypt without anyone noticing. Or maybe Azriel had decided to let me go. The car was still parked outside with the Fallen driver leaning casually against the shiny exterior, ankles crossed. He didn't bother to conceal his wings. He smoked a cigarette as he flipped through a Playboy. When I burst out of the crypt, he glanced up.

"Need a lift?"

"No, thanks."

I'd rather walk than take my chances with a fallen angel. I bolted out of the cemetery and hurried down the street. Luckily, the apartment was a ten-minute sprint but it was the middle of a scorching summer day in Dallas and I wasn't too keen on running. I settled for a brisk walk and hoped I could get back home without running into more unsavory characters.

As I walked, I spotted more and more of the supernatural beings I'd witnessed under the crypt.

The world had shifted suddenly as though my eyes were opened for the first time. I never realized vampires, fallen angels and demons roamed the city. That translucent veil I'd seen before was back again, as though I stood on another plane, in another dimension, in another world that was my own but not my own. I could see them now everywhere. Other people—regular people—could not.

I stopped in the middle of the sidewalk, heat radiating upward from the concrete and burning through the soles of my sneakers. A vampire hissed at me as he walked by, his fangs bared. A hairy beast of a man growled. I wondered if he was a werewolf. Several demons stinking of death and decay passed by me. The stench in the club was that of the demons. Now, at least, I could identify them.

I assumed the Fallen allegiance to Azriel. Then there were angels like the one I'd seen in Emma's dream that had been killed. All mingling with humans and humans not seeing them.

A hand clamped around my upper arm, breaking through the veil. It was suddenly gone and I was back to standing in the heat. I yelped and glanced up into a pair of familiar green-gold eyes. Detective Harrison—if he was a detective—dragged me out of the middle of the sidewalk and into a nearby frozen yogurt shop, his jaw set in a firm line. He was clearly unhappy with me.

"Sit." He pointed to one of the orange chairs.

"Hello, detective." I wasn't going to argue. I sat. Though my insides were a quivering mess, I sounded fairly calm.

"Are you trying to get yourself killed?" He raked a hand over the stubble on his chin, his skin bristling.

He wore a sport coat—in summer? Was he nuts?—over a crisp white shirt, faded blue jeans and those scuffed cowboy boots. He propped his hands at his waist revealing his gun holster and gave me a look of exasperation. Like a dad annoyed with his kid.

"What do you mean?"

He kicked the opposite chair out and swung his long leg over as he sat. He leaned forward on the table, his face low and his voice lower. "You didn't know, did you?"

"I..." Words failed me. I was scared to put into words what I'd seen. As if that would make it all too real. A little piece of me wanted to pretend I'd imagined it all.

He peered at me intently. I peered right back trying hard not to let him intimidate me, even though he was super intimidating with his overbearing presence. His eyes narrowed, he inhaled slowly and then exhaled.

"Who are you, Miss Walker?"

I swallowed a sudden lump. "What kind of question is that?"

He snarled. Actually snarled, baring teeth and everything. "Don't play games with me. Tell me who you are."

I stiffened, defensive. "I already did."

"You said you were a phlebotomy tech. But what else? And don't lie to me again."

I pressed my lips together. Who was this guy anyway?

"You weren't praying with that girl in the hospital, were you?" he asked.

Crap.

His intense gaze made me want to look away. But then he would win and he'd know I'd fibbed.

"The truth, Miss Walker."

"Okay, all right. No, I wasn't praying. I was..." I halted. How could I say it without sounding like I was cracked? I glanced around but there were no customers. The only one in the place was the guy behind the counter. "I was in her mind."

He blinked once, twice. Surprise flickered over his face before he managed to control it. "How?"

"It's just something I do. It's not a big deal. I can...see dreams."

"What did you see?" He was relentless and accepted my explanation without pause. As though it were an everyday occurrence to be in someone's mind.

"Nothing."

"Lie. What did you see in her dream?"

How did he know? "A dead angel. One wing had been ripped out."

His jaw clenched, the muscles flexing. "What did he look like?"

"I didn't see his face." But the image of those bloody wings still very much haunted my mind. "You're not a detective, are you?"

"I'm asking the questions. What else did you see?" Fire flashed in his eyes.

I didn't bother to hide my glare. "Someone else was there. He had black wings. He was tall. Muscular. Had black eyes."

"His name is Azriel." It wasn't a question.

Shit. He knew the guy? "Maybe."

The detective's eyes narrowed. "Maybe?"

"Okay, yeah. His name is Azriel. How did you know that?"

"I've been tracking him for a while. He's responsible for several murders."

"Several murders?"

He stood with such sudden velocity, his chair raked back on the tile floor then tipped over and crashed, bouncing several times before stopping. It got the shopkeeper's attention, who had mostly ignored us until then.

"Are you going to buy something?" he asked.

I piped up before the detective could respond. "You said I could have a frozen yogurt."

Surprise widened his eyes before they narrowed again with annoyance. He waved toward the dispensers. "Be my guest."

I hoped the distraction would move us off the topic of Azriel.

Before he changed his mind, I hurried toward the yogurt. I piled my red velvet cheesecake variety high with all sorts of things that were bad—white chocolate chips, crushed Butterfingers, chocolate sauce, graham cracker crumbs. The detective wasn't too happy about paying but he did it.

A few seconds later, we were out of the shop walking down the street again. By then, I'd practically finished the frozen treat. I licked the spoon clean. "Are you a real detective?"

"You like ice cream?"

"Frozen yogurt," I corrected. "And yeah, I could pretty much eat my weight in the stuff. And ice cream, too. Are you gonna answer my question or not?"

"Not."

"Figures."

"My car is parked there. I'll give you a lift home." He motioned to a black sedan at a meter.

I considered telling him no, but it was hot as hell and sweat rolled down my back. "Okay."

In the car, he cranked the AC to high, then pulled away from the curb.

"I live in the Westin Apartments," I said.

"I know where you live."

I blinked. "You do?"

His answer was sullen silence.

"Look, detective, I told you who I was. You could at least do the same and tell me who you are. You can see these supernaturals, too, right?"

"Yes."

"And you're not a detective, are you?"

He hit the brakes hard for a stop light, making the seat belts lock against both of us. He reached into the inner pocket of his sport coat and pulled out his badge, tossing it into my lap. The badge was shiny gold with a star in the middle with "Police" curving around the top and "Dallas, Texas" around the bottom. No picture ID.

"This is supposed to convince me you're a cop for Dallas PD?" I brandished the badge in the air. "Where's your ID?"

"I'm part of a covert division. I can't disclose it." He practically growled the words and snatched the badge out of my hand. He tucked it back into his coat pocket.

"Huh," was my only response.

He was hiding something. All it did was confirm my suspicions he wasn't a detective. At least, not for the Dallas PD. But I'd play along for now.

"Covert like James Bond or something?"

The light turned green and he floored it, burning rubber. I wondered what he was so bent about. When he skidded to the side of the road and slammed on the brakes again, I figured I was about to get my answer. He rounded on me, his face pinched with anger and his neck turning a bright shade of red.

"Do you think this is funny, Miss Walker?"

"Well—"

"Because it's not."

"I—"

"Azriel is dangerous. I have reason to believe he was responsible for that woman's death in the hospital and you're treating this like it's some sort of joke."

"Now hang on—"

"A guardian angel is dead, Miss Walker. Not to mention a young woman."

"Don't you think I know that? I was there when she died!" I unbuckled my seat belt, preparing to jump ship but he caught my arm. I turned back to him. "What?"

"What was in the girl's mind that you're not telling me?"

"Nothing." I tried to jerk my arm away but he held fast.

"Lie. Try again."

My gaze was locked onto his. It was hard to look away even though I wanted to. "I told you. A dead angel and Azriel. He said he killed her guardian angel."

"And what else?" He nodded agreement. His hand tightened on my arm, his fingers pressing into the flesh.

I had to tell him because he wouldn't think I was a lunatic. Somehow, I suspected he would believe me and maybe try to help me.

"Azriel touched the girl. He pulled her..." Pausing, I tried to think how to describe it, "...essence away from her body, held it in his hand then closed his fist around it. He killed her. I'm sure of it."

He released me as though I were on fire and sat back in his seat, looking me over. The anger had dissipated and was replaced by thoughtful consideration.

"Tell me everything you know about the victim, Miss Walker."

"The victim had a name. Emma. My friend. She'd come to the hospital a few days ago in that catatonic state. There's been fifty patients like that over the last month."

"And had you entered their minds, too?"

"No, I did it with Emma because I knew her. I thought I could help her. I wasn't sure it would work because normally I do it while the person sleeps. I figured her state of mind would be similar and I owed it to her to try."

"Did it?"

I nodded. "It felt like a memory instead of something in a dream. There was a house with green walls. The angel was dead in the kitchen." I waited to gauge his reaction. Then added, "You don't think I'm crazy?"

"No, I don't. In fact, I think you can help me."

I caught a glimpse of a brief smile. Nothing more than a quick lift of the corner of his mouth that gave no indication he was happy. It faded as quickly as it appeared and somewhere, deep in the back of my mind, I knew I was in for a rocky ride with the detective.

CHAPTER 3

KINCADE DROPPED ME OFF at my apartment after we'd come to an understanding. I would help him catch Azriel. Hey, that worked for me since I wasn't interested in the fallen angel's business proposition. If I could remove Azriel from my life by having him arrested, I was all for that. I agreed to meet him after my shift tomorrow. I didn't share where to find Azriel. Kincade hadn't asked that question and I hadn't volunteered the info. I assumed he already had a lead.

I bounded up the stairs to my third-floor apartment, my legs burning with the quick sprint, and unlocked the door. Sweat trickled down my back as I shoved inside, thankful for the blast of cold air in the face. I had enough time for a quick nap before I had to head to the hospital for work. I was dead tired after all the excitement with Azriel and the detective.

Immediately, the scent of strawberries and chocolate assaulted my nose. Nothing in the apartment smelled like chocolate *or* strawberries. Had Ben come home for a mid-afternoon rendezvous? I grinned at the thought of having an afternoon delight.

"Ben? Are you here?"

Our apartment wasn't that big. On the left, off the entry, was a small study with a desk and bookshelf. The kitchen and dining nook were off to the right. The living room wasn't much larger than the bedroom.

"Hello?"

No answer. I walked through to the bedroom, flipped on the light. The French door to the balcony was ajar and the scent was strong there. Humid afternoon air poured into the room warring with the air conditioner trying to keep the place cool. Cautiously, I moved to the door, pushed it open and peered out.

No one. Shrugging, I closed the door and turned around.

A winged man stood on the other side of the bed. I yelped, nearly jumping out of my skin at the sight of him. I pressed a hand against my rapidly beating heart. *He* was the source of the delectable smell.

"You scared the life out of me!"

He was tall with ice blue eyes and short black hair. He towered over me by at least six inches. His wings spanned maybe five or six feet and were white as the purest snow. They looked soft, too. His handsome face was all hard angles, his body toned and muscular. He wore jeans, black boots and a white shirt that hugged his torso, showing off corded abs.

I could only guess he wasn't one of the Fallen since his wings were white, not black. He didn't appear to be as sinister as Azriel. He appeared to be something else. Something divine.

"Annabelle Marie Walker, I believe."

The bottom dropped out of my stomach and my knees threatened to turn to water. Did all these guys know who I was without having to tell them? Kinda creepy.

No one had used my full first name in a long time. The last person who did...well, he was dead to me. It had taken me a while to shed the old Annabelle Walker to become Anna and I wasn't about to backtrack. I wasn't going down without a fight.

"Annabelle Marie no longer exists. It's just Anna now."

"Oh? Last I checked Annabelle Marie Walker was you."

Oh, great. A smartass angel. That's what I needed to end this weird day. "What can I do for you, angel boy?"

He scowled, unappreciative of my nickname. "You have been approached by the Fallen."

Was that the deal with angels? You couldn't hide from them? "Yeah? So?"

He smiled. A smile that said he wasn't amused. "It would be in your best interest if you refused to help them."

"And why is that?" I pinched the bridge of my nose between thumb and forefinger, my head throbbing.

"Because your eternal soul is at stake."

More threats? Did I have a target on my back or something? "What do you want, angel? I'm exhausted and would like to go to bed."

"Mind your tongue, dream walker. I am Joachim and I've been sent with a message for you."

"Oh, yeah? Who sent you?"

"The archangel, Michael."

I fought the urge to laugh. I wasn't sure why that reaction was my first at seeing the messenger angel. Maybe because I was delirious with fatigue. It'd been a long day. Or maybe because I had been visited by enough celestial beings for one day.

"Michael, huh?" He wasn't kidding. My legs gave out as I sank to the edge of the bed.

"The Horn of Gabriel. Azriel asked you to bring it to him, yes?"

"That again?" I rolled my eyes.

"I assure you this is not to be taken lightly."

"Yeah, yeah, yeah. End of the world stuff. That's what Azriel said."

"You do not believe him?"

"Should I?" I met his gaze and all I could hear was the whoosh of blood pounding in my ears.

He stiffened, clearly unhappy with my challenge, and walked to the edge of the bed. The queen mattress was the only thing separating us. "Perhaps it's time to ask yourself what you believe, Annabelle."

"Just *Anna*," I corrected, sounding prim and proper.

"Is it? Strange that's not what's in the Book of Names."

I gave him a flat look. No one called me Annabelle, not even my uncle.

"You don't yet realize how special you are."

I huffed. "I'm nothing special."

A humorless grin creased his mouth. "Soon, you will find your powers and realize who you are."

Azriel had alluded to something similar—that I had powers not yet realized. What was everyone trying to tell me? And why all the mystery? I huffed, breathing hard, like I'd just run the forty. "I'm not sure I believe in all this predestined crap."

He stared at me with an all-too familiar look. I'd lived with disapproval all my life.

"Fine. What do you want me to do?"

"I want you to bring *me* the Horn of Gabriel. In turn, I will hand it over to Michael for safekeeping while you search for the other four relics."

I threw up my hands in disgust. "Are all of you crazy? I'm not searching for the other four relics. I'm not searching for *any* relics."

"It would be unwise to refuse an archangel's request."

"Maybe you didn't get the memo I'm a complete moron." Aggravation clawed through me as I returned to my seat on the edge of the bed, keeping the wide mattress between us. "And if I refuse?"

"Do not try me, Annabelle."

"Are you threatening me?"

"Take it as you will. You mock me and the Fallen. It is not wise to make either of us enemies."

"Noted."

I glanced over my cuticles pretending to be bored while trying to hide the fear shaking through me. That was the second threat I received that day from sources that shouldn't be taken lightly. I didn't want to believe I was anything special because I wasn't. My mother was dead. I had no idea about my father and my uncle...well, even though he was family and he'd raised me for a few years, he'd kept me at arm's length. I'd never gotten close to anyone, even Ben. I liked it like that.

"You really don't know who are you, do you?"

I peered up at him, not wanting to admit the truth for fear he would tell me. He rubbed the back of his neck.

"You, Annabelle, are the key to the coming war. And there *is* a war coming. It will decide the fate of all mankind."

I stared at him as though he'd grown a second head, my heart jumping around in my chest and my stomach clenched. He couldn't possibly mean me. He had the wrong Anna.

There was no way I was the key to save all of mankind. Hell, I couldn't even save myself. I was nothing more than a wanna-be vampire who prowled the hospital at night drawing blood. I don't save people. Let alone the whole fucked-up world.

"You've got the wrong girl."

His lips thinned in anger. He clearly had enough of me. "You will bring me the Horn of Gabriel and the other Holy Relics."

"Oh, yeah? And how am I supposed to get it to you?"

"You're a resourceful girl. I'm sure you'll figure it out."

Joachim walked around the bed and stood before me. I looked up into his icy blue eyes. His wings were within touching distance. I resisted the urge to reach out and stroke them.

"You will bring me the Horn of Gabriel, won't you?"

Something about the way he looked at me, the way he said it made me nod agreement. "Yes."

"If these artifacts fall into Lucifer's hands, the world will be doomed to eternal damnation. I *can* count on you. Can't I, Annabelle?"

I hated he knew my true name and used it whenever he wished. But he was a messenger angel. That gave him the right.

I swallowed the lump in my throat. "You can."

"Glad to hear it." He turned toward the balcony door, opened it and stepped out.

"Wait. How do I find it? Where do I look?"

But he was already gone.

◆————▶

I tried to nap, but it was a fitful sleep. Being contacted by a messenger angel sent by Michael, a handsome detective tracking an angel murderer, and a fallen angel sent by Lucifer all in one day messed with my chi. All I needed was at least one hour of rest to work my night shift but it wasn't working out. Finally, I gave up and dragged myself out of bed with a yawn. It took all my strength to shower and head to work.

On my way, Ben called. I answered it with a forced smile. "Hi!"

"Hey, baby. I'm working late on a brief before heading home."

He always liked to check in with me even though I wasn't there. I grinned. "Don't work too late."

"I won't. You remember Frank Shotter?"

"You mean Shitter?" I laughed. Frank worked with Ben at his law firm. I'd met him at last year's Christmas party where I learned he earned the nickname because of his fondness for using the word shit in creative ways.

"He checked into the hospital today."

"What happened?"

"No one is really sure. I don't think he'd been sleeping much lately."

Alarm bells screamed Red Alert in my head. I wondered if he'd been struck with the latest illness.

"He's at your hospital. I wondered if you could look in on him for me?"

I hesitated. My last episode with Emma didn't turn out well at all. I swallowed hard. Even so, it was hard to say no to Ben. "I'll do what I can, but you know how strict the HIPPA laws are." And I'd already violated them once.

"Thanks, babe. See you in the morning?"

We signed off with our standard exchange of love words.

Sometimes I wondered how our relationship was supposed to work being on two very different schedules.

As I started my shift for the night, I thought back on yesterday's freakiness. What had I gotten myself into? All because I couldn't leave well enough alone and *not* dream walk Emma. What would happen if I said no to Azriel? To Joachim? I didn't think I could defy either of them, but I was going to have to tell one of them no. I knew which was the lesser of two evils.

Either way I was totally in over my head.

The only person on the planet that had answers for me was my uncle. And the thought of going back to Somerset made me want to break into hives. My trust with Uncle Edward had been shattered when I was barely eighteen.

Ten years had passed since then. My uncle had been strict and disciplined. He wanted structure and obedience. He believed in duty and responsibility. My world revolved around lessons and mealtimes. I had to follow strict rules and rigorous classes my uncle shoved on me. I had the best tutors in England since I was homeschooled. I could read Latin and Greek, though not very well.

Until I met someone that could take me away from it all. Edward made sure that never happened.

I shoved all those unwanted memories out of my mind and checked into the lab for my assignments for the night. It was quiet, so I made my way to the wing where all these patients ended up. I found Frank's room with ease. Sure enough, he was in a catatonic state. I checked his chart. The same symptoms were there. Unable to sleep, followed by loss of appetite, nightmares, and then finally the staring into space. Unable to communicate, eat or drink. He had a feeding tube attached, unlike Emma. She hadn't. Maybe she still had some coherency and that was why I stepped into her mind with such ease.

The prognosis for these patients weren't good. Some had been there for months in that trance-like state. None had recovered. A few had died, including Emma.

I had to help Frank. Or at least I had to try.

I perched on the edge of the bed, looking at him. Even though he was in his late thirties, he looked like he had aged twenty years since I'd last seen him. I hesitated reaching for his hand. Should I do this? It was possible the same thing that happened with Emma would happen with Frank.

I took a deep breath and laid my hand on top of his.

I closed my eyes and a moment later, I was in his mind. It was quite easy to push through into his mind, like it was with Emma. But unlike Emma, I was immediately dumped into a scene of chaos.

We were on a rail train, speeding from downtown Dallas to the northern parts of the city. Someone screamed. The lights flickered overhead. And there at the end of the train stood Azriel. He had blood running down one cheek and looked even more menacing than usual.

"Stay out of this, dream walker," he snarled at me. "You're not part of this."

I was going to say he made me part of it when someone shoved me from behind with such force I flew forward. I threw my hands out to catch myself and smashed against the metal flooring. Pain shot through my hands and arms up to my shoulders. I only had enough time to roll over when someone leapt over me and landed in front of Azriel.

I glanced up. His snowy white wings spread open behind him. A few of the feathers drifted to the floor near my face. They were perfect. White. Dotted with blood.

"If you want Frank, you'll have to go through me," the angel said.

"My pleasure, Kaziel." A knife materialized in Azriel's hand.

They charged each other. I heard the slap of skin against skin. Bones crashing against one another. I scrambled to my feet and found Frank sitting calmly in one of the seats. He'd been stabbed. Blood dampened his shoulder.

"Frank, come on. I have to get you out of here."

He blinked and looked up at me with sightless eyes. Then his brows drew together. "Do I know you?"

"I met you once. You work with my boyfriend, Ben."

"Ben?"

I grabbed his arm and hauled him to his feet. "I'll explain later."

I started for the back of the train. Behind me there was a loud bellow and then someone—Azriel—shouted to "stop her." I shoved Frank in front of me and urged him to hurry but he shuffled his feet. I wasn't exactly sure where I was going. Only that I had to get off the train.

A sharp pain speared through my back. I shrieked with the pain. A short-handled dagger stuck out of my shoulder. As I reached to pull it out, I saw a demon charging me, his razor-sharp teeth bared, a knife in his hand.

I froze. I had no idea what to do.

Before he reached me, he flew backward. An arm wrapped around his upper torso and his throat was slit. The demon crumpled to the ground. The angel, Kaziel, saved me. Time stood still for that brief moment. It was as though some silent communication passed between us. His gaze flickered to Frank, then back to me. He gave me a nod of thanks as though he understood I was trying to save him.

"Who are you?" His hands clenched as he looked me up and down, suspicion in his eyes.

"I'm trying to help. I—Behind you!"

I was too late. Before Kaziel could turn to fight off Azriel's attack, the fallen angel grabbed one of his wings and jerked. Hard. A horrifying ripping sound followed by the angel's agonized scream piercing the air. Blood spurted, splattering across Azriel's chest.

Kaziel fell forward, landing on his hands and knees. The color had drained from his skin. Azriel stood behind him holding one of his wings as though it were a trophy. The fallen angel grinned at me before slitting the angel's throat.

Bile surged to my throat. I made a valiant effort not to throw up. And now I was faced with Azriel.

"You should not have interfered." Dark rage creased his face and flashed in those black eyes as he advanced on me.

Terror slashed through me, shredding what little confidence I had left. I backed up a step, standing in front of Frank as though I were a human shield. I wasn't sure how much good that would do since I was defenseless.

"I'd kill you, too, dream walker, but that would displease my lord master."

His threat was a shallow one. He'd already told me he wouldn't kill me because he—and his lord master—needed me alive. "We wouldn't want to disappoint him now, would we?"

His eyes narrowed, making him look more menacing than usual. "Stand aside, girl, and let me have him. He's been marked."

"Marked?"

"Move or die. Final warning." He flexed his fingers, ready to strike.

I lifted my chin in defiance. "If you want him, you'll have to take him."

He didn't like that answer. "So be it."

Azriel flashed around me, shoved me out of his way. My head cracked against the back of a seat and I saw stars. I crawled to my hands and knees, trying not to pass out and forced myself to turn my head in time to see him put his hand over Frank's heart, exactly as he had with Emma.

Like Emma, Frank shrieked with the pain as he aged quickly. Azriel pulled out a blue light, closing it in his fist and then disappeared.

Frank was dead.

CHAPTER 4

I WOKE UP IN a fog. My head pounded with a raging headache. I sat in a chair at the nurse's station outside Frank's room, a Styrofoam cup of water in my hand. I didn't remember getting there. I only had a vague recollection of someone forcibly removing me from his bed.

Azriel had killed him in the dream. In real life, he was dead. The commotion in his room was a distant hum. They frantically tried to save him. But Frank couldn't be saved. Understanding about what I witnessed dawned. Azriel said Frank had been marked. He took his life force—his soul. I had no doubt he'd done the same to Emma. But for what purpose?

That would make two patients dead in less than twenty-four hours. And I was present for both. I was not exactly batting a thousand here. It would call undue attention to me. I'd have to explain. Even defend myself.

But how? How was I going to tell my superiors it wasn't my fault? They would never believe a fallen angel had been responsible. Especially one that wasn't even *here* in real life.

How was I going to tell Ben? What the fuck was I going to do?

Dr. Ortiz, the resident on duty, exited the room and marched across the hall to the nurses' station. The only thing separating me from him was the desk.

"Is he...?" But I already had my answer.

"He's gone. What happened?" Suspicion sparked in Ortiz's eyes.

"I...I don't know." I couldn't tell him the truth.

"What's that supposed to mean? No one else was in the room with you."

I floundered for an explanation. "He was fine one minute. The next he was..."

What? I couldn't remember. I had no idea because I'd hit my head. No, wait. That hadn't been real. But it had *seemed* real. It sure as hell *felt* real. I still had the headache to prove it. I reached up and touched the place where I'd smashed my head. I expected soreness or a bump but there was nothing.

"He coded. Just like the last one. And just like the last one, you were found holding his hand." I wasn't oblivious to the suspicion in Ortiz's eyes. "You're not even supposed to be here."

I wasn't holding his hand. I was touching his hand. Big difference.

"What do you have to say for yourself?" Ortiz asked.

I blinked. What was he saying?

"You didn't attempt to find help for those two patients according to what the others saw."

Hot prickling fear spread over me. My stomach cramped. "Doctor, I...I tried to save them both."

"What steps did you take to do that? What are you doing here?"

I had no idea what to say. Pretty sure anything I told him would sound weird. He'd never believe I was inside his dream, trying to save him. I tried to get Frank off the train to safety but I had no idea where that safety was. I was in his *dream*, for god's sake.

"You have nothing to say, then?" His hands were on his hips. I realized a small crowd had gathered to eavesdrop on my interrogation.

I placed the cup on the desk, my head still pounding as though there was a tiny jackhammer inside my skull. I pressed fingers against my temple, rubbing in a circular motion trying to make the pain stop. I didn't know what to say or what to do.

"I'm going to have a talk with your lab supervisor about this," Ortiz said. "I intend to recommend he remove you from duty until we figure out what happened. Do you understand what I'm telling you, Miss Walker?"

I did. I nodded.

"If it were up to me, I'd fire you."

"You can't fire me. I don't work for you."

"Pity." He stalked off.

I pushed out of the chair aware all eyes were on me. I couldn't stay here. I looked like a murderer. I needed a way to prove my innocence in all this, to show them I had nothing to do with their deaths but I hadn't a clue how to do that.

No one was going to believe a fallen angel was responsible for the murders. I figured I'd start with Azriel and see where that got me. But he probably wouldn't care. He'd have what he wanted—my help. Maybe that was his diabolical plan all along.

I headed down the hallway, my shoes silent on the linoleum as I made my way to the locker room. I grabbed my purse out of my locker. I needed out of there and home before anything else happened. As I approached the bank of elevators, one dinged. The doors swished open to reveal Kincade Harrison. I scowled.

When he made no move to step out of the elevator, I stepped in and punched the lobby button with unnecessary force. It made me feel better, though.

"Just the person I was looking for."

"What do you want?" I was so not in the mood for him.

"Another one dead, huh?"

Did he have some sixth sense that told him or what? I gave the guy the side eye, wondering how he knew already. "So that's why you're here." It wasn't a question. It didn't need to be.

"Azriel?"

"I don't want to talk about it here."

"Then we can talk outside." He suggested it casually as though talking about the weather.

"No offense, *detective*, but I'm not exactly in the mood to talk. I'm probably going to get fired." Maybe even arrested and charged with murder. That remained to be seen.

"Why?"

I looked at him, anger firing through me. "Why do you think? Two patients died while I was the only one in the room. It doesn't look good."

"You're right." He said it with a confident nod.

The elevator halted. As soon as the doors opened, I bolted out. But he was hot on my trail. His boots thumped against the ground as he followed me. The humid summer air hit me in the face, trying to suck the air out of my lungs. Even at close to midnight, it was still ninety degrees.

"Go away, detective." I hurried toward my car, reaching into my purse to grab my keys.

Before I could wrap my hand around them, he grabbed my arm and spun me around to face him. That was getting to be a habit I didn't like one bit. I jerked my arm away. This time, he let me.

"I'm not going away. You're going to tell me everything that happened. Was it Azriel?"

I rolled my eyes. "Duh. You know it was or you wouldn't be here. And how did you get here so fast anyway? The guy died like thirty minutes ago. He hasn't even been carted off to the morgue yet."

"What happened? I can't help you if you don't tell me."

He ignored my question to ask me again. His tone softened. He didn't sound like the hard-ass he had earlier when we met in the yogurt shop. And for a moment he sounded as though he wanted to help. My shoulders drooped in defeat.

"Can we talk about this somewhere else?"

He led me to his car. I expected him to take me to the police station for questioning. Instead we ended up at an all-night diner on the seedier side south of downtown. We sat in a booth near the front window and ordered coffee.

When the waitress left, he said, "Now, tell me."

I fiddled with the napkin wrapped fork, stalling until the coffee arrived a few minutes later.

"I knew him." I poured a healthy portion of cream into the cup, turning the liquid from black to taupe. "He worked at the law firm with my boyfriend."

"And you thought you could help him." Kincade preferred his coffee strong and black.

"Yeah. I failed with Emma. Maybe he would be different. His chart was like hers. He had the sleep disorder, the nightmares. He was prescribed sleeping pills but they hadn't worked. He was admitted because he stopped eating and drinking and basically living. A lot like her."

"But it was different?" He sipped his coffee.

"Frank's dream was violent. Hers wasn't. We were on one of the light rail trains. Another angel was there. Kaziel? I think that was his name."

"His guardian. Go on." Kincade nodded encouragement.

"He and Azriel were fighting. I thought I could get Frank out of there. To where, I didn't know but I had to try. Maybe away from them and wake him up."

"You couldn't, though." A statement. Not a question.

"No. Azriel attacked Kaziel. He..." I remembered the horrific way he'd killed the angel. I swallowed hard. "He ripped out his wing then sliced his throat."

Kincade leaned back in the booth, the aged vinyl squeaking, and blew out a breath. He didn't seem surprised at all by my description. More like it was information he already had and I confirmed it for him.

"The guardian angel for the girl, your friend—"

"Emma," I supplied.

"I found him dead in a house in Plano. I found Kaziel dead on a commuter train in North Dallas. His throat had been cut."

My mouth went bone dry as I stared at him. Blood drained from my head in a whoosh, making me lightheaded. I'd lost the taste for the coffee and pushed it away.

"I don't understand."

"I don't either. But you're seeing the murders happen in a dream as they happen. As if you were there." He leaned toward me, his big forearms filling up the space in the middle of the table. "You said dream."

"Huh?" I didn't follow what he was talking about and he didn't appreciate my response.

He scowled, something he did a lot. "You said Frank's dream. You told me before you could enter minds. You said nothing about dreams."

Oops. He'd caught me in my omission which was kinda sorta a lie. I spun the empty coffee creamer container around in a tight circle. "Did I?"

"What's the truth?"

The waitress returned. She was a young girl with stains on the front of her circa 1975 uniform. "You wanna order somethin'?"

"No," he barked.

At the same time, I chirped, "Yes!"

54

She glanced between the two of us and clicked her pen, the point hovering over her order pad. "Which is it? I ain't got all night."

"Actually, you do since we are the only patrons." She didn't appreciate me pointing that out as evidenced by her glare. I flashed a grin. "Apple pie, please, with vanilla ice cream."

"Don't come any other way, sugar." She scribbled the order on her pad and left.

"I'm waiting." Kincade's eagle-eyed stare never left me while I ordered pie.

"I was hoping you forgot."

"I never forget anything, Miss Walker."

"You're like a bloodhound with the memory of an elephant, aren't you?" It annoyed me he had a talent for ferreting out the truth with such ease. "I sort of have this...super power."

"Which is?" He was unflappable. Admitting my super power didn't even faze him.

God, his forearms were huge. Like the size-of-my-head huge. He had a sprinkling of dark hair that smoothed in a perfect curve around his muscles. I wondered if it was as soft as it looked and then mentally slapped myself. *Ben. Think only of Ben.*

Ben who was at home right now sleeping in our bed.

"What. Is. It?" His teeth clenched so hard his jaw muscles flexed.

I dragged my eyes from his inordinately large forearms and met his gaze. Those green-gold eyes glittered with curiosity and annoyance. "I can enter dreams."

Surprise flickered over his features as he melted into the back of the booth and dropped his hands into his lap. "You're a dream walker."

His words held a kind of reverence that amazed me. Like maybe he thought I was cool. And here I thought I was a freak of nature. But the thing that blew me away was I'd never heard anyone outside my immediate family call it dream walking. Except for Azriel, but I wasn't counting him since he was my archenemy.

"Yes."

"So is Azriel."

"Duh. I already knew that."

My pie arrived and I dug in with vigor. I shoved the plate to the middle to share but he waved it away. More for me.

"How long have you been able to do that?"

I shrugged. "Ever since I can remember."

I was five when I freaked out my adoptive mother. She woke up screaming in a cold sweat. Even though she didn't understand what I could do, she never treated me like a freak. When I got older, she would very kindly ask me *not* to come into her dreams again. The thing was, I couldn't control it like my uncle.

Kincade looked thoughtful for a long moment, the gears turning in his head. I wondered what was going on in that brain of his. He took a sip of coffee.

"Tell me more about Frank's dream."

"Not much to tell." And then I remembered something important. "Wait. Azriel said Frank was marked and then pulled a blue light from his chest. The same thing happened with Emma only hers was pink. He's stealing their souls, isn't he?"

His hand tightened around the plain ceramic mug, his fingernails leeching of color. "It would appear so."

"Why?"

He shrugged. "Beats me."

"You're the detective. Shouldn't you find out?" I shoveled the rest of the pie into my mouth.

"I'm not interested in dead humans, Miss Walker. I'm interested in dead angels."

"So, you're saying dead humans are, like, not your department?"

"That's right."

"Well, they should be," I snapped. "The deaths are obviously connected by one common denominator. Azriel."

"And you're a witness to both."

His response left me momentarily speechless. "Whoa, cowboy. I'm not a witness to *anything*."

He plowed ahead as though I hadn't spoken. "I found his hidden lair beneath a crypt in Greenwood Cemetery. I intend to go after him. And you're going to come with me."

"No way. I didn't actually *see* the murders. I'm not getting involved. I have my own problems." I'd already been to the cemetery once. I didn't want a repeat performance.

"If you're worried about your safety, I can protect you."

And how was I going to explain *that* to Ben? I hadn't breathed a word of these incidents to him. He didn't even know Frank was dead yet. To explain why a strange man was suddenly hanging around the apartment would be awkward. And he wasn't exactly aware of my super power either.

"You think I'm worried about my safety?" I shook my head. "Azriel can't touch me."

He lifted a brow. "What makes you think so?"

Crap. I'd said too much. But I wasn't going to spill about the Holy Relics. "Look, all I'm saying is I'm in hot water at work. They think I had something to do with those deaths. I expect my supervisor to call any second now."

"You said you'd help me."

"I changed my mind. Find someone else to help you because it's not going to be me."

His face hardened into perfect chiseled lines. "Whether you like it or not, you're connected to the murders, Miss Walker. You *are* my only witness."

"You're not hearing me. I can't be a witness because I wasn't *there* when it happened."

"But you *were*. You saw them happen."

I ground my teeth. "We could go around all day about this but I'll still have the same answer. Our discussion is over."

The waitress brought the bill and offered a coffee refill. We both refused. When it was clear I wasn't going for the check, he sighed and pulled out a wad of bills, tossing them onto the table. If I had my car, I'd have stormed out. As it was, I needed a ride back to the hospital parking lot. I had to rely on the detective. The thought of riding all the way back to the hospital with him gave me hives. My apartment was much closer. I could always Uber to pick up my car in the morning.

He slid from the booth, unfolding his six-foot-plus frame with the grace of a cat.

"Let's go." He loved barking orders at me.

I followed him out the door. But when I arrived home, I walked into an ambush.

CHAPTER 5

K INCADE PULLED UP OUTSIDE my apartment building,
put the car in park and turned to look at me. The glow
from the street lamp bathed his attractive features in pale yellow light. If I was single and he wasn't an asshole, then we might
have a shot together. But as it was, a snow cone had a better
chance in the Sahara Desert.

"Sure you won't change your mind?" he asked. "I intend to
go after Azriel tonight."

"Good luck with that, cowboy. I'm out."

I shoved open the door and stepped out, waiting for a retort.
He had none. I slammed the door and headed up the stairs to
the apartment. Ben would be sleeping now and all I wanted
to do was climb in bed and snuggle against him. I wanted
his warmth to envelop me. I wanted to forget this day had
happened. With my erratic schedule, we didn't get many nights
together and I was going to relish this one. Before all the bad
news hit. Before I had to tell him about Frank and Emma.

I pulled out my keys, ready to unlock the door. But as I rounded the corner, I noticed it was kicked in.

My heart picked up speed. The jamb had splintered where someone forced their way inside. I froze in the breezeway, my stomach in a knot and my hands shaking. Had there been a robbery? This was a safe, gated community. Crime like this didn't happen in this area. I pushed open the door with my fingertips and stepped inside.

"Ben?"

A muffled sound came from the bedroom. I hurried toward it, opened the door and halted. Ben was in one of the kitchen chairs, his hands tied behind his back. He had been beaten. His face was bloody. One eye was swollen shut.

"Ben!" I took a step toward him.

"Halt, dream walker."

Azriel stood in the open doorway to the balcony. I had missed him when I came into the room because I'd only focused on Ben. The gagging scent of sulfur and death surrounded me and I knew a demon was behind me. I stared at Azriel, his eyes full of menace and his face creased with hate.

"Let him go. He has nothing to do with any of this." I did well to hide the panic in my voice even though it quaked through me.

"I warned you of the consequences if you did not agree to help us. Did I not?"

Oh, God, but not Ben. Azriel gave a nod of his head and meaty hands seized me by the arms. There was a demon on each side. I recognized the same punks who'd grabbed me off the street and taken me to see Azriel. One I called Switchblade and the other was Bull.

"Those consequences can no longer be avoided." Azriel pulled out a knife with a long blade. It was the same knife he'd used to kill Kaziel.

"No! Please don't kill him."

"Is that what you think I'm going to do?" He gave me that all too familiar wolfish grin. "Not at first. I want you to watch while I torture him. While you understand it was you who did this to him because you refused me. Then I'll kill him. You'll have a ringside seat to the murder of your lover."

He pulled his arm back, ready to plunge it into Ben's side when there was a high-pitched whine followed by an explosion and a flash of light. Switchblade's chest exploded, splattering bone bits and black goo. He crumpled to the floor, blood seeping from him and staining the carpet. Before anyone could react, another high-pitched whine, loud blast and bright flash of orange light. The second demon's head was destroyed, exploding brain matter and other gross stuff all over me.

Surprise and then annoyance flickered over Azriel's face. I spun. The detective stood in the bedroom doorway with a smoking gun in his hand. Kincade was at my side in the next instant—how the hell did he move so fast?—putting himself between me and Azriel. But I stepped to his side, not wanting to be shoved out of the way.

Kincade pointed his gun at Azriel. "You murdered Kaziel and Zaphreal and you'll pay for that."

The fallen angel laughed, unconcerned. "You may have killed my demons, *gardien*, but more will answer my call."

Without waiting for a reply, Azriel stabbed Ben in the ribs. I screamed, trying to get to him. Kincade held up an arm and pushed me back. I clawed him, but he was a human blockade. Ben whimpered, came back to life and looked at me through swollen, confused eyes.

"Anna?"

"Ben, I'm here!"

Demons came through the bedroom dragging their putrid scent with them. Kincade forgot about me and spun to take them out. He shot them but they kept coming. I had to get to Ben. Azriel had cut him loose from the chair and held him, a knife at his throat.

He stood in the doorway of the balcony, the stifling summer air pouring inside.

I knew what I had to do. I had to agree to help him. If it meant saving Ben's life, I had to help Azriel find the Horn of Gabriel. I couldn't stand the thought of losing Ben. He was my only anchor to reality.

"I'll do anything you ask. Just please don't hurt him anymore."

"I'm glad you came to your senses, dream walker. However, you should have agreed when you had the chance. My condolences on your loss."

One slicing motion and Ben's throat was slit. He gasped for air. Blood gurgled in his windpipe. Our eyes met, his full of incomprehension followed by a flash of disbelief. Horror pounded through me as the light faded from his eyes. I screamed as Azriel put his hand over Ben's heart. That evil grin graced his face. My heart leapt into my throat.

"No!"

Azriel kept his eyes on me as Ben took his final breath. He pulled his life force out of his chest. The fallen angel closed his fist around the green glow and then he was gone. Ben's legs folded underneath him. He crumpled to the ground in a heap.

In one horrible moment, something inside me broke, a fracture that ruptured my very being, splintering my perfect world into a thousand tiny slivers never to be mended again. My gut twisted into a sick knot. Even though I knew he was dead, I ran to him and collapsed next to him. I brushed the dark hair away from his forehead, horrorstruck by all the blood at this throat. I closed his sightless eyes as a tear dropped on his cheek.

But the moment didn't last long. Kincade pulled me to my feet. I struggled against him, elbowing him in the ribs. He grunted but held on to me.

"He's gone, Anna." His voice was quiet, full of empathy. I stilled against him. "We have to go."

In the distance, sirens split the night air. Someone had called the cops. The real ones this time. I didn't care. Ben was dead. Azriel sliced his throat and took his soul. Kincade released me and started for the door but I didn't budge. I needed to think, to decide what to do next. I couldn't leave Ben.

"Anna! I'm out of ammo and more demons are coming. We need to go *now*."

When I failed to move, he growled and clamped a hand around my wrist, dragging me through the tiny bedroom. Away from Ben. Through my haze, I could see dead demons littering the floor. It stank like roasted flesh and rotting garbage. Kincade had kept them at bay while Azriel killed Ben, while my life shattered before my eyes.

He pulled me along through the living room. More dead demons. The door was blasted from its hinges and hung by a thread as we fled past it.

"Gonna need a cleaning crew." He muttered it under his breath and I wasn't sure if he was talking to me or not.

My neighbor across the breezeway—an elderly woman whose name I didn't know—peeked out her door. Kincade thrust the gun in her face.

"Get back inside."

She gasped, slammed the door and clicked the deadbolt. But we weren't out of the woods yet. Footsteps pounded up the metal stairs. When the fallen angel disappeared, he hadn't taken them with him. He'd sent more. That bastard.

"Is there another way out?" When I didn't answer, he turned to me, grabbed my shoulders and shook me. "Anna, I know you're hurting right now but we need another way out."

"There's another...set of stairs." I pointed to the backstairs on the other end of the building.

He grabbed my hand again and hauled me along with him. I stumbled behind him down the stairs and nearly lost my footing. I managed to keep my balance by grabbing the iron handrail.

First responders entered the complex. Their flashing red and blue lights lit up the night, bouncing off the brick façades as they came to a halt outside my building. Kincade kept a hand on me and headed the opposite direction. I looked over my shoulder to see a group of demons running after us, their sharp pointy teeth bared.

"I could really use some help."

I had no idea who he was talking to but as we ran, the air shifted around us from hot and humid to cool and windy. Kincade halted and turned to look behind us. A bright iridescent veil came between us and the demons. That high-pitched whine came again—the same one I'd heard back in the apartment when he'd fired his gun. A fiery blast illuminated the night sky in white light. The heat of it radiated toward us. The detective wrapped his arms around me and shoved me to the ground, covering me with his body.

It was the last thing I remembered before waking up in an oversized chair in a dimly lit room that smelled like leather and wood. I had no recollection of how I'd gotten there. My head throbbed like mad. I was covered in demon gunk. I reeked, too. Like something that had been scrapped off the bottom of a Port-A-Potty.

"You're awake."

The detective stood somewhere to my right, but I couldn't turn my head to look. It hurt too bad. He put a cool square glass in my hand, a pale amber liquid glittering inside. The strong scent of whiskey wafted to my nose. Two fingers, neat.

"You all right?"

I failed to answer. How could I be all right? What was he smoking that he'd ask such a dumb question? I'd lost the love of my life.

A demon's head exploded all over me and I stank like a sewer that barfed all over itself.

"You hit your head pretty hard. Sorry about that."

I lifted my hand and my fingers traced along a bump on my forehead. "What happened?"

"The explosion was more powerful than I expected. I had to shield you. I didn't mean to toss you to the ground." Regret tinged in his voice.

I leaned my head against the back of the chair and closed my eyes. Tired. So tired. All I wanted to do was sleep. I didn't want to think or feel or talk. I didn't even want to drink the whiskey.

"Have a drink. It'll take the edge off."

Something about the way he said it rubbed me all the wrong way. Was he *trying* to piss me off? My eyes slanted open and I looked at him. He sat on a plush ottoman across from me, his elbows on his knees as he leaned toward me, peering at me with those green-gold eyes that saw into my very soul.

I splashed the whiskey in his face. He didn't even flinch or blink, that bastard. He rubbed his face dry and shook the droplets on the rug. He said nothing as he stood, picked up a bottle and poured another drink. Two fingers, neat. He must have perfected that long ago.

"I don't want your damn whiskey," I said.

"It's a ten-thousand-dollar bottle of damn whiskey. You'll drink it."

Ten thousand dollar? Maybe it was worth a sip. Maybe it would numb the pain and make the sting of loss go away. I downed it in one gulp, letting the burn go all the way down to my toes. Warming me from the inside out. Blood pulsed in my eardrums, numbing the pain. I held the glass out for more. I was sorry I wasted the first one on his ugly mug.

He poured. I drank.

"You fucking stink."

Like that was my problem? He was the one who shot the demon next to me. It was his fault guts spewed all over me and made me stink.

"Thanks for the newsflash, asshole."

He glared at me. I didn't exactly know what his problem was. I felt like shit. I witnessed my boyfriend die at the hands of a monster. And what exactly did he do?

"I saved your ass."

Had he heard that in my head? But he couldn't save Ben. He hadn't even tried. Why not? What hadn't he tried? Why did he bother to save me? I was irrelevant. Or maybe he didn't want the blood of another human on his hands.

My lip quivered, tears threatening, burning the backs of my eyes. I would not cry in front of this man. I would not give him the satisfaction of knowing how much pain I was in. I held out my glass again and he complied. I downed the whiskey, letting it slide down my throat and burn all the way down to my gut. Numbing all my pain.

"We're safe for now. I have a guest room you can take."

"Where's here?"

"My place."

He'd brought me to his house? I glanced up at the coffered ceiling with the heavy wood beams. As my eyes focused on my surroundings, I realized I was in an office. Bookshelves lined one wall. A desk dominated one corner. There was a leather sofa behind him. He unfolded his large frame from the ottoman across from me.

"Come on."

I *did* stink. When the whiskey wore off, I wouldn't be able to maintain my composure. It took all my strength to hold my emotions in check but the edges started to fray. Numb and not knowing what else to do, I rose and followed him through the dim corridors.

The sprawling apartment had compact rooms that looked like something out of Architectural Digest. No outside noise penetrated through the glass. Down the hall and on the left, he opened a door and led me inside, flicking on lights as he moved deeper into the room. He entered a bathroom and then came back with a towel in his hand.

"You can clean up and rest here."

He tossed the towel on the bed and left, closing the door behind him. But instead of heading to the shower, I sank to the floor and let grief overcome me.

CHAPTER 6

B *EN WAS DEAD. AZRIEL had taken his soul.*

Yesterday Ben was taken from me in the most horrific way. Guilt slashed through me that I couldn't save him. That I could do nothing but stand and watch with a horror-struck expression plastered on my face. I should have done something. Instead, I did nothing.

Less than twenty-four hours ago, Ben was alive and we were living happily together. Less than twenty-four hours ago, I had everything my heart desired.

Now it was all gone. Wiped clean by one slash of a knife. While my inner self complained I wanted more out of life, then a boyfriend and the possibility of marriage, I now longed to have that option back in my future. How quickly life changed in the blink of an eye. How I wished I could go back and do something—anything—different. Maybe Ben would still be alive.

The universe was a heartless, cruel bitch. Whether I liked it or not, life goes on. I lived. He died. It pissed me off.

My hatred for Azriel grew ten-fold over the long, endless night. I held it close to me, letting it fester like an open wound that would never heal.

I wasn't sure how long I stayed curled in the fetal position, letting emotions run the gamut from grief to guilt to hate, back to grief. I cried until I couldn't anymore. I dozed off with my head pillowed on my arms. The dream came almost immediately. I was back in England at the house in Cannington, Somerset.

"Hello, Anna." Uncle Edward greeted me with a nod of his head.

He looked the same as the day I left, wearing that stony expression he always wore while impeccably dressed in an Armani suit and Ferragamo shoes. Not one black hair was out of place on his head and his dark blue eyes still had that same look about them that always appeared older and wiser than they were.

"Are you here in my dream?" Edward could dream walk like me. Though he rarely did it in my dreams. If he was with me, then he undoubtedly came with a message.

He nodded. "Come to England, Anna. Let me help you."

"You can't help me. No one can help me."

"I can. There are things you need to know. Now it may be too late."

"What? What do I need to know?"

"Come to England. I'll tell you then."

The dream faded and was gone. I had no other visitors in my sleep, for which I was grateful.

Sometime in the wee hours of the early morning, I awoke. No doubt the stench emanating from my body roused me. The grief remained, like a tidal wave had consumed me, leaving behind the wreckage that was once my life. A gaping hole had been punched through my chest, the wound still raw and bleeding. I had nothing left—the man I loved, my home, my job.

I peeled myself off the floor, grabbed the towel and headed to the bathroom, halting in the harsh light to stare at a face I hardly recognized.

Dark circles were under my red-rimmed eyes. My eye color would change with my mood. Today they were a dark melancholy purple. My nose was red, my face swollen from crying. I had black demon blood all over me, even caked in my hair. My hands were stained red. Ben's blood. It was caked under my fingernails. The lump on my forehead had turned black and blue tinged with green, giving me a lovely bruise.

I stripped off the dirty scrubs I wore to work that day—night? It seemed an eternity ago—and dumped them on the floor. I wanted to burn them they smelled so bad. I pulled my bra and panties off and stuck them in the sink to soak.

I stood under the hot spray of water and scrubbed until my skin turned red. Try as I might, the stench of the demons was still branded in my nostrils. Hopefully in time that would dissipate but at the moment, I tried not to gag. I washed with the lemon-scented bar soap, washed my hair with shampoo that had the pleasant aroma of lavender and then stepped out of the shower, wrapping in a thick towel.

As I padded out of the room, an oversized blue T-shirt and a pair of sweats were on the bed. Had they been there before and I hadn't noticed? Or had Kincade brought it while I was trying to scour my existence away?

Since my underwear was still soaking and smelly, I'd have to go commando. The sweats were about four sizes too big. Was the guy a giant? I rolled down the top until I could walk without stepping on the legs. I pulled the shirt over my head. It practically fell to my knees and looked like a shirt dress.

I stood in the center of the room trying to decide if I wanted to leave or not. Maybe I could curl under the thick coverlet and go to sleep. Forever. Maybe I didn't have to ever leave this room.

There are things you need to know. Come to England.
My uncle's voice beckoned me. He wasn't an idiot. If he planted the seed in my subconscious sleeping brain, I would have to comply. The seed already began to sprout. Before long, it would take root in my mind and I would have no choice.

But, how could I? My job was on the line. My absence would surely incriminate me. I'd be branded a murdering phlebotomist and there wasn't a damn thing I could do to exonerate myself. Maybe that was Azriel's plan all along.

I moved from the center of the room to the one window and pulled aside the curtain. I peeked through the blinds and was astonished to see nothing but brilliant blue sky. Kincade lived in a high-rise. Down below, people were the size of ants and cars the size of toy cars. Straight ahead in the distance, the freeway was a bustling hive of activity as commuters made their way through rush hour, which was all day in Dallas traffic.

And then some other piece of reality hit me. I probably wouldn't be able to go home again. It had been destroyed as surely as Ben's life.

No Ben. No home. No job.

The universe was definitely a cruel bitch.

Maybe my uncle was right. Maybe it was time I returned to England. I didn't trust him. I didn't even like him that much but he summoned me through a dream. I was hard pressed to resist. The big question was how was I going to return to England? I had no clothes, no money, no mode of transportation.

My only other option was to ask the detective for help.

Fuck all.

I pulled on my demon-blood-splattered sneakers—they still stank—and padded to the door, cracked it open. It was silent on the other side of the door. No movement. No sign of life whatsoever. I stepped into the hallway and found my way through the large apartment to the gourmet kitchen.

Quartz countertops, white-washed cabinets with brushed nickel handles, high-end range boasting the name Viking that I would love if I could cook, sub-zero fridge. And not a speck of grease or dust anywhere. The man must have an awesome maid.

At least he had a coffee pot.

I rooted around the cabinets until I found a large enough mug that suited my coffee addiction. I found creamer in the fridge and not the cheap stuff. Something struck me that nothing about Kincade Harrison would be cheap. He drank ten-thousand-dollar whiskey, for crying out loud.

His booted feet thumped on the hallway carpet before I saw him. He halted in the kitchen doorway and we peered at each other across the expansive room. I held the steaming mug of inspiration in my hand and sipped. I would be damned if I spoke the first word.

"Good morning."

Fuck good morning. "I want to go back to my apartment."

"You can't."

"Why not?"

"It's too dangerous."

"Bullshit."

"It's a crime scene."

"I don't give a shit about that."

"You don't have a fucking clue what I had to do last night, do you?" Anger creased his forehead.

I stared at him, holding the mug close to my lips, letting the heat radiate over my face. "You don't have a fucking clue what I went through last night. Though you should. You were there."

"I saw what happened with my own eyes. I'm sorry for your loss."

"Oh, can it, cowboy. I don't want your fake condolences."

He moved, lightning fast, to the center of the room. Now the only thing between us was the kitchen island with the quartz countertop. His fist landed a loud blow against the stone, striking it so hard it cracked. It-mother-fucking-cracked. I wouldn't have believed it if I hadn't seen it with my own eyes. Rage etched his features as he glared at me, fire flashing in those green-gold eyes.

"I've lost friends, too, dammit. Kaziel was my friend. Azriel slaughtered him the same way. I want him *dead* as much as you do."

I gasped.

I hadn't realized how much I wanted that until he'd said it. Yes, I *did* want Azriel dead. I wanted to pull his entrails out through his eyeballs and stuff them down his throat. I wanted him to writhe in pain as I slowly, methodically killed the bastard with my own two hands. Ripped him from limb to limb. Made him suffer as he'd made me suffer. And my suffering wasn't over yet. I still grappled with the thought Ben was no longer alive.

The violent thought staggered me. I put down the mug on the cracked countertop and held on to the edge with my fingertips, trying to push the ugly thoughts out of my mind. I inhaled a deep breath, let it exhale slowly.

"What does Azriel want with you?"

"I don't know." I had to tread lightly here because he sensed when I lied, which I still couldn't figure out. I wasn't ready to tell the detective anything about the Horn of Gabriel.

Kincade's eyes narrowed. He didn't believe me but he wasn't going to push it. Yet.

"I have to leave." My voice was thin and quiet.

"You're not going anywhere."

That thing that snapped inside me when Ben was killed reared its ugly head. "You're not the boss of me. I go where I damn well please. And I'm leaving."

I started to go around the island and make for the door but he stepped in front of me. "Azriel has demons hunting you."

That was a piece of news I didn't want. Let them hunt me. They couldn't touch me. Azriel said as much. He needed me alive to do his bidding.

"How do you know that?" I asked.

"I tracked them back here but I have wards around the place so they can't get in."

I stared at him, dumbfounded. "Wards? What are you, some kind of witchdoctor?"

His mouth thinned into a straight line. He was far from amused. "No."

He blocked the walkway and I couldn't push past him. His stance was clear—he wasn't moving and letting me walk out that door.

"Last night, after you hit your head, I brought you here. Then I went back to finish cleaning up the mess we'd left behind."

"But the cops—"

"Were there already. I had them stalled while the Watchers cleaned up the bloody mess."

Bloody mess. *Ben.* I had no idea who or what the Watchers were and I was pretty sure I didn't care at that point. I opened my mouth to ask about Ben when he cut me off.

"The coroner removed his body early this morning after they processed the crime scene."

"Then I'm going back."

"The hell you are. Did you not hear me when I said Azriel has demons hunting you?"

"I heard you and I don't care about that. I—"

"You should care. You're going to get yourself killed."

Now my mouth thinned into a straight line. "I thought you weren't interested in dead humans."

His eyes narrowed. "What's so important you have to go back for?"

I gaped at him. What kind of question was that? My whole world had been in that apartment. I needed to snag my stash of credit cards, cash, and my passport.

Somewhere in the back of my head, I'd made up my mind I was going to England. I was going to see my uncle and figure out what the hell was going on. If anyone knew why a messenger angel and a fallen angel wanted me to search for these Holy Relics, he would. He knew everything.

Which also meant somewhere in the back of my head, I'd made up my mind to find this Horn of Gabriel if only to get Azriel off my back. And then I was going to kill the bastard. I had never killed anyone in my life. I was about helping save lives, not taking them. But Ben had to be avenged and Azriel needed to die.

"I don't owe you any explanations."

I shoved past him and headed for the front door, realizing I had nothing on underneath the baggy clothes. Did I really intend to walk out that door? And then what? Walk all the way to my apartment in Uptown?

At least I'd blend in and look like another homeless person.

Kincade's heavy footsteps were behind me.

"Wherever you're going, I'm going."

Fantastic.

CHAPTER 7

I HAD TO LOSE the detective like a bad habit. The question was how. I hadn't figured that out yet, especially since he was hot on my heels.

I quickly discovered Kincade lived in a penthouse condo on the thirtieth floor of a high rise in Victory Park overlooking downtown Dallas. In a world of open-concept floor plans, his was decidedly not. He had symmetrical rooms with walls mapping out all the specific rooms. I liked that. I was all about spatial symmetry.

As I hurried through the living area to the front door, I screeched to a halt. The room boasted ultra-modern yet comfortable furnishings that included a glass coffee table, armless chairs in a plush velvet upholstery with matching sofa, a gas fireplace surrounded by stone. His electronics were state of the art. The twelve-foot ceilings hosted recessed and track lighting.

Two walls of floor-to-ceiling windows looked out at the buildings of downtown. The concrete and glass jungle where fortunes were made or lost, hearts won or broken, dreams shattered or fulfilled. In the distance, the famous ball of Reunion Tower, the pointy top of Fountain Place with its mirrored glass, the Bank of America Plaza that once was outlined in green lights but now sported LEDs that changed color. All gleaming brightly in the late morning sunshine.

Not a trace of clutter or dust in the place. No stacks of unread magazines or newspapers or junk mail. No photographs, either. Nothing that showed a person actually lived there. His apartment could be mistaken for a model home. I cut a glance at him.

"You must make a nice salary for a detective in the 'covert' division." I put air quotes around covert. I wasn't sure I believed he was who he said he was.

"I'm good with money."

"I guess."

I got a glimmer of something about him indicating there was more to him than his outward appearance. He dressed like a cowboy but lived like a tycoon. And I wondered again who he was. Azriel had called him *gardien*. Guardian? Was he more than a homicide cop trying to solve the murder of angels?

I continued through the condo to the front door. I tried to ignore the dining room with the long oak table that seated ten and the tinkling double chandelier hanging over it.

This guy was loaded.

I found it hard to believe a homicide detective on the DPD payroll would live like this.

The ride down the thirty floors was an uncomfortable silence. I didn't appreciate him tagging along. My grief was still too raw and I wanted to be alone when I went back to the apartment. I needed time to process and to figure out how I was going to get out of the country. I needed time to break down.

We made our way through the posh and palatial lobby garnering quite a few looks from bystanders. I flashed a smile at them and then clung to his arm, giving him adoring looks as though we'd had a raucous night together. Most people looked away. Others gawked. He scowled.

At the parking garage, he herded me into his car. He pulled into late morning traffic, blending with ease with commuters. I clasped my hands in my lap, staring through the windshield, trying to decide if I was ready to poke the bear.

"Last night," I began, my voice low and slow, "Azriel called you *gardien*."

"That's right." His response was less than informative.

"What does that mean?"

"It's French for guardian." He never took his eyes off the road.

Jackass. I rolled my eyes. "I *know* that. But the way he said it..." I paused, trying to figure out exactly what I was trying to say. I shrugged. "Just seemed like there was more to it than that."

"I'm a cop. That's all he was referring to."

I cut him a look but he still had his gaze firmly planted ahead. I narrowed my eyes. I didn't think he told me the truth, but since we weren't well acquainted, I couldn't tell. Time to regroup and ask another question.

"Who are the Watchers?"

"Irrelevant."

Gah, he was maddening. "Not irrelevant. Who are they? You said they came to 'clean up the bloody mess.' What does that mean exactly?"

His hands tightened on the steering wheel, turning his knuckles white. He didn't want to tell me.

"I'll answer your question if you tell me why Azriel is so interested in you."

Blackmail. Should have seen that coming. "I already told you. I don't know."

"Then I can't help you. And that was a lie."

I sighed. He was beyond frustrating. I hated the way he could tell whenever I fibbed. I could play that game, too. "Fine, I'll tell you. He asked me to look for something."

"Something like what?"

"Irrelevant." His jaw tightened. "It's kinda personal."

"How personal?"

Persistent bugger. I huffed out an exasperated breath. He wasn't going to let it go. "He asked me to find the Horn of Gabriel."

The shift of his eyes toward me was almost imperceptible. I would have missed it if I hadn't been looking at him. A muscle in his jaw ticked and he swallowed.

"Know what that is?" I pressed.

"No. The Watchers are a clean-up crew." He slid past my question with ease. "Whenever an event happens like last night, they remove the dead demons."

I blinked as I processed the indication there had been more than one incident like that. "Are they on the DPD payroll, too?"

"Not exactly. They're more of a subcontractor."

Interesting. But... "Why?"

"In case you haven't noticed, Miss Walker, humans can't see the angels and demons walking among them."

I scowled and resisted the urge to stick my tongue out at him like a petulant child. I didn't want to admit I had no knowledge until recently when Azriel opened my eyes to them. I didn't understand why I couldn't see them before and now I could. Maybe Azriel did something to me, put a spell on me or something.

"You called for backup last night, too." It wasn't exactly a question but I was hoping he'd answer like one.

"Yeah. So?"

I huffed out a breath, annoyed. "I felt a shift in the air before the explosion. Then I blacked out."

"Full of questions today, aren't we?"

"Yeah, I am." I folded my arms across my chest, indignant. "So, who was it? Fellow covert cops?"

He pulled into a spot outside my apartment building and put the car in park. "Not for you to worry about, Miss Walker. Shall we?"

Before I could retort, he was out of the car and slammed the door. I had no choice but to follow suit. We climbed the stairs in silence to my apartment. The closer I got, the harder my heart hammered. While I was desperate to return to the place, I was also terrified.

Even though the door had been replaced and I smelled fresh paint, crime scene tape still blocked it. I cut Kincade a glance.

"The door was busted open yesterday." In fact, the door had practically been ripped from its hinges.

"And today your door is fixed. Key?"

Last night, he'd called for backup. I wondered if that backup had somehow worked a miracle and replaced the door on the apartment. I stared at it with my heart in my throat. Finally, I shook my head. I hadn't thought through this plan. My keys were still inside where I'd dropped them.

"I don't have them."

He pulled a lock pick from his pocket. In two seconds flat, he had the door open and the crime scene tape ripped out of the way. He pushed open the door. While he was pretty handy to have around, I still didn't want him to cross the threshold with me. But seeing as how I didn't have much of a choice, I stepped inside.

And immediately stopped. On the floor at my feet was a brown padded envelope. My name was written in perfect, neat block letters in thick black marker. No return address and no postage. The handwriting was unfamiliar.

"What's that?" He peered over my shoulder, looking down at the package.

"An envelope."

"That wasn't here last night."

I bent to pick it up as Kincade moved to my side, scanning the place with his sharp assessing gaze. Looking for more demons maybe. I tore open the package and a postcard fell out. The colorful photograph was of Two International Finance Centre in the Central District in Hong Kong. Something else was inside. I upended the envelope and a small gold key slipped into my palm. I pocketed the key quickly as Kincade turned to peer down at the postcard. I flipped it over. In the same hand were the words *begin your search.*

The hairs on the back of my neck stood on end. I got a hot prickling sensation all over. This wasn't an ordinary piece of mail. This was a message. From Joachim? Or Azriel? Or someone else? What did this place have to do with the Horn of Gabriel?

"'Begin your search.' From Azriel?" he asked in typical detective fashion.

"I have no idea. I don't recognize the handwriting and there's no return address or postage."

I knew it couldn't be Azriel. He'd already given me a message loud and clear when he killed Ben. Kincade took the envelope out of my hand to survey it.

"That envelope is too thick to slide under the door."

I noted that, too. It was also too big to fit in the mailbox. How did it get here? Obviously there had been repair work done but the landlord wouldn't leave something like this in the apartment. He would hold it in the office until I could pick it up.

"I need a minute," I said.

Kincade hesitated, not moving.

"Please."

He gave a nod with a slice of his head. As he walked by, he handed me back the envelope, then stepped outside, pulling the door closed behind him and sealing me inside the silence. Knowing he stood guard outside gave me a little comfort. If demons were tracking me, they'd get to him first.

I stepped deeper into the apartment. Last night, dead demons littered and bled all over the floor. The bodies were gone. Today, the carpet looked as though it had been steam cleaned, as though they had never been there. A faint medicinal smell wafted on the air. I wondered if that was the work of the Watchers.

My hands shook as I made my way to the bedroom. I pushed open the door and paused in the threshold, my stomach twisted in a thick knot. I didn't want to see but at the same time I *had* to. My handbag had been kicked under the bed. On the other side was the darkened blood stain where Ben had died. Where Azriel had killed him. I fell to my knees, remembering, letting the thick tears slip down my cheeks.

I would avenge him.

Ben's parents would be notified by now. They'd be planning his funeral. I had to find out where and when. That would be the last thing I did before leaving for England.

I don't know how long I sat there. It felt like an eternity. Finally, I shoved to my feet and staggered to the closet where I flung open the door. I couldn't linger much longer. Kincade would be back inside and I had to find something. In the back corner of the closet, I peeled back the corner of the carpet with ease. Underneath was a small hidden compartment with a pull ring. I opened it and picked up the lock box. Thankfully, I had enough forethought to pick a lock box with a combination instead of a key.

First order of business was to retrieve my passport. I also picked up the one credit card and bank card. I'd socked away money in an account for an emergency. I had no idea I would ever use it.

I slipped the cards and the passport in the envelope with the postcard, shoved the box back in the hidey hole and covered it back up. I heard Kincade enter the apartment as I exited the closet.

"Time's up," he said. "We can't stay here much longer."

"I know. I need to change my clothes, okay? I'll only be a second."

Again, he hesitated. But he knew I couldn't go on wearing his oversized clothes. "I'll wait in the living room."

Fair enough. I nodded and waited until he was out of eyesight. Then I stripped down, quickly found underwear and put it on. Back in the closet, I pulled on a pair of faded jeans, grabbed an oversized t-shirt and a hoodie. I discarded my smelly sneakers for my running shoes. I pulled the key out of the pocket of the sweatpants and dropped it in the bottom of my shoe before sticking my foot inside. Then I shoved the envelope in the inside pocket of my hoodie and zipped it up.

I snatched my purse from under the bed, fished my cell phone out and checked it. Three missed calls and a voicemail. The voicemail was from my boss at the lab summoning me to meet him first thing today. Great.

I had to go. Convincing the detective to take me to the hospital might be difficult, but I had to try. I had to meet with my boss. I had to get my car back. I wadded up his sweats and shirt and dumped them in his hands as I passed by.

"Come on, cowboy. I have one more stop to make."

I didn't look back as I left the apartment for the last time.

CHAPTER 8

"**I**'M NOT TAKING YOU to the hospital."

Kincade was clearly unhappy with my next stop as evidenced in the grim line of his mouth and the way he held the steering wheel as though he held onto the edge of a cliff.

"I need my car. Besides, I have to go back and meet with my boss. If you won't take me, then I'll find another way." My hand inched toward the door handle.

It didn't seem like a smart idea to leap from a moving vehicle, but I was willing to do anything to lose him. I planned to jump at the next traffic light.

"Fine." His voice had a hard edge laced with frost. "But if you get yourself into trouble, I'm not bailing you out."

"Fair enough."

And my heart skipped into high gear. This was my chance to free myself of his unwanted company. What trouble could I possibly get into? I was going to meet with my supervisor so he could fire me and then clean out my locker. Then I'd be home free.

"Just drop me off and park. I'll grab my stuff and come right back."

"Not so fast. I'm coming with you."

Aw, crap. He was totally ruining my plan. "You can't follow me where I'm going."

"Then I'll wait in the lobby."

He was maddening. I was still going to ditch him. As we pulled into the parking lot, I did a quick scan and noticed my car was still parked where I'd left it. That was good. At least I had a getaway.

He parked and we got out. The closer we got to the automatic doors of All Saints Hospital, the more my heart palpitated at a rapid speed. My hands broke into a hot sweat. Tendrils of nervous heat coiled up my back and to the nape of my neck. I was a nervous wreck. I'd never been fired before. I wasn't sure how it was going to go.

We entered. He halted with an unspoken *I'll wait here* look. My running shoes squeaked on the tile floor as I made my way past the elevator banks, to a corridor and through two double doors that were marked *Authorized Personnel Only*. I was personnel but probably not authorized much longer.

With my heart in my throat and stomach churning acid, I made my way to the lab. I garnered a few looks. I'd pinned my hospital ID to the front of my hoodie, though, so no one would stop me as I made my way to meet with my boss.

I presented myself to him in his office. He was less than excited to see me. He waved me in, pointed to the seat across from him.

"Dr. Ortiz contacted me about your unusual behavior. He thinks you had something to do with the death of that patient. Did you?"

A point-blank question. There was no beating around the bush here. "I did not."

"And that woman, Emma. You were found by both of their beds at the time they coded."

"I don't know what happened to them," I said. "Honestly."

"In my experience, if someone adds the word 'honestly' they're not being very honest." He took a deep breath. "You saw nothing?"

I shook my head.

He sat back in his chair and steepled his fingers. "You've been with us a short time, so I don't know you very well. But this...it's very suspicious, Anna."

"I know what it looks like and you're right. But I had nothing to do with their deaths."

"Then what happened?"

I searched my brain for any plausible explanation but had none. I couldn't very well tell him I was in their head when it happened and Azriel did it. He would never believe that. I took a stab at the truth.

"I didn't see what happened. One minute they were fine. The next, they weren't."

"What were you doing?"

"Ah..."

"Witnesses say you were sitting on the bed holding their hands." I opened my mouth to reply but he leaned his elbows on the desk and continued. "Under the circumstances, I can't have you around patients. Therefore, I agree with Dr. Ortiz you should be terminated effective immediately."

I blinked. "I'm fired?"

"You'll need to clean out your locker and turn in your badge to HR. Elaine is waiting for you."

And that was that. I rose and walked out of his office, numb and oblivious to all the looks I garnered as I headed to the employee locker room. When I arrived, my heart picked up speed. My stomach bottomed out. My locker was wrenched open and empty. Everything was gone. Had HR cleaned out my belongings for me?

"Hello, Anna."

The familiar voice was behind me and I spun to face Azriel.

"Having a bad day, *chérie*?" He gave me his famous wolf grin.

Fear tingled the back of my neck. I didn't like the sound of that.

"HR cleared out your belongings, including a bloody knife with your fingerprints on it." He flashed a triumphant grin. "More's the pity the poor woman was found stabbed to death amongst all your personal effects. Elaine, was it?"

A burning knot coiled in my stomach and stayed there. Elaine had been the head of human resources. He'd killed her. He'd killed her and framed me for it.

"You sick bastard."

"Last night you said you'd do anything I asked. Is that still the case?"

I nodded.

"The *gardien*. He is still with you," Azriel said. "What have you told him?"

"Nothing. I've told him nothing," I lied. "I'm trying to ditch him so I can leave the country."

He stared at me as he considered whether or not I told the truth. Outside in the hallway, there was a commotion. Why did he have to block my way out? I couldn't move past him.

"Please, Azriel. Let me go so I can start searching for the horn. That *is* what you want me to do? Search for the horn?"

I must have convinced him because he stepped aside. As soon as he did, Kincade burst into the room, gun drawn.

"Hold it!"

Did the guy have GPS on Azriel or what?

Chaos erupted. Azriel spun, his wings fully extended and charged toward Kincade as he fired. I watched with horrified fascination as the gun charged with that high-pitched whine, illuminating the barrel in blue, and then exploding in a ball of fire straight for Azriel. A bright white flash of light knocked me off my feet. I landed on the floor, banging my elbow.

I rolled and got back to my feet. Behind me, Azriel managed to knock the gun from Kincade's hand. They were locked in hand-to-hand combat.

All I had to do was scoot around them while they were both distracted. The only way out of the lounge was through the one door. I had enough room to squeeze by the lockers. As I approached my escape route, security ran in. I halted, flattened against the lockers and held my breath.

As soon as the security guards came into the room, Azriel disappeared in a flash of light. Kincade, who had been holding onto him, stumbled forward, losing his balance and falling to his hands and knees.

The security guards rushed to his side. Not to help him up but to take him into custody. I took that as my moment to flee. I bolted for the door. Damn Azriel! He must have known I would come here. He wanted to make sure I had agreed to find the horn and he was going to use any means of blackmail necessary.

And he clearly didn't like Kincade. That was something I needed to add to my list of things to remember.

I bolted up the hallway and was almost out of the restricted area when Dr. Ortiz came through the door headed right for me. I screeched to a halt, the blood draining from my head. He came to a stop, too, and we stared at each other for what seemed like forever but in reality, was only a few seconds.

I couldn't catch a break.

My moment of hesitation nearly cost me. I bolted up a secondary hallway leading through the intricate hallways. There was another way out but I had to make it to the exit without being caught.

Dr. Ortiz was on my trail and now people gawked at me as I ran down the hall. He shouted something about stopping me but no one was able to react fast enough to grab me. While I wasn't a fast runner, I was quicker than most and in fairly good shape.

I turned down a hallway that led to the exit and ran right into several cops. I tried to turn back the other way but Ortiz was behind me. He shouted at the cops to stop me.

One seized me by the arm. I went willingly. Now that I'd been caught, I was screwed. Kincade made it clear he wouldn't help me out so I was on my own. Ortiz marched toward me, a triumphant look on his face.

"Thought you could get away with it?"

"With what?" Playing dumb wasn't going to get me out of this situation.

"Elaine is dead. You're telling me you don't have a clue about that?" Ortiz's eyes narrowed as he peered at me.

Dread twisted my gut as my knees turned to water, threatening to buckle. Azriel had gone to great lengths to coerce me into working for him.

"Release her."

Dr. Ortiz spun around. Kincade came up the hallway looking disheveled. He stopped in front of us and flashed his badge long enough for us to see he was some kind of cop. He'd told me in the car he wasn't going to bail me out, yet here he was. There had to be some end game to that. He didn't strike me as the type to help me out of the kindness of his heart.

"Detective Harrison, homicide. That's my suspect you've got in custody. Thanks for nabbing her."

He took my arm and pulled me away from the two cops. They looked perplexed but released me without objecting.

"Homicide detectives were already here investigating and questioning everyone. You weren't one of them," Ortiz said.

This guy was starting to piss me off.

"She's wanted in connection with another case," Kincade said coolly.

Ortiz's gaze flickered from him to me and then narrowed. As if he were saying *I knew it*. Kincade led me away from them. I should be grateful he saved my ass but I was mostly annoyed. I'd never work in this hospital again. Or maybe anywhere. Ortiz thought I was a killer. Azriel made sure of that.

Kincade gave that manly "later" nod to the other cops as we started to walk away.

"You can thank me now," he said, after we were out of ear shot.

The nerve of this guy. "Oh, can I? I thought you weren't going to bail me out?"

"Changed my mind."

"Why?" I didn't bother to hide the suspicion in my voice.

He ignored my question. "That's the second time I've helped you. You could be a little grateful."

"Well, excuse me for being pissed off. Dr. Ortiz is convinced I had something to do with the deaths in this hospital, even the HR lady."

"Relax. Those charges won't stick."

"Oh, how do you know?"

"There's no murder weapon anymore. And besides, you have an alibi." He looked down at me and wiggled his eyebrows. "You were with me this morning."

Heat flashed over my body, from embarrassment and anger and a whole bunch of emotions I couldn't process at the moment. He'd done something with the knife but I didn't want to know what. My boyfriend was dead. My apartment was a homicide scene. I was jobless. And a maniac fallen angel was after me with a vengeance. My life sucked.

"I am *not* using you as an alibi."

"Fine. If you don't want my help, I can take you back to them and produce the murder weapon. I'm sure they'd be glad to read you your rights and park your ass in a county jail."

I said nothing. He was right and I knew it. We stepped outside in the morning air and he led me to his car. I'd lost my moment to escape so I had to think quickly and figure out something else.

"Why did you help me?"

"Because I'm going to help you figure out what that post-card meant and why Azriel wants you to search for the Horn of Gabriel."

Was he serious? No way. I didn't want him involved. I wanted him out of my life as fast as possible.

I glanced toward the parking lot where my car was parked. "I'm taking my car."

"Why? You don't need it."

"I don't care. I'm going." I unzipped my handbag and dug around, looking for keys.

"What are you doing?"

"Getting my keys."

I needed some sort of intervention here. That's when I saw the tiny spray bottle and a memory came crashing through my mind with such force, it nearly knocked me off my feet.

I remembered the day Ben gave me the pepper spray as though it were yesterday. He'd been worried about me working the night shift when I first started at the hospital. He'd pressed it into my hand.

"What's that for?" I asked.

"Just to be safe," he said.

"I don't think I need this, Ben."

"It'll make me feel better if you carry it." He closed my fingers around it. "Okay?"

I lifted the small tube and flicked off the lid, then tucked it in my hand. I grabbed my keys, making sure they jingled and Kincade heard them before dropping them back into the bottom of my handbag. I glanced up to see him watching me with his intense gaze.

"I'm sorry about this," I whispered.

Before he could react, I sprayed him in the eyes. He grunted, cried out with pain and put his hands up to block the stream. By then I was running to my car, pulling my keys out and clicking the lock. Seconds later, I peeled out of the parking lot leaving a very unhappy detective behind.

CHAPTER 9

TEN YEARS HAD PASSED since the last time I stepped onto English soil. I was home again. *Home.* It didn't mean the same to me as it did most people. I never had a home at Walker Manor but I called it that since my uncle was blood.

I had a home with Ben, though. A happy one for two blissful years. Thinking of him sent a sharp pain through my gut. I couldn't help but feel responsible for his death.

In the days after I pepper sprayed Kincade, I cleaned out my bank account, died my black hair blonde, leaving a few streaks of black here and there. I'd picked up a new wardrobe at the local discount store and left everything behind. Then I found some creepy dude in a seedy apartment on the south side of downtown to make a fake ID so I could get out of the country.

Attending Ben's funeral was the last thing I did before leaving for England. I'd stood under a tree in Greenwood Cemetery in the sweltering heat watching Ben's parents lay him to rest.

His mother had been inconsolable. She held a handkerchief against her face, covering her mouth and nose as she wept without pause. Ben's dad was stony faced, his hands clasped in his lap. Ben had been their only son. After he cut his teeth on the law industry, his dad intended for him to work with him and eventually take over the reins of his firm.

Now that would never happen.

I wanted to tell them how sorry I was but I couldn't. It turned out I was a person of interest wanted for questioning in connection with Ben's death. Anna Walker was on the no-fly list and hunted by the authorities. But Zoe Cavanaugh was able to walk through security without a hitch.

At Heathrow, I rented a car and started my journey to the English countryside where my uncle's estate was in the county of Somerset. Because it'd been so damn long since I'd been back, I managed to get lost not once, but twice. It added another hour. Being in the States for so long had my frazzled mind short-circuiting. I had a hard time acclimating to driving on the other side of the road.

By the time I made it to the Walker Manor Estate, the sky turned that dusky shade of pinkish-blue as the sun set. Jetlag hit me hard and fast. Weary didn't begin to describe how tired I was. When I turned up the long gravel drive toward the big manor house, my heart pumped a little harder, my foot lifted off the gas and I came to a coasting halt near the front.

Despite my long absence, the grand Walker Manor hadn't changed a bit. It'd been in the family for hundreds of years. The main house was a late Elizabethan country house built in classic Renaissance architecture. It boasted three floors with a parlor, a drawing room, a ball room, a library, and several bedrooms.

It took a full-time staff to care for the sprawling gardens. My uncle expanded the small two-car garage to house his eclectic and expensive classic car collection that included a 1973 Corvette, a 1957 Austin-Healey, a 1960 Bentley and a 1967 Rolls. He also had a penchant for thoroughbreds—he liked all kinds of horsepower, clearly, and had built sprawling stables that were fit for the best racehorses that were former Derby winners now retired living the life and breeding future derby winners.

The entire estate was surrounded by a six-foot stone wall, as if that could keep intruders out. I drove through the open gates, almost as though the inhabitant of the manor expected guests.

As I sat behind the wheel, gazing through the windshield at the oversized oak door with iron hinges that looked like it belonged in the Middle Ages, the first memory of arriving at the estate flooded back to me.

I was thirteen when lawyers showed up on my mother's doorstep with information that a man claiming to be my blood relative wanted me, that he'd been searching for me since my real mother died in childbirth. Orphaned as an infant, I was put into the system but was lucky a kind-hearted woman took me into her home and her heart. I hadn't thought of her in years. We'd lost touch.

That day changed my life. The woman who raised me for the first thirteen years tearfully told me to be a good girl, kissed my forehead, and bid me farewell.

And then it was me and Edward Walker. Stoic yet staunch. Tall and forbidding. He told me my mother was his younger sister. He didn't realize she was with child when she fled to America. He never shared with me why she ran off. It had only been after her disappearance he tried to find her, especially when he learned she was pregnant.

Twilight edged out the evening light. I wasn't getting any answers sitting in the car and staring at the place. Taking a deep breath, I shoved open the door and stepped out, my booted feet crunching on the gravel drive.

At the front door, I almost lost my nerve. Turned, tucked tail and drove away. But something pushed me onward. Something made me press the doorbell. The church-like bells gonged through the house announcing my arrival. A moment later the door opened to a studious old man who looked about as British as they came. Hook nose, long face, graying hair slicked back from his high forehead. He had a pinched expression said he was annoyed at the disturbance.

"May I help you?" He had a nasal tone that grated on my nerves.

"I'm here to see Edward Walker."

One eyebrow lifted in question as he looked me up and down as though he had a bad taste in his mouth. I suppose he didn't approve of my cheap wardrobe or my striped hair. "And you are?"

"His niece. He'll want to see me."

"His lordship was not expecting company, Miss...?" The question at the end of his sentence prompted me for my name.

"Oh, he's expecting me. Just tell him his niece from the States is here."

Still looking as though he'd swallowed castor oil, he stepped aside and motioned me in. "Wait here, please."

He turned right and took the stairs up to the library, leaving me in the grandiose foyer with the Louis XIV furniture and the massive chandelier overhead tinkling quietly in the stillness. It reminded me of Kincade's chandelier over his dining table. Beneath my feet was an antique Persian rug. The furnishings were different than when I was last here but they were far from modern.

I perused the priceless paintings on the wall as I waited. Monet. Van Gogh. I half expected to hear Mozart playing softly in the background. Instead, there was the soft tick-tock of a clock nearby.

Returning footsteps on the stairs signaled the butler. His lips pressed into a thin line and a dark look on his face said Edward agreed to see me. The butler was perturbed I refused to give him my name almost as much as he was perturbed Edward agreed to see me.

"Follow me, please."

I didn't remember this butler, but then my past was often fuzzy. The man led me through the foyer to the stairs. At the top, we took a right and headed down a long hallway toward the library in the corner of the manor. This was Edward's favorite room. The butler opened the heavy wooden door and gestured me inside.

"His lordship will be with you in a moment," he said in that nasal tone.

He left, the clop of his shoes growing fainter with every step.

The room hadn't changed much. Every wall was lined with built-in bookshelves all full of dusty tomes. The furniture was still heavy, wooden and almost oppressive.

Where there was once upholstered-covered furniture, in its place was now leather chairs, a sofa, a chaise. Another rare Persian rug covered the floor. On the far side of the room was my uncle's oversized mahogany desk, a leather desk chair. A bar with glittering decanters full of various colored liquids.

I ran my hand over the length of the desktop marveling at the neat organization. Not even a speck of dust. Behind the desk was a locked cabinet and more bookshelves.

"Knew you'd come."

His voice startled me and I turned. He was still the same, too. He still had the strong, stubborn jaw I remembered. The same dark blue eyes. His black hair had nary a gray strand, as though he'd forbidden his hair to age. His face showed no signs of aging either—no wrinkles, no age spots, not even crow's feet at the corners of his eyes. The man looked exactly the same as the day I left ten years ago.

He still wore the tailored three-piece suits. This one was navy and his shirt was crisp white. His tie had an intricate pattern alternating in silver and navy. When the light caught it just right, it shimmered.

"Welcome home, Anna."

"Haven't your heard? I'm a wanted woman. It's Zoe now." I didn't bother to hide the haughty derision I became someone else to get here.

Annoyance flickered over his features before he managed to regain his calm composure. "Here, in this house, you are Anna." Then he looked me over with a critical eye. "You changed your hair. I don't approve. You will change it back."

His tone told me there was no room for negotiation. I flexed my fingers, resisting the urge to clench them into a fist. Instead, I tucked a lock of my skunk-striped hair behind an ear. He was back to his old pushy ways.

"Sorry, old man. I had to leave the States in a hurry."

"Tell me."

"Long story. Doesn't matter." I didn't want to go into that sordid tale.

He walked to the leather winged-back chair and sat, waving me toward the other one.

"Please sit. I doubt you came all this way to stand and stare at me."

I perched on the edge of the chair, refusing to lean back. I didn't want to get too comfortable. He, however, leaned back with his elbows resting on the armrests and his hands clasped in front of him.

He wasn't much older than my mother would have been, had she lived. I tried to mentally calculate how many years in age separated her and my uncle but I couldn't recall when she was born. He had a mature—no, ancient—feel about him with an inherent wisdom. His eyes had a primordial depth to them that oftentimes scared me. Like he knew things were going to happen before they happened.

"Has anyone told you it's bloody rude to stare?" His clipped British accent stabbed me.

I flushed and leaned back. I came all this way but now that I was here, I was tongue-tied. I'd practiced over and over in my head what I was going to say. I had my questions memorized, ready to fire off. And now I had absolutely no idea what to say, how to begin, where to start.

"You've changed." He looked me over with a critical eye.

"You haven't."

A knowing smile. "I'd ask why you're here, but I know."

"You should. You summoned me."

"I daresay summoned is a rather strong word, don't you think?"

"No, I don't think." I didn't like he'd been in my dreams.

"You're right. You don't. Exactly why we are in this predicament."

I scowled. "I left because of you. Because of what you did."

"Because you couldn't follow my rules."

"Stupid rules," I spat. "Rules to keep me from having a life. Rules to keep me under your control, your lock and key. You treated me like a...an...inmate." Prison. Yes, that's how it felt living here those years. I hadn't realized how much pent-up anger festered inside me.

His face hardened. Lines of anger creased his forehead. "Do you wish for answers or not?"

"Do you even know what my questions are?"

"A question for a question. Some things never change despite your outward appearance."

Despite my best effort not to, I cringed.

"You are dressed like a man." He sounded disgusted.

Not only did he hate my hair, he hated my black cargo pants, black shirt, black hoodie. I dressed for comfort and anonymity. I stretched out my legs and crossed them at the ankles, showing off my pink combat boots to annoy him. They were the only thing I wore that wasn't black.

"What'sa matter? Don'tcha like my outfit?" I pulled out my acquired Texas accent and watched as he cringed again.

His eyes narrowed. "Perhaps you should get to the point."

"You already know why I'm here."

"Don't be so cocky, Anna, or I won't be inclined to help you."

Annoyed, I blew out a ragged breath and sunk deeper into the chair. The cushions surrounded me, giving me comfort. I realized that was what I need in this house—comfort. The tension between us as thick and hot as sweltering Texas summers.

Edward relaxed, leaning back in his own chair.

"I came to talk to you about the messenger angel that paid me a visit."

He stared at me a long silent moment. I couldn't tell if it was in disbelief or something else. His jaw hardened, the muscles ticking. "You've been contacted."

"Did you know I would be?"

"It was an eventuality, but I had hoped they would come to me first."

"So, *you* could search for these relics?"

"You are not skilled enough. The moment you left my protection, your fate has been out of my hands."

Skilled enough? I was insulted. Yet that wasn't what bothered me the most. "Your protection? That's what you call it?"

"I tried to protect you. In fact, I *did* protect you in many ways. You have no idea."

I knew what he inferred and it inflamed me. It was like that canker sore that just wouldn't go away and was constantly rubbed raw. "If this is about Marcus—"

"Marcus would have bloody well destroyed you." His words were laced with heat.

"Marcus was nothing but a boy. He was sweet and kind and he loved me." My fingers curled, the nails scraping the leather of the chair arm.

His lips thinned into a mulish line. A look I remembered all too well. A look I detested. "People are not always what they appear. It would be wise of you to remember that."

Remembering was like a knife in the gut as that old wound reopened.

I met Marcus Davenport when I was seventeen. He arrived to work the stables and care for the horses my uncle owned. He was charming and handsome and I was immediately smitten. I pined for him until one day a note showed up on my dresser inviting me to meet him in the stables.

From that moment on, our secret romance blossomed. Until the day he was no longer employed by my uncle. He had been removed, abruptly moving to Paris to go to university. I never saw him again.

"He was *exactly* what he seemed. A stable hand. Nothing more."

"This messenger angel. What did he want?" Edward deftly changed the subject and relief plumed through me. Clearly, he didn't want to talk about Marcus and neither did I.

"He wants me to find the Horn of Gabriel before the Fallen do. He wants me to hand it over to him."

"Ah. And so it begins." A satisfied look passed over his face.

"So what begins?"

"The battle for mankind. For eternity. For redemption."

"I don't understand." Only I kind of did. The angel gave me this spiel before.

"No, you wouldn't. You left before I could train you completely. There was still much for you to learn."

Train me? What did that mean?

"I *learned* quite a bit. Your tutors were thorough. My lessons were difficult and demanding. And yet it wasn't enough."

"No." He nodded agreement.

"I know Latin and Greek. Useless languages. I know more history and geography than any normal person. Also, useless. And yet you say there is more for me to learn. What else is there?"

"There is much." He didn't elaborate.

"I'm here now. Teach me."

He laughed a bitter laugh. "As if there is time now to teach you. As I said you are not skilled." He shook his head. "Had you listened to me I could have taught you everything."

"And now?"

"Now you are still a child, Anna. You are still close-minded. You're only interested in what you want and not what is for the good of all."

"Oh, please. The needs of the many outweigh the needs of the one. Yeah, sure. I get it."

I rolled my eyes, unable to stop the famous Star Trek line from leaping out of my mouth. It was that or shout at him, tell him I wasn't a child, close-minded or selfish. But that would only prove his point and I would be *damned* if I proved his point.

I bit the inside of my cheek and remained silent. Maybe he was right. Maybe I shouldn't have left because I was angry Edward destroyed my love affair with Marcus, that he'd taken away the one joy I had in life. That he had removed what little happiness I had in a world of misery.

"That is exactly why you will fail if you search for the relics," he said. "You must have unfailing belief in them, in what you've been asked to do, and you must have the courage to find them."

"And you think I don't?" I couldn't help but feel insulted.

He huffed out a breath. "The messenger angel is correct. You will need to give the horn to Michael when you find it."

He didn't answer the question. That was his way of saying he thought I'd fail before I even began. I'd show him.

"Michael, the archangel, you mean?" I asked and he nodded. "Why?"

"Objects of power need not fall into the wrong hands."

"Into the Fallen's hands. Why do they want it?"

He offered a watery smile though I didn't miss the disgust passing over his face. Maybe he thought I was nothing more than a stupid girl. A girl who longed to fit in, to find a place where she belonged. Who wanted nothing more than a *real* family and yet who was betrayed by her blood relative sworn to protect her.

"You have no clue?" he asked.

"No." It was a small lie. I knew what Azriel told me, but I wanted to see what my uncle said about it.

"The five godly artifacts—the Holy Relics as they are known—are objects of immense holy power. They're hunted by Lucifer so he may dominate the earth and rule mankind. He used Hitler as a vessel to march across the world looking for them. He will do whatever it takes to acquire the artifacts."

"World War II was fought because Lucifer wanted the Holy Relics?"

"Partially. Our family and others were called upon then to stop him. We lost many dream walkers during the war, but we won. As for why now, it seems readily apparent." When I didn't respond, he sighed. "Man is weak. It is the perfect time for Lucifer and his Fallen to strike. I'm sure Lucifer is aware of the moral decay. There are many who try to justify their sins when they are merely fueling the fires, so to speak, for him and his darkness. He will use it to his advantage. To offer promises to those he can seduce. The more souls he can collect, the bigger his army."

"Why does he need the Holy Relics?"

"When used together, he will be unstoppable. The Fallen will rule and Lucifer will proclaim himself as the Most High. He will regain that which he most desires—to return to Heaven."

"But that doesn't explain anything. How do the artifacts work? How will he use them?"

"Only Lucifer and Michael know for certain."

"So, this is all a big mystery?" I waved my hands in frustration. He nodded.

Shit. My stomach clenched in a knot. A wave of sickness enveloped me. I pinched the bridge of my nose. I loved enigmas. *Not.*

"And that's why Michael wants to keep them out of his hands," I said.

"How truly perceptive of you." His tone dripped sarcasm.

My nails dug deeper into the cushion. "Why me?"

"That's the question of the century. You, my dear, are more important than you realize. Had you stayed I could have helped you. You left. Ran away like the ill-tempered child you are. Tell me, Anna, do you know what we are?"

I disliked him even more than I did ten minutes ago.

"Dream walkers. Of course, I know what—"

"No." His tone was so sharp it nearly cut me. "Beyond that."

I shook my head.

"Long ago, the dream walkers were entrusted with the artifacts. Dream walkers are protectors of good, defenders against evil. At our heart that is what we are. But the power corrupted one. He nearly destroyed all there was. Nearly allowed Lucifer to take over.

"The archangels came, took the relics away to hide them. I'm not even sure the angels know where they are. The relics are hidden in our everyday world. Blending in with what once was. No one knows where they are.

"You are more than a dream walker. You are the key. The one who will defeat the uprising of evil. The only one. That is why both the Fallen and the archangels want you."

"Because I'm the key?"

I didn't want to believe this tale. Mostly because I hadn't heard it before. At least not until lately when the angel broke the news. My uncle nodded.

"That's absurd," I said.

"Believe or not, it is the truth."

"I have no idea how to search for these artifacts or even where to begin."

"That's because you're close-minded. Open your heart, Anna. If you do, you will be able to locate the Horn of Gabriel."

Open my heart? What did that even mean? Like it was that easy. Uh huh. As if. I remained silent, pondering his words. I wasn't sure if he was telling the truth or not. I had to trust he was.

"If I do this—"

"There is no 'if'. You have no choice."

"*If* I do this," I repeated, "what happens if I fail?"

"There is no room for failure. And locating the horn is only the beginning."

He frustrated me to the point I wanted to scream. I shoved my hand through my hair and blew out a breath. "What are the other four artifacts?"

Dare I ask? I *had* to know what I was up against, what was expected of me. Knowing this quest didn't end with the horn sickened me further.

"Aside from the horn, the Spear of Destiny, the Staff of Moses, the Holy Grail and the Ark of the Covenant." He ticked them off on the tips of his fingers.

Words escaped me as I stared at him, waiting for the *just kidding* punch line but Edward was completely serious. Prickling heat washed over me, piercing my skin and making me break into a cold sweat.

"This will not be easy," he continued. "Nothing worth fighting for is. But hear me now, Anna. The fight for mankind *is* coming. You can choose to become what you were meant to be or you can go back to your hideaway as the coward you are."

"I'm not a coward." My cold fear was forgotten as anger flared bright inside me. I pushed to my feet. "And I'm tired of your insults. I don't have to sit here and take them. I came here for answers. I should have known you wouldn't give them to me. You never want to give them to me."

In a fit of rage, I stalked toward the door.

"Run away, little Anna. As you did before. As you always will."
I slammed the door behind me.

CHAPTER 10

I STOOD THERE FOR the longest time, listening to the old manor house creak. I had more questions than answers now. I heard no movement inside the library and wondered if my uncle remained seated when I stomped out. Or had he slipped out through one of the hidden doors? Even though I never found them, I always suspected there were hidden compartments in the old place. The old man appeared with such stealth he used to scare the life out of me.

One day you will realize how important you are, Anna. Until that day, you are under my care.

Edward's voice filtered through my memories and I clenched my fists, my nails digging into my palms.

You mean your control.

Control is a harsh word, my dear. I prefer care.

We'd had that conversation a million times. I resented Edward kept me on a tight leash. I was always under the watchful gaze of one of his people.

I peered down the hallway lined with portraits of all the Walkers who had come before me. Walker family portraits lined one-hundred-seventy feet of the gallery. I stood in front of the oil painting of my mother, Annabelle Walker. In the portrait, she was sixteen perched on the edge of an oversized garnet wing-backed chair wearing a lovely champagne-colored gown that hugged her thin frame. Her ankles were crossed and I could see a hint of black strappy heels under the hem of her dress. Her black hair hung long and straight over one shoulder. She peered out of the same purple eyes I had. She had a small smile on her lips, as though she gazed at someone she was madly in love with.

She had a timeless beauty. There was something ethereal about her. I wish I'd known her.

But who was she really? Beyond being her namesake, I knew nothing of her other than she'd run away to America when she was eighteen. In that respect, our lives had been parallel, though I had no idea why she left Walker Manor. Did she flee the country with someone? And why did she leave? Because she was pregnant and her family wouldn't approve?

My grandfather died before I was born. I gazed at his portrait for the longest time. My mother favored him. She had the same jawline, the same heart-shaped lips. The same curve of ears and eyes. My uncle favored my grandmother. Lips in a thin straight line, square jaw, piercing blue gaze. But the only gene consistent throughout our family was our hair the color of ink.

Something pushed me onward, down the hall to the last door on the left. My hand hovered over the brass knob for a long moment, my breathing labored and my heart ramming against my chest. Ten years had passed since I'd entered this room. Did my uncle redecorate when I left?

I twisted the knob and pushed open the door to the darkened room. I clicked on the light. My breath caught in my throat as I gazed around the room. Things were the same as though I'd never left. Everything was exactly as I remembered. The four-poster bed still had the same coverlet with pale blue flowers. A wardrobe in the corner stood partially open, hinting at the clothes still hanging inside. I walked over, put my hand on the edge of the door and pushed it open with a squeak.

Shoes were lined up like soldiers in the bottom. My clothes were still in perfect order by season from dark to light. When I was younger, I'd pretend the wardrobe would take me to Narnia away from my rigid life of nothing but studies.

The bookshelves along the wall still hosted all my favorite books. I ran my finger over the dusty spines, my fingernail halting on each title. Books by C.S. Lewis, J.R.R. Tolkien, Lewis Carroll, L. Frank Baum, Louisa May Alcott, followed by volumes H.G. Wells, Grimm's Fairy Tales, Edgar Allen Poe, and the complete works of William Shakespeare.

Looking at those titles now I realized I had a fixation with fantasy worlds and escapism. I wanted nothing more than to be somewhere else, to live in a land where magic was real, to be part of something bigger than me.

Squeezed in between *The Time Machine* and *Alice in Wonderland* was my journal. My heart tripped as I slipped the thick leather-bound book from the shelf. The pages had yellowed with my careful script. I flipped through the pages, that old book smell wafting to my nose, and smiled. I tucked the hefty tome under my arm for reading later when I wasn't standing awash in memories of a life I'd left behind.

"Hello, dream walker."

Joachim's sudden appearance made me jump out of my skin. I yelped, the fear puncturing through me at lightning speed. He stood in the doorway, leaning against the jamb as though it were the most natural thing for an angel to do. His wings were visible, tucked around him. I pressed my hand against my rapidly beating heart.

"Geeze, you scared the life out of me. Don't do that again. What are you doing here?" I practically snarled the words as I gulped in air.

He stepped into the room and nudged the door closed.

"You have come to your uncle for help," he said matter-of-factly. Not a question.

"Yeah? So?"

"He can help you if you'll let him."

"He can suck it." And then I glanced around as though there were listening ears.

Joachim frowned. "Not very lady like of you to say so."

"Who says I'm a lady?"

"Hate and anger are not positive emotions, Annabelle."

"Yeah, well, I'm not feeling very positive at the moment, angel boy."

Red fury flashed over his face as he glared at me. "You are more than stubborn."

"I've also been told I'm a coward. What else is new?"

"Annabelle." He said my name in exasperation.

"Don't call me that," I said between clenched teeth. "It's just Anna."

He huffed, clearly frustrated with me. I got a little satisfaction from frustrating him. "Annabelle, you must give Edward an opportunity to assist you."

He didn't want to call me Anna. Fine. I didn't want to search for his toys.

"He's an ass and we clearly have nothing more to say to each other."

"Oh, but you do. There is so much more. And if you believed that, you would not still be in the house."

Score one point for the angel. He was right but I was still belligerent. "I don't want to hear about the end of the world shit again."

"It is far more than the end of the world. He is the only one who holds the answers you seek. About who you are."

I glanced over at him. He'd moved to the bed where he sat with his hands clasped in his lap looking at me through those pensive blue eyes.

"You seem to know a lot about me. Spill."

"I cannot. I am not permitted."

"But Edward is?"

"He is your uncle. Your blood relative. He is the one who holds the knowledge. The information lies within your family history book."

An icy sensation prickled the back of my throat. The family history book resided somewhere within those dusty books in the library. I'd seen it when I was a teen. The recollection crashed through my mind on a tidal wave of memory. In my mind, I could see the thick tome resting on my uncle's desk. The pages yellowed. The leather binding tattered. The front cover embossed in gold with the family crest and the name WALKER in thick letters. I remembered running my fingers over the indention of the letters and asking my uncle about the contents.

When you are older, Anna, I will show you. I will show you what you need to know in this book.

What is it, uncle?

The key to who we Walkers are. It is a history of our family beginning with the first Walker. And more.

I never understood why I wasn't allowed to read the book. Uncle Edward kept it under lock and key somewhere in his office. Maybe his desk but I wasn't sure.

Damn Joachim. He was right. The only way I would find the answers was by going downstairs.

"If I return to him, will I find the answers in the book?" I asked.

"The entire history of your dream walkers has been recorded by the hand of Edward I. Your great-grandfather, I believe."

Yes, my great-grandfather, Edward Walker I.

"The family goes back farther than him?" It seemed like a silly question but Edward the First was the oldest relative on the family tree in the book. Of course, the line went farther back. When my uncle said we began with the first Walker, I always assumed he meant Edward the First.

"Yes, of course. Back to the days of the Crusades."

I stared at him in disbelief. I assumed incorrectly. The history of the Walker family went back that far? Back to the early Middle Ages? Uncle Edward never told me. He was stingy with information at best.

"You must return to him, Annabelle. You must accept the quest and search for the relics. You must become the Keeper."

"Hold on, angel boy. I'm not doing anything until I have some real answers."

"And your uncle has those answers."

Now *he* frustrated *me*. Fine. But I wanted to search his office when Edward wasn't around. I was still in the manor. No one had come to throw me out. Maybe it was as simple as walking downstairs and perusing his office.

Viable? Or stupid? Probably stupid but I was willing to take the risk.

"Okay, angel boy."

"Good. I will relay your decision to Michael. He will be well pleased."

Before I could respond he was gone in a poof, leaving me alone once again.

That pesky messenger angel. He intended to tell Michael I agreed to go after the relics, when all I agreed to was going back to see Edward. I sighed. All I needed now was a visit from Azriel and my day from hell would be complete.

I shoved aside that thought almost as quickly as it passed through my head. I didn't want that to conjure the fallen angel.

After the messenger angel disappeared, I perched on the edge of the bed to think. Joachim said I must become the Keeper. Keeper of the Holy Relics? What exactly did that job entail? Finding the artifacts and hanging on to them for what purpose? What was I supposed to do with them once I got them?

Aside from the obvious which was give them to Azriel or give them to Michael. Once I handed them over, was my job complete? Was there no more use for Anna? What would happen to me then? If I was of no more use to either party, did that mean I was expendable?

I didn't like the potential answers to any of those questions. Should I decide to take the job, I wasn't too keen on handing over the relics, angel or Fallen.

I was tired. I'd traveled a lot that day. I should get some rest. But I also didn't want to leave. If I left, I'd lose my nerve and not return. It was now or never.

I stepped out of the room and closed the door. I paused to listen. The house was quiet.

I approached the library, pushed open the door and stepped inside. Adrenaline pumped through me as I closed the door and made my way to the wall behind my uncle's desk. My uncle used to keep the book open on his desk but I hadn't seen it since before I left. I ran my finger down the ancient spines. Nothing. I turned to the perfectly neat desk but no book. I tapped my chin with a finger wondering where he would keep it.

An ancient book caught my eye. The weathered leather-bound cover looked older than the others and decidedly out of place. The spine was tattered and embossed with faded gold letters reading *The Book of Watchers*. Kincade had mentioned the Watchers when Ben had been killed. I slipped the book off the shelf and flipped through the musty pages. There were a few drawings and long blocks of text I had no desire to read. I tucked it under my arm for future reference.

As I stood staring at the wall of books, one stuck out from the rest on a shelf at eye level. The ancient dark green spine was devoid of markings. It looked old enough to be the family history book and big enough. It looked like the book I remembered.

My heart skipped as I pulled it off the shelf and hefted it onto the desk. The cover crackled as I opened it and the musty odor accosted my nose. On the first page, yellowed with age, was carefully written script.

The Book of Dream Walkers
As written by Edward Clifton Walker I

A chill entered my bones and my hands shook. Edward Clifton Walker my great-grandfather. He was the first to pen our story. I recalled his portrait on the wall. He had kind eyes and wrinkles at the corners of his mouth. He held a pipe in one hand as he stood in the portrait.

I turned the brittle page. Our family tree was next. The brackets clearly showed our lineage. It went back to the twelfth century and stopped at someone named John Walker who married a woman named Eliza Jane. They had four children. Joachim was right—the Walkers went back to the 1100s, during the time of the Crusades.

My gaze scanned the first page, then the second to current times. There were my aunts and uncle. Edward, Matilda, Josephina and Annabelle Walker. My father was listed as unknown. There was the shame I bore for twenty-eight years. Who was he? Where was he? My mother never breathed a word of who he was to anyone, not even her beloved brother.

I stared at the unknown for an indeterminable amount of time. It stuck in my craw, made me angry she was so selfish and never told anyone. Could I search for him? Find out who he was? If he was still alive, would he want to see me?

All those memories flooding back reminded me of the void I carried with me. I pressed a hand against my chest, aching for the family I never had. Never would have. My gaze flicked over the list of cousins. I'd never met most of them.

I flipped the page. The handwriting was fancy and the ink faded. After all this time, with all this technology, I wondered why the book hadn't been scanned into an electronic form.

I read the story of the dream walkers, though I found the writing difficult to decipher. A few keywords caught my eye. Angels, demons, Holy Relics. I sat hard in my uncle's leather chair, my heart racing.

The dream walkers were chosen by the archangel, Michael, as guardian of those things the heavens and the Most High, the Holy and Great One, hold sacred. The artifacts were given to us when man became corrupted.

I pondered over that for a long moment. *When man became corrupted?* What did that mean? Did it refer to the Crusades or some time much farther back? Shaking my head, I continued reading, skimming the page to the next passage that caught my eye.

It has been many years since the dream walkers have been guardians. When once we were held in high esteem, now we hide in shame. It is my hope to change that, to once again hold the guardianship.

I cannot blame my ancestors for their actions. Only try to repair the damage. The power can corrupt even the purest heart, but I believe we can overcome. I no longer wish to hide in disgrace. I have asked the archangel to allow us once again to gain the guardianship.

He does not believe it is the right time. He believes one of our kind will come. But it will not be the son of a Walker. It will be a daughter. A strong, powerful woman. She will have a pure heart and will be the one to save Man from the evil that walks the Earth.

I know not of whom he speaks. Only that she is a direct descendant. The only one who will become the Keeper of the Holy Relics. The one to save mankind from Hell.

I stared at the words not breathing. The perfectly written letters wavered. My skin tingled. My heart raced. I traced the words with my fingertip wondering if who he wrote about...was me.

I flipped through more pages of the book and noticed a page had been ripped out toward the middle. I ran my finger down the jagged edge of paper wondering what had been so important someone felt the need to tear it out. The following pages were full of drawings. One of a horn labeled the Horn of Gabriel. It was long and straight with a flared bell at the end. There were no keys or holes like a normal instrument.

"You couldn't stay away, could you?"

I jumped at the sound of my uncle's voice, my heart doing double time and my hands shaking. I never heard him come in and that scared me, too.

"I see you've found the book."

I slammed the book closed, snatched up my journal and the Book of Watchers and stood.

"No, please do continue," he said. "I didn't mean to disturb you."

"Who is the one Edward the First wrote about?" I clutched the books to my chest, shivering.

"Don't you know?" His gaze was hard, unwavering.

More answering questions with questions. I scowled and rounded the desk. "You left the book where I could find it. You knew I'd be back."

"Come now, my dear. You never left because you had to search for answers."

The man was infuriating. I wondered if he and Joachim were in cahoots. It was all too convenient the messenger angel urged me to seek answers from my uncle while I was still in his house.

"Why didn't you tell me?"

"You weren't ready and then you left. I'm not sure you're ready even now." His face hardened, still pissed about my leaving. "Would you have believed me had I told you?"

Probably not. "Am I the one then?"

"Yes."

The word hit me like ice and I flinched. "I didn't ask for that. I don't want that."

"I daresay you don't have a choice. Your destiny has been predetermined."

I shook my head. "No. I don't believe it."

"*For I know the plans I have for you.* Believe it, Anna. The archangel would not lie. Your path was clear to him before it was to me. That's why I was desperate to find you when you were a child. Why I bloody well protected you with my life. Why I did everything for you."

"You did everything for *me*?" Shock rolled through me. "You did nothing for me. Nothing! You kept me locked in this house away from family. Hiding me. Are you ashamed of me, uncle? Do you detest me?"

He glared at me. "That's not the way of it."

"Isn't it?" I snapped. "You did everything you could to keep me away from everyone, especially Marcus."

That had been a thorn in my side for years. It was the only ammo I had against my uncle. The only grudge I had left to hold.

"Marcus would have ruined you. Hurt you. You have no idea what he would have done to you. I saved you from heartache and total ruination. I saved your life."

"You sent him away because you saw how happy I was." Arguing about this was pointless but I couldn't help myself.

Darkness clouded his gaze, turning my blood cold. "Anna, what's done is done. There's no going back to the past. It would be best if you never brought up that...man again."

"I won't speak of it again to you, uncle." Even so, the anger still boiled.

"So be it."

The matter was closed. I wanted to run from the room but he blocked the door. Everything I ever knew was a lie. I didn't just have a "gift." I had a destiny. The family I always wanted was never going to happen. My uncle only found me because he wanted me for *this*. It wasn't because he wanted me in the family. Or because he wanted to protect his sister's daughter. No wonder the family avoided me like I was some sort of blight upon the family. Tears clotted my throat and I hated it. Hated him. Hated everything.

"There is more. Our lifespan is not like humans."

My brows knitted in confusion. "What do you mean not like humans?"

"We age slower. We have been given the gift of longevity."

"Are you saying we're...immortal?" I almost wanted to laugh.

"Not immortal, exactly. We merely live a longer amount of time and don't age as quickly as others."

That explained why he didn't look as though he'd aged in the ten years since I'd been gone. This was all too much. I didn't know how much more I could handle.

"Why didn't you tell me about the relics before?" My voice shook with emotion. I clutched the books harder against my chest, willing the tears to go away.

"You ran away," he said.

"And you didn't bother to find me again."

"Am I supposed to chase after you all the time?" He shook his head. "You left. You disappeared. It was apparent to me you had no interest in our family or your gifts."

Another stab to the heart. He enjoyed pointing out everything I did wrong. I paced behind the desk, still clutching the books.

"But you must have expected this day would come." I couldn't help the accusation in my words.

"I did."

I halted and pierced him with a glare. "Then why didn't you come for me?"

"I did find you. You repaid me by leaving."

Like your mother.

He didn't say the words but they hung between us as though he'd said them with his eyes.

"You did, at last, return," he added.

He suspected I would seek him out after contact with Joachim. It was only a matter of time. I'd run away so why should he trouble himself? And when I did make an appearance, he would make it all too convenient for me to learn about my destiny. I huffed out a breath.

"How am I supposed to find these objects?"

"You have your abilities. Use them."

My abilities to dream walk? *That* will find the Holy Relics? I didn't believe it.

"I don't know how." My voice hitched at the end and I recognized a wail when I heard it. I sounded like a cranky toddler. Like the same child that ran away so long ago. It disgusted me. I lowered my voice to a normal tone. "I have no idea where to begin searching. I came here for answers."

"And I have given you them."

"Not all of them."

"Had you stayed with me you would know where to begin searching."

"You won't help me?"

"You must discover it on your own. You have the power within you. You must use it."

I was at a breaking point. I wanted to snap. I wanted to shout. I wanted to scream. He was no help whatsoever. Why did I torture myself by returning? I wanted out. It was a mistake to return. I walked toward the door, pushing him aside.

"Anna." I looked at him over my shoulder. "Don't trust anyone. When you're ready, I'll be here. Waiting for you."

CHAPTER 11

I RAN OUT OF the house and got in my rental car, slamming the door. A myriad of emotions pulsed through me. Everything from anger to despair to fear to outrage. My breath hitched. Before I could stop them, tears rolled down my cheeks followed by wracking sobs.

My chest heaved. I let it all release for my life that never was, the man I once loved, the uncle I thought I knew. When the tears finally subsided, I gripped the steering wheel, trying to decide what to do next. I was stuck. There was no getting out of this Keeper thing or finding the Holy Relics.

I wiped my face with the edge of my sleeve. My stomach twisted into a nervous knot which was a normal state these days. When I returned to England, I walked into a situation completely out of my control. I had no idea how to regain that control.

I glanced upward at the roof of the car. "Why did you do this to me?"

I got no response. I didn't expect one.

Finally, I started the car and drove down the gravel drive, the tires crunching along the way. After wandering through the country-side in the dark, I finally came upon a small inn. Fatigue hit me between the eyes as I parked and got out. I needed a soft bed and a shower. In that order.

After procuring a room from the sleepy-eyed proprietor, I trudged up the stairs to the room and melted into the bed. A cold-ness seeped through me and I couldn't stop shivering. I wasn't sure what to make of everything yet my mind started to ask questions, to try to figure out what to do.

Why hadn't Edward told me before? What other abilities did I have? Were they in the family history book? Were the answers to all my questions there?

My eyes were heavy. I tried to fight sleep, but couldn't. I closed my eyes and dreamed. I saw nothing but images. Emotions. And cold.

I was so cold. Shivering. Teeth-chattering. Bone-chilling. Then there was warmth. The cold was chased away and I knew who was responsible.

Azriel.

He was with me in my dreams. He took me into his arms, those beautiful black wings surrounding me, pulling me against him. He was dressed in a white button-down shirt, collar open to reveal a sprinkle of dark hair.

I was powerless to resist him. I realized with some horror I want-ed him. I wanted his hands on me. His mouth. His everything. I wanted him to fill me up, take me to heights I'd never before ex-perienced. His gaze never left mine as I slid my hands up his chest, over the divine curve of muscles, wanting skin-to-skin contact.

A sense of familiarity pulsed through me. Like something I dreamed or experienced before. His gaze never left mine as his sultry mouth curved into a smile.

You cannot deny me, can you, dream walker?

I tipped my head and parted my lips and a moment later, he tasted me. That mouth was as sinful as I thought it would be. His tongue traced the soft fullness of my lips, sending a shiver of desire through me. His hands slid down to my lower back and pulled me closer. Closer. Closer still. Until our bodies molded against each other. Until we were nearly one.

You want to help me, don't you?

His words pulled me deeper as heat spread through me from head to toe. I moaned my delight. My hands tangled in his hair. So soft. So perfect. Like his mouth.

You do, don't you?

The longer he kissed me, the more I was powerless to resist. I was swept under the tide of his passion, pulled along the undulating waves. The more he whispered in my mind, the more I was ready to do whatever he asked of me and more.

You want me. I want you. Let me take you, chérie. Our bonding will seal our understanding. You will be mine.

His hand pushed under my shirt, cupping my breast. His mouth was now on my cheek, kissing his way down my neck. His kisses left a hot, damp trail down my neck. The orgasm rocked through me so violently my entire body shuddered.

My hands clawed his shirt, ripping away button after button. Finally, I made contact with his scorching skin, my nails raking down his chest. I left behind a red trail. He growled approval. I leaned into him and licked the hollow of his throat, tasting his heat, his spiciness. Cinnamon.

His hands were on my breasts, kneading, pinching. My weak legs barely held me up. My head swam making it hard to focus.

You could not deny me forever.

All I could think about was straddling that damn beautiful body of his.

And then his handsome face morphed into something horrid. Skin turned to scales. Eyes glowed red. A horn protruded from his forehead. Hands turned into claws. His tongue was forked, seeking a taste of my skin. His mouth opened wide as though he was about to sink those jagged teeth in me.

Something jarred me. I shoved out his arms with enough violence to rip us apart. My senses slammed back into me. I realized with horror what I'd almost done. He snarled.

My eyes popped open and I sat up and screamed, the dream gone. I was alone. My breath hitched in my chest and my hands shook and the cold returned.

Azriel. Damn him. He tried to seduce me. To make me agree to help him by using me in my dream.

Something was clutched in my fist. I opened it. A white pearlized button rested against my palm. I caught the scent of cinnamon in the air. Azriel had been there.

⬥————➤

I couldn't go back to sleep. I didn't want to. I didn't want to open my mind again for Azriel to come through to try to seduce me again. I couldn't shake the familiar feeling I had about him but then, I'd never seen him in real life before a few days ago. Maybe he'd visited my dreams before and I didn't remember. He was powerful. He could do that sort of thing.

Morning light slashed through the open curtain as I paced the length of the small room, trying to decide my next move. A knock at the door made me halt. Suspicion lanced through me. I didn't know anyone in town other my uncle. I told no one where I was staying or even why I was there. My heart jumped into a quickened beat.

Another knock. I padded to the door and peered through the peephole. A woman stood on the other side.

"Who's there?"

"Your cousin."

124

My cousin? I stiffened and cracked open the door.

"Hey," she greeted with a pop of gum.

Her hands were shoved in the pockets of her jeans with holes in the knees. She wore an oversized Black Sabbath shirt that'd seen better days and red Converse that were so worn they were faded and had holes in the toes. A stud pierced her nose and one ear was pierced from the lobe all around the curve. She popped her gum and grinned.

Her face looked vaguely familiar. She looked at me with mirth in her big green eyes. I'd seen her in the house before. I searched my memory banks for a name but came up empty. She pushed past me without waiting for an invitation.

I closed the door. A spicy scent of perfume infused the air, tingling my nose. She continued to pop her gum as she looked me over.

"You're the one, huh?"

"Who are you?" I asked.

Her gaze searched my face as though memorizing every line. "Guess you don't remember me. I remember you."

In all the years I spent at my uncle's manor, I met only a handful of family. They never stayed around for long. Nor did they want to claim me as one of their kin.

"You're Annabelle's kid, right?"

"Yes," I said slowly, cautiously. I hadn't been a kid for a long time.

"I'm Lexi. Josephina's daughter."

I blinked confusion.

"You probably don't remember me." I shook my head. "I was there when ole Uncle Ed brought you to the manor."

The memory flooded back to me with such force I sat on the edge of the bed. Josephina was my mother's sister. Lexi was two years my senior. I'd forgotten so many things about my life at Walker manor. I pushed them into a box in the back of my mind, put a pad lock on it, and let it collect dust. Now I blew away the cobwebs and allowed the memory.

On the day I left with Uncle Edward, we immediately flew back to England on his private plane, landed at Heathrow, and then rode in his chauffeur-driven luxury car to his manor in Cannington, Somerset. Rivulets of rain sluiced down the windows the entire drive. We didn't talk much. I was afraid of him and he was busy brooding. Or reading a musty old book with yellowed pages.

When we arrived, I followed him inside the big house. The manor was bigger than anything I lived in back in America. Edward Walker had money and a lot of it. At the time, my grandmother, Elinor Walker, was still alive and living in the manor. When we arrived, Lexi and her mother were there for a visit.

It was mid-afternoon and still raining. My threadbare clothes were drenched. The butler gave me a look of disdain as my clothes dripped, leaving little circles of water at my feet. Uncle had left me in the foyer only for a moment, ordering me to stay put. But I was never one to follow directions and went exploring. Lexi and her mother were in the parlor having tea.

Little cakes perched on the serving tray and my stomach rumbled. I couldn't remember the last meal I had.

"Well, who do we have here?" Josephina, my aunt, beckoned me closer, deeper into the room. She had the same long dark hair, the same big green eyes as Lexi. My cousin scowled at me. There was another older woman in the room.

"Good God. What street urchin has Edward dragged home this time?"

"Mother, hush." Josephina put down her china cup and waved me toward her. "Come inside, child."

When I refused to move, she said, "Alexandria, give her a cake."

"Don't feed her. We'll never get rid of her then."

"Mother, she's not a stray dog," my aunt scolded.

She picked up the beautifully iced cake and handed it to Lexi with a nod. The girl was reluctant at first but finally walked to me and handed over the pastry. I took it, held the perfect thing in my hand before stuffing it all in my mouth.

"Disgusting creature," the elderly woman said.

Elinor Walker exuded wealth and condescension. As she stared at me with that disgusted look, she touched the pearls at her throat. Even Lexi scowled, scrunching up her face with distaste.

"I simply don't understand why Edward continues to drag these filthy creatures home. We're not running an orphanage here." Elinor sniffed derision.

"You *know* why, Mother." Aunt Josephina eyed me the entire time as I munched on the cake.

"Ha. As if this girl is who he thinks. Look at her. She's a skeleton with scraggly hair. All skin and bones. Dressed in rags. Can she even talk?"

"And she smells," Lexi added. She'd rejoined the others in the parlor.

"*Mother,* please. And Alexandria that is quite enough out of you. She could be the one." She used her best chastising voice and gave them both a glare.

All the while, I chewed the delectable treat. I knew my face was covered in icing as crumbs fell to the floor, but it was the tastiest thing I had in a while.

"Yes, Mother, she could be." Edward's voice boomed behind me. "In fact, I believe she is."

I craned my neck to look up at him. He seemed so...big then. So larger than life. So menacing. A dark angry look creased his features. He was not amused by Elinor's observations.

"She's clearly nothing but a street urchin. How dare you bring her here!" Elinor's snooty voice was thick with disdain.

"She's here because she's your granddaughter and I'll thank you to remember that."

"She's no granddaughter of mine." She sucked in a sharp breath of contempt and turned her head, pointing her nose in the air. "My *daughter* did not give birth to such a creature as *that*." And to punctuate her words, she pointed a finger.

All I remembered was the glittery ring on her index finger. Snotty old bitch.

Scowling, Edward grasped my hand. "Come. Let's take you to Maryanne. And I'll thank you, Mother, to keep your comments to yourself."

Maryanne was the maid who cleaned me up, gave me fresh clothes and a bed.

I pulled myself back to the present and whispered, "I remember you."

Lexi sauntered around the room, surveying the surroundings as though taking a mental inventory. She kept her hands in her pockets as she walked around looking at everything. She finally halted in front of the dresser, leaned her hips on the edge and crossed her feet at the ankles.

"You came back, huh? Why?"

"Does it matter?"

"It matters to him. He was pretty ticked when you left."

"I had no reason to stay," I said.

"Sure, you did."

I scowled. "What do you know about my situation?"

"Plenty. Besides, the whole family knows." She rolled her eyes.

"If the whole family is aware of me and my 'situation,'" I put air quotes around *situation*, "then why hasn't anyone ever told me?"

"Edward thought children should be seen, not heard. Out of sight, out of mind kinda thing. He kept you busy with all your studies away from the family 'cause he wanted to keep you 'pure.' Or something like that." She rolled her eyes again. "He didn't want anyone filling your head with wild ideas about the prophecy."

What I read earlier in the book made no mention of a prophecy. "What prophecy? And why would he keep me from the family like that?"

"Everyone is familiar with the one dream walker that screwed things up for us. Guess he figured you were safer not knowing all the deets."

I stared at her. "What's the prophecy?"

"He didn't tell you about that either, huh?"

I shook my head.

"We gotta lot to learn then, don't we?" She huffed out a breath and sat in the chair in the corner. "You don't know?"

"No."

"It's in the family history book. The one he keeps locked up."

That couldn't be true. I found it right away when I went back to the... Wait. He'd wanted me to find it. He even told me as much. That bastard.

"Like he's scared someone will read it." She snorted. "I mean, isn't that the point? Anyway, it's all about the one who'll stop the downfall of man. The one who'll become the new Keeper of the Holy Relics. Blah, blah, blah. All fire and brimstone and shit."

That wasn't news to me. He told me as much but what he *didn't* say was that there was a prophecy. I wanted to gag but refrained. A prophecy sounded so cheesy and fake. Like something out of a movie. I was living my own action-adventure flick.

"Yeah? So? I know all that already."

"But not the *whole* story." She grinned, like she was holding onto a secret. "I read the prophecy word for word but I didn't memorize it. There's something more about you, specifically."

I stiffened. "I need that book." Suddenly desperate, I wanted to read and ingrain it into my memory. I hadn't found anything about me or a prophecy in the book when I was there earlier, but I'd been interrupted. Almost like Edward intruded on purpose before I could get that far.

"To do that we have to go to the manor."

"I'm aware of that."

"Uncle Ed isn't going to let you have it."

"Why not?"

"Because he keeps it locked up. Duh."

"Not unless he *wants* me to see it."

She cocked her head to the side as if trying to figure out what I was saying.

"He knew I'd come back," I said. "He left it for me to find. But I only read a few pages before he interrupted."

"He wants to parcel out bits of information to you," she said.

My eyes narrowed as suspicion crawled through me. She seemed to know a lot about this family prophecy for someone who claimed the book was "locked up." I jumped to my feet, yanked her to her feet, and tossed her against the wall. My arm rammed against her throat. She gasped for breath.

"Did he send you? Did he want you to feed me these lies?"

"Not...lies... Swear." She held up her hands in surrender.

"How do you know about the book?"

"Not...a...secret..."

"Why are you here?"

"To help." She tried to gulp in air as I pressed harder.

Her gaze cut to my arm on her neck. I eased up only a little. "It's true then?"

She nodded.

I released her and stepped back. She rubbed her throat and coughed, trying to catch her breath. "You didn't have to choke me."

"I don't trust you." Not yet. "I still want to see it. And you're going to help me."

"How?" She still rubbed her throat.

I grinned. "I have a plan."

Convincing her took two hours. When she finally agreed, I wasted no time heading back to the manor. The plan was for Lexi to go in, take a snapshot of the page with her cell and text it to me. Easy, right?

"What if I can't find the book?" she asked.

"It's in the library. I saw it yesterday."

I was still convinced she was working with him. It was the only explanation for her sudden appearance. She must have followed me from the manor to the inn. I suspected my uncle put her up to it. I didn't understand what he or Lexi would gain for her to help me. We were strangers. But she had information I needed and wanted so I planned to use her for that.

She huffed out a sigh. "Fine, I'll go. But no promises."

When we returned to my uncle's, the gates were guarded. Unlike before when I drove through. I figured Edward didn't want any more unexpected visitors.

Suspicion still crawled through me.

The guards let Lexi in since she was a regular house guest. I hunched down in the back of her SUV as she cleared the gate. She parked near the front door, cutting the engine.

"I'll be back as soon as I can."

She slammed the door and clicked the lock on her remote. I listened to her receding footsteps crunch on the gravel drive and then nothing. The minutes dragged by until my phone vibrated. A text from her.

Inside. No book. Ed here.

Make small talk, I replied.

I was going to have to do it myself. I lifted my head and scanned the area. No one was about so I climbed over the front seat and popped the locks. I slipped out of the car, pausing to look around for any sign of life. Gripping my phone, I ran to the back of the manor, hoping the security guards were snoozing and didn't notice me.

I peeked inside the back door to the kitchen and saw no one which was odd. Edward always had a large staff. Maybe not so much these days but he'd surely have a cook. I tried the knob. It was unlocked.

Inside the kitchen, something simmered in a large stock pot on the stove. It smelled divine and my stomach rumbled. I couldn't remember the last time I ate.

He had all the finest in equipment. A Viking oven and gas cooktop with all the fancy grates. A subzero refrigerator. Wine cooler. Trash compactor. Marble countertops. Oak cabinets. This wasn't the old kitchen I remembered. This was updated. New. Modern.

I paused, listening. If there was food cooking, then a chef couldn't be far. Not wanting to linger, I crept through the kitchen to the door. In the hallway, I made for the library, hurrying before I was spotted. The door was ajar and I heard voices on the other side. I flattened against the wall and tried to peer into the room, but I couldn't see anything.

"I thought I told you never to return." That was Edward. But who was he talking to?

"You may have mentioned that." Lexi. She sounded cocky and confident. Not at all like the air-headed gum-popping girl. "I came for the book."

She was trying to get the family history book for me. I smiled, glad to know someone was finally on my side.

"As if I'd hand it over to you. You can't have it. Now get out."

I took that moment to make my entrance. I shoved open the door with a flourish and stepped into the room. They both looked up, startled. Edward recovered quickly but Lexi fidgeted and her face flushed.

"You can't stay away can you, Anna?" He smirked.

"I want the damn book," I demanded.

"Did you send her to get it?" He indicated Lexi, but he wouldn't look at her.

"Where is it?" I asked, ignoring him.

He glanced between the two of us and then shook his head. "Not while she's here."

She popped her gum and grinned. "I can take a hint. See ya 'round, cuz."

We both watched as she sauntered out of the room, slamming the door behind her. He didn't say anything. Instead, he walked to a locked cabinet. He pulled keys out of his pocket, unlocked the door and slid out the book.

"I warned you not to trust anyone."

"Even Lexi? She's family."

"*Anyone.*" He stilled and looked at me. "All you have to do is ask for my help. You don't have to send someone in your stead. Especially her."

We stared at each other for a long quiet minute before he placed the book on the desk. I realized he *wanted* me to come to him for help. He wanted me to beg for it. It was the second time he mentioned it. I'd be damned if I asked him for any more help. I was going to read the book and then get out. But first I wanted to find out what his beef was with my cousin.

"Why did you tell her to get out?"

"Josey is my dear sweet sister, but her daughter is a thief and a liar. Now, do you want to read the book or not?"

"Where's the prophecy?" I walked around the end of the desk.

Edward's eyes narrowed. "Did she tell you about that?"

"It doesn't matter. Show me the page."

With his mouth in a thin line, he flipped it open. Past the family tree, past carefully written pages. He paused halfway through then pushed it toward me.

"There." He stabbed the page with his index finger.

I read the carefully written words. As though someone had a precise hand when scribing.

Darkness will rise. Evil will walk the land. It will be time for the new Keeper to take control of the Holy Relics. My dreams and the archangel both have foretold this Keeper will be a woman. She will carry the Light inside her and she will stop the evil. She will be pure of heart. She will be more powerful than any Keeper before or after her. The ultimate good. She will use her powers to find the artifacts and she will be backed by an army of angels and men.

Her quest will not be an easy one for the relics are hidden upon the Earth. Once she begins, she cannot turn back. And once she begins, her powers will manifest, making her stronger, more powerful than any Walker before her.

But if evil should overcome her, for she will be tempted beyond all temptations, she will falter. If she chooses to follow Darkness, then the world of Man will suffer. Good will be defeated. The world will change forever and the evil cannot be undone.

This is true as known to me and the archangel, Michael. He has come to me again and told me of this prophecy. The destiny of the Keeper has been foretold.

So it is scribed.

So it shall be.

The words wavered. Was it all true? Could I stop the evil? How? And how could an army of angels help me? And then there was the tidbit about me being tempted to the darkness. What the fuck? Did that mean Azriel would be the one to try to pull me into that darkness? How would I resist?

But then hadn't he tried that already? I managed to push him away. I won that round. I refused to fall under his spell, to let him control me.

I didn't have answers to any of these questions. And I was scared. Terrified actually. I didn't want this responsibility. I never asked for it.

"Well?" Edward asked.

"Well what?"

"I would think you'd have a comment since the fate of all mankind rests with you."

Hearing the words aloud sent cold creeping down my spine. My chest tightened. I flexed my fingers, resisting the urge to rub it away. It wouldn't go away with a simple massage.

"I'm not doing this."

"You don't have a choice."

"I *do* have a choice and I'm not doing it!"

"Anna—"

"No. I'm not this person. I never will be." My hands fisted. My face burned hot.

Edward clenched his jaw, the muscles ticking along the edge. He was angry all over again. I didn't give a shit. I flipped the book closed with a thud.

"I'm going home."

"You do that, Annabelle." He put particular emphasis on my name, as though it singed his tongue. "Go and let the world go to hell. And I assure you, it *will* go to hell. There is no one else to do this."

"I don't care. Why have I been chosen? What makes me so fucking special?" I couldn't stop shaking.

"Because of who you are."

He took a deep breath, turned and walked toward the wall of windows overlooking the west side of the property. I clutched my elbows, trying to stave off the cold fear gripping me.

"Since the day I learned my sister was pregnant, I searched for her. She covered her tracks well when she left England. I followed what little clues she left behind thinking I could find her. And your father. She never told anyone who he was."

My mouth went bone dry as I stared at him. I knew my father had been listed as unknown on my birth certificate. But the first glimmer of hope sparked within me. I still quaked. This was the most I'd ever heard about my father. My uncle had never told me he searched for either of them. He exhaled a heated breath, headed to a nearby chair and eased into it.

"Annabelle was my youngest sister. She had a light within her. So bright and dazzling that anyone would have been drawn to it." He glanced at me. Pain and anguish etched his features. Even after all this time he still missed her. "Someone *was* drawn to it. Someone she loved more than she loved her own family. Someone who made her go into hiding."

My heart tripped as he paused, contemplating his next words.

"Go on," I urged.

He gazed off into space, remembering. As though visualizing that life so long ago. "She told no one of the pregnancy. She hid it. Even from me."

I inched closer, desperate to hear more about her. To learn everything I could about who she was and what happened to her.

"She finally wrote me a letter when she was nine months along. She admitted she had been seeing a man in secret while still living here. She'd slip away at night to go to him. She feared what would happen to her and the child once it was born."

He paused again and I slipped into the chair across from him. His level gaze met mine.

"She refused to name him and said he couldn't marry her. Her letter arrived with no postmark. Not even a stamp. As though it was hand delivered but no one on the staff accepted the letter from a courier and no one recalled anyone delivering it. It simply appeared. The writing on the outside was in a neat, perfect hand printed in precise block letters. Not at all like her careful script."

A neat perfect hand. I was reminded of the envelope I found in my apartment with the postcard of Hong Kong and the words *begin your search* written on the back. Eerie tendrils tickled the back of my neck.

"I searched for any thread of evidence as to who he was. She described him as a strong man who loved her and wanted to keep her and her unborn child safe. She begged my forgiveness for what she'd done and asked that I never search for you. She wanted you well-protected, away from this life. I suspect she had no idea she would die while birthing you."

"What happened to my father?"

He shrugged. "Since he wasn't at your birth, I can only assume he was unable to be there or unwilling."

I couldn't believe he was unwilling. If the man loved her as much as she said in her letter and he wanted to protect us, then he'd never leave her. Never leave us.

Edward pushed to his feet and walked back to the family history book. He opened the cover, flipped a few pages. When he paused, he motioned for me to join him. Once at the desk, I peered over his shoulder.

The Keeper of the Holy Relics will be born of the Light on the Winter Solstice. The Bringer of Light into Darkness.

As it is written, so it shall be.

I gripped the edge of the desk to steady the dizziness that suddenly slammed into me. I was born on the winter solstice. I was the Bringer of Light into Darkness. I was the Keeper of the Holy Relics. I was always destined to be the Keeper of the Holy Relics.

"I made it my life's mission to find you, protect you with my life. I combed news stories from every major newspaper I could get my hands on hoping I would find some mention of a girl who had special abilities. I found you once when you were small but then lost track of you. You moved around a lot. That's why it took me so long to find you."

"I know." My voice was only a whisper, the words stinging my throat.

"You see now why I've tried to keep you out of harm's way."

"Yes."

"I meant what I said about trusting no one."

I met his sharp assessing gaze. "But I can trust you."

"No one," he repeated.

It shook me to the core. Was he warning me about himself or someone else? Would he turn on me? Was I to take on this entire task alone? My mouth was too dry. My head throbbed with all the information.

"What does 'born of the Light' mean?"

He cleared his throat and shifted from one foot to the other before he answered.

"I haven't been able to determine if your father is still alive." He pointed to the passage. "However, I believe *Born of the Light* is a clue to his identity."

"Who is he?" My voice was breathy, hopeful. I didn't want to ask, but I would never forgive myself if I didn't. I had to know.

"I believe he is an angel."

CHAPTER 12

*M*Y FATHER WAS AN *angel.*

I wished Edward punched me in the teeth. That would have been easier to take. The pain wouldn't have been nearly as bad as knowing that my father was an angel. I hope he hadn't deserted me when I needed him the most. Why would he? Had he been killed? What happened to him? Though Edward wasn't sure, he suspected the truth because of the wording in the family history book and the mysterious circumstances surrounding my mother's disappearance and subsequent death.

And since our family had a sort of celestial connection, it made sense to him.

Not to me.

I couldn't make sense of anything.

Born of the Light.

I stared in disbelief at him. Time halted as his face wavered in front of me. I wobbled on my feet and the next thing I knew I sat in a chair. Edward pushed a glass of cold water into my hand.

"You all right?" Edward stood near the chair with concern etched on his face.

"What happened?" My voice was weaker than I expected.

"You fainted."

I gripped the glass until my fingers ached and then took a sip, letting the cool water slide down my raw throat to calm me. Too bad it wasn't Kincade's ten-thousand-dollar whiskey. I pressed my palm against my forehead, trying to come to terms with all I'd learned in the last two days.

"I'm fine." I lifted my head finally and placed the glass on the nearby table. Then got to my feet and headed for the door.

"Where are you going?" Edward asked.

I paused, my booted feet scuffling on the floor. The truth was, I had no idea where I was going. "I need to think."

My head hurt. My heart hurt. My very existence had been bruised.

I thought he would try to talk me out of it, but he didn't. He let me go. Maybe because he understood I had a lot of thinking to do. When I stepped out of the manor, Lexi had deserted me. So much for her help. Maybe that was for the best.

Trust no one.

She'd left me stranded with no car. My shoulders slumped. The door behind me cracked open.

"Miss?" The butler swung the door open wider and stepped into the threshold. "The young lady said you would need a ride back to your inn. I called a taxi. Ah, here it is now then."

He shut the door before I could thank him. Indeed, a taxi was headed up the long drive. I was relieved I didn't have to walk. He drove me back and I tossed him a few bills. Frazzled, I opened the door and flipped on the light...and yelped at the sight of the winged man in my room. Azriel. I pressed a hand to my fluttering heart.

His shadowed form was outlined in the pale light. His wings were fully extended and he stood leaning against one of the walls

140

with his hands shoved deep into the pockets of his tight-fitting jeans.

"Welcome back, Anna."

"What are you doing here?" I snarled.

The erotic dream rushed back. I saw Azriel for the demon he truly was. I was aware of what he tried to do. The spell he'd tried to put me under. To make me his. The memory turned my stomach. I'd tossed the button I found in my hand into the trash.

"My apologies, *chérie*, for startling you. Have you given any more thought to my request? I need your answer."

I pinched the bridge of my nose. He already knew the answer to that. He walked my dreams, the bastard.

"My answer is still no."

"Pity." He looked crestfallen but determined. "You realize if you refuse us, I will be forced to hurt you."

"Don't threaten me."

"Your arrogance is going to get you killed one day."

"So is yours."

"We shall see. Your officer friend paid me a visit. He seems to think I had something to do with your disappearance," he said. "We had a lovely chat."

My eyes narrowed. "Did you?"

"Indeed." He gave me a shit-eating grin. "He was quite inquisitive about your whereabouts. Is the detective pining away for you?"

"Hardly," I scoffed. Our last encounter was far from friendly. I'd pepper-sprayed him in the face.

"I believe he was rather disappointed when I had no information to give him."

I stared at him a long moment. Azriel covered for me? Why? "What did you do to him?"

"Far be it from me to injure or threaten someone of his importance. It hurts me you would even think that." He looked abashed

141

before he continued. "I did nothing. We talked. That was all. I couldn't answer his questions. He left."

"So glad to hear you two are chummy now," I said. "Like I care."

"Oh, you care. More than you're willing to admit at this point. Do not forget how well I know you."

I scowled. I would never forget how well he knew me or what he did to me. I would still avenge Ben's death if it was the last thing I did on this earth. My fingers curled into a fist. I didn't answer.

"What's wrong, *chérie*? Are you afraid I'll hurt him?"

He mistook my anger towards him as affection for Kincade when he had it all wrong. Let him think what he would. I didn't care.

"Your honey scent was all over him."

I was disturbed he thought I smelled like honey. Where did that come from? Was there some chemical reaction with my skin and soap? If so, I'd change that immediately.

"He tried to take me into custody, thanks to you," I said. "Or did you forget you murdered an innocent woman?"

"I forget nothing." He took a step towards me, his eyes narrowing. "There *is* something more between you, though I think neither of you realize it."

"Whatever."

I dismissed his thought with a wave. Kincade and I were far from friends, as far as I was concerned. He'd been a thorn in my side. I wasn't about to let him get in my way now. Azriel was smoking crack.

Anger tumbled through me. I was tired of this game. "Get out."

"My Lord Master will be disappointed."

"Tell your Lord Master to suck it."

"I'll be sure and do that, Anna." He gave a little wave and left.

I sank to the bed. It took all my strength not to break down. Now all I needed was a visit from Joachim. Just to round things out.

I was so exhausted—emotionally, physically, mentally—I dozed off. My dreams were all fire and brimstone. The end of the world. The death of mankind. In one dream, the second coming. I woke, shaking and nauseated. But thankfully no one walked into my dreams. No Azriel. No Edward.

I downed a glass of water and crawled back onto the bed. Unable to sleep, I remembered the postcard and grabbed it out of my bag. My fingers traced over the thick handwriting with the words *begin your search* and I couldn't help but think about my mother's letter. Was it addressed to him in the same hand? Why had she written him? I wished I could see the letter, see her handwriting, read her words. Maybe I would feel more connected to her somehow.

I stared at the picture on the other side. The building in the picture was of Two International Finance Centre in the Central District. The tallest building in Hong Kong. How did that place connect with the Horn of Gabriel?

I snatched my smartphone and searched for the building. I came up with the usual Wikipedia entries, stats on the building, etc. Then I researched Hong Kong itself and found a Roman Catholic Church. That seemed too obvious a place to hide the horn.

I stared at the postcard again. Was Two International Finance Centre a clue? In my search, I discovered one of the tenants was a merger and acquisition company from Texas. Another an oil and gas company as well as several banks. Other companies included various financial institutions including the Hong Kong Monetary Authority.

I wasn't sure what any of that had to do with the horn. Yawning, I rubbed my tired eyes and clicked off the phone. I was exhausted again and the bed was a welcome oasis. I curled up, pulling the blankets to my chin and was out in a matter of minutes.

The dream started right away. I stood in a garden with a fountain in front of me. The fountain was a statue of a naked man with mermaids all around. The water was cool and misty.

I wasn't wearing my normal black uniform. I was dressed in a pink gown with flowing sleeves and a scooped neckline. My feet were bare. My hair was pulled back away from my face and adorned with ribbons and flowers.

I sat on the edge of the fountain trailing fingers through the cool water. My face rippled in the reflection. As I gazed down, Azriel's face joined mine in the pool.

Before I could stop it, his control latched onto me. He sucked me in. He cast his spell over me, making me release all restraint.

I turned to him and he took me in his arms. He wasn't dressed in jeans and a T-shirt. Now he wore a long tunic with sleeves cuffed at the wrist open to reveal his chest and all that glorious muscle.

His hand laced with mine as he led me away from the fountain to a meadow thick with wildflowers. His lips were inches from mine. My heart raced with anticipation yet I couldn't stop him or what was to come. As he did before, his power was over me and he controlled this dream.

A gentle breeze blew and we fell to the ground together. Me on my back while he knelt over me. He stripped away the tunic, leaving his glorious wings and exposed chest. His hands ran up my thighs, pushing up the skirt, and my eyes fluttered closed.

Everything about this was wrong. But his hold on me was strong. I couldn't speak or move.

"You want to do as I say. Don't you, *chérie?*"

I screamed no in my head but my mouth said yes. The bastard pushed up my dress and his burning hot hands were on my thighs. Just inches away from my wet core. I hated that he made me respond this way. I wanted him to stop but my body had other ideas.

"You want me as I want you," he said.

"Yes."

No! But I couldn't refuse him. He was going to take me and I was powerless to stop him.

In the dream walk with Emma, I controlled my own movement. But I couldn't leave. Now, his power was so great I couldn't break it. He stretched his arms outward and suddenly a dagger appeared in each of his hands. Morning sun glinted off the silvery blades. His face morphed into the evil one I saw before. He raised his hands above his head seconds away from plunging the daggers into my heart. I was still unable to move or react. I wanted to scream but couldn't.

"My Lord Master sends his regards." He flashed a smile as his arms came down.

My eyes squeezed shut as I waited for the pain to pierce through me. Instead, Azriel screamed. An arrow punctured his shoulder. He was so stunned, his normal face reappeared, the demon face gone. The daggers slipped from his fingers, thumping on the ground next to me. Black blood trickled from the wound. He reached up and ripped out the arrow.

"Release her."

I recognized my uncle's voice.

"How nice of you to join us, my old friend." Azriel pinned his gaze on him behind me. Blood trickled down his torso, mingling with the sweat on his chest.

I heard the distinct creak of a bow and arrow. Edward was ready to fire again. I still couldn't turn my head to see him, though.

"Release your hold on her. Now."

"Why? She has refused to help us. She must be punished."

"The next arrow will be to your heart if you don't let her go."

Edward meant business. I could hear it in his frosty tone. It was so cold it sent chills through me. I imagined Azriel and Edward had a staring match since the fallen angel's gaze didn't waver. He reached for the daggers. Another arrow pierced his other shoulder.

"That was a warning," Edward said.

"Still a decent shot." Azriel yanked out the arrow and more black blood flowed. He didn't even grimace with the removal. "Why don't you kill me?"

"Because you're not worth it," Edward said, his voice razor sharp.

Ouch. He meant it.

Azriel laughed. "Very well. She will live. For now."

"You only say that because you can't kill her. If you kill her, Lucifer will kill you. Unless you want to die..." Edward's threat hung in the air between them.

"Touché, my old friend." He glanced down at me and then blew me a kiss before disappearing.

And just like that I had movement again. I shoved down the dress and rolled to my feet. My uncle held the bow and arrow at his side. He was dressed in the suit he wore the last time I saw him.

"Thanks," I said, though a little reluctantly. "How did you know?"

"The door to your subconscious is always open. That is why he was able to overpower you and how I found you."

"Have you been watching me?"

"What do you think?" He quirked an eyebrow.

The thought of Edward in my dreams made me ill. I didn't want him anywhere near me, much less in my dreams.

"You are the Keeper. And if you don't go after those relics, he *will* try to kill you again. I may not be there to stop him next time."

"You said he couldn't kill me," I pointed out.

He nodded, his head bobbing slowly. "He will be punished by his Lord Master if he does kill you. It will, however, not stop him. Our family has been his enemy for a long time. He would relish making sure you die, even though he knows Lucifer wants you alive."

Odd logic. It didn't make sense, though I supposed killing me was worth facing whatever torture awaited him.

"You said the door to my subconscious is always open. How do I keep him out?"

"You have to learn to control the door to your dreams, Anna. It's what I would have taught you if you stayed."

"Can you teach me?"

He hesitated. "Yes."

"Now?"

"No. You must come to me."

It was inevitable I'd return to him. Eventually. But not now. Now I had to make a decision that would change my life forever. I had to agree to find the horn even though I resisted.

"Your choice now is about the relics. You can no longer avoid the search," he said, as though reading my mind.

I wondered if he was the one responsible for pushing me in the direction of the relics. "Did you send me the postcard?"

"What postcard?" His brows knitted.

He was telling the truth. He concealed a lot from me, but I could tell his response was honest.

"Someone sent me a postcard of Hong Kong. The message was, 'Begin your search.'"

"Then I suppose that's where you should start."

I shook my head. "I'm still not doing it."

His face turned into a dark glower. "Then you will bloody well die. And I'm done trying."

He was gone and the dream was over. I bolted upright in bed, my heart racing. I didn't want to admit Edward was right. I had to do it. But dammed if I didn't want to.

In the morning, I'd leave for Hong Kong.

Cold realization was a horrible thing to hit you first thing in the morning. I hadn't slept well. I'd tossed and turned the rest of the night after my horrible dreams.

When the sun came up and shone brightly through the windows, my decision had been made. I was going after the Horn of Gabriel. At the time, I thought if I got it and handed it over to Joachim, I'd be left to go along my merry way. I'd been so naïve. There was no getting out of this quest or any of the others, nor could I avoid taking on the job of Keeper.

I packed my meager belongings and purchased an airplane ticket online. Even though I wanted to arm myself, I knew I'd never get through security with weapons so I'd made the decision to create my arsenal when I got to Hong Kong.

My cell phone beeped. It was a text from Lexi saying she wanted to help. If she wanted to help me so bad, why did she desert me at my uncle's? He said she was a liar and a thief. What had she lied about? What'd she steal? Why was she so determined to help me?

I stared at the text a long while. I didn't want to go to Hong Kong alone. And even though I didn't trust Lexi, she understood who I was and what I had to do.

Let me help you. I got mad skills. She added a smiley face after that.

My gut instinct was to refuse her help and go alone. I typed out a response.

Meet me at Heathrow in three hours.

Why?

I told her I was headed to Hong Kong and gave her my flight information. She agreed to purchase a ticket and meet me at the gate.

I left the inn and made my way back to the airport where I found Lexi already waiting at the gate. She gave me a jaunty wave and flipped her long auburn hair over her shoulder.

"Hey, cuz." She greeted me with a gum pop.

I scrunched my nose. She grew up in England but she sure didn't sound like it. "Why don't you sound British?"

She laughed. "I went to university in the States. I spent a lot of time there. And other places. After you left uncle's, I went looking for you."

Warning bells. Red alerts. Flashing lights. "Why?"

She shrugged her shoulder. "Figured I'd find you and offer my services."

She must not have been looking too hard. I'd been in Dallas for a long time. And I wasn't that hard to track down especially if she could dream walk as well.

"Uncle probably told you I'm a thief."

I nodded.

"He's not wrong. I am."

"And you wanted to team up with me why exactly?"

"We're two loners. Thought we could help each other out. So, what's in Hong Kong?"

I took her by the arm and led her away from the crowd, not wanting anyone to overhear.

"The Horn, I think. I got a lead."

She clapped her hands. "Sweet. Where'd you find the lead?"

Distrust nagged me. Lexi was the only one of my cousins who'd had dialogue with me in years. Still, I needed someone on my side and it beat having to go it alone.

"I have my sources." Sources I wasn't willing to share. "Did Uncle send you?" Just to be sure.

She scowled. "That crotchety old man? Hell, no. I'm here to help *you*."

"Before I agree to let you come along, what'd you steal?"

"You going to kick me off the trip?"

"Not if you tell me what I want to know. You readily admit you're a thief?"

She glanced around and dropped her voice. "I've been known to lift a painting or two. It's not common knowledge in the family."

"You mean it's *not* common knowledge *to me*," I corrected.

"Oh. Right."

"Is that all you've stolen? Art?"

"Well that and I can hack. I told you I had mad skills." She wiggled her fingers and flashed a wicked smile. "I've picked up a few things here and there. You're not the only oh-brilliant-one here. You gonna let me come or what?"

Lexi could turn out to be an awesome partner. "I don't think it'll be easy. Are you prepared for that?"

"I'm prepared for anything. I'm totally up for the adventure."

"And you have to do what I tell you." I wanted to be clear I was in charge.

"Whatever you say, boss." She gave me a mock salute.

"Good. Then you can come with me."

She whooped and grinned from ear to ear as the airline started the boarding calls. We settled into our seats ready for the long flight to the other side of the world.

<hr />

Eight hours into the flight, I pulled the postcard from my pocket and examined the picture of Two International Finance Centre. It was a night shot and the building was lit up. On the other side, I examined the perfect handwriting, the block letters. I still wondered who sent it and if it was the same person who sent the letter from my mother to my uncle.

It wasn't Azriel or Joachim. They paid me a personal visit. Who then?

"What's that?" Lexi leaned over the arm of the seat for a better look. She yawned.

"Postcard." I flipped it to show her the photograph.

"Ah, the IFC. Next to the Four Seasons. What about it?"

I flipped it over again and she read the words aloud. "*Begin your search.* Huh. Weird. Who sent it?"

"No idea. It arrived in an envelope with no return address or postage."

"So that's your lead. Awesome." She popped her gum one last time before spitting the wad into a scrap of paper and stuffing it into the pocket of the seat in front of her.

Even though she was older than me, she didn't act like it. She was more youthful. I guessed because of her charmed life. She grew up rich with a family. She never knew what it was like to be alone. When I lived with Edward, I was still alone. He never gave me a sense of belonging.

"So, what's the sitch when we get there, cuz?" She took out a fresh piece of mint green gum and popped it into her mouth. "Or should I call you boss?"

"You can call me Anna. I have reservations at the Four Seasons. I need a floor plan of the IFC." I used one of my credit cards with a big balance to book the hotel.

"Why? And sweet on the reservations."

"I think the postcard may be a clue." I didn't tell her about the key I stashed in the bottom of my shoe. She didn't need to know about that yet.

"You think maybe the...thing we're after is in the IFC?"

"Not sure but I intend to find out."

It made sense. It was the most prominent building in the picture.

What if Hong Kong itself was a clue? And, further, how and why did it end up in that city? Edward told me the archangels took the relics away, hid them in our everyday world.

I leaned my head back, thinking. If the Holy Relics were scattered across the world, they would eventually be rediscovered. Perhaps that was what the archangels wanted all along. They wanted them hidden and put in a place of safety. Like a museum. Or a church. There were plenty of museums that held Christian art and relics. Maybe the horn was located in one of them.

A church would be the next obvious place to look. But not just any church. A Roman Catholic Church. Why? It was the world's largest Christian place of worship. The most prominent throughout Europe during history. And Christianity had been part of the world since the first century as well as Catholicism.

"Well, I can totally hook you up with the floor plan."

She pulled me out of my thoughts. I lifted my head to look at her. "How?"

She rolled her eyes. "You forgot already? Hacker." She thumbed at her chest and popped her gum, grinning. "Good thing I brought my laptop, huh?"

We agreed she'd start trying as soon as we got to the hotel and hooked up to the WiFi. Once she was snoring, though, I toed off my shoe and pulled out the key to examine it.

It was like any other key. Gold. Boring. With the number 001 stamped on one side. It didn't look like a house key or an office key—too small for that. It looked like it might belong to a desk. Or some type of cabinet that held the horn.

How was I ever going to find it in a city like Hong Kong? It was like looking for a lost earring in the ocean. I stashed the key again, then leaned my head back and drifted to sleep.

I wasn't a fan of sleeping lately. Too many visitors. Especially winged ones. This time, though, Edward was the only one who made an appearance.

He wore a suit I remembered from when I was a little girl. Did he do that to make me more comfortable? Or did he truly view himself that way?

"Did you send Lexi to find me?" I asked before he could speak.

"Hello to you, too." He tipped his head in greeting. "And no, I did not. Remember what I told you. Don't trust anyone."

"I'm taking her with me. I think she can help."

"Are you sure that's a good idea?" He folded his arms over his chest.

"Is there something I should know about her?" I narrowed my gaze, suspicious.

"I told you before she was a liar and a thief. I want you to be careful. I'm glad you came to your senses, Anna."

"I'm not doing this for you. I'm doing this to save my own skin."

"I suppose that's enough of a noble cause."

I didn't miss the sour note in his tone. The scene shifted and we sat at an outdoor café having tea. Numerous angels, Fallen and heavenly alike, roamed the street near us. A few demons, too. Though they masked their true appearance, I could still sense them.

"Where are you headed?" He dropped a lump of sugar in his cup and stirred with a delicate spoon.

"Hong Kong to follow up that lead. What do I need to know about going?"

"You tell me," he said.

"I'm only going because of the postcard."

"The postcard you received from some mysterious person."

I nodded. "Yeah. That postcard."

"The world is full of Fallen, Anna. You must be cautious. There are many factions who are also looking for the relics. You are not the only one."

I recognized the warning. "You mean Lucifer has sent others to search for them?"

"There are always others looking for them." He reached for the cream, poured it in and stirred. "They will do whatever it takes to keep anyone else from finding it first." He paused and his gaze met mine. "Or stealing it."

Great. I pursed my lips. "I'll be careful."

"You should. It will not be easy, Anna."

I huffed. Like I expected this to be a cake walk. "How can I keep Azriel out of my dreams?"

"Worried, are you?" Edward took a sip of his tea. "First, you must listen. Can you?"

"Yes."

"Keeping him out, totally, is not possible for you yet. When he enters your dream state, you must find a way to maintain control."

"But will I be able to do that? Keep him out?"

"Eventually. Maintain control of your mind and fight him. You can shut down that part of your mind."

"How?"

"Only you know that."

The scene changed again but this time we stood on a cliff surrounded by fire. The smell of sulfur was strong. Now Edward wore a black suit and thin white tie. A heavy hot breeze blew, mussing his perfect hair.

"Try it now," he said.

"What do you mean?"

"I'm controlling your dream. Push me out. You can do it, Anna."

Something deep down snapped inside me and I reached into my mind, looking for that control. I didn't want him there. Answers or no, I wanted him out of my head. I clenched my fists but I couldn't seem to scrub him out of my mind.

"I can't." Frustration clawed through me. Even in my dream state, I couldn't defeat him. I couldn't push him out.

The scene changed again. This time we were in a thick forest. A stream trickled nearby. Trees all around. Sunlight slashed through the overhead canopy, splashing on the carpet of leaves at our feet.

In the distance, the black yawning opening of a cave. The air reeked of sulfur.

"You aren't trying hard enough. I'm still controlling your dream."

I scowled and pushed out a heated breath. "I don't know how."

"Reach down deep inside you. Look for that one thread you can control. Take it."

I closed my eyes and imagined my inner world. My heart drummed a wild beat. My pulse fluttered at my throat. The one thread I controlled was my true self. I was the Keeper of the Holy Relics.

"I know who I am." I opened my eyes.

He stood right in front of me, closer than before. Anger flared through me. Anger he controlled my dream. I gave him a shove and he stumbled backward.

"You can't control me."

"Very good, Anna." He smirked.

But he still controlled the dream. His mind was in mine and I wanted him *out*. I rushed him and gave him another rough shove. He stepped back, bumping into a tree.

"Get out! Get out! Get out!" I shouted. "You don't belong here!"

The control shifted to me so suddenly, it was a punch in the gut. The air knocked out of me. I was winded. I couldn't breathe.

And then he was gone and the dream was over.

I snapped awake. For the first time, I had the power to rid Azriel from my dreams. At last, I had some peace of mind.

CHAPTER 13

AFTER A GRUELING SEVENTEEN-HOUR flight, we finally landed in Hong Kong. I was glad to be on solid ground again. I wasn't much for flying. Something about being shoved into a metal tube at thirty-thousand-feet bothered me. When I booted up the cell phone, a text waited for me from my uncle.

Well done, dearie.

I was mildly disturbed he knew my number. But then I guess he would. He seemed to know everything about me. The man was filthy rich and probably had connections in every nook and cranny of the globe.

Lexi fluffed her hair and chomped on a fresh piece of gum as we de-boarded. "Where to, cuz?"

We made our way through Hong King International, which was a total hub of activity. I stopped at a store and bought a walking map. The airport was at Chek Lap Kok on the island of Lantau. The financial district—where I wanted to be—was on Hong Kong Island in the Central District. I pointed to it on the map.

"That's where we're going."

She peered over my shoulder. "Hong Kong Island? Think we'll find the horn there?" She popped her gum for emphasis.

"I hope so. The first place I'm going is the IFC."

She frowned. "No Four Seasons?"

"Later," I said. "Come on. How's your Cantonese?"

She laughed as if I made the best joke. Lucky for us, folks spoke English since it used to be a colony of the British Empire. Hong Kong wasn't like the rest of communist China. In fact, capitalism and free enterprise were the norm. The four-hundred-square-miles boasted seven million residents. The place was pretty hip and happening with lots of tourism.

I'd never seen so many colorful people in one place as the airport. We elbowed and pushed our way through the crowds. I sensed the Fallen before I saw them. A quick scan of the congested terminal showed a lot walked among humans, their wings hidden with glamour from the human eye.

But not just Fallen. Chinese, Brits, Americans, Pakistani and Aussies all populated the terminal. Lexi didn't have a checked bag either so we made our way through Immigration Hall to check in and then to Customs. While waiting in the lengthy line, my phone beeped again. Another text from Edward.

Good luck.

Creepy. I wished he'd stop that. I had no idea he was so up on technology. I hoped he didn't friend me on Facebook. Or maybe he was tracking my GPS in my smartphone. I made a mental note to purchase a new one.

After a few minutes of studying, we figured out the transportation system. The train they called the Airport Express would take us to Hong Kong Island where we could change to the Island Line. The jam-packed thirty-minute ride took us right to the Central District and to the IFC.

The Fallen frequented the streets, too. They walked by with their hidden wings and their human lovers. There were other supernaturals, too, but mostly the demons. We made our way to our destination and paused out front. Standing on the street looking up at the tall building made my confidence waver. What had I been thinking? The Horn would appear to me in my dreams? That I'd find more clues once I reached the IFC?

"Well, now what?" Lexi asked.

"Hell if I know."

"We can't search every floor."

No, we couldn't. Not all eighty-eight floors. "I need to do more research. And you need to find me that floor plan."

"I will but I'm jetlagged. I need sleep." She yawned.

"You slept on the plane. For sixteen hours."

"And I'm still tired." She rubbed the back of her neck with a grimace. "Plus, I need a massage in the worst way."

Right. She wanted to get to the fancy hotel. Fine. I flagged down a cab and we arrived in record time. Our room overlooked the crowded Hong Kong skyline. Lexi immediately made a spa appointment and then slipped out. She clearly was not as tired as she complained. I might not ever get that floor plan.

But with her gone, I had time to think. I pulled out her laptop and logged into the hotel WiFi to find out more about the Central District where Two International Finance Centre was located. In my previous search, I'd found a Roman Catholic Church. I pulled up the address and got directions.

Seemed as good a place to start as any.

✦———————✦

The church was only two miles from the hotel. I pulled out the postcard and took another look. The IFC was prominent in the picture. Was this the true location of the horn? If so, how? Why? I hadn't found any religious organizations leasing office space but maybe I overlooked something. Maybe Lexi could find something for me.

The more I looked at the photo, the more I was convinced it was a clue. Had to be.

I arrived at the Hong Kong Catholic Cathedral of the Immaculate Conception. The beautiful building had pointed peaks and a cross on top, stained glass windows and brick and granite façade.

I hadn't stepped foot in a church in a very long time. I certainly hadn't attended mass. I wondered if lightning would strike me if I entered. I paused outside for a long time thinking about how long it had actually been. Likely since I lived with my uncle.

The church was gorgeous inside as outside. Heavy mahogany pews sat atop checkerboard marble floors. Columns rose on either side. I had a sense of calm and belonging. Several tourists wandered throughout snapping photos and lighting candles. I paused halfway up the aisle to stare at the confessional off to the side. When was the last time I did that? I couldn't recall.

From the literature at the door, I learned the church was the seat of the diocese bishop, Cardinal John Zhan Xue. Originally built in 1843 but destroyed by a fire fourteen years later. A new site was selected to rebuild and construction began in 1883.

A dark-haired man in a bright orange shirt wandered through the church. He took pictures and looked like a tourist but something was off. I couldn't quite put my finger on it. I didn't sense Fallen—I doubted they or demons could enter the church—so I knew he couldn't be one of them. But something was vaguely familiar about him.

He caught my gaze. His ice blue eyes pierced me to the bone. A sense of cold dread washed over me. He flashed a knowing grin before glancing away. As I approached, the scent of strawberries and champagne assaulted my nose.

"Joachim?"

"Very good, Annabelle," he said. "Welcome to Hong Kong."

"Did you send me the postcard?" I asked, wanting to solve the mystery.

"I did not."

"But you know about it."

"There is much I know about you."

Nice. I looked him over. One thing was missing—his wings. When I looked closer, I could make out the faint outline. Like the Fallen, he could hide them behind a glamour. But a glamour I could see through. "Why are you hiding your wings?"

"I've hidden them from the humans. I wouldn't want to startle them."

"Right. An angel in a church. That'd freak out the even the staunchest atheist."

He wasn't amused with my crack. Even so, he was more relaxed than when we first met in my apartment.

"Is the horn here?" I glanced around the church as though the relic might be hidden in plain sight.

"No."

"Do you know where it is?"

"No."

"Are you here to help me?"

"No."

Infuriating angel. "Then why are you here? Checking up on me?"

"In a sense, yes. We are pleased you have decided to search for the horn."

"'We' being you and Michael?" He nodded. Yeah, well, join the party. Edward was pretty excited, too. I'm sure Azriel will do cartwheels of joy when he finds out. "Calm down, angel boy. I'm aware of the prophecy."

"Ah. Your uncle has told you."

"Does everyone have this information this but me? And yeah. He's told me some, but not everything," I admitted.

"You will in time. When you locate the horn, I will await your arrival."

Right. Like was going to hand it over. Truth was I hadn't quite decided what I was going to do when—if—I found the horn.

"Well, don't hold your breath. I haven't found it yet. And if I do and don't give it to Azriel, I'm pretty sure you'll lose a dream walker."

"You are the Keeper."

"Like that matters."

"Azriel will not harm you."

"Says who? He already tried to off me in my dream."

"He needs you alive and he cannot kill you without an order from his Lord Master."

"You mean Lucifer."

"Indeed."

Lovely. I was anticipating more fun and games with Az. But I wondered, if he needed me alive, why did he try to kill me in my dream? To force me to search for the relics? That was the most logical explanation.

"Then why is he trying to kill me?"

"Because he wants you to fear him. He uses that fear to control you."

That was a better answer than my uncle gave me.

"What happens if I don't give him the horn?" I asked.

"He will want to torture you most likely."

Terrific. "And what happens if I don't give it to you?"

"The archangel will be displeased." He gave me a look of curiosity. "What is your plan, Annabelle?"

I was annoyed he kept calling me that. I didn't much care for it but I'd let it slide.

"Not sure yet. But if I'm the Keeper, why should I give it to you? Or anyone else for that matter."

"You are not prepared for the responsibility."

"Oh, right. I'm just your runner." What a crock. I suddenly wasn't feeling so generous with my help. I gave him a sideways glance. "I still don't know how to find the thing."

"All will be clear to you soon."

"So cryptic. Can no one give me a straight answer?"

He grinned, glanced around the church and then stepped closer to me. "The world is a dangerous place."

"Thanks for that, Captain Obvious." I rolled my eyes.

He scowled. "A couple of half-human, half-demons are following you. Even now they're in the church."

I glanced around but didn't sense the...wait, yes, I did. One in a paisley shirt with a camera around his neck. Another in a Panama hat, plaid shirt and khaki shorts. Seriously? Someone should give these guys some fashion tips. Or maybe they thought they would blend in.

"Weren't aware of that, were you?" Joachim smirked. "They've been sent to keep an eye on you until you find the horn."

"How did they get in here? I thought churches were consecrated ground."

"I cannot say. Something about them allows them to step over the threshold."

I lifted an eyebrow. "Are you sure they were sent to keep an eye on me?"

"Annabelle, when are you going to realize not to question me?"

"You don't have all the answers. Like how they got in here." I thumbed toward the demons. Joachim gave me the hairy eyeball and scowled. I wondered, though, why he popped up here and now. "Are you my guardian angel?"

He scoffed. "I am your messenger angel. Nothing more."

"So not guardian?" I teased him, nudging him with my elbow. "Do I have one of those?"

"Everyone has one of those."

As I suspected. I nodded toward the demons. "Thanks for the head's up, angel boy."

"Be careful." He was gone in the blink of an eye.

I looked over the two demons in their hideous clothes. I wasn't going to allow them to keep me from doing my job. I marched toward them with a purposeful stride and paused next to them.

"It's brave of you both to step foot inside a church."

Their sulfuric scent permeated the air. I somehow missed it before. And that's when I realized while I can sense the demon in them, they are also half-human. An interesting combo. It must be how they were able to step inside the church.

Both of their heads snapped in my direction. I glanced their way, still trying to keep an eye on my surroundings. Paisley shirt boy snarled at me. I could see the reddish tinge in his eyes giving away his true demon self.

"I would have thought you'd fry the second you'd stepped across the threshold," I said.

"Mind your tongue, demon-seer," Paisley shirt said.

Demon-seer? That was a new one. "Or what?" I crossed my arms over my chest. "You'll kill me?" I snorted. "Not even."

Panama hat demon moved to my other side. He reeked of death and rot and general disgustingness. "We may not be able to kill you, demon-seer, but we can injure you."

To press his point, his hand slipped to my shoulder. For a brief moment, his fingers turned into claws that sank into my skin. Pain lanced through me but I refused to wince. I didn't want him to see my discomfort. Instead, I looked him in the eye, defiant.

"You have been warned," he said.

"Good to know." I glared down at his hand. He removed it, but left behind bloody spots where his claws dug in. "I'm not afraid of you."

I sounded brave even though I wasn't.

"You will be," Paisley shirt said.

They both headed for the door. I watched them leave. My heart was in my throat and my knees buckled. Okay, so I put on a brave face. I didn't want them to sense they scared the crap out of me.

I turned and gripped the back of a pew to steady myself. Taking a deep breath, I walked around and sat and for the first time in a very long time, I prayed.

———

An hour later, I walked out of the church with an empty feeling, as though there was something missing. As though Joachim had dropped a few more clues into my lap but I was too dense to figure it out. That and I disliked being threatened. I didn't want to head back to the hotel yet. I wanted to figure out where the horn was, grab it and go home.

I spotted the demon boys across the road looking obvious in their street clothes. Panama hat smiled and saluted. Paisley shirt lifted his camera and snapped a photo. Terrific.

I ignored them and paused to take in the surroundings. I didn't have a clue what to do next and then something caught my eye. A statue near the front of the building I hadn't noticed when I entered. I was drawn to it immediately. It was an angel carved in white marble with magnificent wings. Her face was delicate, with a small smile on her lips and her arms outstretched as if to welcome visitors.

As I gazed at it, a man stepped up beside me. He gazed up at the angel, admiring it. He was a well-dressed Hong Kong local, reeking of money and power. His dark hair was slicked back from his high forehead. He looked refined as though he'd always come from money.

"Beautiful, isn't it?" His English was impeccable.

"Yes," I agreed.

"I had it commissioned for the church. The artist did a remarkable job." He admired it as though it was his own handiwork.

I looked him over. "You work here?"

He chuckled. "No, not at all. Though I do attend mass every Sunday. Forgive my rudeness. I am Chen Tso Lang." He extended his hand.

"Anna," I said as I gripped his hand.

His fingers closed around mine and a sudden jolt shot up my arm. It was quickly followed by an image bursting through my head. It was the Horn of Gabriel in a wood and glass case resting against a garnet cloth of velvet. I inhaled a sharp breath and immediately recovered with a coughing fit. He dropped his hand but I didn't miss the glance he gave the two demons across the way. He had one eyebrow quirked in question.

"Are you all right?"

"Yes, sorry. Just a, ah, allergic reaction. Maybe to your cologne or something."

He looked less than amused but covered it with a cool smile. "Ladies often have that reaction to my handshakes."

I blushed. "That's never happened to me before."

"Perhaps I will not wear the cologne when you have dinner with me tonight."

"Oh?" I regarded him coolly. "I'm having dinner with you tonight?"

"It would be my honor." He took my hand again but nothing happened. He made to kiss the back of it before I gently tugged it out of his grasp.

I had a sneaking suspicion why this perfect stranger wanted to have dinner with me. We'd only met two-point-three seconds ago yet he knew demons were across the street. He must have sensed something too when we shook hands. He took my hand again to test that theory. I was game to find out what was up with him.

Bring it on.

"I'd love to have dinner with you." Not. I smiled. "Name the place and time and I'll meet you."

No way I wanted him to know where I was staying. He gave me the name of a restaurant near the hotel.

"I do hope you enjoy Cantonese."

"Sounds delicious."

"See you then, Miss..." He paused, waiting for me to give him my last name.

"Just Anna." I smiled.

Annoyance flickered over his face before he turned and walked away. I wondered what had just happened. He clearly had an inkling as to who I was or he would have never asked me to dinner. Maybe never even approached me in the first place. I was probably walking into a trap so I needed to make sure I wasn't caught unawares.

I'd been warned by my uncle not to trust anyone. I'd also been warned by Joachim to be careful. I didn't trust Chen and immediately put him on the list under foe. He could be part demon, too, though I didn't smell it on him. I didn't think he was a Fallen. But then Azriel smelled like cinnamon, so who knew?

I hurried back to the hotel. Lexi lounged on the bed watching mindless television. I took a deep breath and closed my eyes. Her lack of enthusiasm for our current quest for the horn irked me. She was completely unconcerned I asked her to find the floor plans of the building. When she saw me, she propped up on the bed and gave me a bright smile.

"Where have you been? I had the most amazing massage." She had a look of pure bliss on her face which did nothing to help her case.

"I had the strangest encounter." I told her about seeing the half-demons in the church and meeting Chen and that he asked me to dinner. "I had a vision of the horn when I shook his hand. I think he has it."

"Are you really going to dinner with him?" She scrunched her nose in distaste.

"Yes. I may be able to get some information out of him. I need you to find that floor plan." I slid the laptop over to her. "See what you can find out about our buddy Chen. If he's a collector. Where his office is. That sort of thing."

"I'm on it, boss."

Two hours later, as I paced the length of the room biting my thumbnail, I tried to keep my mind on something other than the possibility of ending up dead. Because that was a real possibility when I thought about it. Dinner with some strange guy who was probably my enemy was stupid. I was going anyway.

Lexi sat cross-legged on the bed, popping her gum and typing like mad. Her hair was pulled back, cascading in glossy waves. She looked so relaxed I had to squash the jealousy pulsing through me. It had been a long time since I'd pampered myself but I didn't have time to lounge around in spas and primp. I had a job to do.

"Any luck on that floor plan yet?" I asked.

"Working on it. Almost." She tapped away and then stopped and spun the laptop toward me. "Booya!"

On the screen were blueprints of the building she somehow managed to dig up.

"Sixty-two elevators. Eighty-eight floors. Completed in 2003." Gum pop. "It's the big brother to One International Finance Centre. Tenants include Bank of America, State Street Bank, Texas Pacific Group and...drum roll please...Partners for the Sanctified."

"What's that?"

"Only a religious organization your buddy Chen funnels money into. They're religious fanatics. Running all over the planet looking for holy relics." Suddenly she didn't sound like the ditzy tag-along kid.

"Like the Horn of Gabriel?"

"Most likely. He's got tons of dough and he's a collector of fine antiquities. Specifically, religious ones." She popped her gum. "But wait, there's more. He has an office *in the building*, my friend."

Bingo. "That's it. That's where it is."

"How can you be sure about that?" she asked. "I mean, would he really keep it in his office?"

"I saw it when I shook his hand. I know it's there, Lex." I bit my thumbnail. "He seems cocky enough to keep it where he can see it every day."

"All right. What's the plan, cuz?"

"The plan is we get in, steal it and get out."

"Oh, that simple, huh?" She scowled in distaste. "It won't be that simple."

"You got a better idea?"

Lexi grinned. "Not really. But you're gonna be so totally glad you brought me along."

"Why is that?"

"Duh. I'm a thief. Remember?" She thumbed at her chest, the pride evident on her face. "I'll work on a plan."

I grinned at Lexi. She was right. I was glad I brought her along. Her skills had come in handy. Having her was like hitting the jackpot.

I left her to plan the heist wile I prepared to meet Chen. But I wasn't going into this thing unarmed. Before I headed to the restaurant, I purchased a couple of daggers and strapped them to my thighs. My black cargo pants had slits in the pockets for easy access. Lexi insisted we stay connected the entire time, so she figured out a way to pair our cell phones. I used a Bluetooth earpiece that sat deep inside my ear so she could hear our conversation.

I met Chen at the restaurant and realized I was underdressed. Had I known I might have dressed a little better. I might have put in an effort.

Oh, who was I kidding? I totally wouldn't have.

Chen sat at a table by the window. He stood when I approached and gave me a once over. I didn't have on any makeup and my skunk-striped hair was pulled into a high ponytail. I sat at the table, Chen across from me. Could this be any more awkward?

"Thank you for coming," he said.

"Thanks for the invite."

A waiter arrived and took our order.

"I wasn't sure you would come after what happened today."

I stared at him, completely off-guard. It took me a minute to recover. "What do you mean?"

I figured if I feigned ignorance he'd forget. I figured wrong.

"Come now, Miss Anna. I was aware of the jolt when we shook hands. As were you." I could hear the hint of his Cantonese accent coming through. But still he masked it well.

He'd sensed something, too. That confirmed one thing. I gave him a thin smile. "What jolt?"

"You think to play dumb?" He leaned toward me, his elbows on the table. His eyes narrowed as he looked me over. "I plan to find out what you are."

"And here I thought we were going to have a romantic dinner for two. So much for that."

I rested my hand on my thigh, ready to pull out one of the daggers. The guy jumped right to the point. No beating around the bush. No pleasantries. Definitely a trap of some sort. He smiled at my joke and leaned back in his chair.

"What do you want, Miss Anna?"

"I don't follow."

"You would not have accepted dinner with a stranger so readily if you didn't want something in return. What is it?"

As if I was going to tell him.

"Uh, cuz?" Lexi said in my ear. "This guy is bad news. He may be a church-goer and all that but he's kinda wanted for murder."

I didn't let that rattle me. To Chen, I said, "You're right. I do want something."

As I looked at him across the table, the air flickered around him. Shimmering as though I were in some kind of waking dream. And then his black wings were visible. He managed to keep them hidden until now. For whatever reason, they were visible. He also managed to mask his demon scent but now it hit me full force in the face, accosting my senses. Apple spice cake. I glanced around the place. The other patrons weren't aware of the shimmering veil.

What was it with these Fallen smelling like Grandma's kitchen?

The entire restaurant moved in super slow-motion. The only normal speed was between me and Chen. I could only guess he was one of the Fallen. If he had the horn all this time, why not turn it over to his boss? Why was he keeping it? And why didn't I sense the demon in him before? Did he have some way to suppress it?

"Who are you?" I asked.

"I asked the same of you."

"No, you didn't. You said you planned to find out what I was." I slid my hand inside my pocket, gripping the hilt of the dagger. "I can see your wings."

His eyes widened only slightly before he lunged across the table to grab the neck of my shirt. But my knife was at his throat in an instant. He didn't even flinch.

"What are you doing in Hong Kong, demon-seer?"

I sure wasn't going to tell him I was after the horn or I was the official Keeper. I didn't want to give him a chance to move the relic before I could take it. Or kill me.

"I don't think this is going to go your way." I pressed the knife point deeper into his throat, nicking the skin.

His grip relaxed and he righted himself in his chair, smoothing his hands down the front of his shirt. He wiped away the trickle of blood with his napkin, as though unconcerned. His wings disappeared behind his glamour and the restaurant returned to normal speed. The other patrons were oblivious to our little scuffle.

Demon magic was a powerful thing. They could use it whenever they wanted. Chen used it to shield us from the dining humans. He also used it to hide his black wings from them and me. But those weren't the only things for which they could use their magic. I slid my knife back into my pocket.

The waiter returned with our food but I'd lost my appetite.

"Now that I know what you are," he said, "I ask why you are here."

I smiled and shrugged. "Sightseeing."

"Liar."

"Perhaps. But you aren't exactly forthcoming with info." I fiddled with my fork. "Are you part of the Fallen?"

He scowled. "No. They are a group of thugs. I am better than they are with a much more noble purpose." He said this with haughty disdain as he dabbed at the corners of his mouth.

Okay, so...yeah. A different kind of demon who thought he was above the rest. Interesting.

I tried not to snort. "And that is?"

"To save those who wish to be saved. To purify their souls."

Freaky. And something with which I wanted nothing to do.

"Cuz, he means business," Lexi said in my ear. "He's killed several people in the name of religion. He may not be one of the Fallen, but he's still dangerous."

Duly noted. "And how exactly do you purify their souls?" Probably a question I didn't want answered. But I couldn't resist asking it anyway.

"Are you stupid?" Lexi snapped. "He's not gonna tell you."

Chen smiled and stabbed a carrot in brown sauce. "Use your imagination, demon-seer. I'm sure you can figure it out."

Cold trickled over me and gooseflesh rose on my arms. I could imagine a lot of horrible things. Things like people burning at the stake, their skin flayed from their bones. I shoved away the awful images.

"Hello. He's a killer," Lexi sang in my ear. "Likes to butcher people and—"

"I'm sure I can imagine the worst," I said, trying to get Lexi to shut up. I didn't need specifics. My imagination helped me out enough with the gruesome details. "But why?"

"Why?" He looked abashed. "It is the only way to purify them."

"Huh." I wasn't entirely sure how to respond to that. "Is that how you acquire your antiquities?"

He stared at me a long moment then a smile spread on his face. "Ah. So that's what this is about. You're interested in antiquities?"

I shrugged. "I have a passing interest."

"Anything in particular?"

"Not really." I didn't want to give away I was interested in the horn or any of the other relics. And I doubted he'd tell me he had it anyway. Since I had his undivided attention, I pried him for all the information I could.

"There are many Christian relics throughout the world, Miss Anna. But very few of us have the ones that are the most valuable."

"By very few, you mean private collectors?" I pushed food around on my plate.

"Most of the valuable pieces are in museums. However, a few of us have managed to find some of the more precious items."

I wondered if he meant items like the Horn of Gabriel. I bit the inside of my cheek to keep from blurting it out.

"Such as?"

"The Shroud of Turin. The Holy Nails. Jesus's crown of thorns. The sword of David."

Interesting he didn't name any of the relics I'd been tasked with finding. "And a partridge in a pear tree."

My humor was lost on him. He pressed his lips in a thin line. "It would not be wise of you to go poking around looking for such things though."

"And why is that?"

"It's a dangerous pastime."

All these caveats. People were starting to piss me off. "Thanks for the warning." I pushed back my chair, scraping it against the floor, and stood. "I think we're done here."

"For now, demon-seer. I'm sure we will meet again."

As I walked out of the restaurant, I sensed his dagger eyes glaring a hole through my back. As though he could see into me and knew what I wanted. As soon as I was outside, I breathed the fresh air in deep. Lexi was already talking in my ear again.

"You okay? That guy creeps me out."

"Me, too. We need to get to his office as soon as possible. Can you make that happen?"

"I'm on it."

As I headed down the street looking for a cab, I spotted two demons heading for me. The same two that were at the church. Chen must have called for backup.

Fantastic.

CHAPTER 14

"**U**H, LEXI. I'M IN trouble."

"What's happening?"

"Two demons heading right for me."

I was pretty sure the demons could see me, I could see them, but the humans couldn't. The people moved in slow-motion going along their merry way as if everything was situation normal. Much like the day I stood on the sidewalk staring at them all before Detective Harrison snatched my arm and pulled me into the yogurt shop.

"Are you running away from them?" Lexi asked in my ear, panic in her voice.

I wasn't running. I stood my ground to stay and fight. I pulled the daggers from my pockets and widened my stance. These guys weren't going to be so forgiving like Azriel's lackeys. I had no idea how I was going to wiggle my way out of this one.

One of them disappeared. Gone in the blink of an eye. The other advanced on me with long sharpened claws and razor-like teeth with fangs dripping poison. No longer did they have their human appearance. Their glamour was gone and they were full on demon. I was pretty sure I was screwed.

Number Two reappeared behind me and wrapped his arms around my upper torso in a vice grip. Number One still headed toward me, ready to do some damage.

But I still had the daggers in my hands, gripping the hilts so tight my fingers cramped. What the hell did I think I was doing? I hadn't a clue how to fight these guys. With the adrenaline surging hard through me, I listened to instinct and let it kick in. Fight or die. And I wasn't in the mood to die today.

"Get ready to die, demon-seer."

I snorted. So not going to happen. "Ya think?"

I leaned back and pushed all my weight against Number Two, kicking up my feet as Number One lunged for attack. I struck him square in the chest. He stumbled backward, crashing into a sidewalk trash can. Trash billowed down the street. I struggled in the grip of Number Two, trying to get free. The scent of decay and rot assaulted my nose. I wasn't sure which demon emitted it.

The first one clambered to his feet, more pissed off than ever. In a desperate move, I jammed both knives into Two's thighs, digging them in as far as I could get them. Right to the bone. It jarred me to the back of my teeth. I tried not to gag. He yowled in my ear but released me and I dove out of One's way. He collided with his fellow demon. I took off running. I wasn't sticking around for an encore.

Fear and adrenaline were the only things keeping me on my feet. It was then I realized Lexi shouted in my ear.

"...all right? Anna, are you there? Hello?"

"I'm here." I panted, trying to catch my breath. "I'm...okay. But those demons...aren't happy at all."

If there were two, there would be more. I ran through the streets, sweat streaming down my face and back. I braved a glance behind me but they weren't following. As I rounded a corner, I collided with someone. Immediately the stink of rot assaulted my nose.

Shit.

I regained my footing, stumbled backward a few steps. I was unarmed. I had no weapons because I left them in the demon's thighs. The one I faced snarled, drooled and looked at me as though I were a tasty morsel.

"Cuz?"

"Um. Hang on a minute."

I had no choice. I was going to have to fight this one. But hand-to-hand combat with a demon wasn't like kickboxing class. I glanced around looking for something to use as a weapon. The fear pumping through me threatened to take hold.

If my guardian angel or messenger angel wanted to pop in right about now, I wouldn't be offended.

But no one showed up to save me. I was totally on my own. I backed up a step or two, keeping one eye on demon boy and one eye on the street. No one took note of what was happening.

"Hello, demon-seer."

Great. Like I was up for any small talk.

"I'm looking forward to feasting on your pretty flesh."

Fucker. "Are you? You'll be disappointed. I taste kinda sour."

He licked his lips. "I will be the judge of that."

Yeah, I'll bet.

He pulled out the biggest, longest knife I'd ever seen. That was something I could work with. Stealing it out of his hands and shoving it into his sternum was going to take some doing, though. My fingers twitched with anticipation.

The demon was big and slow and kinda dumb. I figured that was going to give me the advantage. He took a lumbering step toward me and swung. I ducked. He missed me by a lot and I jumped toward him to grab the knife. My hands were on his thick wrist, clawing. He grunted and jerked his arm upward.

Since he was bigger than me, my feet dangled about two feet off the ground. We were eye to eye and his breath stank like shit. His entire body reeked. His free hand clamped around my throat and squeezed.

I was aware of Lexi's voice in my ear but I couldn't hear her. I was too focused on what was happening. The demon grinned and licked his lips again. His forked tongue snaked out. The tip grazed my cheek, leaving a hot trail. I gagged.

"You're sweet. Like honey." He inhaled deeply. "Smell like it, too."

I had enough. I swung my legs and kicked him hard. I tried aiming for his groin, but I missed by a few inches. Still, it was enough for him to groan though he didn't release me. His hand tightened on my throat. I swung my free hand but it only wafted by his face. He grinned that evil toothy grin.

Shadows crept around the edges of my vision. Every ounce of energy seeped from me as I passed out.

←——————→

When I came to, cold pressed into all my bones. Not like a little either. Like bone-rattling, teeth-chattering, body-shivering cold. I blinked my eyes open to cool darkness. My arms were shackled above my head, stretching them to the point my sockets ached. I stood in the middle of what looked like a warehouse, the tips of my bare toes barely touching a metal stool.

I idly wondered what happened to my shoes.

I had no clue where I was or even how I got there. My earpiece was gone. The chatter in my ear was silent. That meant my phone was gone, too. I scented the familiar demon odor indicating they were nearby.

A shiver raced down my back.

I hated the cold. It was one of the reasons why I liked Texas. The winters were mild even if the summers were brutal. Heat I could stand. Cold was another thing altogether.

Somewhere a metal door scraped open on rusty hinges. It banged shut, the sound reverberated throughout the cavernous warehouse. Footsteps followed the slamming door. And it didn't sound like one person. It sounded like more than one.

Yep, I was screwed.

Three shapes headed toward me. Two demons and...Chen. He didn't bother to hide his wings as he approached. He paused and grinned.

"As I predicted, we meet again."

"Not the best circumstances," I quipped.

"Miss Anna, we have unfinished business."

"We do?"

"Did you think I would believe you are here to sightsee?"

I knew that excuse wouldn't work. "Anything's possible."

"Why don't you tell me what you're doing in Hong Kong?" he asked, ignoring my sarcasm.

"I'm on a diplomatic mission." I was sorely tempted to add *to Alderaan* but I didn't think he'd get the joke. It wasn't far from the truth, though. I was on a mission, diplomatic or not.

"What sort of diplomatic mission?"

"The secret kind."

I waited for a sign of amusement to flicker across his face but it never happened. I didn't expect him to be amused. He stared at me with a deadpan expression.

"You are not making this easy for yourself, Miss Anna."

An arctic breeze wafted off him and hit me, making me shudder. Or maybe that was the icy fear prickling me all over. Whatever it was, gooseflesh rose on every available inch of skin. I saw him look at my chest. Men were men, even if they were Fallen.

"If you will not willingly tell me, you give me no other choice but to force you."

I never faced torture before. I was a weakling. I'd break and sing like a canary. I could take my chances and tell him, or continue to be an idiot and let him do what he wanted with me. But there was something inside me that bowed up. Some sort of hidden strength that made me refuse to let him win.

Maybe today was a good day to die after all.

He gave a nod to one of his cronies who shuffled off and returned a few minutes later with a bucket of ice water. I ground my teeth, knowing what was to come. One held up my legs while the other placed the bucket on the stool on which I'd teetered. They shoved my bare feet inside the bucket.

I think I mentioned how much I hate cold.

Cold was too mild. The polar vortex was warmer than standing in a freezing empty warehouse with my bare feet in a bucket of ice. It hit me with such force I thought for a second I stood in a cryogenic chamber. It cut through me, slicing into me making me tremble.

An eternity passed in the muffled silence. My teeth chattered as the cold pricked my flesh all the way up my body. Their hushed voices were the only sound in the deep chasm of the warehouse. I went in and out of consciousness.

The clink of a key got my attention. My wrists were unshackled. I fell forward, but one of the demon boys caught me before I face-planted into the concrete floor. My arms, legs and feet were numb from cold and no blood flow. But as soon as my wrists were free, the blood whooshed back into my limbs, making them tingle with tiny pinpricks.

This was turning out to be a fantastic day.

They dragged me to a metal chair and cuffed my hands behind my back. They shackled my ankles together and stuck them back into the bucket.

Chen stood in front of me, pulling on a pair of surgical gloves. An array of scary-looking sharp objects and a couple of syringes were on a nearby table.

"I will ask again. Why are you here?" He picked up a syringe.

"I'm visiting family," I managed through my chattering teeth. I refused to be intimidated and looked him square in the eye.

He smirked, gave the go-ahead nod to one of his demons who pushed up my sleeve, baring the crook of my elbow. I struggled against the restraints but it did no good. Chen didn't bother to swab my arm before he jabbed me with the needle.

"This should help loosen your tongue."

I cringed. He'd given me pentothal. As soon as the stuff hit my veins, the nausea followed. A second after that the reek of rotting onions hit me, filling up my nose. An awful tang of garlic hit the back of my throat. It was some horrid side effect of the nasty drug.

The world spun and the edges darkened to black. I awoke when Chen smacked me in the face. My head bobbed and my cheek stung. When I looked at him through squinted eyes, he had a wicked-looking blade I imagined would do serious damage.

My mind was fuzzy. My eyes were blurry.

"She doesn't know anything," Chen said. "Kill her."

Had I been through the interrogation and not remembered? Biting cold blistered through me still. I managed to focus on my fingernails and noticed they were blue.

"W-wait," I said through chattering teeth.

His eyes narrowed. "Too late, Miss Anna. You refuse to tell me anything and now you are nothing but a nuisance who must be dealt with."

"I'll t-tell you want you w-want."

"Will you? Then tell me why you're here in Hong Kong."

"I'm...on t-tour." I couldn't help it. Sarcasm came as second nature to me.

He didn't like that answer. One of the demons punched me so hard my head snapped back and my teeth clacked together. Pain exploded across my numb face.

"Hit her again."

The demon complied and punched the other side of my jaw. At least I had matching pain. Through the haze, I saw Chen pick up a pair of pliers.

"You think you are such a comedienne, don't you? I'm tired of your games. Now I want to make you suffer. I will start removing body parts unless you tell me why you're here and why you are so interested in my antiquities."

Shit. I spit the blood pooling in my mouth but it did nothing but dribble down my chin. I nodded for him to come closer. I had a raging headache, either from the face pummel or the drug. I wasn't sure which and didn't think it mattered.

"I have a r-request."

He leaned toward me, genuinely interested. "And what is that?"

"Could you start with my toes? I can't feel them anyway."

He grimaced.

He placed the pliers behind the first joint on the forefinger of my right hand. I squirmed. I had no idea how I was going to escape this with all my digits intact. Seconds before he clamped it down to remove my finger, a crash startled them all.

I couldn't see what happened but there was definitely some kind of commotion. The demons bolted into action. Chen shouted something in Cantonese. A high-pitched squeal like something charging and then one shot fired and then a second. The two demons dropped dead. Chen ran toward the door as another shot rang out, deafening me.

I knew that sound. I knew that gun.

It couldn't be. It just *couldn't*.

My chair tipped backward. I was dragged, the metal legs scraping across the floor with a screech loud enough to make my teeth ache and wake the dead. The door squeaked open and slammed. Whoever was behind me spun the chair so I no longer faced the dead demons.

Then silence. A deathly silence. At least my feet were out of the damn ice bucket.

A second later, Kincade stepped in front of me. He held his still-smoking gun in one hand as he looked at me with annoyance etched on his face.

"You sure cause a lot of trouble." He removed the restraints on my wrists and ankles. He pulled me up from the chair. "Let's get you out of here and warm."

Well, that was just great. Kincade Harrison saved my frickin' life. His arms started to wrap around me but I shoved away, stumbling a few steps out of reach.

"J-just take me to my h-hotel."

His faced darkened from annoyance to anger. "And leave you there alone?"

But I wasn't alone. Lexi was at the hotel waiting for me. Probably wondering where I was and if I was okay. I clutched my elbows and stumbled backward, shaking my head.

"I'm f-fine."

"Fine, huh?"

It was the last thing I remembered him saying before I passed out.

I woke up wrapped in a cocoon of warmth in a room I didn't recognize. I sat up, clutching the blankets to my chest and staring at the palatial suite that was the size of my old apartment.

I was lucky to escape. I could be dead. But I wasn't dead. I'd made it out alive. I made a valiant effort to ignore the pounding of my head. If it hadn't been for Kincade... *Shit.* I was in his suite. He'd saved my ass. Why? How did he find me?

I realized I was in my underwear. I frantically glanced around for my clothes and shoes. They were tossed on the nearby chair. I scooted off the edge of the bed, thinking only about the little gold key and hoping it was still there.

My legs didn't seem to want to work but I managed to half-crawl, half-drag myself to the chair. I picked up the left shoe and stuck my hand in it. Nothing. I tried the right. Nothing again. The key was gone. I slumped to the floor, still holding one boot.

"Looking for this?" Kincade leaned against the doorjamb of the bedroom, holding the small key. Light glinted off the shiny surface.

Realizing I was in my underwear, I scooted back to the bed and tugged a blanket off to cover up. Not that he hadn't seen me already in this state. Likely he was the one that got me there and coming to that conclusion made heat burn in my cheeks.

Kincade, for all the gentleman he was, kept his gaze firmly planted on my face.

"Where did you find that?"

"In the bottom of your boot."

I'd been barefoot through the whole ordeal and didn't recall seeing my boots. Yet, somehow, Kincade managed to grab them before rescuing me.

"Which," he added, "I found by your chair. Demons didn't find this on you, did they?"

I ignored his question. I held out my hand but he refused to bring it to me. And I was too weak to move. "That's mine. Give it back."

"Not until you tell me what it is."

"Duh. It's a key."

He scowled. "I *know* it's a key. Do I look like an idiot to you?"

"Well—"

"What does the key go to?"

I shrugged. "No idea."

He regarded me coolly. "That, at least, wasn't a lie."

He walked into the room and perched on the edge of the bed. He extended the key down to me and I snatched it from his hand.

Uncomfortable that he was close and I was nearly naked, I pulled the blanket tighter around my shoulders.

"Don't worry, sweetheart. Your virtue is safe with me."

I stuck out my tongue. Could I be any more childish? But I was tired, hungry, had a hangover the size of Texas and it felt like cotton had started growing in the back of my throat. My face throbbed. My lip was split and I generally felt like shit.

"How did you find me?"

"I've been tracking your ass since you sprayed me in the face with pepper spray."

"Oh. Sorry about that." I couldn't stop the blush that crept into my cheeks. "But I had to get away from you."

"Did you, *Anna*?"

My heart stilled. For a second, I stopped breathing. It was strange hearing my first name on his tongue. It made the pit of my stomach tingle.

"I thought it was weird when Anna Walker fell off the grid. And yet there had been sightings of a woman who looked remarkably like her. A woman named Zoe Cavanaugh who made it out of the country to England to visit her long-estranged uncle. How about that?"

Shit. Shit. Shit. How did he know all that? He'd tracked me to Edward's? So not good.

Who was I kidding? The man was a detective, for crying out loud. Finding me was probably as easy as solving the Sunday crossword puzzle. I wasn't that hard to find. I did leave a paper trail and even though Anna was off the grid, Zoe totally wasn't.

He twirled a strand of skunk hair around his forefinger before letting it fall back to my shoulder. His finger grazed my neck.

"Nice hair."

My skin tingled where he'd touched me, leaving a sizzling trail behind. I didn't want to notice his masculine scent or the way his muscular hands looked resting on his thick thighs.

"Shut up." I shoved to my feet, wobbling a little before regaining my balance. I still hadn't fully recovered from the pentothal. He reached out a hand to steady me but I batted it away. "You know nothing about me. Nothing. And I'll thank you to stay out of my business."

"I know enough." He pinned me with that sharp assessing gaze that made me want to peel back the carpet and hide underneath it. "What do you think happened when Chen gave you the pentothal?"

I blinked. The first thing I remember hearing Chen say when I woke up was that I didn't know anything. "Nothing happened. I didn't tell him anything."

One brow rose. "You sure about that, sweetheart?"

Um. Now I wasn't. He'd placed that seed of doubt in my mind. "I passed out?"

"Guess again."

I huffed out a heated breath. "Why don't you tell me, already?"

"You told him you were on a mission looking for Christian antiquities and you wanted to see his."

I swallowed hard. Crap. Did I spill the beans?

"Luckily for you, I showed up right about the time they started using your face as a target practice."

"He was going to kill me."

"Yes, he was."

I bit my lip then winced with the pain. I *would not* cry like a baby. Not in front of the detective. "I suppose I should thank you then."

"You can thank me by telling me what the hell you're doing in Hong Kong. Your uncle wouldn't tell me."

"You questioned my uncle?"

"You have an interesting past, Miss Walker. Or do you prefer Annabelle?"

"Do *not* call me that. I prefer Anna."

185

He shrugged. "You can call yourself Mata Hari for all I care. What are you doing in Hong Kong?"

"Why? Are you here to take me back to Dallas? I didn't kill that woman or those patients."

"That's why I had all the charges dropped."

I stared at him in utter shocked silence. "You did? How?"

He gave me a wicked grin. "I'm good like that."

Relief spilled through me and I exhaled a deep breath. "I sort of feel like hugging you right now."

"Don't push it. Now answer my question."

"I can't tell you." When he started to say something else, I rushed on. "I *am* on a mission for my uncle. That much was true. And I *am* looking for Christian antiquities."

"Is it this Horn of Gabriel?" he asked.

Crap. I forgot I told him that. I bit my lip again and winced again, letting my silence be my answer. His eyes narrowed with a glimmer of suspicion.

"For what purpose?"

"I can't tell you that either. It's important I keep it to myself. I can't have you involved in this."

"I'm already involved in this. Whatever *this* is. I know who Chen is and what he's capable of. You're in over your head, sister."

It almost sounded like he was offering me help. The last thing I needed was him underfoot along with Lexi. I had enough help with her.

"I'm aware how dangerous he is."

"Sure, you are. Now." He nodded agreement.

"And I can handle myself." I sounded a lot more confident than I felt. "Please go home."

He stared at me, dumbfounded, as if he couldn't fathom I didn't want his help. "I disagree, doll."

"I'm not your sweetheart or your doll. I don't need any of your help."

He shrugged. "All right. If that's the way you want to play it. By the way, your room with your cousin is two floors down." He rose and started for the door.

Was there anything this guy didn't know? He probably already knew why I was in Hong Kong. Questioning me was a technicality.

He left the bedroom, closing the door behind him. I shuddered, mildly disturbed we were staying in the same hotel. I quickly dressed. This time I stashed the key in one of the pockets in my pants. When I left the bedroom, Kincade was gone. I was glad. I didn't want to have any awkward goodbye's or see-you-laters.

When I finally made it to my room, I entered and sagged against the door trying to control my shaking. Lexi leapt from the bed as soon as she saw me, hugging me. Relief was evident on her face.

"Where have you been? Are you okay? What happened to your face? You scared me to death!"

"I scared me to death," I said. "Chen sent those demons after me. One caught me. How long have I been gone?"

"Two days. I combed the city looking for you. Thank God you're all right." She wrinkled her nose. "You reek of demons. Come on." She released me, walked into the bathroom and started the shower.

As she prepped the shower, I explained to her what happened but conveniently left out the part about Chen administering pentothal and Kincade coming to my aid. I didn't want her to know about Kincade. It would add another layer of complications having to explain who he was.

"How did you escape?" Her eyes were wide.

"I managed to free myself and kick some serious demon ass."

A thoughtful look crossed her face, her brows drawing together. For a minute, I thought she wasn't going to buy my story. Then she blew out a breath.

"Well, I'm glad you're all right. I was about ready to file a missing person's report." She pulled a towel off the rack and handed it to me. "Clean up. We have work to do."

A hot shower was exactly what I needed. I lingered, letting the warm water sluice over me. Once I'd toweled off and wrapped in one of the hotel bathrobes, I examined my face in the mirror.

The demon did a number on my face. I had matching bruises on each side. My jaw still throbbed with dull pain. Luckily, I still had all my teeth and the swelling was starting to go down. My neck and arms were sore and the manacles left abrasions on my wrists and ankles.

At least I wasn't dead.

I exited the bathroom, padding across the room to the empty bed. Lexi sat cross-legged on the other one with the laptop in front of her.

"I found Chen's office on the eighty-second floor. If you think the horn is there then that's where we need to go." She was all business again.

"I *do* think the horn is there and that *is* where I'm going. I need to figure out how to steal it without being detected."

"You mean *we*, right? And I've got that all planned out. I'm going with you." She propped her hands on her hips, giving me a stubborn look that said *and you can't stop me.*

"I think after what happened to me I should go alone."

But she was already shaking her head. "Hell, no."

I wasn't going to win this one. I wasn't sure I wanted to. I might need someone to watch my back. "Okay, fine. What's your plan?"

"Thief and hacker, remember?" She grinned as she balanced the laptop on her knees and typed away. "While you did your disappearing act, I managed to find out the name of the cleaning company that takes care of Two International Finance Centre. They have about two hundred people cleaning the office building at night."

"Okay?" I wasn't sure where she was going.

"The building has a lot of security. In fact, they check badges of the crew every night to see who's coming and going. And we can't waltz in after hours expecting to get inside," she said as she continued to type. "So, I made us these."

With a broad grin, she spun around the laptop. On the screen were two picture IDs. One for me and one for her.

"So?" I asked.

"Hello. They're fake IDs. Tomorrow you and I go to work for Chingshung Cleaning Service."

Awesome.

CHAPTER 15

I WOKE UP THE next morning with more energy than I had the day before when I woke up in Kincade's suite. Part of me was glad he was in the city. The other part of me wanted him to go back to Dallas. But, if he hadn't been following me, then I probably wouldn't be around.

I doubted he went back to Dallas just because I said so. I had a hunch he was going to hang around and keep an eye on me. I wasn't sure *why* I felt that way but there had been too many coincidences since I met him. He always seemed to be in the right place at the right time when I needed him the most. I didn't want to admit that gave me a weird sense of comfort.

Lexi and I decided to plan the heist for that night. I was still not one-hundred-percent sure she wasn't working for my uncle but at the moment she was all I had. She was smart and totally computer-hacker savvy. Even if she was working for Edward, who cared? She was clearly on my side which gave me some ease about the whole situation.

While she procured two uniforms from Chingshung Cleaning Service, I headed out in search of a store to buy daggers and arm myself. No way was I walking into that with no weapons and I'd left my last two in the thighs of that demon thug.

I asked the concierge where to shop. He sent me to Sheung Wan where there were lots of antique shops and other stores. Even amidst the tourists and residents, I sensed the Fallen. Uneasy, I kept aware of my surroundings. I assumed if I sensed them, they sensed me, too.

Armed with my walking map, I left the hotel and made my way down Queen's Road, curving toward the shopping area on Bonham Strand. The brisk walk was invigorating after the previous days' events.

The shops were full of eye-popping color. The district in Sheung Wan was crammed with open-air stalls and people. They sold everything from eggs and exotic fruit to dried fish on the street. As I made my way further to West Lok Street, street vendors and women wearing straw hats crowded the area selling their wares. That was where I found some of the oddest things—snakes and monkeys' glands—to some of the most normal things—copper mirrors, gems, watches, necklaces, ancient coins, stamps.

I wandered my way through the streets. Some vendors sold traditional Chinese medicines. Shops sold incense and funeral offerings. Everything one might need in the afterlife. Moving along the street, I found sellers of handbags and matching shoes, electric fans, cognac. But nothing that sold daggers.

I passed Man Mo Temple which was a famous landmark according to my map. I turned up the road from the temple and descended several steps until I reached Upper Lascar Row. I found a collection of vendors selling bric-a-brac, souvenirs and memorabilia. I finally reached the heart of the antique district where shops displayed pottery, jade carvings, vases.

And antique daggers.

I stepped across the threshold of one of the antique stores. The bell on the door jingled my arrival. The store had more than knives, though. Figurines cast in gold, vases, pottery and jewelry lined the shelves. It was a smorgasbord of everything you never knew you wanted. I was greeted by a short woman with dark hair graying at the temples. She smiled, her wrinkled skin crinkling in every corner of her ancient face.

"Can I help you?" She spoke English with a thick Cantonese accent. Her gaze lingered on my bruised face but she didn't ask questions and I didn't offer explanations.

"I'm looking for a couple of daggers."

"Ah, I help you. You come to the right place."

She showed me several old ones. Still in the case was one with a jade handle. The blade was shiny with an intricate design etched into it. I couldn't stop staring. Something about it spoke to me. The shop owner eyed me ogling the dagger and pulled it out of the case.

"You like this?"

"It's beautiful."

She placed the blade carefully on the glass. Hesitation trickled through me for fear it would ensnare me in a spell and I'd have to buy it.

"Very special knife," she said. "Probably the oldest I have."

"But it looks new." The blade was in such pristine condition, I would have sworn it was made yesterday.

"Ah, but it is in good condition, yes?" she said. "You take."

She said it even as I reached for it. My hand closed over the handle. The blade warmed against my palm. A sense of calm washed over me. It was lighter than it looked and felt as though it was meant for me and only me.

"Very special. Meant for only one person to wield. One...particular person."

Even though I heard her words, they didn't sink in. I was still mesmerized by it. By how good and right it felt in my hand.

"I love it," I breathed.

"It's yours."

"How much?" Mesmerized, I turned the blade this way and that watching the light catch on the steel.

"No charge."

That stopped me cold. I looked at her, eyes wide with surprise. "I can't do that."

"Yes, you can. A gift to you." And then she gave me a very slow smile. "Demon-killer."

My heart thumped, tumbling around in my chest. I was dumbstruck and had no idea what to say or how to respond. She laughed.

"I sensed demon-killer." She waggled her eyebrows as if we were in on a secret together.

"I...Yes, I am." I sounded confident. Like I believed in my abilities.

She grinned broadly. "Then you need one thing more. I show you."

The lady picked out several more for me. They weren't as fantastic as the jade-handled dagger but they were still as awesome. I strapped a dagger to each thigh and slipped one in each boot. But the jade one...that was special. She gave me a sheath to attach to my waistband. She refused my money but I insisted I pay her something for the blades.

"You must keep. Better than staying here collecting dust. They are with their rightful owner now."

"Are you certain?"

"Yes, yes. Certain. More certain than anything and I've lived a long time." She smiled again and her face crinkled.

"And you want nothing in return for them?"

"Promise you slay many demons. That is the price."

"That you can count on." I extended my hand. "I'm Anna."

"Li Mei." She grasped my hand and gave it a firm shake. "Come back, Anna, and tell me of all the demons you kill."

"I will. I promise."

I bid her farewell and stepped into the afternoon air.

The second I was outside I saw them. Three demons headed straight for me. The world descended into slow motion whenever they were around. The humans didn't see them. Only I could. And it was unnerving. I scowled.

I wasn't ready to break in my new daggers but I had no choice. I palmed the jade-handled one, the weight heavy in my hand. I widened my stance and squared my shoulders. I was ready to take on the three demons. They trotted to a slow stop before me. One had the hide of a snake, all scales and forked tongue. Another had flaming red skin as though he stood outside in the sun for a prolonged period of time. He had a giant horn protruding from his forehead. The third could pass for human if he didn't have red snake eyes.

"Hello, boys. Fancy meeting you here."

"You can't seem to take a hint. Can you, demon-seer?" This from snake eyes. His S's were more pronounced, giving a hissing sound.

I smirked. "I'm like a bad penny. I always turn up."

The other two stepped behind snake-eyes. Both of them eyed my dagger. I decided to test the waters a little and used the tip to dig dirt from underneath my fingernails.

"Where did you get that?" snake-eyes asked.

I shrugged. "Found it."

"Lying bitch."

As he advanced, the overwhelming scent of rot permeated the air. I casually glanced up and met his red-eyed gaze. He halted in front of me. He was within inches of me. I slid my free hand into my pocket and grasped the hilt of another dagger. The jade-handled one glowed brightly and pulsed as if the demon standing so close disturbed the thing. Like it was a sentient being.

Weird.

"Why don't you toddle off back to your boss," I said.

He snarled. "You're dead."

"Maybe but not today." My confidence swelled but deep down I shook like a coward. My uncle was right. That was exactly what I was.

Snake-eyes clamped his hand around my throat. His fingernails elongated into claws, their poisoned tips pricking my skin. I didn't think. I reacted and plunged the jade-handled dagger into his chest. Right to the hilt. Right through the heart.

It took a second for him to realize what was happening. Then the searing began. It was a slow sizzle at first with smoke rising from his chest. I didn't remove the dagger. I watched the smoke thicken. His hand released my throat and dropped to his side. He tried to stumble backward but he couldn't.

The hilt heated up and nearly burned my hand but I held fast. Deep in my psyche I believed I would be all right. The blade wouldn't hurt me.

His red eyes were wide now. Black ooze leaked from the wound. And still that persistent sizzle. His entire body smoked and his comrades refused to come to his aid. He jerked backward trying to dislodge the dagger but it wouldn't budge. His hands clawed mine but I wasn't letting go. Not a chance.

More seconds passed. The edges of his skin turned to ash. He dissolved into nothing more than a heap at my boots. The blade was covered in black blood but the pulsing glow remained. I glanced over to his buddies.

"Who's next?"

They turned and ran and the world righted itself. I had no need for the knife in my left hand and slipped it back into its holder. I wiped the black blood on my pants. A second later, the door behind me popped open. Li Mei poked her head out with a broad grin on her aged face.

"Forgot to mention, demon-killer, it's enchanted." She nodded to the dagger in my hand and then promptly shut the door.

For the first time in a long while I laughed out loud.

The daggers gave me a sense of security. I could protect myself should any more demons attack me and try to kidnap me. The frigid warehouse experience was something I didn't want to repeat ever. As I headed toward Queen's Road, a little more bounce to my step, I had hope Lexi and I would actually succeed at this harebrained idea of stealing the horn.

Hope was drained and replaced with annoyance. Three men headed for me. Locals by the look of them. One had a definite scowl on his face and seemed to be the leader. I heaved a sigh.

As they neared, I realized they weren't Fallen or demons. They were angels. Their wings were hidden from the human eye yet I could see a shimmering outline of them. I had that same weird sensation of the world slowing down and the humans once again oblivious.

"Demon-seer," the leader called out as he halted in front of me.

He gave me no other option but to halt, too. I glanced at all three of their faces. They seemed harmless enough. Maybe Joachim sent them to check up on me.

"Angel." I nodded at him in acknowledgement.

"Your presence has been brought to my attention."

Ooo-kay. "And so...what? You've been sent here to deal with me?"

"In a way, yes. You're not wanted here."

"Well, too bad because I'm here until I've found what I'm looking for."

His eyes narrowed. "What are you looking for?"

"None of your business, bucko. Now move aside and let me pass."

He stood his ground. "You are treading on dangerous ground, demon-seer. We have our region well in hand. We need no other help."

Region? There were regions? Man, there was a lot I didn't know. Not a good feeling.

"Trust me when I say I'm not here to step on any toes. I'm here for one thing and one thing only. When I achieve that, I'm gone." I held up my hands in surrender, hoping to convey my sincerity.

He stepped a little closer to inspect me. His eyes narrowed. His gaze went over me. "Who are you?"

I lifted my chin a little higher and looked down my nose. "I'm the Keeper. Who are you?"

"The Keeper." His eyes widened and he took a step back. "I did not realize. Forgive me." He bowed his head and then fell to one knee.

Embarrassment flushed over me and I was grateful for the veil that hid us from the humans. "Get up. You don't have to bow to me."

"But you are the Keeper. It would not be fitting if I did not bend to you."

"Has everyone heard of me but me? You don't have to bend to me. No one does."

"It would honor me to have your name, Keeper."

I hesitated for one split second. "Anna."

"Anna Walker, it is my supreme pleasure to meet you." He took my hand in his and kissed my knuckles. That wasn't awkward at all. "I am Genghis. Seraphim leader and protector of the Hong Kong Region. And this is Huan and Ling."

"Genghis?" I couldn't help the snicker that escaped me. "Is your last name Kahn?"

He scowled. I guess he didn't think I was funny. "As in Genghis," he said stiffly.

"Pleasure to meet you then."

"The pleasure is mine, Keeper Anna Walker."

"Just Anna," I said, trying not to be agitated. "You seem to have a demon infestation. Is that normal?"

"The population continues to grow daily," he said. "Unfortunately, there is only so much my brethren and I can do to keep them contained."

He indicated the two that stood next to him. I suspected more of his brethren ran around town. I hadn't seen any, though, except for the trio in front of me. And then it occurred to me if he was the protector of this region, he might have information about Chen.

"What do you know about Chen Tso Lang?"

His eyes widened. "A very dangerous man. You would be wise to stay far away from him."

A little too late for that.

"Why do you ask, Keeper?"

"I had a run-in with him earlier. Thought you could give me some intel."

"Trust me when I say the less contact you have, the better. If you've already had a confrontation with him, then you're on his radar and he'll likely not leave you alone until he gets what he wants."

He wanted me dead. Of that I was sure. The warehouse experiment was proof of that. He didn't want me to find the horn. He'd likely send more demons after me if I continued the quest.

"I'm sure he wants my head. But that's not going to happen."

"Perhaps I should offer you my protection. As leader of this region, it's my duty to make sure you're safe."

"I'm good on my own but thanks." I didn't need any more fingers in the pie. I had my hands full enough with Lexi and Chen and now Kincade. "I can take care of myself."

"If you're certain..."

"I'm sure."

"Very well. We will allow you to be on your way. However, should you ever have need of me, I hope you'll contact me."

"That'd be great." I didn't think I'd need him but it was nice to know he had my back. "I'm kind of new at this. How do I contact you?"

"Say my name into the wind."

"That's it?"

He nodded. "Until next time, Anna."

And just like that the world started moving again. Genghis and company were gone. No matter how often that happened, it was always disconcerting.

I headed back down Queen's Road to get back to the hotel when I smelled several of them. Vile, stinky demons. Did I have a freaking GPS attached to my forehead or something? Was there a bull's eye painted on my back? How did these demons and angels keep finding me?

I was ready for them now though. I had the jade-handled dagger that would turn the creatures to a pile of ash. I flipped open the sheath and rested my palm on the hilt as I scanned the crowd of humans. I sensed them. And then there were, um, a lot of them.

Didn't that beat all?

I palmed the dagger and prepared to fight. I had no idea how many since they hadn't come into my line of vision. The world still moved as normal and not in that slow motion that happened when the demons—or angels—spotted me.

Sidebar. I couldn't help but wonder why that didn't happen when Azriel or Joachim were around. Maybe because they had more power? Or were a higher power?

I didn't have time to reason that out because demons appeared. I counted six so far. Slimy, slithering, scaly. They were disgusting with their poison-dripping fangs and their claw-like hands. Forked tongues. One had a wicked tale with sharp spikes up and down ending in what looked like a mace. I sensed more behind me and stole a glance over my shoulder. Sure enough, more crowded in. I sighed.

And then the world slowed down. The humans were blurred behind a haze. This was turning out to be a spectacular day.

"Hello, boys. Come to play?"

I got no response. The leader charged me. I charged right back not willing to give into the fear. The dagger was in my hand and ready to strike. As the first demon neared me, I jabbed him. It didn't take long for him to turn into nothing but a pile of ash.

The ones behind me closed in and there wasn't much I could do about that. I had enough trouble with the ones in front of me. I glanced to the left and right. I was near the corner of Ladder Street and Queen's Road. I couldn't fight them all. I took off running down Ladder Street, heading toward Man Mo Temple. But at Hollywood Road I hung a left and ran back toward the antiquing district where I met Genghis and his buddies. Maybe they were still in the area and I could call for help.

The demons were hot on my trail. Sweat poured down my face and back as I ran at breakneck speed down the street. At least I didn't have to dodge humans. They were already out of the way. Did they sense the evil? Did they know something was happening? I tried to focus on their faces as I ran by but they were a blur.

"Genghis!" I shouted, hoping he was still close.

The park was up ahead. Maybe I could hide inside it. My boots pounded the pavement as I bolted for it and dove through the pagoda-style entrance. I came to a screeching halt. Genghis stood like a guardian, arms crossed.

"I thought you could take care of yourself?"

"I...was wrong." I bent over to catch my breath. "Demons...chasing...me."

He was instantly on high alert. "Where?"

But the clamoring of the demons through the entrance gate was all the answer he needed. He spouted something in Cantonese to

Huan and Ling and they flew into action. They bolted around me with such force I nearly lost my footing. I stumbled but managed to stay on my feet as I turned to watch the carnage.

Genghis wielded a sword made of blue fire, ready to attack. It was like he drew it out of thin air. Who knew with these angels? He and his buddies attacked the demons with relish. With renewed strength, I gathered myself up and joined the fray.

We killed several of them. Mine turned to ash. His merely curled up and died on the pavement. All the while the humans around us were blissfully unaware of our battle.

When the demons realized they were not going to defeat Genghis and company—or kill me for that matter—they gave up. The last few remaining tucked tail and ran.

I slipped the dagger back into the sheath. Genghis's sword disappeared into thin air. He turned to me with a sharp smile.

"That was exhilarating."

I still tried to catch my breath. "Thanks."

"Anna, perhaps you can tell me why you have so many demons on your tail?"

I shrugged. Because honestly, I didn't know. Maybe Azriel put a hit out on me. Maybe Chen did the same thing. I was hacking off all the wrong people lately.

"Just a lucky girl, I guess."

He cocked his head to one side, as though something occurred to him. "You said you were looking for something. Your presence in our city means only one thing. Are you searching for something? One of the relics, perhaps?"

I regarded him coolly. I still wasn't certain I could trust him even if he did do a bang-up job killing demons. And if he was the leader and protector of this region, then why didn't he know the horn was here? "What's it to you?"

"If you are here for one of them, then I must know."

I didn't want to tell him anything. The less he knew the better. I flashed him a wide smile. "Sorry. That's classified."

"We can help you," he said. "Give you the protection you need while you search."

"Thanks, but no thanks. I already have a good idea where to find it."

"As you say. Choose your friends wisely, Keeper. Many seek the relics for their own nefarious reasons."

"You're not the first person that's told me that. I consider myself warned."

"Good luck. Do try to stay out of trouble."

"If I could do that, I wouldn't be here in the first place." I gave him a jaunty wave. "See you around, Genghis."

CHAPTER 16

I WAS UTTERLY EXHAUSTED by the time I got back to the hotel. Sweat trickled down my spine. The nape of my neck was damp, too. We had a long night ahead of us. Even though every muscle hurt from the rundown, I had to push through. The horn awaited. I needed to find it before Chen moved it.

When I arrived back at the hotel room, Lexi had ID badges as well as uniforms ready for us. She had a sort of nervous energy as she popped from one side of the room to the other smacking her gum. She packed up her laptop and organized her suitcase. I wondered what she was up to.

"Here. You'll need to put this on." She handed me the drab tan jumpsuit. The name JiaLi was embroidered on the left breast pocket.

"You okay?" I hadn't seen her this way. Her hands shook and she was out of sorts.

"Fine. I'm fine. Just nervous." She punctuated that with a pop of her gum. "I'm always nervous before a job. This one is big."

I put a hand on her shoulder to make her stop moving. "Hey, everything is going to be okay. Take a deep breath." She met my gaze and inhaled then exhaled. "We can do this. I know we can." I gave her a reassuring smile.

She nodded as if trying to convince herself. She noticed the black stains on my hands, shirt and pants. "What happened to you?"

"I had a run-in with some demons in the shopping district. They didn't fare so well." I stepped into the bathroom to wash the demon blood off my hands.

"Another run in? Are you okay?"

"I'm fine but you should see the other guy."

The sun dipped toward the horizon. We didn't have much time but I didn't want to go in reeking of demons. I took a quick hot shower and dressed in clean cargo pants. I used a fair amount of make-up to hide the bruises on my face and then pulled my hair back into a ponytail.

I strapped daggers to my thighs and stuck one in each boot. My jade-handled one was in a special holder on my hip. I checked to make sure I had the little gold key in my pocket. I hoped it belonged to whatever held the horn. After getting situated, I pulled on the jumpsuit over my clothes.

Lexi was dressed and ready to go. She still fidgeted. Her nervous energy radiated off her in waves. The stakes were high but I wasn't as edgy as her.

She scrutinized my make-up job. "Looks better. I can't see the bruises."

"Good."

She snatched a baseball cap and handed it to me. "For your hair and to hide your face."

Chen would be looking for me, no doubt.

"Good thinking." I pulled the cap down low. "What's the plan?"

"We enter through the service entrance by the loading dock. We'll need to show our IDs once we arrive to go through security.

The cleaning service will issue us an access card to enter into the building."

"And then we find the horn," I said.

"Right." She bit her thumbnail.

The building was only a few minutes' walk from the hotel. We decided going on foot would be better especially since I was armed to the teeth. Once at the service entrance, Lexi shifted from one foot to the other. As if she thought we might not make it past building security. She was right about that. Armed guards flanked the entrance. They searched people before letting them pass through.

I leaned close to her and dropped my voice. "Lex, how am I going to sneak my weapons past them?"

"You may have to leave them behind."

Forget that. I wasn't going in unarmed. I gave her a stiff shake of my head. Now I shifted from one foot to the other. If they gave me a pat down, I was doomed.

We were next in line. Cold sweat broke out on my palms. Fear prickled my nerve-endings. My daggers were going to be discovered. I'd be arrested and shoved into a Hong Kong prison for the rest of my life. At least that was what I imagined.

As we approached, Lexi took in a deep breath and exhaled. The spearmint scent of her gum filled the air between us and the security guards. We showed our fake IDs. They looked over them and gave us a cursory glance. To my shock, they waved us through. They searched everyone before us. How was that possible? That was far too easy.

"I can't believe we got through." I gave her a cursory glance.

Lexi flashed a nervous smile. "We were lucky, I guess."

Something wasn't right about the situation. I didn't want to look a gift horse in the mouth, though. Once we passed inspection, we met the cleaning crew. The manager handed us an access card for the building and pointed us in the direction of the elevator banks.

The elevators were controlled by the access cards. Once we were inside, she swiped her card and punched the button for the eighty-second floor. The ride was long and silent. There wasn't even cheesy elevator music to break up the quiet. The nervous energy coming off Lexi was palpable as she continued to pop her gum and bite her thumbnail.

At last the elevator dinged and the doors swished open.

"This way," she said.

She led the way down the hall like she knew where she was going. She probably had the floor plan to the place memorized. We stopped outside the office of Partners for the Sanctified that housed Chen and his demon cronies.

She pulled out two silver instruments and knelt in front of the door. A few seconds later and she had the lock picked. As soon as the door was cracked, an alarm sounded. She shoved the door wide and punched in the security code. All fell silent.

"How'd you get that?" I asked.

"Trade secret." Her voice held a tense edge.

I shoved the thought aside. I wanted to be impressed with her hacking and thieving skills but something didn't jive.

Once inside she closed the door and flipped on a light. The small office looked like any other with a reception desk, a couple of guest chairs, some magazines scattered on the coffee table. A short hallway led to a break room and four offices. All the doors were closed and locked.

"Chen's office is the corner one. It's up this way."

She pointed to the office at the end of the hallway. Lexi picked the lock on the door and then we were inside. Two of the four walls were floor-to-ceiling windows with the fancy electronic shades. His office boasted a breathtaking view overlooking Victoria Harbour. Lights from the buildings and boats reflected on the dark water from across the waterfront.

An oversized desk dominated the center. Several bookcases lined one of the walls and next to those was a strange-looking credenza. The credenza was a custom case with a glass top. The Horn of Gabriel rested on a red velvet cushion. Just like in the vision when I shook Chen's hand.

He did have it. The bastard.

"Look," Lexi breathed, awestruck.

And it was hard not to be. The silver Horn of Gabriel was beautiful. Shiny and perfect, the horn was long and straight with a flared bell at the end. The horn had no keys or holes. No etchings, no fingerprints, no nothing. Like the drawing in the family history book.

The glass case had a gold lock. I realized I must have the key. The small gold key currently resided in my pants pocket. Lexi started to pick the lock.

"Wait."

My hands shook. I stripped out of the uniform and kicked it aside. I reached into my pocket for the little gold key.

"Where did you get that key?" Lexi didn't bother to hide the surprise in her voice. "You didn't tell me you had that."

"That's right, I didn't."

I didn't bother to answer her question as to where I found the key. That wasn't important. I slipped it in the lock and turned it with a click. With a slow hand and my heart pounding a wicked beat, I pushed open the lid.

"It's beautiful," she said, peering into the case.

"Yes."

"What's it doing here?"

"You said Chen was a collector of religious antiquities. This has to be his prized possession," I said.

My fingertips brushed the cool metal. A vision exploded in my head. A battle scene played out with both dark and light angels and humans and demons fighting each other. All engaged in a bloody battle against a backdrop of sweeping mountains and rolling hills. The ground was red and black with demon, angel and human blood.

A man stood behind a large gold chest with lightning bolts shooting out of the sides, striking down all those in its path. The man laughed next to him. Lucifer had a look of satisfaction on his face.

Beyond them was a wall of angels. White-winged, silver-winged, gold-winged. They were magnificent and deadly. They fought for all mankind.

The vision was so powerful and so vivid I inhaled a sharp breath. But I couldn't remove my fingers yet.

Then the vision changed. The Horn was in the hands of the archangel, Gabriel. How he entrusted it to the dream walkers. The man with the dark hair. The one who laughed as he used the gold chest to kill. That was no ordinary chest. That was the Ark of the Covenant.

I snatched my hand back, holding my wrist. As though my fingers had been scorched. I knew the outcome to that. I knew my ancestor betrayed Gabriel's trust.

Holy shit. My heart beat double-time. What battle had I seen? The future? The end of the world? Judgment Day? Or something in the past?

A knot formed in my clenched stomach. Was this why I was made to search for them? Because I saw visions in the relics? Apprehension and fear prickled through me.

"Anna, you okay?" Lexi's concerned voice brought me back to the present.

"I-I..."

"You spaced out for a sec," she said.

She hadn't seen because she didn't touch it. Which made me wonder...

"Touch the horn," I commanded. My voice was strong and hard and she flinched.

"Why?"

"Just do it."

She brushed her fingertips along the length of the horn. She didn't cringe or jerk her hand away. She didn't see the vision.

Only I could. As the Keeper of the Holy Relics.

"The metal is cold." She looked at me then with an inquisitive eye. "Isn't that what you felt?"

"Yes."

The lie slipped easily from my lips. I didn't want to tell her about the vision. I needed to discuss it with Edward. I wondered if it was part of my abilities he told me nothing about.

I reached to pick it up but Lexi grabbed my wrist. "This is too easy, cuz. Don't you think there's some sort of alarm? Chen wouldn't let this sit here unprotected."

She was probably right but I had no idea how to get around an alarm. "I'm not leaving without it."

"Let me take a look."

Lexi fell to her knees and crawled around the floor and the back of the case. She ran her hands over the carpet, the wood surface, the back of the cabinet. Then she stood and peered around the ceiling, the bookcase, the desk.

"I don't see anything. No wires or anything."

"Maybe we're safe then?" I asked.

"Maybe Chen is arrogant enough to leave it here unprotected," she said.

I glanced back at the horn, glittering in the half-light of the office. I came too far to worry about traps or alarms. If there was, so be it. I lifted it and held the slight weight in my hands.

Nothing happened. No alarms. No flashing red alerts.

"Let's go," I said.

I didn't have to tell her twice. We headed for the door and got to the elevator in record time. My heart pumped wildly. A cold sweat slicked my palms. I wish I'd thought to bring something to put the thing in. I didn't know how we'd avoid the security cameras and make it out of the building.

"We can use one of the trash carts on the bottom floor," Lexi said as though she read my mind.

I nodded. An eternity passed before the elevator dinged. Lexi pushed the lobby button. The doors slid closed and we started to descend. My stomach was in knots. My nerves were on high alert. At the fortieth floor, the damn elevator came to a jarring halt.

"Fuck," I said.

"Not good," Lexi said.

A clanging noise vibrated the elevator and then it lurched. My stomach plummeted to my shoes. Bile rose to my throat and I swallowed hard to keep from vomiting. Lexi produced a knife in one hand. She frantically pushed buttons but nothing happened. She tried the emergency call button with no results. All I could do was clutch the horn.

Scraping noises reverberated in the elevator shaft over us. Or around us? I couldn't tell. A drop of sweat rolled down my back. This was worse than standing on the street watching the two demons head straight for me. This was worse than having my bare feet shoved in a bucket of ice water. This was like standing in a death cell waiting for shit to go down.

The escape hatch over our heads blew open. Lexi squealed and I ducked down, clutching the horn to my chest. Two demons jumped inside. One went for Lexi, the other for me. I swung the horn, connecting with his skull. A resounding *bong* echoed through the confines of the elevator.

He was momentarily stunned, giving me enough time to grab my favorite knife. Gripping the horn under one arm, I jabbed the blade into his gut and sliced him from navel to neck. He crumpled to the floor, black blood spilling everywhere. A moment later he turned to ash.

Lexi, meanwhile, managed to dispose of her demon. But we weren't be in the clear yet. I realized there *was* an alarm on the horn—a demon alarm I tripped when I picked it up. Above our heads, more scraping sounds in the elevator shaft. Like little claws on metal.

My heart pumped overtime. Any harder and it was going to burst through bone and skin. I scanned the small area trying to come up with a plan. An idea. Anything.

"Uh, cuz?"

"I'm working on it."

"Can you do it faster?" She shifted from one foot to the other. I realized then she was covered in black blood.

I clutched the horn under my arm again. "Boost me up. I need to see what we're up against."

She cupped her hands as a foothold. *Scrape, scrape, scrape* in the elevator shaft didn't inspire a lot of confidence. I stepped in her hands and pulled up to peer over the edge of the opening. My heart stopped. There were so many I couldn't even count. Like cockroaches with pointed teeth just waiting for their kill.

"What do you see?" she asked.

Words froze in my throat as I jumped down. Lexi's eyes widened when she saw my face.

"Your face is white." Her voice wavered.

"There are more."

"More?"

Thousands. But I couldn't tell her that. I nodded. I had no idea what we were going to do but we couldn't stay and die. They had us cornered. What were they waiting for? Why hadn't they attacked yet?

I glanced down at the horn in my shaking fingers. Could the horn help? Legend said blowing the horn signaled Judgment Day but I wasn't Gabriel. I was the Keeper. Could anyone blow it? Or was it simply restricted to the archangel? If I blew it, would I cause the end of the world?

I had to try. It was the only way to save our skins. If Judgment Day came, then maybe it'd blow up the damn demons, too.

They were getting closer. Taking a deep breath, I held the horn to my mouth.

"What are you doing?" Her voice was a panic, as though I'd lost my mind. Maybe I had.

"Saving our skins." I hoped. "Get ready."

"For what?"

"For whatever happens next."

As the first demon fell into the elevator, Lexi sprang into action. I placed the horn to my lips and blew. Nothing happened. No sound. Nothing.

"It didn't work!" She sounded like she was on the verge of tears. She kicked the demon then stabbed him in the chest. "Try again."

Another had already taken its place. I tried again but still nothing happened. Out of desperation, I tried three times before abandoning the idea and joining Lexi in the fight. There were too many in the shaft. We'd never defeat them all. They'd come to kill us and they wouldn't stop until we were dead.

We could die trying, damn it.

The elevator gave a violent wobble. Lexi and I lost our footing with the violent movement. She banged against the wall. I fell into the demon I battled. His claws wrapped around my arm while the other reached for the horn.

No way in hell I was letting him have it.

A loud explosion rocked the cab. Then a burst of light above us. A minute later, the elevator plummeted downward. Much faster than normal speed. Lexi killed her demon and then frantically punched the stop button but the elevator didn't stop. Demons still poured inside one after the other.

I was in the middle of a tug-of-war with the demon guy. Poor Lexi was bombarded. She screamed. I had to help her but I couldn't let go or I'd lose the horn.

I kicked the demon where his balls should be and ripped free the horn. The demon clawed my arm in retaliation, leaving a burn in his wake. I stabbed him in the neck and watched him turn to ash.

Suddenly there was a flash of light, a pressure around me and another flash of light. The inside of the elevator was gone and I stood on a rooftop overlooking the city. My stomach heaved as dizziness assaulted me and I fell to my knees, spilling what little food I had all over the roof.

When I managed to recover, I glanced up. The angel peered down at me with narrowed eyes. He was tall, blond, gorgeous. His wings were snow white and fully extended. Why were all the angels so hot? He clamped a hand around my upper arm, his fingers biting into flesh.

"Who are you?"

I glanced around for Lexi but she wasn't there. "Lexi! Where is she?"

"You blew the horn, did you not?"

"Is it like a dog whistle or something? No sound came out," I snapped. "You left my cousin!"

"The one who blows the horn is the only one who receives aid." He said it so matter-of-factly and unemotionally I actually wanted to smack him.

So maybe it was like a dog whistle...but in this case an angel whistle. I managed to jerk my arm out of his grasp. "But she'll die. Please! You have to help her."

He pressed his lips together in a thin line and then flashed away. A moment later he returned with my cousin unconscious in his arms. He laid her gently on the ground. I fell to my knees at her side and smoothed away the hair from her face.

She had scratches and claw marks all over her. Her blood was mixed with the black demon blood and I couldn't tell where one started and the other stopped. Her clothes were in tatters. She was barely breathing. This was my fault. Lexi didn't deserve that death.

"Will she live?"

It was almost too much to hope. The angel knelt across from me on the other side of Lexi. He peered at me intently, his eyes a gorgeous chocolate brown.

"Please," I begged. "Don't let her die. She helped me get the horn."

"How did you get that?" He eyed it. I clutched it tight against my chest, protective.

"I was charged with finding it which I did. Can you help my cousin or not?"

He looked down at Lexi, considering. Then he passed his hand over her body and her wounds were healed. Her clothes were no longer shreds. Her eyes were still closed as though she slept.

"Thank you," I whispered.

"You must return the horn to Gabriel." He stood and held his hand out to me. "Come. I will take you at once."

Seriously? Totally not going to happen. Although meeting Gabriel would be awesome and all, I wasn't giving it up. I'd gone through too much to steal it. "No way. I'm keeping it."

His jaw clenched and anger flared in his depthless eyes. "You do not know what power you hold."

"Uh, yeah, I do, winged warrior. I blew the horn and summoned you, didn't I?" Which was an awesome power to have, by the way.

He considered this and then his eyes narrowed again. "I will ask you again since you failed to tell me. Who are you?"

I raised my chin higher. "I'm the Keeper."

Recognition flashed over his face and he bowed his head in a curt nod. "My apologies, Keeper. I did not realize you were the dream walker. Even so you must return the horn to its rightful owner."

I sort of wished he bent on one knee and called me "your majesty" or something but that didn't happen. And Gabriel? Yeah, well, he wasn't getting it. I needed the horn to bargain for my life with Azriel and Joachim. "A messenger angel was sent to me. I'm to give it only to Joachim."

Which wasn't going to happen either but I didn't want him to know that.

"I am a warrior angel. I assure you I can take you to Gabriel myself so you can return the horn. It's not necessary to give it to the messenger angel."

"You're not listening. I'm keeping it until I find the other relics. You can pass that message along to your boss."

He bestowed one last glare then the jerk of his head in a nod. "As you wish."

And then he was gone, disappearing before my eyes.

CHAPTER 17

AFTER THE WARRIOR ANGEL left, I realized I was stuck
on a gravel rooftop with my unconscious cousin. Great.
I had no idea where I was. I had to admit, though, the view
was spectacular. Two IFC, the tallest in the city, rose up from
the cluster of buildings illuminating the bay like a beacon. I
wondered if it was overrun with demons. Or did they die in
the elevator crash? Assuming the elevator did, in fact, crash.
Victoria Harbour was lit up. Numerous boats glided over the
glassy water. It was a lovely view of all the lights and buildings.

But that didn't help me figure out where the hell I was.
I clutched the horn and walked to the edge of the roof and
looked down, my boots crunching on the gravel. The bustle of
activity on the ground below reminded me of a disturbed fire
ant hill. Except these ants had cars. Lots of tourists and locals
were out for a night on the town. A sharp stabbing pain of envy
shot through me. I wished I was one of them, hurrying off to a
bar to enjoy drinks with friends.

The only friend I'd ever truly had was murdered in cold blood. I clutched the horn tighter, reinforcing my vow to avenge Ben.

Lexi groaned behind me. I hurried over to her, dropping to one knee as her eyes fluttered open.

"You scared me to death." I blew out a breath of relief.

"What happened? I have a raging headache. The last thing I remember was being in that elevator and getting attacked by demons while plunging to my death. And then you...you disappeared. How did you disappear?" She squinted at me, her brows drawn together in confusion.

"Lex, the horn worked. It called a warrior angel. He got us out of there."

She sat up quickly and then groaned and grasped her head. "Is he still here?"

"No, he's gone."

Perplexed, she looked back at me. "Where are we?"

That was a great question and one to which I didn't have an answer. I helped her to her feet. She seemed fine. Completely healed from her injuries.

"That's the million-dollar question. I have no idea."

"You're a mess."

I glanced down. Blood stained my clothes and hands. Cuts and claw marks covered every inch of exposed skin. I only remembered the one clawing me when he tried to take the horn. The others must have happened during my skirmishes.

I managed to make it out of the elevator with the jade-handled dagger in hand and the others still firmly in place. I was grateful for that at least.

"What happened to me? I had cuts and gashes all over me." She checked over her arms and legs.

"You did," I agreed. "I thought you were going to die. The warrior angel saved your life."

"Really?" She looked at me wide-eyed before grinning. "Was he cute?"

Sure, he was cute. But that wasn't important right now. We needed off the roof and back to street level. Then out of Hong Kong. I had the horn. I wanted out of town as soon as possible. I'd worry about getting it through customs later.

I rolled my eyes. "We don't have time for that. We need to get out of here."

"Yeah. You're right. So how do we do that?" she asked.

I looked around and found a door with a sign indicating Stair B. "That's how."

We hurried across the roof. I muscled open the door. Inside the stairwell was musty and smelled like dirty rubber. There didn't seem to be a lot of oxygen either. Or that was my imagination running away with me. The signage said we were sixty stories up. It looked like I'd be getting my fair share of exercise. Down, down, down we went.

And then I saw the shadows coming up. I halted on the stairs around the thirtieth floor. My heart was in my shoes.

"What is it?" Lexi whispered.

"More demons."

"Didn't we just leave that party?"

Yeah, we did. But demons who wanted their shit back would follow you anywhere. I turned and pushed her back up the stairs. We couldn't go down. Nor could we fight another horde. I was too exhausted and Lexi had no weapons. My winged warrior would be pissed if I blew the horn again so that idea was out.

"We're going up now?" she asked.

"Got any other bright ideas?"

"Well...not exactly."

We ran up the stairs, our feet pounding on the metal. My thighs burned from the exertion and it took everything I had to keep going. My breath see-sawed in and out of my chest. Sweat ran down my face and back. It took all my strength to keep going.

Lexi breathed so hard, her face turned bright red and her hair was damp from sweat. I didn't know if I could go another step. She came to an abrupt halt in front of me. I couldn't stop in time and fell into her.

"What are you—?"

And then I saw him. Chen stood at the top of the stairs with two demon henchmen flanking him.

"I knew you were after something. I didn't realize you would be stupid enough to steal the Horn of Gabriel."

"Hey, Chen. Fancy meeting you here." I had a surprising amount of calm and false bravado.

His gaze flickered to Lexi and then back to me. His face was dark, menacing.

"My demons failed to stop you on the street yesterday afternoon. You even got lucky when your guardian came to your rescue in the warehouse."

"Guardian?" Lexi whispered out of the corner of her mouth. "You said—"

Chen cut her off, thankfully. I didn't want to explain that but I wondered why he'd called Kincade my guardian.

"Now, tonight, my demons failed to stop you in the elevator. And so, I am forced to come myself and retrieve what is rightfully mine."

"It's not yours, dude. It's Gabriel's." Judging by the grimace on his face, he didn't like that answer. I wasn't feeling so generous or giving, either. I stepped around Lexi, putting her behind me. "I stole it fair and square. Not giving it back."

"Then you and your friend will die." He said it as though he talked about the weather.

My fingers twitched. I wanted to pull out my dagger and stab him in the neck but if I made a move, they'd attack.

"And if I give you the horn?" I asked.

"Cuz..."

I shushed her with a wave of my hand. I didn't know what my plan was exactly. I hoped I could talk my way out of this impossible situation. Chen narrowed his eyes.

"Then you may live."

I didn't want to give him the horn. But if it was the only way to make it out of this alive I would. I clutched it tighter in my grasp. My palms were slick with sweat.

"I thought you'd say that."

Behind us the horde of demons approached. Ahead of us Chen and his two cronies. We were trapped in the stairwell. The air closed in. Maybe I'd suffocate and then it wouldn't matter. I shifted from one foot to the other wondering how to get my daggers out of my boots. How to get Lexi and me out of this.

"Make your choice," he said.

Too bad no one was going to rescue us. I wished the wall would burst open with a white knight. Where was Kincade when I needed him? Not here.

"I don't want to die that's for sure. It would ruin my day."

"Then hand over the horn."

"There's the rub. I don't want to do that either."

He scowled, clearly impatient with me.

"But since I don't want to die," I continued, "I guess I have no choice."

"Yes," he said.

"Have you lost your mind?" Lexi's rough whisper was in my ear. She wondered what the hell I was doing. So did I.

Currently, I was stalling. Trying to come up with a way out with the horn. Behind us was the clamoring of demons as they closed in.

"Ya know, it's kinda hard to decide with your demons breathing down my neck."

"What demons?" he asked, his brow crinkling.

"Duh. The ones behind us."

Huh. He didn't know about the demons behind us? Was I the only one that sensed them?

"Anna," Lexi urged.

"Give me a minute." I wasn't sure if I was talking to her or Chen.

"No. Time is up, demon-seer. You have wasted enough. Give me the horn." He held out his hand.

"Okay. Sure. Right after I tie my boot."

I bent down. He watched me the entire time. My heart palpitated hard in my chest. I was sick with nervous energy. The adrenaline pumped hard through my veins.

I had to be quick. As fast as I could move, I snatched the dagger out of my boot and threw it. To my horror, Chen anticipated. I wasn't the best knife thrower either. He leaned out of the way and the dagger clattered against the floor, useless.

He emitted a low growl and then snapped his fingers. Two demons leapt into action. I palmed my dagger, ready to attack.

"Anna!" Panic etched Lexi's voice.

I clutched the horn and prepared for imminent death. I could take on one but not two. If I killed one, the other would already be attacking.

Before the demons reached me, there was a flash of light and my view was blocked by a six-foot white wingspan. The warrior angel returned holding a glowing sword. He easily took out the two demons and advanced on Chen.

But the chicken shit took off running up to the roof. The warrior angel followed, his feet silent—really? Silent?—on the stairs. I grabbed Lexi by the hand and followed them up, dragging her the whole way. He chased Chen now. The horde behind us followed.

Terrific.

My legs burned as we reached the top. Lexi and I both panted, trying to catch our breath. The angel cornered Chen. Behind us the door to the stairwell banged closed and I chewed on my lower lip, worried about the other demons.

"Uh, hey, warrior angel guy—"

"You think to defeat this demon, Keeper? You must be mad."

"Hey!"

"Despite his human half, he is a high lord. One of the vilest. One of Lucifer's commanders," the angel said.

"He said he wasn't a Fallen!" I glared at him.

"Not a Fallen, Keeper. A high lord. There *is* a difference."

"Oh. Well, I stole the horn from him. He's pissed off at me."

Chen's glare seared through me. "And you'll be punished for it. Others will seek vengeance for my death."

"Yeah, we'll they'll have to find me first," I said.

"Stupid girl." He spat. "You've stolen a holy relic from me. They already know who you are. Tracking you will be easy. Killing you will be even easier."

He was trying to scare me but I wasn't going to let him. I cut a glance at the warrior angel. His hand tightened on the hilt of his glowing sword.

"You threaten the Keeper's life. For that you must die."

Chen started to retort but the warrior angel didn't give him a chance. He swung the sword wide and decapitated the high lord. Buh-bye, Chen. Good riddance. The angel turned to me. Fury lined his handsome face.

"I knew you could not be trusted. You do not understand what power you hold in your hands."

"Is this the warrior angel? He *is* cute," Lexi said.

I rolled my eyes and ignored her. "I wasn't going to give it to him. How stupid do you think I am?" He started to answer but I waved him off. "Never mind. Thanks for the save, angel boy."

"My name is Darius," he snarled.

"Thanks for the update, *Darius*. You might want to know Chen has more demons following us."

The stairwell door burst open and demons poured out. Like the cockroaches they were.

"You might have mentioned it sooner." He gave me a sour look.

"I tried." I shrugged innocence.

"Those are not Chen's minions," he said.

There was a difference between high lord's minions and regular minions? Weren't they all the same? Demons were demons in my book. And they all had to die.

Before I could reply the angel flashed in front of me and Lexi and launched into attack. He killed demons right and left. Indecision flashed through me. I wanted to help him but I couldn't fight so many at once.

The stairwell door banged open again. The three Seraphim charged out. Genghis, Huan and Ling to the rescue. I was so happy to see them, I wanted cry. They quickly joined the fray, wiping out the demons. More poured out of the stairwell and then the most absurd thought crossed my mind—it was like clown car. Would the parade of demons ever end?

"Who are they?" There was a catch in Lexi's voice.

"Seraphim. I have to help them."

I clutched the horn in one hand and the dagger in the other. Fighting with the thing was seriously hampering my limited abilities. There wasn't much I could do but I had to help instead of standing there like a dumfounded idiot.

Lexi backed up a step toward the edge of the roof as though ready to bolt. There was no place to go, so I didn't give it another thought. A demon charged toward us and I lunged, shoving the blade into his chest. He immediately turned to dust. I took several backward steps to reach her.

"Guard this with your life. Stay behind us." I shoved the horn toward her.

As the horn landed in her hands, her eyes widened and then a look of sheer pleasure passed over her face. It didn't register in my frantic mind. All I thought about at the time was killing demons. I should have seen it. I should have known.

I slashed and cut my way to Darius and the Seraphim. I was impressed with Darius's precision as he hacked the demons like they were nothing but thin air. I slashed and killed as many as possible but, honestly, I sucked compared to the others.

"Hello, Anna!" Genghis gave me a giant grin like it was the best time he'd ever had.

"Nice of you to join us." I stabbed another demon.

"I wouldn't miss this party for anything."

He and his buddies hacked away into the crowd. But Ling broke off and took up a station at the open doorway. He cut them down before they stepped onto the roof. Nice tactic. Wish I'd thought of that. Huan took down several before kicking them off the edge. I wondered what happened to them when they plummeted to the street. Did the humans see them?

I had other things to worry about than the Seraphim. I fought my way to Darius's side.

"What did you mean...they weren't Chen's minions?" I panted, trying to keep up with him and not die.

"They belong to another high lord." He wasn't even winded. Totally not fair.

"Who?"

A demon lunged for me but I stabbed him and turned him to ash.

"Azriel," Darius said without missing a beat.

Azriel?

Why would Azriel's demons...Shit! He must have tracked me here to get the horn. I spun around to warn Lexi but the sight that greeted me turned my stomach sour. Azriel stood beside her while she casually held the horn in one hand and looked over the cuticles of her other.

The realization of what she'd done hit me so hard my knees buckled. I wobbled on my feet but managed to remain standing. I was so wrong. She wasn't working for my uncle. She was working for Azriel. Cold fury scalded my heart, searing my nerve-endings.

She was the only one I trusted. She was the only blood relative I *thought* gave a damn about me. She came to me offering her help and now understood why. She used me. She betrayed me. It slashed me to the very core. It turned my heart to a block of ice and I shivered.

My uncle was right. *Trust no one.* I would never make that same mistake again.

"You bitch."

"Sorry, cuz, but I had to. He gave me an offer I couldn't refuse."

"And that is?" I was oblivious now to the battle going on behind me. Darius and the Seraphim killed demons but I couldn't pay attention to that right now. All I focused on was Lexi and her treachery. *How could she?*

She only helped break into Two IFC for the horn. Maybe she knew where it was all along. That's why it was so easy for her. And the gum breath she blew at the security guards—they must have been demons. She used some magic spell to mask their scent. Everything clicked into place now. She'd been working with Azriel since the beginning. What a fool I was.

"She brings me the horn and she will be rewarded."

Azriel slid an arm around her waist and pulled her close. They kissed in a display so sickening I wanted to puke. Not only were they working together, they were also lovers.

"Everything was a lie? Is that it?"

"Pretty much." She flashed a smile. "I hoped the demons in the elevator would kill you and then I'd have the horn free and clear. But then you summoned...what did you call him? Oh, yes. Angel boy. It sort of ruined my plans."

I clutched the dagger tighter trying to decide what to do. I stole a glance at Darius but he didn't see me. Neither did Genghis or Huan or Ling. I couldn't grab their attention without looking obvious.

"But you almost died in that elevator," I sputtered. "You were surrounded by demons. You only lived because I used the horn and called Darius."

"Yeah and you nearly ruined everything with that stunt. I would have been okay if you'd died like you were supposed to," she said.

The pain of her words stung through to my core. She wanted me dead. Out of the way.

"Anyway, I wasn't sure I could pull it off but then things sort of worked out," Lexi said.

"And you made it so easy." Azriel didn't hide his smug grin as he said it. "Lexi, my darling, agreed to help me. She has similar dream walking abilities as you." He kissed her cheek. "We couldn't have found the horn without your help."

"Yeah, so thanks for the help, cuz." She waggled the horn at me.

My emotions got the best of me. In a rage, I rushed them. I didn't know what I was thinking, only that I had to kill him. Kill her. Take the horn. Something sharp slammed into my back between my shoulder blades, bringing me to my knees.

Oh, God. The pain was awful. Another sharp pain and I realized I'd been stabbed. There must have been poison in the blade because I leaned over and retched. Behind me there was a scuffle. I heard Darius shout something but I couldn't respond. Lexi grinned before giving me a pinky wave.

Bitch.

I crawled toward them and pulled myself to my feet. I wasn't finished yet. I wasn't going to die, damn it. I was going to kill them. *Them.* I was going to get that horn back if it was the last thing I did.

"How cute. You think you can take it back," Azriel taunted. His gaze landed on the demons behind me. "Finish her off!"

"You bitch. I'll kill you for this," I vowed as another sharp pain seared through me.

"I'm sure you will."

"Anna!" That was Genghis. Then he shouted, "Huan, Ling! Get to the Keeper!"

Lexi laughed. *Laughed* as Azriel took her in his arms. He lifted off from the roof into the night sky and disappeared against the inky blackness.

The horn was gone. The horn was gone and demons swarmed me. I couldn't move. I couldn't react. I could only sit on the roof, numb.

Darius flashed in front of me. He grabbed me by the arms and hauled me to my feet.

"Don't you give up, Keeper! Don't you dare give up!" Fire sparked in those chocolate eyes and he gave me a little shake. "Do you hear me?"

"I lost it," I muttered.

Demons sliced my ankles. The pain shot up both my legs and my knees crumbled. Blood smeared my clothes. Red, mine. Black, demons'. The angel released me and shoved me roughly behind him. I stumbled to the rooftop and threw out my arms to catch my fall. My palms met gravel, abrading the skin. It was the least of my worries. I was going to die.

I was tired. So tired. I laid my head down. Through my hazy vision I saw Darius and the Seraphim still fighting the demons. All with their glowing swords. They cut down several more and then Darius turned back to me. His face swam into my vision. Blood was splattered all over his face and there was concern in his eyes. He scooped me into his arms, cradling my tired body against his chest.

It was the last thing I remembered before darkness consumed me.

CHAPTER 18

T HE WORLD WAS ABLAZE. Fiery chasms surrounded me. Lava poured out of a nearby volcano and spilled down the mountain. The heat was so intense I thought my skin might melt off my bones. Behind me, death screams and a raging battle.

I focused on the fight before me. Angels. Demons. Humans. All trying to survive. But some didn't survive. Their bodies were littered everywhere, both humans and angels. Their blood pooled beneath them, turning the ground red. Demon blood looked like a dark oil slick pouring out of their wounds. The smell of sulfur and death and rot permeated my nose.

And somehow, I understood this was the end of days. Azriel held the Spear of Destiny. Lucifer held the Staff of Moses. Four of the Seven Seals had been broken heralding the arrival of the Four Horsemen of the Apocalypse. My eyes fell on Death whose skeleton face was smiling as he sat astride his pale destrier. His bony hand held a scythe and his red eyes surveyed the destruction with a satisfied glint.

The other three seals broke. The souls of martyrs dressed in white robes wailed, calling for the blood of the ones who persecuted them. Who destroyed them for their beliefs.

A great earthquake shattered the land, breaking it in two.

I heard Gabriel blow his horn. On a ridge, there were seven archangels with their seven trumpets. This was the signal. The beginning of the end. This was Judgment Day.

Armageddon.

While the ground still rumbled, I met Azriel's gaze. His eyes blazed red like the lava. Across the field, Kincade fought a demon. I couldn't understand how or why he was there. Azriel rushed him, the spear clutched in his hands. I tried to shout a warning to Kincade but my voice was lost among the battle noise. Among the wailing martyrs. The rumbling ground. The blasting trumpets.

I ran down the mountain but the hot ground scorched my feet through my shoes. I screamed Kincade's name but he couldn't hear me. Azriel halted in front of him. He gave me a wicked smile as he plunged the Spear of Destiny right through Kincade. I watched in shocked horror as he fell slowly to his knees and turned to look at me. Kincade's eyes didn't meet mine. They were Ben's. A screamed dislodged from my throat. Hot tears scalded my cheeks.

Vengeance would be mine.

But then the scene changed and I was whisked from the fiery peaks of the mountain to a rose garden fragrant with the morning dew. No death and destruction. I realized it was nothing but a dream. The end of days scenario wasn't real. Azriel didn't have the Spear of Destiny. I glanced down. I was dressed in a Victorian gown with a bustle in pale blue water silk. It was the finest gown I'd ever seen. My hair played about my face in the gentle breeze.

I followed the maze of sidewalks past the rosebushes, my shoes clicking a muffled sound along the stone. The gown made a swishing sound as I walked. I rounded the corner of a giant bush and halted. My uncle perched on the edge of a stone bench. He was dressed in a suit. He's always dressed that way when he's in my dreams.

"Hello, Annabelle."

The last thing I recalled was the attack by demons. Lexi stealing the horn. I wondered now if I was dreaming after all.

"Am I dead?" I asked, fearful of the answer.

He chuckled. "No. You are still very much alive." He waved me over. "Come. Sit. Let us talk."

A dream then. Could one feel in dreams? I certainly did as the punch of relief hit me. I perched on the edge of the bench on the opposite end. I couldn't look at him. For whatever reason, I was aware he knew I'd lost the horn. I was afraid of the backlash.

"Fine day, isn't it?" He inhaled a deep breath and gazed up at the clear blue sky.

"What are you doing here, Uncle Edward?"

"You need me."

My breath hitched. I didn't want to admit it. I didn't want to admit I needed anyone. "Because I lost it."

"I know." He nodded.

"I'm sorry. I failed."

"You did not fail, Annabelle. You merely experienced a setback. That is all."

"Are you here to give me a pep talk?"

"I'm here to encourage you, yes." He looked at me then, his gaze pressing into me. "To help you."

"I don't need your help."

"Don't be so bloody arrogant. I'm aware Lexi betrayed you. I warned you not to trust anyone."

"She made a fool of me and now Azriel has the horn."

"She deceived you and gained your confidence and trust. She made you believe her. I cannot fault you for that. She used you to get what she wanted for Azriel. Now we must deal with the consequences. You must take it back."

"How?" Warm tears leaked from my eyes and rolled down my cheeks. Damn, I hated crying. I hated showing weakness.

"You have help."

"Do I?"

"The warrior angel can help you," he said. "Among others."

"Darius."

And who else? Kincade? He showed up in the warehouse when Chen tortured me. Could he help? And Genghis. He was there for me in the streets of Hong Kong and then again on the rooftop. I swiped away the tears, annoyed, and met his gaze. I couldn't help the smile tugging at the corner of my mouth.

"But can I trust him?"

He returned my smile. "You learn well, Anna. Believe me when I tell you any messenger of the Most High can be trusted. Darius is a warrior angel. He will serve you well."

He reached for me and placed his hand on top of mine. "Use your gifts to find the horn again, Anna. I have faith in you."

Then I woke up.

➤————➤

I bolted to a sitting position, my heart hammering. Sudden light pierced my eyes. I blinked furiously until they finally adjusted. I had never seen the place before. I had no idea where I was. The small room was dominated by the large bed in which I sat. Across the bed was a low table with a vase holding white flowers. The scent of roses lingered in the air.

Roses and sunshine.

I wore a white nightgown and briefly wondered how I came to be in it. I could guess and a blush warmed my cheeks. I checked over my body but found no wounds or scars. Someone cleaned me up and healed me. And I was pretty sure I knew who that someone was. I'd passed out in Darius's arms. The last thing he said to me was not to give up. There must be some hope since my uncle paid me a visit in dreamland.

Dreamland. The dream rushed back to me. The fire. The death. The destruction. Azriel murdering Kincade. Or Ben? I wasn't sure. Was that a harbinger of what was to come?

And my uncle. What a puzzle. He'd been so hostile toward me when we first came into contact with each other after so long. He'd said he had faith in me. Me. I couldn't believe it. Had I *really* dreamed that or was he walking? Did my subconscious conjure that simply because I wanted to believe my uncle had faith in me to find these Holy Relics?

The door cracked open. Darius poked his head in. When he saw me, he opened it wider and stepped through. He smiled.

"Good to see you awake finally. Thought I'd lost you."

Realizing my nakedness underneath the nightgown, I pulled the blankets up to my chin. "Where am I?"

"My home."

"And where is that?"

"In the heavens."

I blinked, unable to comprehend. "I'm in...?"

"The clouds, yes."

"I'm not dead, am I?"

He chuckled. "No, you are quite alive. Fear not, Keeper. You are safe here with me and my brethren."

"Your warrior buddies?" I asked.

"You could say that."

"Are they...here?"

"They guard us even now."

Relief made me relax. Knowing I was safe from Lexi and Azriel gave me the security I needed.

"Genghis? What happened to him? And Huan? And Ling?"

"You ask many questions, Keeper. They defeated the remaining demons and banished them from the area. I was grateful for the help of the Seraphim."

"How did they know where I was?"

"He rules that region. As such he was alerted to the presence of the demons."

"Wish I could have thanked them," I said. "Sorry I passed out."

"How are you feeling?" he asked.

"Fine, actually. I suppose I have you to thank for that."

"You do."

"Well...thank you. I would have died had it not been for you."

"Yes, you would have. And for a while I thought you could not be saved."

"How long have I been here?"

"Three days."

"Three days?" I shoved off the blankets. As soon as my feet hit the cold floor, dizziness assaulted me. My head spun and I groaned. I sank back to the edge of the bed, my head in my hands. I needed to find my balance, to make the swaying floor stop.

"Rest, Keeper." Darius was at my side, nudging me back into the bed. Reluctantly, I complied.

"I can't. Lexi has three days lead time on me. I have to find her. I have to get back the horn. Where are my daggers?" Especially the jade-handled one.

"I have them. I will return them when you need them."

"I need them now. And where are my clothes?"

"They were unsalvageable. I will get you whatever you require."

"I require my clothes," I snarled. Even though I didn't feel so good. I convinced myself the nausea would pass.

"No. You will rest. Your wounds were deep. You were poisoned by the demons. I could not heal you."

I lifted my head and met his gaze. "I thought you said you healed me."

"I agreed you had me to *thank*. I did not say I healed you myself."

Tricky angel. "Who healed me?"

"Someone we can both trust," he said.

I narrowed my eyes at his cryptic message but said nothing. I left some things behind in Hong Kong. My smartphone and my overnight case. Lexi left behind her laptop, though she probably didn't need it wherever she was going. Maybe it would give me a clue as to where she took the horn.

"What about the laptop I left in the hotel room in Hong Kong?"

"I retrieved it for you and will return it whenever you are ready."

Darius was a regular jack-of-all-trades. "Thanks." I leaned back in the pillows, still clutching the blankets. "Before I passed out, you told me not to give up. Does that mean you intend to help me?"

"That is to be discussed later, Keeper. Now someone would like to see you," Darius said.

Surprise flickered through me. Before I could respond, he opened the door and my uncle stepped into the room. I stared at him a long quiet moment, wondering how he managed to get up here. He'd already visited me in my dream. Why was he here now? Darius and Edward exchanged a silent glance and then the angel stepped out of the room, closing the door softly behind him.

I realized the "someone we can both trust" was my uncle. Darius must have brought him here. Edward was the one who healed me. Yet another surprising thing about my uncle.

"What are you doing here?" Even though I already had the answer.

"I came to help you."

"Did you dream walk me?"

"I did."

So, it *was* in my dreams. And he *did* tell me he had faith in me. My breath hitched suddenly in my throat and I thought I might cry. Again. Damn.

"You said you...had faith in me."

"I did." He nodded.

"I, uh, don't know what to say."

He leaned his back on the door and looked me over with a curious glint in his eyes. "Is there anything left to say? Let us let bygones be bygones. Let us move forward. We have a mission."

"We?" I gave him a sharp look, wondering when *my* mission turned into *our* mission.

"You cannot do this alone. I realize that now. I was a fool to allow you to leave. I should have foreseen Lexi would double-cross you." There was no mistaking the regret in his voice. "Whatever happened in the past must be let go if we are to successfully find the Holy Relics."

"Are you saying you're going to help me?"

"I offer my help to you, Annabelle, if you will accept it."

I considered this, wondering how I could ever accept his help. The past was so muddied. Maybe he was right and it was time to let the past die. Maybe he *did* get rid of Marcus to protect me. Maybe there was more to my uncle than met the eye.

"All right," I said slowly.

A weight lifted from my shoulders. Even the tension in the room dissipated. He blew out a slow breath. "When you are fully rested, we will convene and begin to plan our attack. We'll find the horn, Annabelle. That I vow to you."

He turned to leave. "Uncle...one more thing." He paused to give me a glance over his shoulder. "I would prefer if you called me Anna."

It pained him. I understood why he insisted on calling me Annabelle. I was his last living link to his beloved sister. Her namesake. Instead of disagreeing, he merely nodded. As he left me alone, I realized we had reached a crossroads. After all this time, I felt as though we had finally reconciled.

A few hours later, I shoved out of bed and procured clothing from Darius. He dropped a pile on the bed before leaving again. I dressed in the black cargo pants and layered two tanks underneath a black button down. He even returned my daggers. I was happy to have my jade-handled dagger back on my hip. I tucked one in each of my boots. Cracking open the door, I peered into the hall.

Darius's decorating taste left a lot to be desired. There was nothing on the white walls. Even the floor was white. Though I noted with some girlish glee the tiles sparkled. They shimmered under the overhead lights, delighting me at every turn. And when I glanced up to the lights, there was nothing more than a glow. Nothing high-tech there.

I headed down the hallway and found Edward standing at the corner of an ornate—white, of course—marble fireplace. He leaned on the mantle and smoked his pipe. I was immediately reminded of the portrait of my great-grandfather, Edward I, with the pipe clamped between his teeth. The place smelled of rich tobacco and a memory surfaced so suddenly I was nearly knocked back a step.

I recalled Edward, my uncle, standing at the fireplace of the Walker manor not long after he took me to England. I hadn't seen him smoking his pipe in many years and wondered if he tried to kick the habit but couldn't.

He looked so studious. So larger than life. He always had.

"Darius allows you to smoke here?" I asked.

He started at the sound of my voice. He must have been lost in thought.

"I allow it for certain individuals," Darius replied from behind me. He entered the room, his wings tucked neatly against his back.

"When are we going after Lexi?" I didn't want to waste any more time.

"Patience," Edward said.

"No. Every passing minute is another minute between me and the horn. I have to figure out fast where to start searching and right now I don't have a clue."

"Are you going to tell her, or shall I?" Darius sounded angry.

"Tell me what?"

"She is not ready," Edward said.

"She *is* ready. She is the Keeper. She needs to know."

"I would prefer if you wouldn't talk about me as if I'm not here. What's going on?"

I glanced between the two of them. Edward gave Darius a look of distaste before blowing out a puff of smoke. He tapped the bowl of his pipe on a nearby crystal bowl emptying it of gray ashes.

"You have the ability to find it," he said. "It is one of your gifts."

"I don't understand."

"You have touched the relic. You are now forever connected to it. All you have to do is close your eyes and think of the horn. The location will be revealed."

"This is another one of my mysterious 'abilities'?" He merely nodded. I crossed my arms over my chest. "Why have I not known about this before?"

"Because you have not been called to find the relics until now," Edward explained in a patient voice as though talking to a child. I sometimes felt like a child. "You received the call and with that your talents have begun to manifest."

"The call being a visit from Azriel and Joachim?" I asked.

"Yes."

"I don't believe you." Defiance surged forward. This journey had been so strange and despite my resistance, I felt myself changing. My abilities were surfacing yet I wanted to deny them. Push them back into the dark cavern whence they came.

I couldn't believe I thought the word *whence* and scowled.

"It is written," Edward said. And to prove it to me—because I would demand it—he picked up the family history book from the cushion of a chair. He cracked open the tome and flipped a few pages before holding it out to me. "Here."

I, James Edward Walker, write this now as I have spoken with the archangel, Michael. The future Keeper, one of my line, will be more powerful than those who have preceded her. She will know where to find the Holy Relics when the time comes, when Man has fallen to hopelessness and when Lucifer prepares to fight for the right to rule Earth. And should those relics become lost to her she only needs to envision them in her mind's eye. And if they be in Heaven, she will see them. And if they be in Hell, she will see them. And if they be hidden on Earth, she will find them. As it is written, so let it be done.

I stared at the words for the longest time, pulse thrumming in my throat. Edward closed the book with a thud and tucked it under his arm.

"I have faith in you, Anna. Have faith in yourself."

I gave him a sharp look. This time when he told me he had faith in me, it was in person instead of a dream. I glanced at Darius who nodded encouragement.

With a sigh, I closed my eyes and thought of the horn. I imagined what it looked like. The shiny surface, the belled end. It appeared in my mind's eye as I saw it in Chen's office resting against the velvet material. And then the scene moved in fast-forward. Lexi and I rushed out of the office fighting the demons in the elevator and then on the rooftop where I stupidly handed it over to her. Where she betrayed me.

This was my last memory but the scene did not die. Lexi clutched the horn as Azriel took her in his arms and lifted up. And for a moment, I realized I *was* the horn. The scene playing out in my mind moved fast. It was hard to follow the horn changing hands, from Lexi's to Azriel's. And then it rested somewhere. The two of them were together, naked. Fucking.

My stomach turned and I winced. I wanted so much to open my eyes, to kill the scene in front of me. Thankfully it lasted only a few seconds and then the horn was on the move again. There was a flash of light, darkness, and then light again. Caverns. Sulfur. Fiery rivers. Death.

I gasped and opened my eyes. Edward and Darius stared at me with anticipation.

"I know where it is. I know where to find the horn," I said.

"Tell us." Edward took a tentative step toward me.

"It's in Hell."

CHAPTER 19

E DWARD'S FACE BLANCHED. IT wasn't often he had a look
of apprehension. He was always the calm, cool, collected
one in control of every situation. Seeing him look as though he
were about to toss his cookies made me a little anxious.

Okay, a lot anxious.

Darius didn't look all that thrilled with my announcement
the horn had made its way, quite literally, to the pit of Hell. I
had to admit I wasn't all that excited. I shifted from one foot to
the other, waiting for one of them to say something. Anything.
They didn't.

"Well? How do we get there?"

"It is forbidden for me to go," Darius said.

"Why?" I asked.

"A price must be paid."

"What kind of price?" He had saved my skin. I considered
him an ally and didn't want to lose him.

"He'll be punished," Edward said. "Azriel will no doubt take
the horn to Lucifer. Anna, you must find a way to stop him."

He made it sound so easy. "Yeah, right. Like how am I supposed to do that? I'm sure I can't walk up to the gates of Hell and knock. It's not like they'll send a welcoming party for me."

They were both silent and exchanged a glance between them. It was like they had some silent communication going on. Which made me want to put up my hands in exasperation. Edward's gaze leveled on me.

"I will go with you," he said. His tone was clear. It wasn't up for discussion or debate.

It shocked me to the marrow of my bones. He wanted to come with me? Had he lost all his marbles? "I don't think that's a good idea."

"Why? Because you think I'm too old? I'm not that fragile and I can help you."

"It's not that, Edward. I need to know you'll still be here if I fuck up."

He pressed his lips together in a thin line.

"Perhaps the Keeper is correct," Darius said. "Should anything happen to her—"

"Nothing will happen to her if I'm there to protect her."

Oh, please. Edward protect me? Was he serious? We may have come to some sort of understanding about our past but that didn't mean I wanted him tagging along. This was something I had to do alone. It wasn't like he could keep a watchful eye on me anyway should something happen.

With that thought, an idea struck me.

"Edward, you're the most powerful dream walker I know. You can even enter waking dreams and consciousness." Like Azriel.

He stiffened, looking proud and sure. "That is a well-known fact, yes."

I shifted my weight again, unsure if I should suggest it or not. It made me uncomfortable but it might be the only way I'd do it alone. "What if you...stay in contact with me? Then if anything should happen you can call for reinforcements."

"And what reinforcements would that be?"

"You know people, don't you? Can't you call in the cavalry or something?"

I struck a chord. He stared at me as he considered. Deep down, I always thought there was more to my uncle than meets the eye. The fact he didn't deny it right away confirmed my suspicions. He *was* the most powerful dream walker and he had connections. Probably to powerful, dangerous people. I respected him even more.

At last, he said, "All right we'll do it your way. But at the first sign of trouble, I'm coming after you."

Like there wasn't going to be trouble. I was traveling to Hell, after all. Anything that could go wrong would go wrong.

"Fair enough. What's the plan?"

"There are certain entry points around the world," Darius said. "I will take you to one."

"Take me as in flash me there? No, thanks." As much as I enjoyed the idea, the flashing made me sick.

"Be reasonable, Anna," Edward said. "We haven't much time before Azriel delivers the horn into Lucifer's hands. Once he has it, we'll never get it back."

"I realize that. And for all we know, he's already delivered it to Lucifer. But the flashing thing makes me sick. I'll need an alternate method of transportation."

"I will fly you," Darius offered.

"Great. When can we leave?"

"I am at your disposal."

"The sooner the better."

"Anna, be careful," Edward said. "You are the Keeper. The only one who can lead us out of this darkness."

"I know. And I will."

His brow crinkled with worry. I'd never seen him look at me that way before. For a minute, I thought he was going to hug me but he didn't. Instead, he picked up his pipe and crushed fresh tobacco into the bowl.

"Good luck."

When I left, he'd monitor me. Even though we'd cleared the air, it still made me apprehensive he'd be poking around in my head.

Now I needed to concentrate on Darius taking me to wherever that place was so I could start my decent into Hell.

Totally wasn't looking forward to that.

❖────────❖

I did a cursory glance over my room but found nothing left of my belongings. All my daggers were securely strapped to my body. As I stepped out of the room, Darius waited in the hallway with the sparkly tiles.

"I'm going to need some supplies," I said.

"Of course." He nodded agreement. "Where do you want to go?"

I paused. What sort of supplies did one need in Hell? I had no idea and I was momentarily stymied by the idea. I blinked, my mind racing as I tried to figure out what to bring. Darius grinned. The sort of grin that lit up those gorgeous eyes of his. I swear I nearly melted into a puddle.

"You need guidance."

"That'd be great." I gave him a sheepish smile.

"Come then."

He held out his hand in invitation. I slipped my fingers in his and he pulled me to him. My heart did a funny thing in my chest as I realized how close we were. He was devastatingly beautiful. His features were carved into hard lines but there was something soft about them. Something that rendered the heart inside out. I couldn't explain it. He was...angelic. Really that was the only word for him.

His lips were perfect and full. His eyes were a gorgeous glittering dark brown. His body was all hard planes and angles and deliciousness. Silver threaded his snowy white wings, giving them a shimmer. An ethereal glow all their own. They stretched behind him and I marveled at the span, wondering what the length was from tip to tip. I imagined the feathers softer than anything I'd ever touched before. Softer than silk. Then a kitten's fur. My fingers curled, itching to touch. To stroke those beautiful iridescent wings. Every muscle curved into perfection. He was flesh-and-blood art.

"Ready?"

His voice rumbled around in his broad chest. I licked my lips and nodded. Before I could make a move, he spun me so my back was to him and wrapped his arms around me. They were solid arms. Safe arms. And he was a wall of sexy muscle behind me.

"How does this work exactly?" I was suddenly apprehensive about this little trip. This was a first for me.

"Do not let go." His warm breath trickled over my ear, raising gooseflesh on my arms.

Before I could reply, the floor dropped out beneath us. My breath hitched. Fear coiled in a tight knot inside me. We plunged downward. Cold air rushed over me and somewhere in the distance was the faint flap of his wings.

As my heart pounded a wild beat in my throat, I realized we were in the heavens. Stars and wispy clouds surrounded us as we plunged toward the ground. Darius tightened his grasp as the cold seeped into my bones and I shivered.

The scene changed in another instant and we were surrounded by blue sky. The ground below was patterned now and I could see rooftops and farmland, rivers and lakes, mountains and hilltops. It was incredible and breathtaking. Before long, we were back in

Hong Kong within a part of the city I didn't recognize nor had been in.

If I had any idea flying with an angel was so awesome, I would have put it on my bucket list.

We landed with grace and ease to the concrete. Dusk settled over the sky but it was still summer and the air was sticky and warm. As we stood there, I realized my hands clutched his arms. When I released him, my nails left behind crescent shapes on his skin.

"Sorry about that."

He continued to hold me, his warmth cascading over me. A girlish blush crept along my neck and flushed my cheeks. Was he...did he...like me? He'd seen me at my worst. Covered in demon blood and stinky.

"Thanks for the ride."

I pushed away. He let go with some reluctance. I turned to him, completely aware of the awkwardness between us. Wondering what to say, how to act.

"We're back in Hong Kong?" I asked.

"Yes. We can find help here. Come."

He took my hand as we headed through the busy Hong Kong streets. I stole a glance at him. His wings were hidden. We looked like any other tourist couple enjoying a night out. Except we weren't a couple and we weren't enjoying a night on the town.

He entered an ancient looking shop with a bell that tinkled our arrival. Once inside, he led me past the shelves of dusty artifacts. Vases and trinkets were all over the place. We went through a dusty velvet curtain to a backroom. Dimly lit, we passed numerous shelves as we made our way to the back where we stopped in front of a door. He knocked twice and a second later, the door cracked open. I could see one eye peering out, looking at first Darius and then me.

"Valiance," Darius said.

The man opened the door wider and stepped aside and we walked inside. He closed the door behind us. Before I could even take in my surroundings, Genghis rose from a chair and greeted us with a broad smile. I couldn't hide my surprise at seeing him here. "You have returned with our Keeper," he greeted. He kissed me on both cheeks. "I am relieved to see you are unharmed. What can I do for you?"

"Darius brought me. I need supplies for a trip I'm taking," I said.

He cocked his head to one side and looked at first Darius and then back at me. "What sort of trip?"

"I'm taking her to Dante's Cave," Darius said.

Genghis looked at him as though he'd grown a second head. "For what purpose?"

"To retrieve the horn Azriel stole from me," I said.

His gaze swung to me and he looked at me a long quiet moment. "A very dangerous place. Are you sure you're up for it, Keeper?"

I wasn't sure about anything. "I am and need supplies. Can you help?"

"You're going alone?"

"Yes."

"Are you sure that's a wise decision?"

"I have to," I said.

"Can you help?" Darius asked. "You have experience with Dante's Cave, do you not?"

"I do, but..." He trailed off. I noticed Darius glared at him. "Very well. Come with me. I will take care of you."

Genghis waved me after him. I realized I was still holding Darius's hand and released him to following the Seraphim leader. He took us to his office and closed the door.

"First you need this." Genghis leaned down behind his desk and produced an old-fashioned knapsack with a shoulder strap.

I peeked inside. It was packed with energy bars, a flashlight and a couple of daggers. Mine were strapped to my thighs, in my boots and my favorite dagger rested on my waist but I could always use more. I lose them a lot. There was a small vial with a cork stopper containing water tinged with a bluish haze.

"This is not an ordinary knapsack. There's food for the journey as well as a small vial of holy water. However, when you run out of something, it will resupply you."

"A magic knapsack. I love it. What's the holy water for?" I asked.

He shrugged. "You may need it."

He walked across the room to a shelf, where he shuffled books back and forth. Not finding what he wanted, he then went to a cabinet and pulled open the door. He rummaged around inside it before turning, holding a small glass bottle. It looked empty but he handed it to me anyway.

"What's that?"

"The light of the North Star for the dark places," he said.

"Cool. What else you got for me?"

He spread his empty hands. "I wish you luck, my friend. God speed. Come back safe."

"I will." I hoped.

We bid him farewell. The two of us left the little shop. I was relieved I was armed to the teeth. Despite the sense of power it gave me, my innards were a nervous wreck. I had no idea what I'd do with the holy water or the light of the North Star. I'd use them both if the opportunity presented itself.

As we headed down the street and turned a corner, I had the distinct sensation someone followed us. I halted and turned to look behind me. Darius paused, too, but no one was there and I sensed no demons.

"What is it?" he asked.

I sniffed the air, then shrugged. "Nothing, I guess."

We continued walking down the street, mirrored glass buildings on one side. I knew Darius was trying to get away from all the foot traffic to a secluded place where we could take off again for Dante's

Cave. But I still had that feeling of being followed. I glanced at our reflection in the mirrored glass as we walked. Several paces back, trying to be inconspicuous and doing a terrible job, was Kincade Harrison.

"Son of a bitch," I muttered.

I spun on my heel and stalked toward Kincade, who realized with some horror, he'd been made. Instead of trying to hide it, though, he stopped and faced me. He was dressed in his typical garb of scuffed cowboy boots, jeans and button down.

"Why are you following me?"

"Where have you been? I've been looking for you everywhere." He gave Darius a cursory glance. "Who's this?"

"I might ask the same of you," Darius replied, tone sour.

I glanced between the two of them. For a second, I had a vision of two roosters with chests puffed out and crests pointing upward. I stepped between them.

"He is none of your business, nor is where I've been," I said to Kincade.

"I saw the carnage on the top of the building. I was concerned."

I would have laughed if I hadn't been so annoyed. "You tracked me there, too?"

"Anna, you're in over your head." That wasn't the first time he'd told me that.

"I told you to go home. There is nothing to be concerned about. I don't need your concern. I don't need your help. I don't need *you*. Now beat it."

He huffed out a breath, his hands at his waist as he looked me over. As though he was ready to continue arguing his point. Or pummel me. It was a toss-up.

I didn't want to admit I was a little flattered and touched by his words. He was the one who saved my ass from Azriel and his demons when Ben was murdered. He was the one who got me out of the hospital in one piece without getting arrested. He was the one who got me out of that warehouse alive. I probably owed him a debt of gratitude. But the fact he kept following me was pissing me off.

The dream I had when Azriel stabbed Kincade with the Spear of Destiny flooded back to me in a rush of memory. So much so, a sharp stabbing pain went through me and I stifled a whimper. In the dream, I saw Ben's face when he looked at me. I worried that was a sign of things to come.

"I wish you'd tell me what this is all about," he said.

Frustration pierced through me. "Why? Why do you care so much?"

He hesitated, ran his hand through his hair making the ends stick up. He looked at Darius again, his lips peeling back from his teeth in an agitated snarl.

"Can I talk you a second? Without your guard dog?"

Darius growled in return.

I turned to the angel. "Give us a minute, okay?"

He gave me a reluctant nod before moving a safe distance that wasn't within earshot but close enough to keep eyes on me. I turned back to Kincade, still paused on the sidewalk of the busy street. Pedestrians streamed around us, laughing with each other, talking on their cell phone. Cars and taxis whooshed by. The cacophony of sirens, horns honking, trucks rumbling surrounded us. I wanted to be a normal girl on a normal night hanging out with a normal guy on vacation in an exotic city. That wasn't in the cards for me.

"You have three minutes. Talk." He hesitated again. I was losing patience. "Or I'm leaving."

"Fine." He snarled again and glanced away, struggling with whatever internal monologue was inside his head. "I'm here to..." He stopped, clamped his jaw shut and then ran his hand through his hair again, blowing out a heated breath. "You clearly need help."

I stiffened at his insinuation. "Why? Because I'm a stupid woman?"

He practically growled. "No, Anna, damn it." He moved closer to me, dropping his voice. "Azriel tried to frame you for those murders. He's so desperate to get something from you he killed for it. What is it? Is it that Horn of Gabriel you mentioned?"

I sucked in a sharp breath. Regret filled me. I wish I hadn't told him but it was too late for that. I clenched my jaw until it hurt. I forced out my reply. "Nothing. And if you know what's good for you, you'll keep your mouth shut about that horn."

His eyes narrowed. "Lie. I didn't follow you to your uncle's on a lie. The difference between you and him is he hides it much better than you do. He wouldn't tell me anything, either."

That, at least, was a relief. Damn Kincade and his internal lie detector. I gave a shrug of one shoulder. "I have nothing to tell."

"You do," he insisted. "Why are you here in Hong Kong?"

The last person on the planet I wanted help from was him. "That reason no longer exists."

The vision played again in my head. Azriel holding the Spear of Destiny and shoving it through Kincade's heart.

"Someday you're going to tell me everything. All of it. From the very beginning."

I didn't much like the demanding tone and the hard glint in his eyes. He meant business. He intended to ferret out the truth from me one way or another but I was a stubborn girl.

"Don't bark orders at me. I'm not one of your subordinates. I don't need any of your help."

I stepped around him and started for Darius, annoyed he was like a bad penny that continued to turn up.

"Anna."

I turned to look at him.

He started to say something else but it was all forgotten as a blast rocked the entire street. Kincade was blown away from the curb. Away from me. The intense heat shoved me backward. A nearby car was engulfed in flames. Debris rained down everywhere. Screams and mass hysteria erupted on the street. The explosion sent passersby running for cover. Others stood and gawked.

Darius wrapped his arms around me, pulling me away from the flames. I struggled against him. When the smoke and haze cleared, Kincade's crumpled was body on the sidewalk. The sight burned into my corneas forever as terror curled through me. I may dislike the guy, was annoyed at him even, but I certainly didn't want him dead.

"Let me go!"

He released his hold on me. Maybe because he didn't want to fight me. I didn't know. I didn't care.

I rushed to Kincade and fell to my knees at his side. Blood caked his face and neck. He had burns over part of his body. His clothes were singed to his skin. I was scared shrapnel was lodged in him. It was too dark for me to see. I checked for a pulse and found a weak one. Fear coiled in my gut. I pulled him into my lap and cradled his body. Already I could hear the sirens in the night air.

"Kincade, can you hear me? If you can, open your eyes." He didn't respond.

Darius was at my side then. "He's badly injured. I can take him."

But the first responders were on the scene already. Firefighters extinguished the flames of the nearby car which was nothing but a burned-out shell while the paramedics rushed to help the others injured in the blast. As they approached, Darius faded into the shadows.

Several paramedics shoved me out of the way to help Kincade. Within minutes, they had him strapped to a gurney and in the back of the ambulance. An impulse shot through me.

"I'm going with them," I told Darius.

Before I could take a step, the warrior angel took my arm and turned me to face him. "Are you sure that's wise?"

I shook my head. "No, but I have to make sure he's all right. How do I find you when I'm ready to leave?"

"Call me."

"How?"

His hand skimmed along the side of my neck and suddenly I realized what he intended to do. I should have stopped him. I should have pushed him away. But I couldn't make my stubborn limbs do what my brain told them. His lips were a breath from mine. The whoosh of blood in my ears was so loud I almost missed what he said next.

"All you have to do is say my name into the wind, Keeper."

And then he kissed me. My eyes fluttered closed. His mouth was warm and gentle and surprisingly delightful. I drowned in that kiss as his tongue slid against mine.

But that was all he did. Nothing more. No other touching. He removed his hand from my neck and stepped away, disappearing into the shadows.

CHAPTER 20

D ARIUS TASTED LIKE RED velvet. Decadent. Sinful. Rich. The flavor lingered on my tongue after he was gone. I shook it off. I climbed into the back of the ambulance with Kincade and the paramedics.

At the hospital, they took him straight to surgery and forced me to wait. There was somewhat of a language barrier but I got the gist the waiting room was as far as I'd get. I paced the length of the room, acutely aware of those waiting for news of their own loved ones, their eyes on me.

I hadn't stepped foot in a hospital since I left Texas. I was fairly certain I could get to Kincade if I wanted. I stared at the emergency room doors and considered my options. Didn't I owe him that? He tracked me to England and then to Hong Kong. He came back for me insisting I needed help. His help. He knew Azriel tried to frame me for those murders and he knew I'd lied about why I was in Hong Kong.

I bit my thumbnail while I waited for news and continued to pace.

The air in the waiting room whooshed away suddenly and I halted. Everyone around me stopped moving. I stiffened as cinnamon wafted over me. Dread clawed through the lining of my stomach. Bile rose to my throat. I swallowed it back down.

"Hello, Anna."

Azriel. He leaned casually against the wall his black wings spread out behind him. He looked as he always did. Dangerous. Sexy. Evil.

"You son of a bitch." My fists clenched. I forced my feet to stay rooted in place. I wanted to lunge toward him, wrap my fingers around his throat and choke the life out of him.

"I'm glad you got my message." He grinned a slow seductive grin.

"You stay away from him. He has *nothing* to do with this."

"But he has everything to do with *you*." He stood straight and walked toward me. "All you had to do was cooperate. Instead, you betrayed me."

"I found the horn. I was—"

"Don't." Warning flashed in his dark eyes. "Save your lies. I know the truth."

"Because you turned Lexi. What was the price for her? Her soul?"

"She came willingly." He smiled. "I wanted it to be you. Oh, how I wanted it to be you. There was so much we could have done together. I tried but you..." His gaze raked over me, then he shook his head. "You're a stubborn girl." He traced the line of my collarbone.

I slapped his hand away. "Don't touch me. Have you forgotten you tried to kill me in my dreams?"

"I never forget anything. I enjoy playing with you, Anna." A dangerous gleam glinted in his eyes. I couldn't ignore the awful dread still crawling through me. "You have some...allegiance to this man. Why? Is he your lover?"

"He's not my lover. He's nothing. We have no allegiance. We were only recently acquainted."

His eyes narrowed. "Why would he go to so much trouble to clear your name if you are mere acquaintances, hm?"

He had me there. I didn't know the answer to that. I bit the inside of my cheek to keep from responding.

"I am no fool. I know who and what he is. This *gardien*. Next time he dies, *chérie*."

"Don't threaten me or him."

"Or what? You'll kill me? Hardly," he scoffed.

He taunted me but I couldn't stop the flash of prickling anger. Azriel wasn't done with me yet. He stepped closer, crowding my personal space and sucking up all the oxygen between us and not in a good way. Not in the way Kincade had before. I tried to back up but he pushed me against the wall. Cornered me. My fight or flight instinct wanted to kick in but I managed to keep my composure.

"When are you going to realize you are nothing? You don't have the experience to be the Keeper of the Holy Relics. Nor do you have the courage. You're only doing this because you think you have to. Because you think once you have the relics, then all will be right with the world. That we will quietly go away. We will not quietly go away, Anna. We are only just beginning."

"Fuck you." It was a lame comeback.

He laughed. "I have the horn and soon I will hand it over to Lucifer. And then the war for mankind truly begins."

Bastard. I clenched my fists harder, my nails biting into my palms. I didn't want to tell him I intended to go after it. I needed the element of surprise. My jaw tightened as I ground my back teeth together. I wondered, though, why he hadn't given it to Lucifer yet. Why did he keep it?

"I hoped to convince you to help me find the other relics. But clearly, I cannot. You may lack courage but you do not lack honor. I cannot trust you to find them for me," he continued.

"That's right. I won't find them for you," I snapped. "But I don't intend to find them for Michael either. I'll find them because I'm the Keeper."

"Your confidence is admirable," he said. "You give me no other alternative than to hunt for them."

"You intend to go after them yourself? Good luck." My tone was haughty.

"Lexi will help me. You and your detective friend should stay out of our way." His tone was conversational but the look on his face said otherwise.

"If you harm Kincade, I *will* kill you." I wasn't a threat to him. Fine. He thought I lacked courage? We'd see about that.

"Ah, so he is more than *nothing* to you. I look forward to your attempted murder. Until next time, *chérie*."

Frustration clawed through me as he disappeared. The waiting room returned to normal. I shoved my hand through my hair and sat in the nearest chair. Pacing didn't help. The ball of worry and fear coiled in my gut remained. Fear I'd fail and not find the horn again. Fear Azriel would come after Kincade again. Fear Kincade wouldn't recover and he'd die and it would be my fault. I already had Ben's death on my conscious. Must I suffer with Kincade's, too? Much as the man annoyed me, I'd grown accustomed to his sudden visits. Knowing he lurked somewhere in the shadows gave me comfort.

Fuck fear. Now I was all the more determined to find the horn. To find the rest of the Holy Relics. To become the Keeper I was meant to become. To fight this war for me, my uncle and mankind. Screw Azriel. Screw the Fallen. Screw Lucifer.

I *could* do this. I *would* do this.

With Kincade finally out of surgery, the doctor arrived with news. He managed to stop the internal bleeding but Kincade wasn't out of danger yet. He was lucky and had only first-degree burns on the right side of his body. They listed him in critical condition and kept him in ICU until he was stable.

"Can I see him?"

"He's in recovery. Tomorrow would be better."

Right. Tomorrow wasn't good for me.

I nodded. I watched the doc walk away, renewed conviction flowing through my blood. The horn would be mine again and Azriel would pay with his life.

CHAPTER 21

I WALKED OUTSIDE THE hospital. Numb. The only thing left to do was find the horn. And then what? I shook my head, uncertain what to do once I had it. I didn't want Azriel to have it. I sure as hell didn't want that traitor, Lexi, to have it. Nor was I going to hand it over to Joachim.

But...if I stole it from Azriel what would he do? Would he kill Kincade? Me? I shoved the thought away. I'd worry about that later.

I left the emergency room and stepped into the balmy night. My nerves were raw. My head pounded. All I wanted was to go home and climb into my own bed. I couldn't do that because I didn't have a home anymore. I didn't have a job anymore. All that was lost to me when Azriel showed up in my life.

I missed Ben. The way he smiled when I came home in the mornings. How he'd cook bacon just the way I liked it—crispy and a little black. His endless chatter about work or nothing. Cuddling on the sofa on Saturday night with a bad movie, a bowl of popcorn, and a couple of beers.

I walked into the parking lot, my feet shuffling on the pavement. My heart hurt but feeling sorry for myself wouldn't get me anywhere. I had a horn to steal. I had a mission to complete.

I had to call Darius.

I glanced up at the night sky. The city lights blotted out the stars. One or two twinkled in a sea of black. The full moon burned bright, shining down and bathing the pebbled pavement in a bluish glow. I clenched my hands and turned toward the wind. I was scared but I had to keep going.

"Darius."

As soon as his name escaped into the wind, a mist shrouded me from the hospital parking lot. Then his arms slipped around my waist from behind.

"Keeper." His voice, soft and dark and tempting, was in my ear. His warm breath tickled the sensitive skin on my lobe.

I closed my eyes as his warmth wrapped around me, seeping into me and filling me up. I couldn't revel in him for long.

"Take me to the entrance, Darius. Let's go."

"It will not be easy," he said.

"I'm aware."

"If I could come with you, Keeper, I would."

"I know."

His words stabbed me in the heart, the sharp pain adding to the already tortured organ. I'd love if he fought by my side. I turned in his arms to face him. "I'm ready."

With a nod, he pulled me closer and launched into the night sky. We went straight up but I didn't want to watch the world flash by. I slipped my arms around his neck and buried my face there. His scent was decadence and warmth and a hint of sunshine. His nearness gave me comfort and hope in a world of discomfort and hopelessness. Maybe I could do this thing. Maybe I could find the horn and return. Maybe I would survive.

Maybe.

Doubt crept into my mind. I shoved it away as quickly as it appeared. We flew through the night for what seemed like hours. I drifted to sleep. The dream started right away.

Kincade was in that dream, walking with me on that street in Hong Kong. The same one where the bomb went off.

Then Azriel came along. I couldn't shake the stalker even in my dreams. He charged toward us. Kincade shoved me behind him. They engaged in hand to hand combat. As in the other dreams, Azriel placed his hand over Kincade's heart and slowly pulled it back.

He was taking Kincade's soul.

I screamed and dove for Azriel, gave him a mighty shove until he released Kincade who stumbled backward. Azriel came for me then, his hand a claw as he reached for me. Kincade tackled him and body slammed him to the ground. Azriel's head smacked the pavement with a sickening crack. They rolled and fought and then Kincade flew backward toward a couple of trashcans, crashing into them.

Azriel got to his feet, his mouth bloody, his hair tousled.

"This isn't over, *chérie*."

I hurried over to Kincade and helped him to his feet. He grasped my hand as our eyes met.

"Admit you need me, Anna."

The dream was over.

I awoke in a cold sweat, unsure what to make of this new dream. I chalked it up to worry about Kincade and hoped he'd be all right.

As I came back to reality, I realized I was in a dense forest. Sunlight trickled through the leaves, slanting to the foliage-covered ground. I was no longer in Darius's arms. I sat on the ground against a tree.

Darius stood in front of me, his back to me. The silver in his wings glinted in the morning light. He remained perfectly still as though a sentry guarding his post. I pushed to my feet.

"Where are we?" I asked.

"Dante's Forest."

I blinked. Of course, I knew Dante's Inferno. I never knew there was a forest named after him, too.

I glanced around. Thick foliage carpeted the ground. The leaves weaved a ceiling overhead. It wasn't hot here like back home. The chill in the air seeped into my bones and made me shiver. A well-worn path led through a patch of dark trees where no light punctured the shadows.

"The entrance to the cave is nearby. It will take you to the First Circle." He motioned toward the darkness.

That figured.

Was I going to do this armed with my five daggers in a knapsack? I realized I hadn't thought it through very well. I shoved my hand through the length of my hair.

"You are apprehensive, Keeper."

"Yes."

"As you should be."

That didn't help. He took my hand and led me through the bracken. I assumed he was taking me to the darkness but instead he veered to the right and paused at the edge of a stream. He produced an empty water bottle out of thin air. Kneeling at the edge of the stream, he filled the bottle then handed it to me.

"For your trip."

"Thanks."

"It will refill when you need it."

I nodded understanding. "Like the backpack."

"Yes."

I took a deep breath. "I think I'm ready now."

He took my hand again. The warmth of his fingers pressed into mine. I still got a whiff of that faint scent of sunshine emanating off him. I took comfort in that. We walked from the stream into the darkness. It took a minute for my eyes to adjust but he didn't seem bothered. My boots crunched on leaves and limbs as we pushed onward. The forest was strangely silent here and the deeper we went the warmer it got. The chill in the air was gone.

"Are we getting closer?" Because I was an impatient sort and I wanted to this over.

"Almost there," Darius said.

I smelled the cave opening before I saw it. Like I could smell demons before I saw them. It had that same peculiar metallic twang. That same sulfuric odor. My eyes were still adjusting but as we neared, I made out the opening, the way the rock curved and opened inward. And for a moment it looked as though it was a yawning carved face with stony eyes peering down. Like it anticipated enjoying me as a snack. My heart drummed a rapid beat. My stomach was scraped by a twinge of something icy.

I stopped to stare at the blackness trying to imagine what was in there. The yawning abyss beckoned me closer. Horrors awaited in the gloom.

I took a deep breath and my first step toward fate.

"I'm coming with you."

The familiar voice stopped me and I whirled. Edward walked toward us. He wasn't wearing his traditional three-piece suit. Instead, he was dressed ready for battle in dark camo fatigues and black boots. I stared, dumbfounded, as he approached.

"I thought we decided you would stay behind." I wanted to pretend I didn't feel relieved but I did. I couldn't deny I wanted him to come with me.

"No, *you* decided. I did not agree." He glanced at the warrior angel who seemed to have flushed red. "Thank you, Darius."

"He brought you here. While I was..." I halted, cutting off my words.

I didn't want to share anything about where I was. Uncle Edward would no doubt question me. It was bad enough Kincade had met with my uncle. I didn't need Edward questioning me about Kincade. He was just a cop. A cop laid up in the hospital because of me.

"Kincade will live," Edward said.

I stiffened. "How do you know about that?"

"When he came to England looking for you..." He paused, considering his words. I wondered what went on in that head of his to make him stop. "I had to find out who he was and why he was looking for you."

"He's nobody."

He lifted one dark eyebrow. "He doesn't seem like nobody. You are quite transparent in your own dreams."

Annoyance and irritation chafed me, abrading what was left of my patience. I despised he knew more about me than I intended. If he found Kincade in my dreams, that meant one thing. He dream walked me.

"You aren't the only one who dreams of demons and Fallen, Anna. He does, too. Just as he dreams of you."

A flush so hot threatened to blister the skin off my bones.

"You son of a bitch. You dream walked him, didn't you?" Fury released in my gut like a spring-loaded catapult. "You had no right. None! He's not one of us. He wouldn't understand."

"He understands more about who we are than you realize. He is not the enemy."

"Then who is he?" I demanded.

The wheels clicked in his head as he decided how to respond. "I'm not sure yet."

I wondered if that was a lie. Kincade mentioned he was adept at it, more so than me.

"Enemy or not, you still shouldn't have dream walked him." I tried to ignore the part where Edward indicated Kincade dreamed about me. I also tried to ignore the tingling of excitement the thought gave me.

I was unsuccessful.

"If you believe I overstepped my bounds then I do apologize. He seemed to be someone you cared about. I thought you'd want to know he would recover."

I did but I didn't want Edward taking liberties with Kincade.

"He has an interest in you, too," Edward added almost as an afterthought.

I spun away from him so he wouldn't see the scarlet blush encase my face. I wasn't stupid. I suspected Kincade had a passing interest. He followed me all the way to England and then Hong Kong, after all. I wasn't sure I could trust him. I wanted to but I wasn't sure.

"Let's get this over with." I slung the backpack over my shoulder. "When we get back, Darius, you can return my uncle to his estate." I turned to Edward and pressed the tip of my finger against his chest. "And you stay out of his dreams. And mine."

"Would that I could, dear niece, but you walk in the shadow of danger."

A reminder I was his blood relative with the *dear niece*. I was not dear to him any more than he was dear to me. Darius made no reply. I stomped toward the cave, my boots crushing leaves and sticks with a snap, crackle, pop. Behind me, my uncle followed.

"Hope you can keep up, old man."

"Don't worry about me. Worry about getting the horn," he retorted.

I fumbled in the backpack for the flashlight, then flipped it on. The light illuminated the cave. Water trickled down the rough-hewn walls. Almost like it wept. In the light, it didn't seem so scary.

"I can't let you do this alone, Anna."

I didn't want to talk to him. I wanted to brood.

"I'm a big girl. I can handle things on my own."

"That may be true, but can you handle what Lucifer throws at you?"

He moved to walk beside me. Even though I wanted him to come along, it annoyed me he was with me. Maybe I didn't know what I was getting myself into but I couldn't allow fear to consume me.

"You cannot go into this thinking that getting the horn will be easy."

I whirled on him. "I don't know what I think! But you sure are willing to tell me, aren't you?"

We stopped walking. His face was lit by the garish glow of the flashlight. He looked grim. I could see the lines in his haggard face.

"This is only the beginning, Anna. There are four more relics to locate."

"Don't you think I know that? And Azriel will do everything in his power to get his hands on them before me. He's probably searching for them now."

"No. He will not search."

"Why not?"

"Because he needs you to find them for him." He pushed out a heated breath.

"He told me he intended to use Lexi."

"He can try but she won't be as effective as you. She's not as strong as you are, nor does she possess your gifts. She's merely a dream walker and not a very good one at that," he said. "As the Keeper, you are the only one who can recover the relics."

"Why?"

"You must touch the relic first before it can be handed to an angel. That is why they cannot search for them."

I assumed he meant any angel, fallen or otherwise. I understood now why the archangels appointed a Keeper. Why I had to be the one to find them. Azriel was able to take the horn away from me because I'd touched it first and then, like an idiot, gave it to Lexi.

"You do not yet understand you are a beacon. Once you locate the relic, he can track it through you."

"How? By getting into my dreams?"

He nodded.

Like I could track it once I touched it.

I straightened. "Then I'm going to have to keep the bastard out, aren't I?"

"Once we complete this task, you will return with me to England so I may teach you."

"You're springing this on me *now*?"

"It's the only way to protect yourself from Azriel or any others."

"No way. I'm not going with you." Even after everything that happened with me, Kincade and Lexi, my stubborn streak remained. I realized I needed to listen to Uncle Edward. I needed to learn everything I could from him. He was truly my only ally.

Well, except for Kincade. He might be an ally.

He lifted an eyebrow. "We shall see."

I swung the flashlight back toward the cave opening and started walking again. He fell in step next to me. As we made our way through the cave, I noticed the change in air temperature. It was damper, colder. I realized the walls morphed into faces. Not ordinary human faces either. Demons. Tortured by fire.

Their silent screams lined the wall. I shifted the beam of light from the walls to the pathway in front of us so I didn't have to see them. Tortured wails echoed in the distance. The deeper we went into the cave, the louder it got.

Up ahead, I made out an opening of bright white light. An exit? Or an entrance to some other horrible place?

"We're journeying toward the First Circle," Edward said.

As the opening grew larger and larger, the cave became hotter and hotter. Sweat broke out on my brow and trickled down my back. I felt death. I smelled decay. I heard cries of pain. It sickened me, twisting my stomach into a tight knot.

At the edge of the light, we paused. It took a moment for the sight to sink into my mind. There was a flowing river of lava streaming left to right through the center of the cavern. Skeletal figures writhed in pain along the banks. Some with skin barely hanging onto their charred bones. Others with skin beginning to melt away. A woman's skin melted away only to return moments later and start all over again.

"Let's find the horn and get out of here," I said.

We walked into the cavern. My boots crunched on what I thought were rocks. It was remnants of bones. If I thought about it too long, I'd vomit. I focused on the lava stream.

Heat poured off it and slammed into me. It was like standing in an oven. The scrabbling of claws on stone heading toward us echoed though the cavern. My stomach twisted. I glanced at Edward who was the epitome of calm.

"Minions alerted to our presence," he said. "A word of warning. If they have weapons, do not let them stab you. Their Hell blades are poisoned."

"Great. I'll file that away for future reference."

Minions. The cockroaches of the underworld. Little annoying bugs that were nothing more than mindless attackers. They were lowest of the lowest. Lower even than the demons sent to kill me in Hong Kong.

"Be ready."

I unsheathed my jade-handled dagger. It was my best defense against the monsters.

They skittered into view on the other side of the lava river. I snorted. Their way was blocked by the molten rock. My answer came a short minute later when they simply rushed through it. There were so many I couldn't differentiate one from another. Some perished in the lava while others used their dead smoking bodies as a bridge to cross.

Next to me, Edward stepped his feet hip-width apart as if readying for battle. I couldn't imagine him fighting. I opened my mouth to ask him how he thought he was going to when he grabbed the backpack from me. Before I could protest, he had it open and pulled out a sword.

I didn't bother hiding my surprise.

"How did you...?"

"Not now, Anna."

He tossed the backpack to me and then sprang into action. He slashed through the minions as though they were nothing more than air. He cut a path through them, even using their dead bodies to cross the lava. I was stunned and rooted into place. He was a force to be reckoned with for sure. And not at all the man I thought he was. My uncle was a total badass.

"Anna, come on!"

His shout spurred me into action. With my dagger in my hand, I slashed away as I followed him through the throngs of minions trying to kill us. Or at least deter us. They didn't seem to be trying all that hard. At the edge of the lava river, I hesitated for only a brief second before I took a deep breath and stepped onto a quickly disintegrating body.

Gross.

The heat singed my exposed skin, threatening to make me burst into flame. I took a tentative step onto a body but my foot sank. I had to move and fast. I jumped to the next one and the next one. The lava licked at the bottom of my boots. Holding my breath, I kept my eyes on where my next step would go. The last thing I wanted to do was take a bath in lava.

Edward was already on the other side still killing minions. I was seconds away from the edge but finally made it across. Relief pulsed through me when I stepped on solid ground.

"That was fun," I said, panting.

"More fun ahead." He nodded toward our destination.

The minions gave way to a group of beasts. Demons. These wouldn't be so easy to kill. But Edward didn't seem disturbed by their appearance at all. They charged. He slashed. They attacked. He killed.

I couldn't stand there all day watching him do his thing. I leapt into action after him. Killing demon after demon but all the while I kept an eye on him.

I watched him move with grace and ease. As though he'd been doing it all his life. And maybe he had. I often thought Edward seemed more mature than the twenty-eight years separating us. There was something otherworldly about him. Something *ancient* but not elderly. Something dangerous to anyone who wronged him or his family.

For the first time, it struck me how much I didn't know about my uncle. Who he was. He didn't appear to be who or what I *thought*. One thing for sure, he proved to be an accomplished killer of demons.

"Stop daydreaming!"

Edward's harsh voice snapped me out of my thoughts. I was seconds away from being impaled by a demon's lance. I jumped out of the way as he lunged, missing me. He jabbed again as I put up my dagger in defense. The lance slammed against the blade, jarring and rattling every bone in my body. Intense pain slammed through me, making the veins in my head throb.

We were in a deadlock. I tried pushing the demon back but he was stronger than me. He shoved me backward. I stumbled and crashed to the hard ground, rolling out of the way of his stabbing lance. In one fluid motion, I jumped to my feet, spun toward him and thrust the dagger into his side. He immediately turned to ash.

"What is wrong with you?" Edward snapped. "You nearly got yourself killed."

"Nothing. I'm just...I'm...nothing."

"This is no time to forget where you are or what you're doing, Anna," he scolded.

We were deep into the First Circle and faced with a black gate nestled at an entrance. The gates of Hell? A demon guard stood in front of it armed only with a sword.

"Why hasn't he attacked?" I asked.

"He is not to leave his post."

"What is this place?"

"The entrance to the First Circle."

"The entrance? I thought we were already there."

"We have hardly begun our trek."

"What now?"

He turned to me. "Now you will dream walk Azriel."

"What? No way." The thought made me ill. The last person anywhere I wanted to dream walk was the fallen angel. "I can't do it if the person isn't asleep."

"Wrong. You did it with Emma and Frank."

I stared dumbly at him. "How did you know about that?"

"It doesn't matter." He waved it away, impatient. "Azriel has the horn. You can find it through him. You *can* do this."

"The second I step into his mind he'll sense I'm here. There's no guarantee he's sleeping or dreaming right now anyway."

"You can walk his subconscious. You have the power."

"You expect me to step in and poke around?"

"Yes."

"He'll try to control me. I'm not putting myself in that position."

"You have to. He threatened your friend's life. He gave you a warning. Now he knows you will come for the horn and will do whatever you can to get it back."

"Then you dream walk him," I said. "Are you like an all-seeing eye or something?"

"Do it, Anna. If you intend to find the horn, it is the only way."

"You want me to do it here? Now?"

"Yes."

I glanced around the cavern, at the demon guard, at the gate. "Here?" I asked again.

"Yes. Here."

"But what if—"

"I will guard you. No harm will come to you while you dream walk."

I hesitated. While I was certain he would protect me from more demons, I was not so certain I wanted to willingly enter Azriel's mind. But if it was the only way to find the horn, then I had no other choice. I closed my eyes and prepared to step into the Fallen's subconscious.

CHAPTER 22

I COULDN'T STOMACH THE thought of stepping into Azriel's dreams. So instead, I looked for Lexi. If what my uncle said was true, she was weak. Getting into her dreams would be a snap. Maybe I could manipulate her into telling me the location of the horn.

It didn't take long to find her. She was somewhere in the depths of the First Circle in a chamber. Azriel's? I wasn't sure. She lounged on a bed doing disgusting things with several minions. My stomach turned.

I was sad and disappointed she fell that far into debauchery. I blamed Azriel for that. He ruined her and turned her. I hated stepping into that sick, twisted dream but wondered if it was rooted in some reality. How could she allow this to happen to her? Then again, she fucked Azriel so anything was possible.

"I hate to bust up the party..." I said, making my presence known.

At the sound of my voice, the minions' heads snapped up and beady red eyes peered at me. They scampered away, leaving Lexi alone on the bed. She propped up on her elbows and scowled, clearly unhappy about the interruption.

She looked different. Thinner. She had scars all along her body from lashes or burns, I couldn't tell which. Had she allowed the fallen angel to torture her in the name of pleasure?

"What are you doing here?" She snarled as she slid off the bed, snatching a pair of pants and tugging them on over bony hips. She grabbed a shirt off the floor and pulled it over her head.

"I thought that was obvious."

"You don't belong here." She punctuated her words with a shove to my chest.

I stumbled back a step but remained firmly planted in her dream. "No, you know what I want. What I've come for."

She laughed a hideous guttural laugh. "It's hidden in a place you'll never find."

"You mean in the First Circle?"

Her eyes widened a little before she quickly recovered. "As if you could get there."

"You sure about that?"

I took a tentative step toward her for a closer look. What I saw was beyond disturbing.

Sweat glistened on her pale skin. She was thinner than I remembered. And her face...God, her face. There were deep circles under her lower lashes. Her eyes look hollow. She hadn't looked this bad before. I wondered how long she'd been down here, doing unspeakable things with those hideous creatures. I wondered, too, if this version of her was how she saw herself—as a plaything for dark creatures.

"What's he done to you, Lexi?"

"What do *you* care?"

"You may have stabbed me in the back but we're still family. Let me help you."

Why I wanted to help her leave him was beyond me. Something pulled me toward that compassion even though she betrayed me and left me to die while she and Azriel took off with the horn. If not for Darius, I would be dead. Azriel brainwashed her but maybe there was still hope.

"Fuck you. Get out of my head!"

She knew I was in her dream. Yet she hadn't tried to control the dream or push me out, so Edward was correct in that she wasn't that strong.

"Tell me where the horn is and I'll leave."

She spit at me. The saliva landed on my hand and sizzled. That was different. "You're wasting your time, *Keeper*." The name she called me sounded as though it left a bad taste on her tongue.

"Lexi, tell me where you are."

"Why?" Her hands clenched into small tight fists, leaching her knuckles of color.

"Because he's killing you."

"I don't need you to rescue me." She prowled the room, pacing back and forth, back and forth. As though she couldn't decide what to do. She halted abruptly then and stared at me out of those hideous sunken eyes. "There is no saving me."

"Tell me where the horn is, damn it."

Her upper lip curled into a snarl. "In a place you'll never find. Guarded by a prince so dark and so evil you will never be able to get close to him."

Finally, some useful information. "Who?"

She snorted. "Like I'll tell you that easily. Why don't you go find him yourself?"

"Tell me and I'll—"

She charged and rammed into me with all her force. Her bony hands smacked into my upper chest. I stumbled backward and crashed to the floor. She was on me, her nails scratching my face.

She looked inhuman. I grabbed her by the wrists to still her hands. My fingers pressed into her flesh, leaving bruises.

Her paper-thin skin revealed her bones. I didn't want to hurt her but she gave me no other choice. I brutally shoved her backward. She flew away from me and crashed onto the floor. She curled into a ball, flashing her best death glare.

I climbed to my feet. She managed to bloody my nose and lip. She smacked me good. I wiped the blood away with the back of my hand.

We stared each other down. She wasn't going to give me what I wanted. I could take a hint. She didn't want my help, nor did she want to help me.

I released the dream and blinked my eyes open. I looked up into the face of my uncle. Concern creased his brow as he helped me to a sitting position.

"What happened?" he asked. "Did you find the location of the horn?"

"Not exactly." I tasted blood and wiped my nose. My fingertips came away smeared with blood.

"Your nose is bleeding. Did he hurt you? All of a sudden you fell as though you'd been hit," he said.

"I was hit. But I didn't dream walk Azriel. I dream walked Lexi."

He stared at me in disbelief. "Lexi? Why?"

"I thought she'd tell me where to find the horn."

"Did she?"

"She said it was guarded by a prince so dark and evil we would never get close to him."

He blew out a heavy breath. "One of the Seven Princes of Sin."

"You know this guy?"

"We all do. They are the ones that influence humans to sin. Lucifer is their leader."

As in the seven deadly sins. I guess it made sense but I never thought about them personified.

"So how do we know which prince has the horn?" I asked.

"Did she give you any other information besides that?"

I shook my head, disappointed I didn't have more to go on.

"We'll have to enter the First Circle and find him."

"That could take an eternity. I don't want to be trapped down here that long. Can't I use any of my special abilities to find the horn?"

A slow grin spread across his face. It wasn't often my uncle smiled. "Now you're thinking like a Keeper. Yes. Use your abilities to locate the horn as you did before when it was in your mind's eye."

I couldn't help but feel a little pride at having deduced the correct answer. Finally, we were getting somewhere. Hopefully, I found the thing with my new visionary powers.

"Will we be safe here if I do it again?" I asked.

"We are for the moment. But hurry. We don't want to tarry here much longer."

I couldn't agree more. I closed my eyes and pictured the horn. The way it was shaped. The weight of it in my hands. The memory of stealing it from Chen's office played out like a movie. Then the vision fast-forwarded to the fight in the elevator and then on the rooftop when Lexi handed it over to Azriel.

Another fast-forward. Azriel gave the horn to someone else. His face wasn't clear but he had dark shimmery wings. Rich black feathers were threaded with gold. Did the gold indicate his elevation as a prince of darkness? He held the horn in his hands. Hands with black pointy fingernails. Hands that were paper white.

He shifted in the vision so his face was visible. He grinned triumphant at holding the horn. His mouth was full of sharp pointy teeth, black lips, black tongue. Black eyes. Sharp cheekbones protruding through his pale skin. His hair was also black and slicked back from his high forehead.

It was as if he stood in front of me.

With a gasp, I opened my eyes.

"Did you see him?" Edward's face was full of hope.

I nodded. If this was the guy who had the horn, he was the last one I wanted to confront.

"What does he look like?" Edward asked.

I described the prince of darkness. Edward stood quietly as I recounted my vision. When I finished, his lips formed a thin straight line. "The Prince of Greed. Mammon."

Did I want to know how Edward knew that? "So how do we find him?"

"Through those gates." He nodded towards them.

The black gates guarded by the sentry that hadn't moved a muscle since our arrival. "Okay. For my next question, I'll ask how we get through those gates."

"We will have to fight our way in."

"I was afraid you'd say that." I sighed.

"It is the only way."

"Are you sure about that?" I asked.

"You have another idea?"

Well, no, I didn't. But I was the Keeper. And I was there for the Horn of Gabriel. There had to be a way through without fighting this guy. I didn't want to chance calling any more attention to ourselves if we could avoid it. We got through the lava river unscathed. What were the chances the sentry would allow us to walk through the gates? Probably slim to none.

But what if I traded him something for passage? Something like...say...a dagger?

"I have an idea."

Maybe one of the daggers would entice him. I slipped the backpack off my shoulder and dug around until I found one with a nice shiny blade and a jewel-encrusted hilt. The stones glittered in the half light.

"What do you think you're doing?" Edward asked. "Are you going to stab him?"

"No, I'm going to bribe him."

Before he could stop me, I stepped toward the gate. The sentry immediately wielded his sword and pointed it at me.

"Hi, there." I flashed a winning grin but all I got in return was a snarl. "I don't suppose you'd let me and my friend here through the gate."

The response was a guttural growl.

"How about I trade you something for safe passage through the gate?" Holding the blade, I waved the hilt end of the dagger toward him. Light from the torches in the cavern glinted off the gems. "How about a weapon you can use?"

"Anna, I do not think this is good idea," Edward said.

I ignored him. "This is better than your sword. You can get up close and personal with this baby."

And if this didn't work, I'd toss the holy water on him.

I caught his attention. His eyes gleamed with a delicious relish. Drool trickled down his chin. "I'll give you this dagger if you'll let us through those gates." I took another tentative step and stretched the dagger toward him. "Do we have a deal?"

He reached out and tried to snatch it from my hand but I whipped it back. "Not so fast. Open the gate first."

He never spoke but he clearly understood me. He opened the gates, swinging them wide. Then he spun back toward me holding out his hands in a "gimme" gesture.

"Not until we're through the gates," I said.

He looked at the open gates longingly, as if he wanted to rush through them, then back at me. He gave me a nod. Edward and I hurried through. After I entered, I turned and handed him the dagger. He grabbed it out of my grasp and then patted it as if it was the best present he ever got.

"That is not the best idea you've ever had," Edward said, his tone sour.

"Nope," I agreed. "But we got through the gates, didn't we?"

"Yes, but how do you propose we get back out?"

"We'll worry about that when the time comes. Let's find this Prince Mammon."

"With pleasure."

Chapter 23

W E WERE THROUGH AND officially into the First Circle. I couldn't say I was wild about the idea. It was a necessary evil. I nearly snorted at the thought.

"Where can we find this Mammon?" I asked.

"We'll know him when we see him."

Somehow that wasn't very encouraging. I knew what the guy looked like, even though I'd rather not know. It was something that would haunt me for a very long time. In fact, the whole journey was going to keep me up nights. Not that I could sleep anymore anyway with Azriel roaming around in my dreams.

We journeyed through the First Circle largely ignored by those who encountered us. Maybe we weren't worth the trouble. Sweat poured down my back and dampened my clothes. My head hurt and my mouth was dry. I remembered the water bottle Darius gave me and fumbled in the backpack for it. As we walked, I took a long swig but it wasn't enough to stave off the heat. Even my eyeballs were hot. Like they could burn out of my sockets any minute. I handed Edward the water bottle. He took a long drink then handed it back to me. I stuffed it back into the pack.

I blindly followed Edward. "Where are we going?"

"I'm following the path."

"There's a path?"

I glanced down but I saw no path. Nothing was there. Maybe he saw something I couldn't. Typical of my relationship with Edward. Always withholding information. He liked to keep secrets.

"Are we supposed to keep walking until we find him?"

I couldn't help whining even a little. It was hot. My feet hurt. I wanted to go home. And why didn't Edward have a drop of sweat on him? I was dying of the heat and thought I'd burst into flame any second.

Two demons approached us. They looked more than mindless minions. Life sparkled in their eyes. Maybe they actually had a brain of their own.

Edward readied his sword. I readied the jade-handled dagger. There was something reassuring about having it in my palm, giving me the confidence to face any evil thrown at me.

"Humans. You are not welcome here," one said.

"Where is your prince?" Edward asked.

"You know these guys?"

But Edward didn't answer. He widened his stance, ready to fight. I followed suit. I was tired of all these demons and minions.

"Our prince is currently engaged."

They both looked at me. One ran a black tongue over his black lips.

"Pretty girl. We can do fun things with you," the first one said then grinned. "To you."

"I don't think so," I said.

"Pity. But you may not have a choice."

I gripped the dagger tighter as a vision of Lexi flashed through my mind. I shifted from one foot to the other waiting for something to happen. At the sound of scuffling behind me, I glanced over my shoulder to see more demons.

Would this never end?

"Tell us where to find the Prince of Greed," I said.

"Information comes for a payment, pretty one."

"Which is?"

"Let us feast on your flesh," he said.

"So not going to happen."

I glanced at Edward. He had a fierce look on his face. His hand clenched the hilt of his sword. He looked behind us then back to me. With some sort of silent communication, I realized he intended to take the two behind us. I'd take the two in the front, which were the ones that wanted my flesh. I could easily kill them with the dagger. They'd turn to ash in seconds.

"Shall we, Anna?"

"I'd love to."

We sprang into action at the same time. I leapt toward the demon on the right and stabbed him in the heart. He immediately turned to dust. The other one, the one that hadn't spoken, tried to back away but I wasn't letting him get away so easy. I charged him as he scampered out of reach. On a whim, I threw the dagger hoping to hit my mark. It didn't work in Hong Kong so I wasn't sure why I thought it'd work here. The blade flew end over end and buried between the demon's shoulder blades. He went down and then he was nothing more than ash. The dagger clattered to the ground.

Good riddance.

I retrieved the blade and checked on Edward's progress. He handled the other two with ease. They were both dead, bleeding black blood.

"Nice work," he said.

"Thanks."

We continued through the cavern. We crested a small ridge. Down below, the throne perched atop a dais. A throne made entirely of flayed skin and bones. The Prince of Greed sat there, a beast panting at his side, while demons and minions engaged in an orgy all around him. I did my best to keep my eyes averted so I wouldn't hurl. He surveyed the action with a gleam in his eyes. Mammon looked as he did in my vision. The same ugly mug. I couldn't stop the shudder of fear coursing through me as I looked at him. His gaze landed on us. He rose from the throne.

"Who do we have here?" He beckoned us forward.

"We must be cautious," Edward warned.

I wanted to believe I was ready for anything. But I didn't know what to expect from Mammon. He stepped down from the dais as we approached. The beast also rose to all fours and snarled. It was big. The head hit Mammon hip-high. It had matted fur and looked as though it was ready to take a bite out of us.

Edward and I paused in front of the prince as he looked us over. He sniffed the air.

"Humans. But not *any* humans. You've been looking for me." He smiled, showing off all his pointed teeth.

"Word travels fast," I said. "Who told you?"

"Does it matter?"

Probably not. Maybe Lexi found a way to send him a message. Or she delivered it in person. I scanned the crowd trying to find her but not focusing because...ick. I didn't find her which was a relief and a worry.

"I understand you've come to take something from me," Mammon said.

"If you already know who we are and why we're here, then why the questions?" I asked.

"I merely wanted to see if you'd confess your identity, Keeper."

"I am the Keeper of the Holy Relics. I've come for the Horn of Gabriel."

A nightmarish smile creased his lips. "I do not intend to give it up."

"Then we'll have to kill you for it." Edward's threat surprised me.

Mammon laughed. "Stupid dream walker. As if you can defeat me." His dark gaze raked over me with a lascivious glint in his eyes. As if he knew what I looked like naked.

"Don't look at me like that," I growled.

"Why, Keeper? Do you not like it?"

"No. And you're not the Prince of Lust so knock it off."

He laughed again. It made my skin crawl. "How right you are."

"Where is the horn?" I asked.

"The fool Azriel gave it to me for safekeeping. I have no intention of turning it over to Lucifer. I intend to keep it for myself."

The Prince of Greed. Should have known he wouldn't give it up so easy. And why did Azriel think it was a good idea to give it to him? I couldn't even fathom a reason. It was beyond my comprehension.

"It doesn't belong to you," I said. "It belongs to Gabriel."

"Gabriel." He snorted. "He shouldn't have lost it to begin with."

"We will fight you for the horn if necessary," Edward said, impatience lacing his tone.

"We will?"

I wasn't too thrilled he volunteered me for some ass kicking fun with the Prince of Greed. He had enough of Mammon. I'd never seen him this way. He was normally the epitome of calm. Perhaps the heat got to him, too.

"You wish to fight me?"

The beast at his side growled. I didn't spare it a glance, afraid to make eye contact with it for fear it would choose me as the perfect snack.

"If we have to, yes," Edward said.

I placed a hand on his arm to calm him. "No, we don't." I gave Edward a *back off before you get us killed* look. What had gotten into him? Had he lost his mind?

"Give up the horn and we'll leave," I said.

"I haven't made myself clear, have I? I'm not giving it to you." His clawed hand landed on the pet by his side. The snarling beast drooled. Mammon stroked the matted fur between the pointed ears as his gaze flickered from me to my uncle. "To either of you. If you wish to fight me for it, then you may try."

Edward started to reply but I cut him off. "We don't want to fight you."

"Then we are at an impasse," Mammon said.

"There must be some way to negotiate for it," I suggested.

"What are you doing?" My uncle hissed the words under his breath. "Fighting is the only option."

I angled my body so Mammon couldn't read my lips or hear what I said. "What's wrong with you? Fighting the Prince of Green is the worst possible idea ever. I'm not fighting him."

"Killing him will get us the horn," he insisted.

"You think we can kill this guy?" I shook my head. "Hello, he's a prince of sin. Did that last demon fight knock the sense out of your head? What's wrong with you?"

His lip quivered. Beads of sweat lined his brow. A distinct *plop* landed on the ground between us. I glanced down to see a drop of blood. Edward's blood. He was injured. One of the demons must have hurt him in the last fight. If the demon stabbed him with a Hell blade, then his blood was poisoned. Was that why he was talking crazy?

I had to take him back to Darius for help. Darius could heal him. Maybe.

"Okay. You're not well," I said. "Stay quiet and stay back and let me handle this."

"You don't know what you're doing."

"You don't know what you're saying," I retorted. "Now shut it."

"Are you quite finished with your sidebar?" Mammon asked. "I'd like you to tell me how you think you can kill me."

"My uncle is not well," I said. "I don't intend to fight you. *We* don't intend to fight you."

Mammon lifted one thin black eyebrow. "Then how do you propose to take it from me?"

I hesitated, my mind racing. I came up with an idea on the fly. "I'll give you something in return."

Hearing that snapped something awake in Edward. He gripped my arm hard, his fingers digging into my flesh.

"*Anna.*"

Warning laced his tone. I wasn't oblivious to the fact he practically hissed my name. I ignored him.

Maybe striking a bargain with Mammon would help us obtain the horn. But what to give him? The jade-handled dagger was the only thing I valued. He was the Prince of Greed after all. I was sure he'd want something in return. Some sort of worldly possession. If the dagger didn't do, then maybe something else. I had no idea what since I didn't have a lot of possessions myself. But I was willing to bribe him.

"Now that is interesting. I like her, Edward. She's dangerous. She would make a wonderful ally."

My head snapped toward my uncle. He knew this creepy dude? What the fuck?

"She will not. You can't have her." Hard conviction was in his voice. He sounded like his old self but the poison had to be doing something to his mind. He'd never gone to bat for me before.

Mammon chuckled, a low guttural sound. His gaze swung back to me. "What will you give me in return for the horn, Keeper?"

"Don't do this," Edward urged.

I dug into the backpack and pulled out a dagger. Another one with jewels on the handle. "This dagger."

"Not interested." He shook his head.

I dropped the dagger back inside. My fingers skimmed the vial of holy water. I held that up next. "A vial of holy water."

"Now what would I do with that?" Another shake of his head. "No."

"What do you want?" I lifted my chin a little higher.

"This is a mistake, Anna. You don't know what you're doing."

"Silence, dream walker," Mammon snapped at Edward.

Edward clenched his jaw, the muscles ticking in anger. An all too familiar look. I'd gotten it on many occasions. He swayed on his feet. I grasped him by the arm to steady him. He groaned and put a hand to his head. His face leeched of color. I had to get him out of there sooner rather than later.

Mammon's searing hot gaze burned right through me.

"I am willing to discuss a trade, Keeper. You give me something I can use. In turn, I will give you the horn."

That sounded too easy but it was worth it to me. "This dagger." I held up the jade-handled dagger. It pained me to part with it.

He shook his head again. "Weapons do not interest me. I cannot use them. Offer me something else."

I opened the backpack and peered inside again. Energy bars but I doubted he'd want those. A flashlight. The light of the North Star. Probably not interested in those either. I didn't have anything else. I glanced back up at him wondering what to give him.

A smile. "Offer me your word, Keeper. I will accept that."

"My word?" Despite the heat, a cold chill burned the back of my neck. All the hairs stood at attention. I was aware this was probably a mistake, but it was the only choice I had.

Edward's hand tightened even more on my arm. "This is too dangerous. Don't do this. There is another way. I can kill him."

That crazy talk again. I ignored Edward.

"You agree to grant me one favor of my choosing at a time of my choosing. Promise me that, Keeper, and the horn is yours."

"She will *not*," Edward said.

My stomach dropped as I peered at him.

Mammon smiled that unnerving smile. "This is the price I seek. Your promise. Your word. One favor."

I swallowed hard, my throat suddenly dry and itchy.

"Don't do it, Anna." Edward's voice was in my ear. He groaned again and fell into me so hard he nearly knocked me off my feet. I grasped hold of him to steady him. "He will expect you to keep your word and he *will* cash in on that promise."

I didn't expect anything less.

"Do not let Edward change your mind, my dear. I cannot be defeated but if you wish to try..." He spread his hands in invitation, a malevolent gleam in his eyes.

"No."

"You can be killed. By beheading." Edward glared at him.

"Again. If you wish to try..."

I wasn't strong enough or fast enough to behead a prince of darkness. Neither was Edward. I dragged my lower lip through my teeth. This was what I had to do. Despite my uncle urging me otherwise. I took a deep breath and hoped it wasn't a huge mistake.

"You have my word."

As soon as I said it, Uncle Edward sucked in a hissing breath. I didn't have to look at him to know he didn't approve.

Mammon looked well pleased. "I look forward to working with you, my dear." He snapped his fingers. A demon rushed forward holding the horn. Mammon took it from the demon then extended it to me in his clawed hands. "The Horn of Gabriel. As I promised."

With shaking hands, I took the horn, sealing the deal.

"As you promised, I have your word," he said.

"You do." My gut churned acid.

"Until we meet again." Mammon patted the head of his beast one last time then returned to his throne. The animal padded after him.

We were dismissed. There was nothing left to do but return home. I clutched the horn under my arm. I should feel elated I had what I came for but I didn't. A sickness trickled through me like never before. Jagged fear sliced down my throat.

In some ways, I wished it would tear me open and let me bleed out. Let me die. Then I could be free of all the misery. Then I remembered Kincade in the hospital and my vow to accept my fate as Keeper. I couldn't give up. Not yet.

"Let's go, Edward."

I steered him back the way we came. He wobbled on his feet but he managed to put one foot in front of the other. His sword hung by his side, forgotten. He shivered uncontrollably and his teeth chattered. His hand was covered with a steady stream of blood. I found a place to perch him against a rock to inspect his wounds.

A wet spot spread across his shirt under his ribs. I tried to shove the material up for a look at the wound but he pushed me roughly away. There was a slash in his shirt sleeve where his arm bled.

"Leave off."

"You're hurt, damn it."

"There is nothing you can do."

"Bullshit. I take you to Darius. He can heal you."

"No, it's too late for me. You should have...let me kill Mammon...when I had the chance."

I got it. He thought if he tried to kill Mammon then the prince would kill him. Put him out of his misery. But then if Mammon killed him, how did he expect me to get the horn? Impossible man. He had to be in terrible pain and definitely not in his right mind. I didn't even want to think about what the poison coursing through his body did to him.

"And then have all of Hell chase after us? I don't think so. Let me see your side, Edward."

He was too weak to fight me. I pushed away the material to reveal the cut slicing across his side up his ribcage. It was deep and beyond any sort of healing skills I had. Damn it.

I stared into the backpack wishing for a first-aid kit. Low and behold, one appeared. I grabbed it, and then rummaged around for bandages. I tore open gauze and balanced it carefully on one knee. Then I opened antiseptic wipes.

"This is going to sting," I warned.

As the alcohol hit his open wound, he sucked in a sharp breath. His hand lashed out and for a second, I thought he might punch me in the face. Instead, he grabbed me by the collar and hauled me toward him. He gritted his teeth. We were face to face. So close I could see every hair follicle, every pore, every bead of sweat.

"Told you it might sting," I said.

"Let me die, damn you, Anna."

"No."

I pushed him away. I swabbed the wound again. It oozed something black. I assumed it was demon poison. I had nothing to cure that. I patched him up as best I could with the gauze but already he bled through it. I bandaged his arm, too, but that didn't seem to help much either. I couldn't stop the bleeding.

"You've been poisoned. How do I cure it?" I asked.

"You can't. Not here," he said through clenched teeth.

"Then Darius is our only hope."

I slung the backpack over one shoulder and cradled the horn with my free hand. I placed my shoulder under his arm and hoisted him to his feet. He was dead weight pushing me down. I was determined to make it out of there, though, and I wasn't going to leave him behind. We stumbled along a few steps. Edward didn't even try to help me. It was like he gave up the will to live.

It was hard to juggle the backpack and Edward and for a minute I considered leaving behind the pack. But there were things in there I might need.

"Damn *you*, Edward. You're giving up. You've never given up on anything. Not even me. So, don't start now. I'm not going to let you."

"You...made a deal...with him."

"I had to."

"No..."

"Yes! I have the horn. We can go home."

"He will...find you...make you do...something...evil. Something you will...regret."

"Is that what you're worried about?"

More scrabbling behind me. I didn't want to turn around. More demons or minions followed me. Edward was in no condition to fight. And I was in no position to fight.

Fuck all.

Numbness spread through my body. The little needles prickled through me as a reminder Edward was far too heavy to carry. He didn't seem to *want* to live. Maybe the poison ate through some of his good sense and destroyed the smart brain cells.

It took all my strength to continue walking through Hell. I *had* to keep going. The demons behind me were getting closer. Closing in the remaining distance.

Up ahead were the black gates. The gates of hope. I wasn't sure I'd make it while dragging a sickly Edward. We were close to the exit of the First Circle and then we'd be home free. Sort of. Making it through those gates would be one more step closer to the opening of the cave. Hope glimmered inside me.

And then died immediately as Azriel stepped in front of me. His face was a mask of angry terror. His black wings spread, rippling in fury. Well, wasn't that grand?

We stared each other down. I waited for him to say something trite like, "Not so fast," or, "Where do you think you're going?" But he didn't. We had an intense staring contest.

"Get out of my way," I said finally.

"Your uncle will die."

It wasn't what I expected him to say. "Not if I get him out of here first."

"He was stabbed by a demon. There is no saving him. And then you'll be on your own." He grinned that wolf-grin as if that was the best news he'd heard all day.

"He's not going to die. And fuck you."

"You think you can make it out of here alive? Have you even looked behind you?"

"Yeah, I do." False courage. I clung to it like a cat clinging to a tree limb. I hoped when I fell, I'd land on all fours, but now I dug in with all my claws.

His gaze slid over the horn tucked under my arm. "I'm impressed you managed to manipulate it away from Mammon."

"He said he had no intention of giving it to Lucifer." Smug satisfaction warmed me knowing I tattled on the prince to Azriel. He didn't look shocked and it didn't have the effect I wanted.

"What was his price for it?" Azriel asked. "Nothing comes without a price."

"That's between me and Mammon and none of your damn business."

"You are a foolish inexperienced girl. I cannot allow you to leave so easily with the horn."

I sighed. Fine. If he wanted to do this the hard way. I eased Edward to the ground and stepped away from him. I'd be damned if I let go of the horn. I learned my lesson the first time.

"What do you want from me, Azriel?"

He moved so fast he was nothing but a blur. I didn't have time to react before his fist landed on my face. Starbursts exploded in a shower in my vision. I stumbled backward a few steps, the horn slipping in my grasp. I tightened my grip and held on for dear life.

My face hurt. I had a lovely throbbing over my left eye which immediately swelled closed. I blinked my one good eye trying to bring him into focus. He came at me again and I didn't have time to react.

His fist landed on my other eye. More starbursts. More exploding pain. More swelling.

Fists pummeling my face. Pain everywhere.

Jaw hurt. Head hurt. Lip hurt.

Couldn't see. Couldn't breathe. Couldn't think.

He didn't even try to go for the horn. My fingers tightened on it anyway. So tight they ached.

He landed a good punch to the side of my head. I fell backward, landing hard on the ground. My head smacked against the stone with a sickening crack that turned my stomach. I wanted to roll to my side and curl into the fetal position. I sensed him coming and kicked my feet up. I made contact and he grunted. But it wasn't enough. He was back to battering my face with his fists. Like he enjoyed it way too much.

"I. Will. Kill. You." He punctuated each word with a blow.

Oh, yeah. He enjoyed it way too much. I understood what his plan was then. Kill me. Retrieve the horn.

I wanted to tell him he couldn't kill me. That he needed me. That I was the only one to find the other relics. No words formed. All I could think about was making him stop. I kicked my foot up again but only hit dead air.

Sharp, harsh laughter followed. I pried a hand off the horn and fumbled for my jade-handled dagger. He slapped my hand away. Clawed my arm. Scraped against the horn.

I clutched it again.

Sharp searing pain burned through my neck. It quickly dissipated. I only felt it for a few seconds. Most of the pain was in my face. Fire burned through my cheekbones.

My face was wet. From tears or blood, I wasn't sure which. Light dimmed. I was going to pass out. Then the pain would stop. It would all be over.

And suddenly it was. A scream. Shrill. Ear-piercing. Deafening. Right in front of me.

It took me a minute to realize I was huddled on the ground clutching the horn to my chest. I couldn't defend myself because I refused to release it. I lifted my head and peered through the slits that were my eyes.

Azriel was gone as were the other demons. My uncle stood, his chest heaving as he sucked in breath. His sword hand was covered in blood. Black blood. It dripped off his blade. His face was paler than before. He looked like he might pass out any minute.

"Edward..." I cradled the horn and crawled toward him. "What did you do?"

"Stabbed...Azriel. Saved...you."

I climbed to my feet. Every movement was painful. But I had to get him out of there. Even if it was the last thing I did. The last breath I took. Darius was my only hope. The only one who could save Edward.

Digging deep for more strength, I shouldered Edward again and started the long journey toward the black gates.

CHAPTER 24

I COULDN'T EXPLAIN WHY the minions left me alone. They hovered at the edge of my vision ready to pounce, salivating at the very thought of sinking their teeth and claws into both of us. I didn't know what Edward did to Azriel. Somehow, he managed to save my skin.

Too bad my face couldn't be saved. Blood trickled down my nose. My lips were the size of the Goodyear Blimp. My eye sockets throbbed with intense pain. Through my half-open lids, I saw the black gates looming ahead. My heart skipped a happy beat knowing our time in Hell was nearing an end.

The demon I gave the dagger to stood on his side of the gate. He held the blade in one hand and stared at me with those black eyes emanating a sort of menace and hate I hadn't sensed before. Just what I needed. Another fight with another demon. I couldn't catch a break.

He barked and the sound made me think of a sick dog. Maybe this demon didn't talk.

"Let us pass," I said.

He snorted.

"I gave you the dagger."

He waved it toward me as if to say *stay back or die*.

"I need out of here," I said. "Tell me what you want for passage."

He glared. This was not going well. Instead of grunting or barking or making any other sound, he opened his mouth wide and showed me his missing tongue.

Gross.

The only thing I had left was the light of the North Star and the holy water. I doubted that would do him any good. But the holy water might work.

Holy water and demons didn't mix. The vial was in my backpack which was slung over the shoulder Edward currently occupied.

I lowered Edward to the ground. He didn't grunt or respond. I peered through swollen eyes but it was hard to focus. Somewhere along the way, he'd passed out. I fumbled for a pulse in his wrist. It fluttered faintly under my fingertips.

"Don't you dare die on me, old man," I whispered.

Quickly, I unzipped the backpack and pulled out the holy water. The insanity of the situation dawned on me but, really, the whole situation from the time I stepped foot in the First Circle was insanity. There I was, in Hell, handing holy water over to a demon while my uncle was near death from demon poisoning.

Life was grand.

I rose and turned to demon boy. I stretched out the vial to him. He looked at it and then at me as if considering if I tried to trick him. He snatched it out of my hand and held it up, shaking it. He turned it upside down and shook it again. He grunted frustration. His clawed fingertips tried to pull out the cork but it was wedged in tight.

"Let me show you."

I clutched the horn under an arm. When I reached for the vial, he jerked it away.

"I'll give it back. I promise." I waggled my fingers indicating he should give it to me.

He considered a long time until he finally extended the vial. I pulled out the cork, then handed it back.

"See? Open. I told you I'd give it back."

He snatched it, the liquid sloshing inside.

"You drink it."

I made a motion with my hand like I tipped an imaginary glass into my mouth.

He wasn't going for it. I slipped my hand into the backpack and closed my fingers over the handle of my jade-handled dagger, if he didn't do it, I'd have to kill him. But then the demon tipped up the holy water and guzzled it in one gulp.

I watched him but nothing happened. I wasn't going to stand around and wait. I slung the backpack over my shoulder again. Juggling the horn, I muscled Edward to his feet. His weight was heavier than a ship anchor.

The vial of holy water appeased the demon. The black gates opened. I hobbled through as fast as I could with the extra weight of Edward, the horn and the backpack, trying to put as much distance between me and the demon as possible. As I trudged through the gate, an awful screeching exploded on the air. I craned my neck around to see smoke emanating off the demon. A moment later he burst into flames.

One less demon to worry about.

I made it to where I dream walked Lexi. I couldn't help but think I should rescue her but I didn't have time to find her now. I hobbled through the cavern. Up ahead was the lava river. I'd forgotten about the nasty minions who tried to kill us before. I wasn't sure how I was going to cross the lava river carrying Edward much less fight more of them, but I was determined to find a way.

The nasty little minions clambered over themselves to attack us. I couldn't fight them. I didn't have the strength.

I glanced down at the horn. Blood was smeared along the shiny surface. If I blew the horn would Darius appear? He said he couldn't go with me. He couldn't help me here. But if I blew the horn...then what? Technically we weren't in the First Circle anymore.

I had to give it a try. I put the horn to my swollen lips and blew. I waited and listened. Nothing happened.

"Please, Darius. I need you."

I gave it another try. The only sound in return was that of the minions. And they were getting closer, ready to tear us to shreds and eat us alive. My vision clouded. I thought from tears, but my eyes were so swollen it was hard to tell.

A sudden flash of light burst in front of me. I tried to pry my eyes open but it was useless. Then I heard the sharp intake of breath followed by a shrill screech. I assumed those were the minions Darius scared away.

"Darius?"

"Give him to me."

Relief slammed into me so hard I wanted to crumble. Edward's dead weight was gone followed by another flash of light. Darius left but he'd be back for me. He wouldn't leave me to the minions. My numb arms hung listlessly at my side like nothing more than a wet noodle. I couldn't hold myself up any longer and fell to my knees.

Another flash of light and Darius returned. He scooped me into his powerful arms and cradled me against his chest. Knowing I was safe and on my way out, I allowed the darkness to consume me.

✦————✦

I startled awake. I was discombobulated at first as I glanced around, trying to force my brain to recognize the place. I remembered the room. I was in Darius's home again. My eyes were no longer swollen.

But my head still throbbed. I brushed fingertips over my nose, felt the rough bandage. My nose was broken.

"Rest, Keeper."

Darius. He stood like a sentinel over me. His wings were spread behind him. They were shadowed, though, not as pure white as they once were. He moved next to the bed and the shadows moved with him. It was wrong but my muddled brain couldn't figure it out. Why did the shadows move with him?

I remembered Edward then and panic hit my gut like acid. I shoved the blankets aside and tried to stand.

"Where's Edward? Is he okay? He was injured by a demon. He was poisoned—"

"Rest." Darius pushed my shoulders back down to the bed.

It hurt to talk. My voice sounded funny. Scratchy and painful. Like I had eaten sandpaper or swallowed a box of tacks. I tried to swallow but my mouth was bone dry.

Darius reached for a glass of water on the nearby night table. He lifted it to my lips. "Sip."

The cold water splashed over my mouth. It was like monsoon season in my desert mouth. I couldn't get enough and tried to gulp more than he'd allow. He took away the glass but I smacked my lips wanting more. He gave me another sip and then took it away again. I licked my lips to dampen them. I had more questions.

"Is he...dead?" I couldn't comprehend my uncle not walking the earth.

"He lives," Darius said.

"Thank God."

"No, thank me."

I giggled for the first time in a while. "Yes, thank you, Darius. I'm glad you helped him."

"He nearly died." Darius sounded grim. I focused on his face. Worry lines that hadn't been there before creased his face. "It took all my healing powers but I managed to remove the poison out of him."

I looked at him again but this time focused on his wings. The shadows were not shadows at all. They were black feathers. I nearly choked on the sob wanting to erupt.

"Your wings..."

"Will heal. I am fine." He dismissed it.

"But...there are black feathers." Tears clotted my throat. I hated seeing those black feathers intermingled with his lovely white ones. I wanted to reach up and touch them. Stroke them. Pluck them out. Remove the black and return his wings to pure white. To good. To banish the evil.

"A side effect of removing the poison. They will go away."

"Are you certain?"

"Yes." But the word sounded like ice.

It was my fault. I shouldn't have blown the horn. Even though we were out of the First Circle, it wasn't safe for him to rescue my dumb ass. And he'd come anyway when it was forbidden. Guilt constricted my chest. "I'm sorry, Darius."

"Why, Keeper?"

"I-I don't know." My breath hitched. "Thank you for saving his life."

"What happened to your face?" He changed the subject abruptly and I flinched.

"Azriel happened."

"He fought you for the horn?"

"The horn! Where is it? Is it safe? I had it when you came back." I'd been so distracted by Darius and his shadowed wings I'd forgotten about the horn.

"Keeper, you must be calm or you will injure yourself further. The Horn of Gabriel is safe."

He pointed to the table across from the bed. The horn rested on a garnet pillow. No longer was it smeared with blood. Darius cleaned it, polished it until it gleamed. I imagined he did it with reverence and a gentle hand. I blew out a heated breath of relief and leaned back into the pillows.

"This job sucks."

"Did Azriel fight you for the horn?" He repeated the question, his voice hard as ice. He clenched his fist as though it angered him Azriel landed a punch on me.

"Yes. No. Sort of."

"Which is it?" he said through clenched teeth.

"Azriel gave the horn to the Prince of Greed. I made a deal with him to get it back."

His face blanched. "You made a deal with Mammon." His voice didn't rise at the end like a question. He repeated it as though he wasn't sure he understood.

"Yes."

"Now I understand what Edward was saying."

"What do you mean?"

"He kept muttering about a deal with sin. I didn't understand. Now I do."

"It was the only way," I said, defending my actions. Though I shouldn't have to defend them to Darius or anyone. I did what I did to get the horn back and I'd do it again.

"What was the deal?" His voice was calm, cool.

"I owe him a favor. He picks the favor and the time."

He stared at me as if I grew a second head.

"What?" I asked.

"A favor for the Prince of Greed is not a wise deal to make."

"It was the only deal I *could* make. Edward wanted to fight him but he was already injured then. Mammon would have killed him and me."

"Your uncle wanted to die with honor," Darius said. "And would have. Was Azriel the one that injured you?"

"Yeah, he used my face for a punching bag."

"And the stab wound?"

I blinked, unsure what he meant. "Stab wound?"

"On your neck." He motioned toward it.

I touched the side of my neck, my fingers grazing another bandage. I had no recollection of being stabbed. No wonder my voice sounded funny and why my throat felt itchy and dry. I had a gaping hole in my neck.

I thought back and remembered a sharp pain down my side. That must have been when it happened.

"He must have stabbed me," I said. "I don't remember."

"You're bleeding again."

If I was stabbed, too, then had I been poisoned as well? I watched Darius peel away the bandage. He tossed the blood soaked one away.

"You removed the poison from me, too," I said. "Didn't you?"

He wouldn't look me in the eye as he swabbed the wound with antiseptic. The stinging shot through my entire body. I grimaced, clenching my teeth to keep from crying out in pain. He placed a fresh bandage on my neck.

"A dead Keeper is no use," he said.

I couldn't stop looking at his feathers. Nor could I stop myself from reaching for them. "Darius—"

He swatted my hand away. "The black feathers are not for you to worry about."

Clearly, he was uptight about the feathers. I dropped the subject for another one that also didn't make sense.

"Edward told me Azriel wouldn't try to kill me. But he had."

"You made a mortal enemy today," he said. "Now he will do whatever it takes to kill you, whether or not you are the Keeper."

"But Edward said I was the only one able touch the Holy Relics before handing them over to an angel. Or a Fallen."

"That is true but it clearly no longer matters to Azriel. He wants you dead."

"Yeah, him and half the demon population."

I couldn't help but wonder how it would affect my future relic hunting. Would Azriel haunt my every step now? How determined would he be to kill me? I couldn't worry about that. I had to worry about getting well and getting back to Kincade.

"Rest your throat, Keeper, and sleep. I must check on Edward."

He left the room and suddenly there was a big empty hole in my gut.

It took me a while but I forced my eyes to close and sleep. My dreams were haunted with the trip through the First Circle. The deal I made with Mammon. Edward nearly dying. Azriel trying to kill me.

Then the dreams changed to something more serene. I was in the garden of my uncle's manor where I spent my teen years. Roses were in full bloom and the air was fragrant with their scent. I saw my true appearance in the reflection of the fountain. Black hair instead of skunk striped. No bandage on my neck. No bruises on my face.

Kincade's handsome face appeared in the reflection next to me, his face wavering in the water. I straightened and turned to him. Instead of his normal cowboy attire, he was dressed in combat boots and black fatigues. A black T-shirt stretched over his muscular chest. He was alive and well. Had I somehow dream walked him unintentionally?

Something was off. When I dream walked, I was in control of everything happening. When someone else dream walked me, I wasn't. Like when Azriel appeared in my dreams. This dream had a similar sensation, yet I couldn't pinpoint exactly what that was. I was in control...but wasn't.

"Kincade."

"Anna." His hand slid along my neck where I was stabbed. The bandage was gone. "You have a scar." His palm was rough and warm against my skin. I didn't mind.

"Yes."

"What happened?"

"It doesn't matter. Are you all right?"

"I'm alive. Where are you?"

Did he understand I dream walked him? That it wasn't real? "I'll come see you soon. I promise."

"And when you do, you'll tell me everything about Azriel and the Horn of Gabriel."

"Yes. Everything, I swear."

I couldn't keep him in the dark any longer. I'd tell him the whole story. And I'd remove myself from his life forever. To keep Azriel away from him. The thought of never seeing him again sent a sharp pain shooting through my scar as if a poisoned blade sliced me there. I wasn't sure why. We weren't close. We weren't even friends. He'd seen me at my worst.

"Good."

I knew by the look on his face he wanted to kiss me. I knew by the way my heart pounded I wanted to let him. Others' dreams were nothing more than images flashing through their sleeping minds. Mine were different. In mine, when I dream walked, I had sensations and emotions almost as though I were awake. When our lips touched, it would be as if it happened in real life.

His mouth melded against mine as though they were made to fit. So perfect. My hands ran up his chest to his shoulders. I liked the power of his muscles under my palms. His mouth was warm, soft, sensual against mine. I never wanted this moment to end even though it was nothing more than a dream.

His hands moved to my face, his thumbs brushing across my cheekbones in a way that made my insides turn to water.

This was not the Kincade I remembered. This dream version of him was less abrasive than the real-life version and I wasn't used to it. I had to remind myself it was nothing but a dream and dreams weren't real, no matter how real mine felt.

Then I woke up. The weird dream with Kincade left me feeling odd. I was still in Darius's home and not the pit of Hell. Cold emptiness surrounded me. A palpable loneliness pressed through me. I had a sudden longing for the life I once had. I thought of Ben and Emma. I thought of the woman who raised me until Edward came for me. All I wanted was that normal, family life.

I pushed off the blankets. There was no need to throw a pity party. I needed to get out of bed. My bare feet hit the cold floor, sending an icy chill up my spine. I wore a long nightgown. My clothes were nowhere to be found but that was okay. They were covered in black demon blood anyway. I didn't want them back.

My daggers were another story. I did want those back. They were lined up neatly next to the horn. Even the jade-handled one. All polished and clean.

I grabbed one of the thick blankets off the bed and wrapped it around my shoulders. I stepped out of the room into the stark hallway. Darius was nowhere to be found. There were several other doors. My uncle was behind one of them. It was merely a matter of picking the right one. After several failed attempts, I found him propped up on pillows looking much like himself.

"Anna, do come in."

I wondered how much he remembered. I closed the door softly, and then pulled up a chair by his bedside.

"How are you?" I asked.

"Exhausted. I'm getting too old for that sort of thing."

I wanted to laugh. What did he mean that sort of thing? Had he visited Hell before? "No, you're not. I couldn't have made it through that without you."

"Perhaps not. But what you did was..."

"Stupid. I know."

"Mammon is a very dangerous demon."

Of course, he remembered. "I'm not sorry. I would do it again."

"It was a bloody poor decision. One I'm not happy about."

"Edward, if you had been in my place what would you have done?"

He thought about that, staring blankly at me. He pressed his lips together as though he didn't want to answer. He didn't want to admit he'd do the same thing. There may be animosity between us but I didn't want my uncle dead.

"You were injured. I had to help you. I wasn't going to let you sacrifice yourself for the horn," I said.

"It was the best way. It was the only way."

"I disagree. What's done is done. I can't go back and change it."

"Well...you have my thanks for saving my life," he said.

"When Azriel attacked me, what did you do to him?" The suspense was killing me.

"I stabbed him." He closed his sword hand. For the first time, I noticed the bandage wrapped around it. "He won't bother you again."

Hot pinpricks skittered along my spine. "Did you kill him?"

"Sadly, no, but I injured him."

"Darius said I made a mortal enemy."

"A valid assumption," Edward said.

That didn't make me feel any better. "Are you sure he won't come after me again?"

"No, but I'll kill him if he does."

The vehemence in his words startled me. "And what about the minions? Why didn't they bother us when we were trying to get out?"

"I stabbed their leader. Why do you think?"

"Right." They were scared of him even if he was nearly dead. Awesome. I needed a superpower like that.

"I hope what you did was worth the horn. Where is it?" he asked.

"In my room."

"How did we get out?"

He didn't remember that part because he'd passed out by then. "I blew the horn and Darius came for us."

"You blew the horn..." His voice trailed off as he stared at me in disbelief. "Darius came?"

"Yes."

"To the First Circle?"

"We were past the black gates. I thought it would be safer there to blow it. I couldn't carry you anymore. And the lava minions were coming after us."

"And Darius came," he repeated.

"Yeah, so. What's the big deal?"

"It's forbidden for him to enter Hell without permission from the heavens."

Crap. "Is that why his wings have black feathers?"

"His wings have black feathers?"

"He told me it was a side effect of removing the poison from us," I said.

"He removed poison from us?"

"Yes, by God, he did. Why are you repeating everything I say?"

He leaned back heavily and closed his eyes. "Yes, the black feathers are an indication he not only removed the poison but he will be punished for entering Dante's Cave. The cave of Hell."

"No. He can't be punished. He came because of me."

"Nevertheless, he will. It cannot be undone."

"He said he would be fine." My breath hitched. The threat of tears warbled in my words.

"He will never be fine, Anna. When he removed the poison from you and me, he took it into himself. It was the only way he could save us both."

"Is that why he didn't take the poison out of me before when he rescued me in Hong Kong? Because he knew this would happen to him." I tried hard not to weep but the damn tears wouldn't stop. They fell, scalding hot, down my cheeks.

"Yes. He absorbed the poison from both of us into his being. His wings will continue to turn black and eventually he will be a Fallen."

"No, damn it, no." I brushed away the tears. The angry tears. The sad tears. The tears I wept for Darius and Kincade and Edward. "There has to be some way to save him. Who do I talk to about that?"

"No one. Nothing can be done."

I stood up so fast the chair scraped back on the floor and tipped over. The back hit with a clack. I gripped the blanket around my frame as I paced. "No. There has to be someone I can talk to. I'm the Keeper, damn it. I'll talk to Joachim. He has Michael's ear. I'll go to the archangel myself if I have to. There has to be—"

"Anna." He said my name quietly.

I flung around the room in a panic, pacing and thrashing and now stopped to look at him. He looked calm, serene, sad. He understood, unlike me, there was nothing to be done for Darius. My heart hurt.

This was all my fucking fault. Everything. Every bit of it. If it hadn't been for me making that stupid error in judgment and giving the horn to Lexi in the first place, I wouldn't have gone to the First Circle. Nor would Edward be injured. Nor would Darius have had to come save my stupid ass.

I hated myself.

"Sit," he said.

"I don't want to sit."

"Sit so we can talk about your training once I'm strong enough."

"I'm not going back to England with you. I have things to do. I have another relic to find." I had to save Darius and Lexi but I didn't tell him that.

"You've embraced your destiny at last."

"I'm not doing it for you, uncle. I'm doing it to keep myself alive."

"You will do it for all mankind, too. And for Darius. And perhaps even Kincade." He said the last so softly, I almost didn't hear it.

I wish I didn't care about all of mankind but that was wrong. Who I did care about was Darius, my uncle and, yes, even Kincade. Even Lexi. I planned to return to the First Circle to find her. But I didn't know if she'd still be alive. Or even if she'd let me rescue her from what she'd already become.

I had to try. I had to try to save her and Darius.

"Anna, you must believe in the Holy Relics. Do you?"

"I believe in the horn," I said. "It works."

"The horn is more powerful than you realize. It belonged to Gabriel for a reason. It is written he will blow it and when he does, it is the beginning of the end."

The signal Judgment Day was upon us.

"Right. The Book of Revelation and all that."

I waved away the thought as if it didn't matter. But it did matter. I wasn't stupid. I was smart enough to be scared of the Book of Revelation. The Four Horsemen of the Apocalypse were in that book. I'd also seen them in my dreams.

"If he blows the horn, the Seven Seals are broken and Armageddon cannot be stopped. Do you understand that?"

"And how am I supposed to keep the Seven Seals from being broken with the Holy Relics?"

"If the Holy Relics are in your hands or the hands of the archangels, then there's nothing to worry about."

Smart ass remark.

"I have the horn. I can find the others."

"Do not let overconfidence cloud your judgment, Anna."

Oh, I was far from overconfident. I was terrified of what was to come. I didn't want to face it yet. I didn't know how to keep the world from falling into total damnation. I didn't know how to save Darius or keep Kincade safe or even stop Azriel from entering and controlling my dreams.

This was only the beginning for me. The beginning of a long terrible nightmare that would not cease. Embrace it? No. But I *would* accept my fate.

Chapter 25

I LEFT MY UNCLE with too many things unsaid. He wanted me to return to England with him but that was the last thing on my mind. I wasn't going. I couldn't. I wouldn't.

Darius waited outside my uncle's room. Pained sliced through me seeing the black feathers interspersed within the white ones. We stared at each other, the painful silence stretching between us. A single white feather released and drifted to the floor. He was molting. The black replaced the white. I searched his face for some reaction, some hint of despair or anger, but there was nothing. His face remained impassive. I wanted him to tell me how to save him, why he lied to me, why he didn't want me to know the truth. He had to realize eventually I would find out, that my uncle would tell me.

"Darius, I—"

He didn't give me a chance to finish. He pulled me to him, his mouth on mine before I could react. The quick movement knocked the blanket from my shoulders. It pooled on the ground behind me. I wore nothing but the nightgown and it was thin at best.

His arms wrapped around me. His hands, hot and burning, were on my back. His mouth overtook mine, stealing my breath and senses. His lips moved over mine as though he wanted to possess me. As though he needed me. As though he would never release me. My brain wanted to push him away, but my body refused.

His tongue slid against mine and I tasted his name. He put it there again should I ever need him. All I had to do was whisper it into the wind. That rich taste reminded me of red velvet and sin and self-indulgence. There was something magnificent about kissing an angel. Something so daring and dangerous and defiant. And not any angel. A *warrior* angel. A brawny, broad, bold, warrior angel who was a powerhouse of muscle and steel.

I snapped back to my senses, remembering where I was and who I was with. I wiggled out of his arms, breaking the kiss and took a step away from him. I sucked in gasps of air trying to still my jumpy beating heart. I gulped a lungful of air.

His breath see-sawed out of him. His chest pumped up and down with his erratic panting. His lips were still damp from kissing. Pain and regret flashed over his handsome features for a brief second before he regained his composure.

"Forgive me."

"Why?" I didn't want to say his name for fear I'd release it. I wanted to hang on to it for as long as possible. Like a toddler hanging on to her favorite toy. It was *mine*. I wanted it. Forever.

"I should not have taken such liberties."

I stared at him, mute. He apologized for being too forward? I dragged my lower lip through my teeth.

"You gave me your name," I said finally.

"Yes."

"Why?"

He took a step closer, his body heat radiating over me as though I stood next to a wood burning fireplace. I looked in his eyes and thought I might fall into those depthless pools.

"In case you ever have a need."

His voice was a roughened whisper of promise and desire. I understood his underlying meaning. In case I ever had a need *for him*. Those were the two words he left unspoken. But I knew what he implied. My heart *thunked* hard. I liked Darius, the warrior angel.

"Now, come. I will return you to your home."

"I thought my uncle would make you take me back to his estate."

"He requested that, yes," Darius said.

"But you're not taking me back?"

"You wish to go there instead?"

"No." I shook my head slowly, thinking of my abandoned apartment. The crime scene. The place Ben was murdered.

I couldn't stay here with Darius. I didn't want to go to my uncle's in England, and there was nothing for me back in Hong Kong.

Except Kincade.

He was still in the hospital recovering in a foreign city. Alone. Why did that trouble me so much?

"You are worried for the detective."

I wasn't sure why it bothered me Darius was aware I worried about Kincade, but it did. I nodded because I didn't trust my voice to remain steady if I spoke. It pained me to admit it to Darius. Especially when something akin to disappointment flashed across his face.

"Your uncle thought as much, as well," he said. "He instructed me to take you to your new apartment in Hong King."

I stared at him, dumbfounded. "I don't understand."

"He made arrangements for you to have a place in the city. He wanted me to tell you it was a peace offering."

I rubbed the side of my head, wondering if Uncle Edward was trying to push me and Kincade together. What was that about? He must have anticipated I would refuse returning to England with him. He'd made arrangements in Hong Kong for me to stay near Kincade and that was weird.

"You will need proper clothing."

I glanced down at the nightgown. The blanket was still on the floor at my feet. I bent and picked it up, then pulled it around my shoulders, suddenly subconscious of my attire in front of the warrior angel.

"There are clothes waiting for you in your room," he said.

My room. He said it as if I might return. My stupid heart skipped a stupid beat. I wanted to shout for it to stop it. Instead, I merely nodded and returned to the room.

On the bed was a tank top, a shirt, a leather jacket, cargo pants, boots and socks and, um, underwear. Darius thought of everything. I wasn't going to let it bother me he figured out my size. Every single one of my daggers were accounted for including the jade-handled one. I strapped the daggers to their usual places within reach in case I needed one of them quickly.

The horn rested on the garnet material. I picked it up with a carful hand. Overhead light glimmered off the polished surface. As I gazed at the horn, it warmed in my hands. An inscription appeared with three words that sent a frosty sensation skittering through me.

Judgment Day Cometh

I wanted to fling it to the ground but I couldn't. I couldn't let go of the relic. The longer I gazed at it, the more I realized I couldn't let it go. A vision burst into my mind. The last person who touched the horn was Darius when he lovingly cleaned and polished it. Then me clutching it to my chest as Azriel beat in my face. And then the Prince of Greed holding it in his hands.

The vision continued backwards in a rush. As if I pressed rewind on a DVD. It sped up faster and faster and faster. The horn was in the hands of someone unfamiliar. A dark-haired man with a mole over his left eye. He was hideous and had sharp teeth like a shark. He was not a man but a demon. And then it was in the hands of someone else. A sharp pain shot through me. My gut instinct told me this was one of my ancestors. The one who betrayed us? The one who wanted the relics for himself?

Then the vision fast-rewound again and I saw it in the hands of...the most beautiful angel I'd ever seen. He was breathtaking. He held the horn in both hands as though it was a reverent gift, gazing upon it with awe and admiration. I realized it *was* a gift. A gift from the only person who gave such a gift. And the beautiful angel was none other than Gabriel.

His golden hair was like a halo. His green eyes were like perfect emeralds. His moonstone wings threaded with gold spanned six feet. He wore golden sandals. He stood on a pathway paved in gold bricks. Seven gold lampposts burned brightly. Peace and joy and love burned bright here.

Was this Heaven? It was more beautiful than I ever imagined or had seen in the real world. Maybe Joachim was right and I had the ability to see into both Heaven and Hell, as well as the history of the relic. My stomach clenched. What I held in my hands was a precious object. No. It was more than a precious object. It was, well, holy for lack of a better word.

Someone called my name over and over. I realized it was Darius. He stood in front of me gripping my shoulders shaking me gently. I blinked several times to clear the vision from my mind and focused on his face.

"Are you all right?"

"Yes...I...I'm fine."

"What did you see?" he asked. His face was creased with concern and worry.

"Heaven and...Gabriel. When he received the horn as a gift from...God."

He inhaled a deep breath slowly and then exhaled. "Only the true Keeper can behold the history of the relics."

"I'll be able to do that with all of them?"

"You will."

"How do you know this?"

"All of my kind knows of you." He smiled.

As he spoke, another white feather drifted to the floor, spiraling in the air until it landed at his feet. If I had the ability to see the history of the relics, then maybe I could find a way to save Darius. That's what I intended to do.

"Edward told me what's happening to you."

"Nothing can be done." His expression turned stony. He closed himself off. No longer did his heat radiate over me.

"I will find a way," I said. "There must be something or someone that can help you."

"It is already too late for me, Keeper. Now allow me to take you home."

It sounded like the subject was closed but I refused to believe it was too late.

Darius took me into his arms like he did the last time. I buried my face in his neck and smelled the sunshine lingering on his skin. The world fell away and we soared through the clouds.

I had a lot of things to think about. What to do about Edward, Darius, Lexi, Kincade. I couldn't allow Darius to turn dark and into one of the Fallen. He was too pure. Too strong. Everything that happened to him was my fault and I was going to fix it. I had a soft spot for the warrior angel.

As for the horn, I couldn't hand it over to Joachim. He was a messenger angel who hadn't paid me a visit in a while. Did he understand what I had to do to get the horn back? And why should

I hand it over to him anyway? I was the Keeper. He wasn't. I'd decide what happened with the horn and the other Holy Relics.

Azriel would expect me to keep it or give it to my uncle for safekeeping. That left me and Edward open for attack. I wondered if he was able to track it like me. He touched it, but did he have that power? Or was that something only I possessed? It needed to be in a place he couldn't reach.

There was only one person I trusted to keep the horn safe.

Darius landed on the sidewalk outside my new apartment building. It was a moonless night and far too quiet. No one was out and about. Not even drunks or the homeless.

I stepped out of his arms, putting distance between us. I possessed his name again and was glad I'd see him at least one more time. All I had to do was speak his name to the wind.

"I need you to do one last thing for me." I extended the horn to him. "Take this. Keep it safe for me until I need it again."

He shook his head before I finished. "I cannot do that, Keeper."

"Please. Azriel will hunt me down for it. He'll expect me to give it to Edward and then hunt him down for it. I can't allow that to happen. I need you to take it. Take it and keep it for me."

"No, Anna."

"Why not?"

"I cannot be trusted. I am...tainted."

"I trust you," I said softly. "I owe you my life. And I do not nor will I believe you are tainted."

He considered my words. Indecision flashed in his eyes. I had to convince him further.

"Right now, I don't have anywhere to hide it. This place isn't secure." I nodded to the apartment building behind me. "If you believe you can no longer hold on to it, you can always return it to me."

He nodded at last. "Very well, Keeper. But this is only temporary."

He slid the Horn of Gabriel from my hands with ease and a careful hand. He cradled it in his palms and gazed at it with awe. He held it like a newborn, like something precious. I was confident he'd guard it with his life. It'd be safe with him. I breathed a sigh of relief.

"Yes. Definitely temporary. As soon as I figure out a place to hide it from Azriel, I'll get it from you."

"Then it's farewell for now."

"For now."

He pressed a set of keys into my palm and then leaned in to whisper the apartment number in my ear. He kissed my cheek before flashing away. He left me standing on the sidewalk feeling lost and a little alone.

CHAPTER 26

I FORCED MY FEET to walk. To take one step and then another and another. I was bone weary. The exhaustion finally set in from everything that happened. Looking back, I didn't remember a moment when fear didn't grip me. It was always pressing into me.

My current situation was no different. Worry gnawed at me like a dog gnawing the gristle off a bone. The pulsing knot of fear refused to diminish. There was so much unknown. I had never seen the words on the horn before. One minute they were there. The next they were gone. They were branded in my mind's eye.

Judgment Day Cometh.

Would more words be on the other relics? Would they warn of what was to come or something else? Would I even be able to find them?

The apartment my uncle procured for me was in a high-rise overlooking Victoria Harbour. So far, I was impressed with the grandeur of the lobby. It had all sleek, modern furniture, marble floors and the coolest floating water feature I'd ever seen. I made my way to the twenty-first floor to the corner apartment and stood outside it, staring at the numbers. Twenty-One-Twenty-Four. Day and year of my birthday. My uncle was sly.

I unlocked the door and swung it open. It looked like every apartment I'd ever seen on House Hunters International. Sleek, modern, and oh-so-European. Marble floors flowed throughout. The kitchen was small but functional and opened up into the large living room that hosted floor to ceiling windows. It was fully furnished, too.

The view overlooking the harbor was spectacular. The lights from the port and surrounding city flooded through the windows, illuminating the place in an eerie bluish glow. It was only a few blocks from the hospital where Kincade was recovering.

How convenient and thoughtful of my uncle to make sure it was so close.

In the morning, I'd visit the detective. It was the least I could do after I nearly got him killed.

As I stood contemplating my life choices, I caught a whiff of chocolate and strawberries.

Joachim. I knew he was there before I saw him.

I closed my eyes and took a cleansing breath before clicking on a nearby lamp. I wasn't ready to face him. He'd come for the relic. How would he react when I told him I didn't plan to give it to him?

He wasn't in the living room, which left only one other place. I trudged the few steps to the bedroom. My feet felt like they were encased in concrete. And any minute I was going to sink to the bottom of the ocean unable to breathe. I'd suffocate from all the pressure surrounding me.

I entered the bedroom but it was empty. Again, I caught a whiff of the decadent smell of strawberries and chocolate. I flipped on the light but no one was there.

"Joachim, show yourself."

"Hello, Annabelle."

His voice was behind me. He stood in the doorway of the bedroom like he'd come for a midnight booty call. I was so not interested in any kind of booty call. He looked much the same as he did when I saw him in the church. Except this time with no bright orange shirt. That was the last time we spoke. Before I had the horn. Before I nearly died. Before Darius stepped into Dante's Cave.

He was dressed in his normal angel attire. The jeans, T-shirt and boot thing must be a uniform of sorts. That was all they wore. Even Darius.

"At last you have returned." He grinned, happy to see me. But his smile quickly turned sour when he noticed I was empty handed.

"Keeping tabs on me?" I asked.

I motioned to move by him and he followed me into the living room. I sank into a nearby chair. I wasn't happy to see Joachim in my new place wearing an expectant look on his face. His ice blue eyes punched through me like the iceberg punching through the Titanic. There was only one reason he tracked me down. I dreaded telling him.

I pinched the bridge of my nose between my thumb and forefinger trying to relieve some of the pressure. "I can guess why you're here."

"You can guess, yes." His brows drew together. "Where is it?"

"Safe," I said.

"Michael sent me to retrieve it for Gabriel. I must have it."

"Well, you're not getting it."

His look was shy of scorching. "Not because you haven't found it. Tell me the truth."

"I found it." I wasn't forthcoming with any more information and he knew it. Why would I be? He wasn't an open book about everything either.

"Then, where is it?"

Didn't he know what I'd been through to steal it back? It took a hell of a lot to keep from being incinerated, to keep Edward from dying. The anger hit me like a blast of hot air.

"Don't you know?" I asked.

"If I did, I wouldn't ask." Impatience laced his tone.

"You mean you haven't been watching my every move?" I couldn't help but needle him.

"No." The word came out low and tight.

"Then how did you find me here in Hong Kong?"

He pressed his lips together in a thin line. "I looked for you at your other home, but it was vacated."

I stared at him a long moment to let that sink in. All my worldly possessions were gone. Not that I wanted them. Ben was murdered in that apartment. I didn't want to ever go back and only now realized it. Perhaps my uncle already understood and that was why he gave me this place.

"It took me a few days to track you down," he added. "Where is the horn?"

"I went through a lot to find it. I nearly died and so did my uncle and you were nowhere to be found."

My hands shook. I was on the verge of exploding. Joachim was the last person I wanted to explain any of this to. He stiffened at my sharp tone but yet his implacable eyes never wavered from mine.

"You are upset because you nearly died?"

"No." I clenched my teeth so hard they ground together. "No, I'm not upset I nearly died. I'm upset because my cousin betrayed me. Because I lost the horn to her and to Azriel. And then I had to track it down to the First Circle where the Prince of Greed had it. My uncle was seriously injured. And Dar—" I clamped my mouth shut. "Never mind."

Heat flashed over me. I didn't want to risk saying his name, even though no wind was inside the apartment. I shouldn't have mentioned Mammon either. Joachim didn't need to know I owed him a favor.

Joachim was unflappable. When I didn't continue, he folded his arms over his massive chest. "You were saying?"

"Nothing. Never mind."

"What is this about the Prince of Greed? You saw Mammon?" he asked.

"Azriel gave it to him. I had to take it back from him. I had no other choice."

"What did you do, Anna?" His voice cracked with concern.

"Save it, Joachim. I did what I needed to do to get back the horn."

"Which is *what*? You must tell me."

"Why? Because you want to help me? So far you haven't exactly been there for me." I folded my arms across my chest, defensive.

"Tell me!" Annoyance creased his features. I'd pushed him far enough.

"I promised him a favor," I said.

His face leeched of color. "You...stupid...girl. Do you realize what you've done?"

Every muscle in my body tensed with irritation. "I'm not stupid. And yes, I realize exactly what I've done."

"Where is the horn?" His jaw clenched so tight the muscles popped along his chin.

"Safe. Like I said."

"Where. Is. The. Horn?" His tone was demanding. It was clear he was done with me.

"It's in a place Azriel can't find."

"And where is that exactly?" His face pinched tight like he might implode any second.

"It's just...safe, okay? You're going to have to trust me on this."

"My trust is something you have not earned yet."

"How nice of you to say so." I pressed my lips together in disgust. "If you don't trust me then why send me to retrieve these bloody relics in the first place?"

He grabbed my arms and jerked me toward him. His face was an inch from mine. Fire snapped in those cold blue eyes.

"You are the Keeper, yes. But in name only. You have no right to these relics. You were sent to find them because of your gifts. Because Michael commanded it. Not because you have earned any trust or right to call yourself the Keeper."

He shoved me roughly away. I stumbled out of his grasp. His words sliced through me, opening a deep wound. I meant nothing to anyone. I was merely a pawn to get what everybody wanted. I resented being used as a Relic GPS. I resented being used period.

"Fine. Then I don't have to search for any more relics. Tell that to Michael."

I sounded like a bad-tempered child. I was sick of these angels and demons. I'd be happy if they disappeared from my life altogether. All I wanted was to go back a normal life, maybe find another job as a phlebotomist. Do some dream walking on the side.

He huffed an exasperated breath. "You must tell me where the Horn of Gabriel is, Anna. I'll not ask again."

If he thought I was going to hand over the Horn of Gabriel, he was clearly insane.

"You can ask until you turn blue but I'm not telling you, angel boy. Only one other knows its location and that person has it for safekeeping. And it's *not* my uncle in case you were thinking that."

I clearly agitated him by the way a muscle ticked in his cheek. His face was still pinched tight. I didn't care. No way was I going to tell him Darius had the horn.

"Michael will not approve."

"Michael will have to get over it." I was all pithy and high and mighty.

His face burned with fiery anger. I realized I was talking to a messenger angel who had the ear of *the* archangel but I had enough of these winged wonders pushing me around. I was playing with fire. The only thing I had going for me was I was the Keeper and they all need me alive.

Oh, no, wait. That wasn't even true. I was a nobody. The Keeper title didn't mean jack shit according to Joachim. Well, it meant something *to me*.

"I'm the Keeper, whether you like it or not. Whether I earned the title or not. And until I'm dead, I'm not handing over the relic." I didn't bother to hide the smug tone of voice.

"You have no idea what power you hold. You cannot possibly understand it. Nor can you contain it. That is why I was sent to bring it back to Michael."

Cocky replaced anger and I tipped my head to the side. "Yeah about that. How do I know you're a messenger for Michael anyway?"

I looked him up and down the way he did me the first time we met. That critical, unimpressed look. He wasn't a Fallen. He smelled different. Fallen had a certain sulfuric scent. A death scent. Except for Azriel who smelled suspiciously like cinnamon. I assumed that was a ruse to make me to trust him.

I wanted to piss off Joachim so he'd leave and I could change my clothes and go to bed.

"You do not believe I am a messenger? Or are you saying this now because you wish to anger me further?"

"Well, it's not like you can flash some credentials, is it? Unless you got an angel ID in those jeans or angel wings of yours. You showed up in my bedroom the same day I met Azriel and demanded I bring this relic to you. How do I know you're not one of the Fallen?"

He bristled. His wings ruffled with the insult.

"How *dare* you imply such a thing." It wasn't a question. Waves of annoyance undulated off him. He was clearly offended. He grabbed my wrist and jerked me to my feet. "If you disbelieve me, I will show you."

"I don't—"

I was silenced by the vision exploding in my head. It was brilliant and bright and singed my optic nerves, nearly frying them to a crisp. It was so painful I fell to my knees. The vision was much like the one I had when looking at the horn, when I saw the past and all the hands that touched it. When God bestowed the gift to Gabriel.

This was not a mere vision. Joachim brought me to this place. Where the streets were paved in gold with unconditional love and there was no fear and no hate and no demons.

Only Michael, the archangel.

His golden hair was like a halo. His eyes the color of the ocean after a storm. His alabaster wings had a tawny glow to them and I realized they were more than white. They were threaded with fine gold. Beautiful and brilliant and bewitching.

"Annabelle Marie Walker." His voice was like a song. Like a beautiful hymn sung by a choir. So beautiful I wanted to weep.

"Michael?" I whispered his name as a reverent prayer. Joachim told me the truth. I shouldn't have provoked him. But standing with Michael was magnificent.

He nodded with one tip of his head and a faint smile. I bowed my head in shame. In reverence. He placed his hand on the crown of my head and gave me one gentle pat.

"Rise, Keeper. And tell me what news of the Horn of Gabriel."

Heat flashed through me. My throat threatened to close tight. Now was my chance to tell him about the horn, to prove to him I was the one to trust with the relics. Now was the time to make him believe I was the one true Keeper.

I should ask him about Darius while I was at it.

I stood and looked him in the eyes.

"I found the horn as you requested. Forgive me, Michael, but I cannot give it to Joachim."

One blond brow rose in question. "Why is that?"

"He doesn't trust me. He said I haven't earned it."

"Have you earned it?"

"I went to the First Circle for it. I fought demons and battled the fallen angel, Azriel. My uncle nearly died. I believe I earned your trust by retrieving the horn and bringing it out of the depths of Hell."

He was silent as he gazed at me, a thoughtful look on his handsome features.

"You entrusted the dream walkers with the relics once long ago," I continued. "Now I ask you to trust me as the true Keeper of the Holy Relics."

"You dream walkers betrayed us."

"No. Only the one. Not all of us. Not my uncle or my grandfather or me."

"'Tis true. Do you know the story, Anna?"

I was ashamed to admit I didn't. Edward never shared that information with me. I never asked. I thought someday I'd find out the truth when I needed. Someday was now. When I shook my head, he continued.

"It was many centuries ago when the world was a different place. Dream Walker Ezra had many powers. Almost as many as you. His gifts included the ability to see into Heaven and Hell, like you. He also had the ability to see into the hearts of men. He knew what they wanted even before they did.

"But it wasn't enough. When he couldn't bend the will of some to fit his needs, he used the Spear of Destiny to force men to riot against their kingdom. To destroy their king. And when the land was leaderless, he took the power for himself. But not all men were corruptible. There was an uprising. By now, Lucifer took notice of him and promised him eternal life and eternal power. He would give him an army. He would help him defeat the men and give him the world. And when the rebels tried to take back their kingdom that was rightfully theirs, Ezra used the armies of Lucifer to destroy them."

I had a sudden shortness of breath and a sinking feeling in the pit of my stomach. A numbing dread filled me. The vision I had when touching the horn for the first time exploded into my memory and suddenly, I realized what I saw. It was *this*...the story of Ezra, the dream walker who had been entrusted with the relics.

"With Lucifer's army, Ezra was invincible. He and his army conquered any land they chose, took any kingdom they wanted, pillaged any village they desired. Raped as many women as he pleased. His evil had no bounds. His path of destruction stretched across continents.

"But it was still not enough. He craved more. He coveted fortune and glory like no other. He used the Staff of Moses to change straw into gold and cotton into silver. He turned the staff into a weapon. He killed all those who defied him.

"All of this did not go unnoticed by me or the other archangels. We realized, too late, something had to be done. I sent my own army to take back what was given to Ezra. It was a great war. Many died. Eventually, Ezra was destroyed on the battlefield and the archangels seized the Holy Relics. But there was a price for Lucifer's help. The dark one still had Ezra's soul."

My heart pumped wildly. I had no idea. My uncle never shared the story of what happened with Ezra. I understood now why it was a stain on our family for centuries.

"I chose you, Anna, because you are born of the Light. You have many gifts bestowed upon you because of your unique lineage. If you ask me to trust you, can I? Will you betray us as Ezra did? Will your lust and greed drive you as it did Ezra?"

I looked up at him, met his gaze. My answer was on my lips before it even formed in my mind. Michael told me who I was—unique, special, gifted. I intended to do all within my power to regain his and the others' trust, to redeem the family name, and become the true Keeper of the Holy Relics.

"I will never betray you. I will never allow myself to become as corrupted as Ezra." I said it and meant it. I believed it in my heart. I would keep my word until I took my last breath. "I have the horn in secure hands. I promise you nothing will happen to it." Confidence swelled through me. I was so sure of that promise, I'd bet my life on it.

He made no immediate reply as he considered, gazing at me. "Very well, Keeper. I will entrust these relics with you. I will trust *you* to keep them safe."

"Thank you." Relief surged through me and I exhaled a great relenting sigh. I bowed my head in thanks. But the relief didn't last long.

"The burden of redeeming your family's name rests upon your shoulders. I hope you're up for the task."

I knew that, as he did. I was up for it. Never mind all the other pressures I had going into it already. Would Edward want the family name redeemed? I was sure he would. A jumble of emotions flickered through me. So many I had a hard time deciding which one took precedence. In the end, I knew what I had to do. Who I ultimately had to become.

It scared me more than Mammon or Azriel.

"I am." I gave a nod of confidence.

"I must request you tell me where the horn is, though," he said. "If it falls into the wrong hands, it would be tragic."

"It's in the hands of a warrior angel."

"And you trust this warrior angel?"

"Implicitly. He is a true hero. I would trust him again with my life. He saved me and my uncle from the poison of the demons. Because of that his wings are turning black."

"It is the penance for such an act."

"An act that saved my life. Please...Please, there must be something I can do to help him."

"Only one thing can stop him from turning Fallen. But there is more to the story, isn't there, Anna?"

I tried to swallow the hard lump wedged in my throat. "My uncle and I couldn't make it out. I blew the horn and he...came to Dante's Cave."

"That is forbidden."

"He did it to save me. If he hadn't, I would surely be dead." *And then you'd have no Keeper*, I wanted to add, but I bit the inside of my cheek.

"Only one thing will be able to save him and turn him back." He paused as though considering whether or not to tell me. Finally, he said, "The Staff of Moses can perform miracles."

"You said the staff had been used by Ezra as a weapon."

"I did. And it has. But in the right hands...the hands of good...it can perform miracles."

"All I have to do is find the Staff of Moses?" I asked. It was that easy? Seriously?

"And then you must know how to use it."

And that was the hitch. I figured out the horn. I'd figure out the staff, too. "Great. Then I'll go after that next."

But he shook his head before the words were out of my mouth. "No. They must be found in order."

"There's a certain order?" That was news to me.

"Yes."

I waited for more clues but he didn't elaborate. I huffed and rolled my eyes. "This is new information to me. What's the order?"

"As a Walker and the Keeper you should already have the order."

Edward. The family history book. It had to be in there. He deliberately held the information back from me so I would have to return to him.

"I'll find out. I know who to ask."

"Now return to Joachim. Tell him you have my faith and trust. Tell him to return to me for I have another task for him to perform."

"I will."

"And Anna...God be with you."

His smile was the last thing I saw before the vision ended.

I jerked back from Joachim, stumbling a few steps away. Sweat dripped down the side of my face. My breathing was erratic.

"Do you believe now, Anna?"

"I believe."

He held out his hand. "Give me the horn."

"Michael said he would trust me to keep it safe."

He dropped his hand, crestfallen.

"He also said to tell you to return to him because he has another task for you to perform."

"I will go. But it is not the last you will see of me."

He disappeared in a flash of light. I didn't doubt his words. I believed I would see him again. Hopefully when I handed over all five relics and was done with this entire thing. With him gone, exhaustion took over. My shoulders slumped and I headed to the bedroom, ready to sleep.

CHAPTER 27

A QUICK GLANCE AT the clock made me realize why I was so
tired. It was shortly after two in the morning. I snapped off
all the lights, stripped and climbed into bed. My body sank into the
mattress. I was sure the sheets were three-hundred-count Egyptian
cotton. The softness against my skin was far too luxurious to be
anything else.

I wondered how my uncle came about this place. I guess he
thought I needed a new home because he found out about Ben's
death. Maybe Kincade told him. It didn't matter. I didn't want to
return to Dallas any more than I wanted to go back to my uncle's
estate.

I fought sleep for a long while until finally my eyes drifted closed.
I fell into a hard, dreamless sleep. I needed it and was so grateful I
had no more encounters with Azriel or anyone else.

I woke up refreshed. I stumbled to the kitchen, thankful there
was a coffeemaker. I put on the pot and headed to the bathroom to
shower. I paused at the closet and peered inside. My uncle thought
of everything. Clothes in my size hung along with several pairs of

shoes. Even multiple pairs of pink combat boots. Maybe my uncle knew me better than I thought. At least I'd have something to wear.

Upon inspection of my face in the mirror, I discovered it wasn't the same face I remembered. Despite Darius's healing job, I still had faint bruises. I wore them as a badge of honor. I went to Hell and survived. Another weird thing I noticed was the white streak at each temple. Not the crappy dye job I did to disguise my appearance. This was clearly stark white strands. As though I'd suddenly aged and gone gray. The blonde I put in had faded, showing hideous black roots. I needed to do something about that. Maybe it'd be a nice conversation starter with Kincade.

After showering and drinking a pot of dark roast coffee, I was wired and ready for my visit with Kincade at the hospital. I chose black cargo pants and a comfy oversized T-shirt. I armed myself and left.

Kincade was at Hong Kong Methodist Hospital, about a ten-minute walk from the apartment. It seemed rude to show up empty handed, so I stopped in the gift shop and bought him a king size chocolate bar. Who didn't love chocolate? After getting the runaround, I finally found his room. He was moved from ICU to a private room. The staff wasn't exactly a wealth of information and their customer service skills left a lot to be desired.

As I made my walk down the long hallway to his room, my stomach erupted with butterflies. The coffee churned like acid. I regretted drinking so much and not eating breakfast. Twice I halted, considered turning back and leaving. I didn't. I forced my feet to walk. I resisted breaking the wrapper on the chocolate.

I knocked on the door and then pushed it open. He was propped up in the bed barking at the poor assistant to leave him alone when it was clear she was there only to check his vitals. She took it all in stride, though, and gave him a sweet smile as she took his blood pressure.

I leaned against the doorframe. He hadn't heard me knock. I had to admit, I liked seeing him bark at someone other than me.

"Not a very good patient, is he?" I asked.

They both looked up. She laughed while he tried hard to mask his surprise at my sudden appearance.

"He's been asking to be released for days," she said.

"That's right. I have shit to do."

"You need rest, Mr. Harrison. One twenty over eighty. Perfect."

"Of course, it's perfect. That's why I need to be released."

"That's up to the doctor."

He scowled. She added a few notes in the electronic chart. She gave me friendly smile as she passed by and exited the room.

"I hate hospitals." He frowned with his disdain.

"Don't we all?"

"Not you. You worked in one," he said.

Of course, he'd remember that. It seemed like a lifetime ago I first met him outside that hospital in Dallas.

"What are you doing here, Miss Walker?"

I didn't miss he was back to calling me Miss Walker.

He cut right to the chase. I entered the room and stood by his bed, feeling awkward and weird. Why was I there? To satisfy some morbid curiosity he wasn't dead? His left forearm had a bandage from elbow to wrist. His hands were unscathed. He had stitches on one side of his head. I suspected more bandages and stitches were on the lower half of his body where some of the shrapnel from the explosion hit him. All in all, he was lucky to be alive.

He was still hooked up to an IV. His face sported a three-day growth of beard.

He looked me over, as though inspecting a piece of precious art. I didn't miss the way his gaze lingered on the bandage at my throat, my bruised face, my broken nose.

Maybe he wouldn't ask.

"What happened to your throat?"

Damn. He asked. "Got into a knife fight. It's no big deal."

"Would this knife fight involve Azriel?"

Azriel and a few demons, but who was counting? "It's no big deal. How are you feeling?"

"I'll live." He looked out the window though there was nothing to see except another building. "Thought you'd be in Dallas by now."

"There's nothing for me in Dallas."

"Sure, there is. I cleared your name. I got your job back."

But I didn't want it back. "That's not my job."

He was silent as he looked at me, then, "What is?"

I ignored the question and pulled the chocolate out of my pocket. "I brought you contraband."

His eyes narrowed as he peered at it with suspicion. "You brought me chocolate?"

He wasted no time tearing open the wrapper. He broke the bar in half and handed it to me. Something about sharing a chocolate bar with him warmed my heart.

"All I've had to eat is crappy hospital food. Even the Jell-O is disgusting," he said around a mouthful. "I don't suppose you could smuggle in some ice cream next time? Or maybe a cheeseburger?"

Hearing him say next time surprised me. Did he want me to come back for a visit? And then what? Would we end up going our separate ways?

"I'll see what I can do. How long are you in for?"

"Another week at least. The burns weren't as bad as they first thought but I still have some healing to do. All this sitting around is pissing me off."

I doubted that not one bit. I didn't know much about him, but what I did know was he was a man of action. Laying in a hospital bed had to drive him crazy.

We looked at each other, munching on our respective chocolate in silence. His intense gaze locked on the faint bruises. I braced myself for what came next.

"Someone beat you up?" His tone left no room for a non-answer.

I shifted from one foot to the other. Why did I feel like an errant child about to be scolded by a parent? "You just noticed that?"

"The truth, Anna."

And back to using my first name. That hard tone that told me I better confess.

"I had a run in with Azriel."

His hands curled into tight fists around the blankets. His knuckles leeched of color. When my gaze flickered back to his face, controlled anger pulsed. The air in the room sucked away which was something I experienced with him before. I was very aware of the smells of the hospital—that antiseptic and chemical scent hadn't bothered me before but now burned the back of my throat. I swallowed hard.

"That is, we had a bit of a, ah, fight," I added.

"A fight that involved him punching you?"

"Well..."

"What the fuck happened? I want the whole story, too."

Oh, crap. I was going to have to tell him the whole sordid tale? I didn't wanna. "You mean from the explosion on?"

"No." His voice was hard and cold as the arctic. "The *whole* story from the beginning. And no lies."

Like from the day we met. I got it. I had the sudden urge to run away. Kincade had this weird built-in lie detector and knew when I fibbed. There was no getting around it. A brittle silence stretched between us as I tried to figure out how to begin. I inhaled a deep breath.

"My mother left England when she was pregnant with me and moved to America. The day I was born, she died, and I was immediately an orphan."

"I'm sorry." He sounded sincere.

I shrugged. "Shit happens."

"No father?"

I shook my head. "She never told anyone who he was. Not even my uncle. I entered the foster system. I was lucky and ended up with a woman who took care of me until my uncle came along. She never treated me like a freak because of my ability. I've been able to do it all my life." I paused and bit my lower lip. "I can see into other people's dreams."

His gaze lingered on my mouth before returning to my eyes. "You mean walk into dreams?"

"Yes. Walk into them. Interact with them. All while they're dreaming. When they wake up, they think it was nothing more than a dream. They remember nothing."

He gave me a thoughtful look. I wondered what was going on in that head of his. I realized how lucky I was to live with a foster mother who didn't think I was odd. She accepted me as I was without question, though there were times when my ability startled her. She made me promise I wouldn't dream walk her and I agreed because I didn't want to upset her. Looking back, I was grateful for the time I had with her. For the first time in a long time, I had an urge to make sure she was okay.

"Go on," he said after a long pause.

"We call it dream walking. When I was thirteen, my uncle tracked me down and took me to his estate in England. Apparently, it runs in the family."

"Even your uncle can dream walk?" he asked.

I nodded.

"That explains a weird dream I had with him as the starring role. He wanted to make sure I was alive, I think."

I cringed. "I'm sorry. He shouldn't have done that. There are boundaries that should never be crossed."

"You mean like dream walking someone without their consent?"

"Yes, exactly."

He was silent a moment, his intense gaze still on mine. "Did you dream walk me?"

The dream I unintentionally walked with him flashed through my mind. Warmth rose to my cheeks but I resisted the urge to press my hands against them. Instead, I bit my lip.

"You did, didn't you?"

I flushed again, the heat pulsing in my face. "I haven't learned to control it like my uncle."

It was as much of an admission as I was willing to give.

Kincade nodded slowly. I wondered if he remembered the dream the same way I did, if he remembered telling me I needed him.

"You have more to tell me, don't you?" he asked. "About this Horn of Gabriel."

He wasn't going to let that go. It was time to spill my guts about the Holy Relics. I took a deep cleansing breath. "A messenger angel came to me with an assignment from the archangel, Michael. He wants me to search for and recover five Holy Relics."

He melted into the pillow, tension releasing from his body. "Michael, the archangel." He didn't sound surprised. More like he was in awe.

"It can't be all that shocking to you. You can see angels and demons, too."

"Yes, but I've never been visited by one of them that high up."

My brows knit as I wondered what he meant by that. I was happy to omit the part about talking with Michael. I wasn't sure how he'd react to that bit of news. Instead, I explained to him the Holy Relics were hidden by the archangels.

"How does Azriel fit into all this?"

"He came to me, too, wanting me to hand the relics over to him for Lucifer so he could bring the downfall of mankind. Michael wants them to save mankind."

"Why you?" he wanted to know.

I didn't think he'd care about my family drama or the history book or the prophecy, so I omitted those nuggets of info. I also wasn't sure he'd buy the line I was the chosen one, the one deemed Keeper of the Holy Relics. That I had all these special abilities I was only starting to understand and learn. If I lied, he'd know it, so my answer had to have some veil of truth.

"My family was entrusted long ago with their protection but they've since been scattered around the world. I'm the next logical choice to look for them because I'm my uncle's heir."

That last bit about being the heir to Walker Estate was a bit of a stretch. Edward had no heirs of his own. I was his favorite niece as far as I was concerned.

"How did you find me in Hong Kong?" I asked.

"I tracked you here from England. Your uncle and I don't exactly see eye to eye. The only thing we agree on is your safety."

I bristled. "I can take care of myself."

He lifted an eyebrow and eyed the bandage on my neck, the bruises on my face. "Can you?"

I scowled. "Yes, I can. I don't need your help." I thought of the dream again and annoyance flashed through me. "What exactly did you tell my uncle, anyway?"

He clenched his jaw. He didn't want to tell me. "You won't like it."

"I spilled for you. Now you spill."

"I told him about Ben. He had no idea you had a boyfriend."

I clenched my fists until the muscles ached. My nails dug into my palms. "Why did you do that?"

"I assumed he already knew. I'm sorry."

Sorry didn't fix it. Sorry was an afterthought. Now I understood why my uncle arranged for my apartment so close to the hospital. He *was* pushing us together because he thought I needed protection and Kincade was the man for the job. It irked me but I could do nothing about it.

"It doesn't matter." I unclenched my fists and waved it away, trying to be nonchalant about it when in reality I seethed inside. "Anyway, I already found the first relic. I have the Horn of Gabriel safely hidden away."

"And the others?"

"I'm working on it."

There was a lot more I didn't tell him. The trip to the First Circle, the promise to Mammon, how my uncle nearly died and Darius saved us both.

"Who was the angel you were with before the explosion?"

"Does it matter?" I sounded defensive even to my own ears. And did he have mind-reading skills, too? It was freaky.

"Yes."

Crap. "A warrior angel."

His gaze burned hot. "What's his name?"

I opened my mouth to reply then quickly snapped it shut. He almost tricked me into giving up Darius's name. I had a horrible vision of the warrior angel showing up in Kincade's hospital room. Talk about awkward moments.

"It doesn't matter," I said.

"Strange name for a warrior angel." His hands curled into tight fists again.

Was he...jealous? No way. "He doesn't matter. What does is I have to find four more relics."

"Right and I'm coming with you as soon as I get out of this joint."

This wasn't going how I planned. How did I veer off course so far? I was going to tell him the truth about myself and then get away from him. I planned to never see him again once I walked out of his hospital room. Helping me find the relics was the last thing I wanted him to do.

"It's okay. I got this—"

"You don't. I'm helping you and that's non-negotiable."

"But—"

"No. No more arguments. Don't tell me it's too dangerous or any other bullshit. I've been in dangerous situations before, for fucks sake. This is no different."

There was a hard edge to his voice. He left me no room to argue.

"I'm going to help you find the other relics. Whether you want my help or not. I've already made up my mind."

"Kincade, I can't ask you to do that."

"You're not asking. I'm telling you what I'm going to do. And you're going to like it. I'm coming with you. I'm going to make sure that bastard, Azriel, never puts another hand on you. If he does, I'll fucking kill him."

I stared at him, dumbstruck, wondering why the sudden need to protect me. Emotions plunged through me. Everything from relief to fury. I'd never had an ally in my life. Or had someone wanting to keep me safe and out of harm's way.

Except for Ben. He was my ally, my friend, my lover. I wondered how he'd take all this with me chasing Holy Relics. Would he understand? Would he run? If he was sane, he'd run.

But none of that mattered. He was dead. He was the last man who pushed his way into my life. Kincade was another, along with my uncle. I didn't much care for it and I wasn't sure how I was going to handle Kincade. How would I save Darius? And Lexi?

How was I going to find the other relics with him hovering over me? I had a job to do and so did he, though I had no idea what that was exactly. He was a mysterious guy who claimed to be a detective that kept showing up when I least expected it.

I plastered a smile on my face, trying to hide my discomfort. "If you insist."

"I insist."

Great. The first opportunity I had I'd ditch him.

"I guess I have a new partner." I backed away from the bed. "And I've been here long enough. I'll let you rest."

I took a step toward the door.

"Anna?"

I turned back to see the question on his face. "Have you ever known anyone else to dream walk? I mean someone not of your line."

I considered. Azriel could. But he was Fallen. I shook my head. "The Fallen and maybe angels, too, I think. Why do you ask?"

He leaned his head back into the pillow. "No reason. See you tomorrow?"

"Uh, sure," I said. "I'll bring cheeseburgers."

He cracked a rare smile. "Good."

I pushed out the door into the garish light of the hallway, trying to forget his odd question about dream walking.

CHAPTER 28

I LEFT THE HOSPITAL with a dark feeling looming over me. Telling Kincade things about me did not make me feel better. In fact, it made me feel worse. I managed to squeak by his internal lie detector. He hadn't called me out on anything.

Yet.

But I was sure that would come.

Why couldn't I tell him everything? Why did I want to hold information back, keeping it close to me?

If I psycho-analyzed myself, maybe I'd realize a part of me was afraid of getting too close to him. He had a brush with death but Azriel didn't want him dead. He wanted him alive. He wanted to send me a message that if I didn't cooperate, there would be dire consequences.

I tried to tell myself Kincade didn't mean anything to me. He didn't matter. Ben meant a lot to me. Ben mattered. Ben was dead. Azriel killed him to force me to cooperate.

And still I refused. Did I have a death wish?

I walked down the street back to the apartment with my thoughts rolling around in my head, trying to discern my myriad emotions. I was confused by Kincade's sudden involvement in my life as much as I was hurting with Ben's sudden departure.

It was mid-afternoon. The streets were full of tourists and locals alike. I paused to take it all in and looked, really looked, at my surroundings. Demons roamed the streets next to humans. Their decaying scent permeated the air. Some spotted me as they milled through the crowded street but for the most part, they left me alone.

What I hadn't seen before were the angels following people who had no clue they were there. I marveled at the angels and demons. All of them. A lady with her eyes glued to her smartphone screen not paying attention came to the street corner. She glanced up only briefly before stepping into traffic as a car barreled around the corner. I opened my mouth to shout a warning but it wasn't necessary. The angel behind her clamped a hand on her shoulder and jerked her backward out of harm's way.

My mouth dropped open as I watched her jump back, her eyes wide and her face drained of color. She looked from side to side, as if looking for the person who'd saved her life. There was a commotion on the corner. People asking her if she was all right, to which she replied with a nod. She backed away from the corner, the angel with her.

It struck me, then, that these were no mere angels. They were guardian angels. Guardian angels mere humans couldn't see.

What was it Kincade said to Azriel that day in the hospital locker room?

You murdered Kaziel and Zaphreal and you'll pay for that.

Azriel laughed before replying. *You may have killed my demons,* gardien, *but I have more that will answer my call.*

Azriel called Kincade *gardien*.

Icy pinpricks danced up my spine. Did it mean Kincade was my *gardien*? I believed Kincade harbored some secret he didn't want to share with me. A secret that, perhaps, my uncle knew because of his determination to push us together. As soon as I got back to the apartment, I intended to call Uncle Edward and ask him.

I walked the rest of the way at a brisk pace with that one thing on my mind. I was out of breath by the time I unlocked the door and shoved it open.

And then stopped cold.

A padded envelope was on the floor. Someone couldn't shove it under the door because it was much too thick. The handwriting was in the same block lettering that was on the package I received with the Hong Kong postcard and key. My name was written across the front.

I tore open the flap. Inside was another postcard. This one was of the Blue Mosque in Istanbul, Turkey. On the back, written in the same handwriting, were the words Spear of Destiny.

My hand shook. This was my next clue. The Spear of Destiny was in Istanbul. Something else was in the envelope. When I pulled it out, the paper was so ancient, it nearly crumbled in my hands. It was parchment. Very old parchment folded into a strange shape with numerous corners.

Gently, I placed it on the nearby kitchen counter and unfolded the delicate paper. It was a map to a palace in Istanbul with no labels. I had no idea what it was or where it was in the city. Was the spear there? Finding the horn was easy. I doubted this one would be that simple. There were demons on my tail who knew who I was, not to mention the pissed off fallen angel who wanted my head.

I slipped the postcard and the fragile map back into the envelope. It occurred to me to research the place, but I'd left Lexi's laptop with Darius.

I placed the envelope on the counter and headed to the bedroom, rubbing my tired eyes. On the bed, almost as if my thoughts conjured it was the laptop resting on the coverlet.

I reached for the laptop, and despite my yawn, booted it up. As I waited for the startup screen, there was a brisk knock on the door. My head snapped up. I stared in the general direction of the door and wondered who could be on the other side. Darius wouldn't knock. Neither would Joachim. Maybe Uncle Edward? I doubted he'd show up here though.

Another knock, more demanding. I padded to the door, then peered through the peephole. A woman was on the other side. A very beautiful, tall woman with mocha skin and chocolate eyes.

I had no idea who she was.

"Can I help you?" I asked when I opened the door.

"Anna Walker, my name is Isobel Marques. I must speak with you on an urgent matter."

She pushed her way inside before I could invite her. I closed the door and turned to her, folding my arms over my chest. She stood in the center of the room, her dark eyes fixed on my face. Her skin had a sort of ethereal glow to it. As though something golden shimmered there. Her eyes were alert, dark, depthless. Her long black hair cascaded into beautiful shiny waves over her shoulders and down her back to her waist. She was dressed in the most expensive pantsuit I'd ever seen. I sniffed money. Old money.

I didn't sniff anything else, though. Not a demon. Not a Fallen. Not an angel. Then what?

She flipped her hair over her shoulder.

"I'm sorry. Do we know each other?" I asked.

"We do not. But we will become acquainted very soon." She stretched out a hand to me. I couldn't help but notice her long slender fingers and perfect French manicure. Her hands and wrists were devoid of jewelry. The only adornment she wore was a small gold cross necklace. "Forgive my abrupt intrusion. Let us start again. Isobel."

I couldn't place her accent, but it was something exotic.

"Anna." I shook her hand. She had a firm grip. "If we don't know each other, how did you find me?" Unless, of course, my uncle pointed her in my direction.

"We have no time for pleasantries. I've come here—"

"Hold on." I held up my hands. "I have no idea who you are or where you came from, but me asking how you know who I am isn't exactly a pleasantry. 'Hi, how you doing' is a pleasantry so why don't you answer my question?"

She huffed out a breath, exasperated. "You are the Keeper of the Holy Relics, are you not?"

I stared at her. My mind emptied of all response and thought. How did she know about that? Who the hell was she? I was starting to wonder if I had a built-in GPS that everyone in the world had access to but me.

"I've been told," I said. "What's it to you?"

"I have come to warn you about the Spear of Destiny. You must exercise great caution in your search for the spear."

Okay, this was getting weirder by the minute. I ran my tongue over my top teeth, trying to decide if I should kill her or merely throw her out.

"How do you know about that?"

"We all know about that," she said. "You must understand the spear is the most dangerous relic. Do you not know what it is capable of?"

"Yeah. It bends the destiny to the bearer's will. So?" It didn't escape me she said *we all know*. I'd have to find out who the "we" were.

She clasped her hands in front of her and spoke slowly as if talking to a child. "It is that. But it is more. It can destroy all that you know."

I cocked my head to the side and regarded her coolly. "How so?"

"It will not only change the destiny of the world but yours. If you are not cautious, you will alter your path."

That didn't sound like a bad idea to me. Maybe I could pick another Keeper and get out of this thing altogether.

"You do not yet understand the power it possesses."

"Yeah, yeah, yeah. A lot of people keep telling me what a dunce I am about the power of the relics. I get it. They're powerful and I'm a weak-minded fool." I couldn't stop the anger snapping through me. "Cut to the chase, sister. I haven't got all day."

Annoyance flickered through her gaze before she squelched it. She stepped closer to me. We stood inches apart. I caught a whiff of her expensive French perfume. Who was this chick?

"Your path has been foretold. If you alter it, if you change the direction of your destiny...then...you will most certainly die."

She paused to give me a chance to allow that to soak in.

"And if you die, Keeper, all hope is lost. Without you, mankind will suffer. Without you, darkness prevails."

So much for finding another Keeper to take my place.

"Thanks for the head's up." I grabbed her elbow and led her toward the door. "I'll keep your advice in mind." I opened the door and shoved her out into the brightly lit hallway. "Have a nice day."

"But—"

I slammed the door and locked it, shutting off her retort.

"You cannot shut me out, Anna," she said through the door. "Nor can you deny the truth."

I peered through the peephole, watching as she stood there a few more seconds before walking away. I sagged against the door. That old familiar ball of cold fear didn't want to go away no matter what I did.

She was right about one thing. I couldn't deny the truth about who I was. My waking nightmare was only beginning.

NEXT IN THE SERIES: BLOOD AND BONE

Can Anna save Kincade before he loses his soul forever?

Dream walker and relic hunter, Anna Walker, is on the most important quest of her life—find the Holy Relics before Lucifer and his forces of evil destroy mankind. She's now after the legendary Spear of Destiny with the power to alter the future of the world. But when her archenemy, Azriel, captures her friend and ally, Kincade, the world's destiny must take second place to getting him back.

The price? His soul for the spear.

As her search heats up, she stumbles upon a sinister plot by a group known as the Knights of the Holy Lance. Their leader has genetically engineered a race of dream walkers with the intent to gain the relic for his own demented means. When he discovers Anna is after the spear, he sends an elite genetically-altered dream walker to take her out.

With the destiny of the world riding on her shoulders, and a terrifying enemy determined to destroy her, Anna must track down the powerful relic before Kincade's soul is lost forever.

Find it at your favorite retailer!

SNEAK PEEK OF BLOOD AND BONE

Somerset, England, Late September 2038 A.D.

At five years old, I was called a demon child. I dream walked my foster mother's younger sister by accident. Ruby's dreams were erratic and scary and I didn't understand them. Naturally, she thought I was a freak. She'd come to visit and spent the night with us and, well, she wasn't the most upstanding young adult on the planet. She drank, smoke, cussed, had a boyfriend named Ricky who rode a Harley. They were both part of a motorcycle gang. They both enjoyed the use of recreational hallucinogens.

Ruby and Ricky were quite a pair.

As a curious five-year-old, I caught her stealing my foster mother's wallet to support her habits and her boyfriend. She smacked me hard and threatened me within an inch of my life if I told her sister.

I tattled anyway and got in trouble for telling lies. But when my foster mother found her wallet empty and her credit card gone after her sister disappeared, she apologized. I remember the conversation as clear as if it happened yesterday.

"She called me a name, Mama. And she hit me."

"She shouldn't have done that." She patted me on the hand to reassure me. *"You went into her mind, didn't you?"*

I nodded. "I didn't mean to."

As she often did, she pursued her lips in thought. Worry flickered in her eyes. "People don't understand what you can do, Anna. It scares them."

"Like it scared you?"

"Yes, like that. You mustn't do it without permission. You must learn control. Can you do that for me?"

As a child, I gave an emphatic nod. "Yes, Mama."

I did manage to control my dream walking—by never doing it again. At least until that fateful day in Dallas.

I never saw Ruby again. If she returned, my mother kept her far, far away from me.

Funny the things you remember. Only now as an adult did I understand Ruby's completely fucked up mind. I forgot a lot about my childhood until I flipped through the pages of the journal I found in my old room at my uncle's manor. I spent late nights reading it and remembering with fondness the woman who raised me the first thirteen years of my life. I missed her.

I hadn't thought of her again until recently. My life changed dramatically when, at thirteen, my uncle found me and brought me to England. I spent five years in England with Edward and his tutors. During that time, I corresponded with her but somewhere along the way, her letters and emails stopped coming. When I returned to Dallas, I searched for her only to discover she had moved. Forwarding address unknown.

One thing was for sure. I wasn't a demon child. I was a demon killer.

Demons called me a demon-seer. Archangels called me the Keeper of the Holy Relics.

Back in June, my life was turned upside down by the archangels and the Fallen, a band of fallen angels led by Lucifer intent on hunting down human souls to build his dark army. They both wanted me to do a job for them—find the five Holy Relics. A job I reluctantly agreed to take. I went after the Horn of Gabriel because my archenemy and fallen angel, Azriel, gave it to Mammon the Prince of Greed.

I lived with regret and guilt on a constant basis. I regretted a lot about the decisions I made over the last several months. The biggest regret was dream walking a patient at the hospital where I worked. Her name was Emma. We were friends once. That's when my life utterly derailed, when I met Azriel, and, in a weird twist of fate, Kincade Harrison.

Two thorns in my side.

And, of course, there was the messenger angel, Joachim. He was another prickly thorn. I was cursed with thorns.

Gideon's fist crashed against my cheekbone, the pain exploding across my face bringing me back to the present. I should focus on my training instead of reminiscing.

My head snapped back and my teeth clinked together with a sickening snap. I refused to go down. I retaliated with a left hook which missed his face. I caught nothing but air. His right fist landed in my ribs and pushed the wind out of my lungs. I doubled over, coughing. He jabbed me in the back of the head with his elbow. Stars burst into my vision. I collapsed to my hands and knees, staring down at the gray workout mat while trying to catch my breath.

My uncle's idea of training stunk.

"Too slow, chickadee."

There was a sneer in Gideon's voice. He got a sick kind of joy out of beating the shit out of me. I flopped over, resting my forearms on my drawn-up knees. Peering at him, I squinted against the harsh fluorescent light as a drop of sweat slipped into my open eye. The salt stung.

He grinned at me, his lips stretching over his teeth. A dimple pierced his left cheek. Beads of perspiration dotted his forehead. He flexed his fingers in his fingerless gloves.

"Being that slow will get you killed."

Gideon was hired by my uncle, Edward, to kick my ass and teach me to fight and defend myself. The old man didn't like the way I rescued him from Hell.

"Step aside, Gid, it's my turn."

Gilli cracked her knuckles and licked her lips in anticipation. She was his twin. I called them the Wonder Twins. She had a matching dimple, the same brown eyes, the same brown hair and was as pretty as her brother. She relished kicking my ass, too.

I held up my hands in surrender. "I think I need a break."

"No breaks." And it was punctuated with the slamming of the door.

I peered around Gilli and Gideon to see my uncle standing inside the workout room. The one he made for me in one of the outer buildings on his estate in Cannington, a small village in Somerset, England.

"You trying to kill me, old man?" I climbed to my feet and stalked across the room to snatch up my water bottle.

"You don't have time to rest," Edward said, his voice hard.

"Ah, give her a break, Eddie. She's worked hard this week."

I suppressed a snicker. Every time I heard Gideon call my uncle Eddie, it took all my strength not to burst out laughing. He was about as far from an Eddie as he could get. An upper-class Englishman, he always wore a designer three-piece suit. His jaw was set in a straight stubborn line as his dark blue eyes assessed me from across the room. His black hair had nary a strand out of place.

Gideon snatched his towel off the floor and wiped the two beads of sweat off his face. Seriously, I hated him. Why couldn't he sweat like the rest of us? Sweat dampened my hair, neck and back.

"Time is of the essence," Edward said in that clipped British accent.

I rolled my eyes.

"You should be out searching," he continued.

Your Free Book is Waiting!

Find out how the Dream Walkers began!

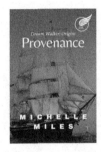 In 1147 England, John of Yorkshire is ushered to his mother's side as she lay dying. When she tells him the secret she's harbored his entire life, it alters his destiny forever. He sails for the Holy Land on a quest to find his absent father. But the ship is pushed off course due to bad weather forcing them to port in Lisbon, Portugal. There, he reluctantly enters a fight to return the city to Christian rule only to discover something more divine awaits him.

Dream Walker: Origins is an origin story to enrich your reading experience for **Call of the Dark***, Book 1 in the Dream Walker series.*

Get a free copy of the prequel
Provenance: Dream Walker Origins!

https://subscribe.michellemiles.net/provenance

ACKNOWLEDGEMENTS

This book has been a long time coming. I wrote it by hand in a journal in August of 2012. I have a vivid memory of when the story hit me in a flash and I knew I had to write it. But it took time and a whole lot of revision to get it where it is today. I finally decided 2020 would be the year I would polish it and release it. I'm proud of the results.

There are people who need some really big thanks, though. It went through several beta readers: **Kathy Ivan, Karilyn Bently, Sara Reinke, Andi B., Kat Baldwin, Janice Lindstrom**. They helped shape the story to what it is today. Another big thanks to **Cathy McElhaney** for her editing skills. Thanks to **Erin Dameron-Hill** for the beautiful cover art. She always knows what I want and how to bring to life my books.

A super big thanks to **Jennifer August** for all the lunches and brainstorming sessions about the book and future books. I love our book/writing lunches and miss them! I can't wait to get back to doing that again. Another thanks to **Misty Evans** for letting me crash her house in the summer of 2019 for friendship, fun, a fairy tea party, and writing talks. I loved that and hope we get to do again soon.

And, finally, to **my husband, Robert**, for always believing in me and this book when I had doubts.

Thank you for purchasing and reading this book. I hope you love Anna's story and look forward to the next books in the series.

About the Author

 MICHELLE MILES believes in fairy tales, true love and magic. She writes heart-stopping urban fantasy, epic fantasy and paranormal romance with an action/adventure twist that will leave you breathless. She is the author of numerous series that includes everything from angels and demons to fairies, dragons and elves.

She is a member of Romance Writers of America (RWA) and Science Fiction and Fantasy Writers Association (SFWA). A native Texan, in her spare time she loves reading, listening to music, watching movies, hiking, and drinking wine. She can be found online at Facebook, Instagram, Pinterest and Goodreads.

Your Adventure Awaits

Read more at MichelleMiles.net

Made in the USA
Columbia, SC
01 June 2025

58775300R00200